ALT-ZOMBIE
THE ALTERNATIVE ZOMBIE ANTHOLOGY

Edited by
PETER MARK MAY

Deputy Editors
STUART HUGHES
ADRIAN CHAMBERLIN

HERSHAM HORROR BOOKS

Hersham Horror Books
Logo by Daniel S. Boucher
Cover design by Mark West

Copyright © 2012 Hersham Horror Books

Hersham Horror Books
ISBN: 978-1466200470

All rights belong to the original artists, and writers for their contributed works.

All rights reserved. No part of this book may be reproduced, scanned or distributed in any form, including digital and electronic or mechanical, including photocopying, recording, or by any information storage and retrieval system, without the prior written consent of the Publisher, except for brief quotes for use in reviews.

This book is a work of fiction. Characters, names, places and incidents either are the product of the author's imagination or are used fictitiously, and any resemblance to any actual persons, living or dead, or undead, events, or locales is entirely coincidental.

First Edition
First Published in 2012

DEDICATION

This book is dedicated to the tireless efforts behind the HHB scenes of Stuart Hughes, Adrian Chamberlin and Mark West.

Also from
Hersham Horror Books:

Alt-Dead
Fogbound From 5

CONTENTS

FOREWORD 1

GARY MCMAHON
Thus Spoke Lazarus . . . . '2

MARK WEST
In Cars 15

DAVID WILLIAMSON
Blind Date 23

SELINA LOCK
Lone and Level Sands. 34

STUART YOUNG
White Light, Black Fire 46

JOE MCKINNEY
Bugging Out 77

ZACH BLACK
The Rhyme of Albert Greentree. 91

SHAUN JEFFREY
'Til Death Do Us Part 107

RICHARD FARREN BARBER
Checking Out 120

ALISON LITTLEWOOD
Soul Food. 132

JAY EALES
Imaginary Kingdom. 143

ADRIAN CHAMBERLIN
The Third Day.. 154

JAN EDWARDS
Midnight Twilight 173

STUART HUGHES
Ded End Jobz 189

KATHERINE TOMLINSON
Pyramid Power 220

R.J. GAULDING
Ultimate Ana... 226

WILLIAM MEIKLE
The Silent Dead... 254

DAVE JEFFERY
Ascension?... 268

RACHELLE BRONSON
Lullabelle 294

SHAUN HAMILTON
Acceptable Genocide 308

STEPHEN BACON
Scarlet Yawns... 333

BONUS STORY
Old Bones 350

BIOGRAPHIES 355

COMING SOON 368

FOREWORD

THE ZOMBIE; it took a while for this rotting remnant of mankind to drag itself out of its sodden grave to the top of the adult supernatural tree. Why so? They don't look good or smell nice, none of us really wants to become one, like our hankering to become our monster of choice, a blood sucker that haunts the night and lives forever.

So why the slow rise since the sixties, and why do zombies have the staying power now? Is it because, in the post *Dracula/ Lestat/Twilight* era, maybe there is a power vacuum at the top, that the poor relation the werewolf could never fill. Is it that zombies are a classless crowd, not the upper-class vampire Counts of old, and being a waking corpse is the great social leveller. Like death that afflicts every man woman and child on the planet.

Many people want them to go away and can't stand another dumb zombie book or film. So what we are hopefully trying here is to bring you 21 stories that will breathe new life into those unbreathing decaying lungs, or at least chill you some more, if you are a zombie fan.

Once more I fling the lych-gates open and let you in to wander in the graveyard mist, to experience these 21 stories, where all things are possible, foul reeking and Alt-Zombie.

—*PMM*

THUS SPOKE LAZARUS: A REVISIONIST FABLE

Gary McMahon

"I am the resurrection..."
—John 11: 1-46

HE COULD REMEMBER NOTHING before the desert and the sun and the sight of the birds wheeling in the clear blue sky above him, and a man's rich, soothing voice calling him away from death.

Death.

Yes, he had died: he had passed over. Of this one fact he was entirely certain. For wasn't he still dressed in his grave robes, and had he not torn the covering napkin from his face?

That voice, it had pulled him from the darkness, its soft and insidious tones settling deep into his flesh, his bones, and tugging like an ox, like a simple beast of burden. Tugging him out of the black and into the heat of what felt something like the love of a parent for a disobedient child. Three blank days he had spent inside the tomb, aware of nothing beyond its thick stone walls and floating in an endless, shifting sea of black. And then, that strange, soft voice had filled his head, at once filling all his empty spaces:

"Lazarus, come out!"

"Lazarus." He spoke his own sweet name, relishing its bitter taste on his tongue. The illness that killed him had initially robbed him of all senses other than sight, and now that he stood resurrected he vowed that he would no longer take things like the taste or the sound of his own name for granted.

The man who had brought him back—the one that some called the Christ and others called the Holy Fool—had ordered him unbound from his grave robes, and watched, smiling, as Lazarus had stumbled, blinded by the cloth that covered his face, out of his tomb and into the hot, heavy air. The rock had been rolled away; an unexpected breath of warm air ruffled his hair and kissed his chill cheek.

But now he was here: in this desert, miles away from the township of Bethany, not even aware of how long he had been away. Time no longer meant anything to him.

Terrified, he had fled from the astonished crowd, from the man who had raised him, even from his sisters Mary and Martha. Leaving his home to disappear into the vast empty spaces which echoed those that existed deep inside him.

To flee into the desert and atone for his sins.

But why had he been brought back? What purpose could it serve? He was a simple man, an ordinary man who worked hard to make an honest living: an affluent man, yes, compared to some of his friends. But he was no one special; never an important man.

Until now.

The people he knew had surged around him, touching his skin, kissing his hands and feet, and proclaiming him a miracle. And when he had turned to that man—that *Christ*—the quiet, bearded stranger had merely smiled, and nodded his head.

Lazarus sat now upon a flat rock, trying to shade his eyes from the merciless attention of the sun. He fumbled with the rag that had covered his face in the tomb, wrapping it around his head as a protection from the heat.

He sat there for a long time, watching the shadows form at his feet and listening as the birds flew off to other destinations, deciding that he would not fall and provide them and the other scavenging desert animals with a free carrion meal.

The desert let out a slow breath, releasing the heat of the day as night approached. Lizards popped their heads up out of the sand, breaking free of the burrows that had served them so well during the unforgiving heat of the day. Darkness began to fall, coldly caressing the sands, filling up the shadowed valleys and hollows created by the endlessly shifting dunes.

Soon a figure passed by. An old man dressed in rags, a beggar. He walked with a stick and had a bundle thrown over his narrow, bony shoulders—his earthly possessions, all wrapped in the old, tattered skin of a calf. He glanced at Lazarus, and sensing something unwholesome about his bearing, the old man continued on his way without breaking his stride.

Lazarus withered beneath the man's gaze, then felt something…something that he could not define. It was a sensation that began in the pit of his stomach and then spread out into his extremities, finally reaching his throat, his mouth, and his lips.

Only then did Lazarus recognise it as hunger.

He followed the man across the sand, gaining slowly, confused; at once unsure of his own motives. His bare feet scudded across the surface of the uncaring desert; the old man's sandals scuffed in the sand and the dust as he tried to run.

"Old man," said Lazarus, reaching out and grabbing the other by his scrawny arm.

The old man turned, his mouth opening, eyes widening in fear. "I have no wealth, sir. I am but a humble travelling man, with nothing to my name but my name. I'll trouble you to let me pass and be on my way."

"I am…I am so hungry." Lazarus had no idea what he would do, but a grasping chill crept into his stomach. Something within him reached out, grasping, needful, and relentless.

"Hungry."

Then he fell upon the traveller, pulling him down onto the sand behind a high dune and tearing at the rags to expose his pale throat. Lazarus opened his mouth and bit down into the aged, wrinkled flesh, ripping away a sizeable piece of the sun-toughened meat and chewing, chewing, sucking down warmth into his cold, cold body in the hope that it might reach his heart. His dead heart. And that it might take away the dreaded hunger.

The traveller screamed, too weak to fight, too confused to do anything but cry out the garbled name of his god and rake at the sand with his stick-like fingers. Blood dyed this terrible corner of the desert bright red; Lazarus bit down again, swallowing the warm flesh as if it were a meal lovingly cooked by one of his sisters.

He ate until he could hold down no more, and then he voided

the contents of his stomach onto the cooling sand, horrified at what he had done.

Then, tired and ashamed and needing the comfort of darkness, Lazarus slept.

Next morning he walked again, covering miles and aware only of the growing hunger at his core—a cold hunger, a frozen desire. He walked and walked, making shallow lines in the sand, until he came to a small encampment. There he paused by a fire and watched as a swarthy man in expensive robes cooked his breakfast.

"Greetings, stranger," said the man, scratching his head beneath the gold-studded red turban that adorned his head. "I offer you a share in my meal. It is not much, but it is better than eating sand." The man smiled, and his brown teeth shone with a dull lustre.

"I'll not partake of your food, traveller, but I will ask if I can warm myself by your fire."

"Then come, friend. Be warm."

Lazarus shuffled over to the fire, his body cool as the water from the well in Bethany. It was still early; the sun was young. The heat of the day had not yet begun to burn.

"What is your name, stranger?" The man warmed his loaf on the rocks that circled the flames, testing it now and then with his road-callused fingertips.

"I am Lazarus."

The man paused, glancing at Lazarus without turning his head; *seeing* him for the first time. "I heard tell of a man of that name in Bethany some weeks ago. This man, this son of Bethany: it is said that he has risen from the dead. That he was but a corpse, and the one they call the Prophet brought him back from the tomb."

Lazarus said nothing; he was unable to get warm.

"Are you that same Lazarus, friend? Have you come back from the dark?"

Lazarus closed his eyes. The hunger had returned, but he had no wish to devour this wise man. A man who had offered him food and companionship, who had given him flame and a place to warm his tired bones.

The stranger broke off a piece of bread and offered it to Lazarus, who took it gladly and placed it in his mouth. He chewed, praying that his hunger might be sated, but knowing deep down that he would gain no sustenance from its bland, doughy texture.

"They say that the Prophet is to be crucified up in Calvary, near the gates of Jerusalem. I am travelling there to pay my respects. Would you join me, Lazarus, and thank the man who resurrected you?"

"I remember…" Lazarus struggled to find the words. He was not a particularly clever man; his education had been basic. He could read, yes, and write, too; he even knew numbers, but really he was not a knowledgeable man. "I remember a great empty darkness. A void. And in that void was a voice that came from a horrible presence, something that made me think of a horde of angry insects scrabbling across a rotting corpse.

"'I am the Fallen One,' said that awful voice. 'I am here to give you something that you might take it back into the light. One will call you, and you will answer. Then you will walk again on the Earth, changed, different. A man, yet something both more and less than that: one who is neither living nor dead.'"

The stranger bit into his bread, a faraway look in his eyes. His camel muttered nearby, grinding its hooves into the desert floor.

Something disturbed it, but the man did not even glance in its direction.

"And someone did call my name; and told me to rise. They rolled back the stone and I stepped out from my tomb, the words of that Fallen One ringing in my ears like a bell."

The camel made a sound in the back of its throat: a low, gurgling cry, almost like a woman's weeping.

"And what did he give you, that Fallen One?" The man had stopped eating; his hand had frozen mid-journey to his mouth, the bread between his fingers crumbling.

"He gave me hunger."

And Lazarus ate once more.

When he came out of the desert three nights later, Lazarus was not alone. The old man and the traveller were with him, their terrible wounds hidden by the folds of their clothing, and the inhuman hunger of the Fallen One lodged in their flesh and bones. Like a plague, it had passed between them, allowing them, like Lazarus, to rise from the dead.

Bethany was silent; many of those who were fit enough to travel had followed the Prophet, trailing him to wherever his great journey might next lead him. The rest slept, unknowing. Lazarus smiled; this would be a simple feast.

First he called at the home of a local moneylender, still aware enough to be entertained by the concept of justice. The man was sleeping with his wife, one arm slung across her taut belly, the other trailing the floor, where his hand rested upon a bag of gold.

"A rich dish," said Lazarus, nodding at his companions. "Eat well, my friends." The silent pair advanced into the dwelling, almost soundless on feet not yet weighted down by the dirt of the grave. They went down on their knees by the rough bed, as if in worship, and gently caressed the sleeping couple.

When they finally bent to the task, the moneylender and his wife remained speechless; they struggled in sleep, but death came quickly. Their attackers were ravenous; no flesh was spared.

Lazarus watched from the shadows, his previous sickness at the sight of consumption now passed. He took pleasure from the sight of flesh shredding like river reeds, and of the blood that flowed like wine. The grinding sounds of feasting caused him no offence; he had come to accept what he was—what *they* were.

He turned away from the carnage and entered the dwelling next door. A slumbering child, clutching a ragdoll and murmuring in its dreams. Mere days ago, Lazarus—or what little had still remained of the old Lazarus—might have spared the mite, but now he moved in close, his mouth moist and his teeth on edge. The hunger orchestrating his acts.

The young meat was as tender as any slaughtered spring lamb, and filled but a small part of the empty space that yawned at his centre, the place where the hunger dwelled.

No one bothered to count how many fell that day, and how many would rise again in three days time. It was not important. All that mattered was the hunger, and filling the void that it created.

Three days hence, Lazarus stood before his new apostles, imagining that he, not the Christ, was the Prophet the world needed. His congregation was one of the dead, and his church was a moveable feast, a banquet for the eternally damned.

The dead opened their mouths as one, clamouring for meat. They were not capable of speech; only he could communicate.

Lazarus was the source, the focus of this great and desolate hunger, and these others were like cattle; they would follow him to the ends of the desert, if that was where he chose to lead them.

"Sleep now," he said. "And tomorrow we dine."

He watched with something approaching pride as, one by one, they lay down where they stood and closed their unseeing eyes.

Morning came with the noise and bluster of many horses approaching. The alarm had been sounded; citizens from somewhere beyond Bethany now knew of his ragtag company of the living dead.

Swords shone in the morning air, dazzling and deadly and possessing their own acute hunger.

But how to kill those who are already dead?

Steel bit into sallow flesh; limbs flew; innards were exposed. But the dead did not fall. They simply walked (not ran; they were incapable of great speed) through the fight, shrugging off wounds that would have been fatal to the living, seeing nothing but meat, aware of little else but their constant craving. Only if a head was severed from an undead body, or a skull was shattered beneath a heavy blade, emptying the brain pan, did one of Lazarus' children crumple to the ground, dying for a second time. Dying forever.

The soldiers were pulled from their mounts so that the staggering dead might feed. Clasping hands shed armour and snapped bones, and Lazarus' risen people did what they always did. They fed. They took their fill.

Lazarus watched from a height, standing on a slight rise. The smell of blood reached him, and he was surprised to find that he was still able to sense its aroma on the reddened air.

"*All this can be yours,*" said a chittering voice in his ear. "*The entire world can reflect this chaos, and you will be the master of what you have created. The master of the dead.*"

Lazarus did not dare turn to face the Fallen One. The sound of his voice was enough: the crackling hiss of flame, the sundering of flesh from bone, the tiny screams of a thousand stillborn infants.

"*Do my bidding, risen one, and all the world will be meat. Let the hunger I have given you spread like a contagion around the earth. Let the dead hordes rise!*"

Then the voice was gone, carried away on a wet red breeze that was heavy with the weight of blood.

Lazarus climbed down from the hill and walked among the dead, the dying, and the ones who would rise again. He stroked the faces of those whole enough to join the ranks of his army, and bent down to partake of the ones too ruined to get back on their feet. The meat went down well; by the time afternoon shadows began to slant, the hunger had receded to a gentle throbbing in his chest.

Again he wondered why he had been called back from death. What did this Prophet expect of him? There must be some purpose to this, some greater scheme whose far edges he was unable to see.

Surveying the results of his grand folly, Lazarus recalled the words of the Prophet as he had left his tomb. "Lazarus, come out!"

At first he'd thought this was an instruction to leave the tomb, but now he realised that it meant so much more. To rise above, to exalt, to come out of the darkness and offer up his soul to something higher and greater than himself. To rise up from the Fallen One and never look down.

Lazarus discarded his grave robes and walked naked into the desert, heading for the sun. The light was waning, the heat of the day lifting from the sands in beautiful shimmering waves. He walked through them, feeling nothing; not the breeze on his brow or the tears that ran down his dusty face. His hands were bloody; his heart was cold and heavy, like a rock in his chest – the rock that had been heaved away from the entrance to his tomb to allow him back into the land of the living from the realm of the dead.

The risen followed him, dumb as dogs, eager to feed. To feed and nothing more.

He looked to the east, towards Jerusalem (which lay too distant to see), and had the sudden and violent realisation that he would find there whatever it was that he was looking for. The thing he was meant to do. The reason for his resurrection. Black clouds sullied the clear azure sky, raging in silence above the spot where he guessed the distant city walls lay. Then, as Lazarus watched, the clouds broke apart and a brilliant column of light shone down, like a mighty finger pointing the way.

Lazarus, risen, went looking for death; and death followed on his heels, stupid, ponderous but indefatigable.

The soldier watched as the fool bled out his final minutes on the cross at the Place of Skulls, which was also known as Golgotha. He did not condone the sheer brutality of what had happened here, but he was paid to do his job and keep his eyes and his mouth tightly shut.

The man was insane, calling himself the Son of God—and, laughably, the King of the Jews, the very people who had helped put him up there, on the cross between two common thieves! Arrogant claims like these could not go unpunished.

The day was almost over; the crowds who had arrived throughout the day from Jerusalem and beyond wept, refusing to move until his body was taken down so that they could bathe and bury it. More madness. These people believed in him, and that belief was not only mad but also dangerous, and terrifying.

The soldier had already been told that he was to be part of the small legion responsible for taking down the bodies. He feared what the restless crowd might do when the time came. Despite what some may have thought, he took little pleasure in the senseless killing of bystanders.

Then he saw them: a slow, shuffling procession of stooped and bedraggled figures that marched past the city walls and climbed the long hill towards the three crucified corpses (for by now they were all surely dead). The soldier gripped his spear as he watched their calm and silent approach, the anticipation of battle roaring in his ears.

But no, he realised, there would be no bloodshed here, no massacre of rioting believers. These people were clearly exhausted; they looked as if they had walked for months, living off the land, being burned crisp by the sun. The flesh was tight on their bones and they were dressed in rags. Indeed, he thought, they looked near-dead themselves!

The newcomers paused at the top of the rise, staring at the crosses. A man entirely without robes, and who looked to be their leader, stepped forward and approached the body of the one who had called himself the Christ.

The sky-clad raggedy man knelt before the body and caressed the stained wood at the base of the upright. Then rising, he slowly parted his lips and kissed the leg of the crucified Prophet—it must have been a kiss, even though, from this angle, it had looked to the soldier more like a bite.

Later, as he helped collapse the wooden cross and strip it of the dead, the soldier experienced a strange sensation as he handled the body of the would-be Messiah.

The cold flesh beneath his palm seemed to pulse; a muscle twitched beneath the bloody surface. Then, when he looked up into the eyes of the corpse, he could have sworn that one eyelid—the one pierced by a thorn from that terrible crown they'd forced upon his head—fluttered like the wing of a moth.

Then, as he dragged the stiffened cadaver from the cross, the soldier heard someone shout a hoarse message that was gradually taken up by other voices in the grieving crowd:

"He will rise again! In three days, *Christ will rise!*"

IN CARS

Mark West

ON THE MORNING THAT IT ALL STARTED, the air had a distinct chill to it and mist clung resolutely to the ground as the sun made its way across the sky.

PC Mike Dougan, carrying the breakfast and drinks, walked back to the Ford Focus patrol car. He and his partner, PC Andy Hedges, always followed the same routine when they pulled the early shift. Their route took them out on the A4300, up the hill out of Hadley Hall and on to Northampton. Part of the road was dual carriageway and in the layby just before, with a wonderful view down on the town, was a little caravan. Lucy's Lunchbox, as it was cheerfully emblazoned, did the best sausage and egg baps in the county.

Dougan put the two wrapped baps on the roof of the car and waited for Hedges to open the passenger door. When he had, Dougan passed him the polystyrene tea cups, grabbed the baps and got in.

"Bit fresh this morning," Dougan said, settling into his seat.

"Did you remember to put your vest on this morning?"

Dougan looked at his partner, who was prising the lid off his tea carefully. Steam rose in plumes, to smother his face. "Of course."

Hedges grinned and took a delicate sip of the tea. "Jesus, that's hot."

"Every day," muttered Dougan, "you think you'd learn."

Dougan put his own tea in the cup holder and started to unwrap his bap. As he did, he glanced up at the rear view mirror secured on his side of the windscreen.

There was a red Nissan Micra in the offside lane, moving at considerable speed, edging across the lane all the time. As the car passed over the rumble strip, Dougan expected the driver to swerve back into his life, but he didn't.

One of the patrons from Lucy's Lunchbox must have noticed the sound and stepped back from the caravan. His tea dropped out of his hands and it was only when the hot liquid splashed up his legs that he moved. But by then, it was too late.

The Micra drove into the layby fast, skimming off the first car parked there and shunting it over the kerb. Its trajectory now shifted, the car hit the Lunchbox patron square on, smashing his legs completely at the knees as he buried his face into the windscreen.

"Fuck," said Dougan.

The Micra glanced off the Lunchbox, rocking the caravan on its tyres. Bottles of sauce fell forwards, smashing against the road in a rainbow. The caravan tipped back, causing buns and sausages to slide out onto the ground.

What remained of the patrons legs caught on something and the body was pulled down the bonnet and under the Micra. The car bounced over the obstacle, but didn't slow.

Dougan could now see the driver, sitting bolt upright in his seat, looking out of the side window as if nothing untoward was happening.

"Move," he said, tapping Hedges's arm hard. "Move the car, move the car."

Hedges, still trying to cool his tea down, looked into the rear view mirror. "Oh shit."

The Micra clipped another car, pushing it towards the road and Dougan was relieved to see that it wasn't going to hit them dead-on now. Hedges had turned the engine on, but was still holding his steaming tea. Dougan reached over to grab it.

The Micra hit the Focus on the offside corner, jerking Dougan and Hedges in their seats. A second later, Hedges yelled as the hot tea splashed over his hands. The force of the impact shunted their car forwards, the handbrake ensured they didn't go far. The front tyres bounced against the kerb and then the car was still.

"You okay?" asked Dougan.

"Yes, no, burnt my fucking hand."

"The impact, Andy, are you hurt from the impact?"

"No."

"Come on then," said Dougan getting out of the car.

The Micra was still moving, crossing the carriageway now. It hit the rough of the central reservation and then clanged into the safety barriers with a thud that Dougan felt in his gut. The front end crumpled, but the car bounced back onto the carriageway, the safety barrier and wires singing in protest.

A horn blared and Dougan turned. At this time of the morning, there wasn't usually a lot of traffic but there were still cars and, whilst some had slowed upon witnessing the incidents, other hadn't even seen it.

A dark blue Vauxhall Vectra swerved out of the way of a braking Escort, until it was almost aiming at the cracked remains of Lucy's Lunchbox. The driver fought for control of his vehicle—Dougan could see the look of terror on his face—and managed to point it back towards the carriageway. But he'd over-corrected and the vehicle almost toppled. Somehow, it managed to stay on its wheels and, as Dougan turned, he knew what was going to happen.

The Vectra caught the remains of the Micra across the driver's door and front panel, shunting the smaller car across the carriageway and onto the hard shoulder. The Vectra, compressed slightly after the impact, shuddered into the central reservation and stayed there.

A chorus of brakes screeched from the oncoming traffic and Dougan noticed, with dismay, that drivers were also stopping on the other carriageway. All around him, it seemed, the air was filled with the sounds of skidding and the smell of hot rubber and smoking brake pads.

He looked to his right and managed to step back out of the path of a car that went past in a blur of light and colour - how it'd managed to get this far without clipping anything, he didn't know. No more cars were coming. Hedges came around the back of the Focus, wiping his hand with a handkerchief, the skin red. From the other carriageway came that curiously dull thud or vehicle impact and further wild shrieking of brakes.

"Call it in," called Dougan and, after checking that nothing was coming, ran across the carriageway. On the other side of the road, a car went up on the verge, its tyres smoking, as it tried to avoid the cars that had managed to stop in front of it. It managed to cling to the small incline and slid back down onto the hard shoulder with a loud thump, stopping as steam started to escape from under the bonnet.

Dougan reached the Vectra and, with some effort, managed to pull open the passenger door. He took in the details in an instant. The driver was moving, but had cuts to his face and forehead and a deep laceration on his left cheek. The airbag was deployed, sagging now. The windscreen was cracked in two places, neither point of impact being the driver's head.

"Are you okay?"

The driver looked at him with eyes that probably wouldn't focus properly for an hour or more. "Think so."

"Don't move, the ambulance will be on its way."

The driver raised a shaky hand and Dougan stepped back from the car. Some of the drivers from this carriageway had abandoned their vehicles and were walking towards the incident. That was the last thing he needed. He looked over at the other carriageway and saw that some of the drivers there, too, were making their way to the central reservation.

"Andy! We've got company."

There was no reply. Dougan glanced at his partner, who was leaning into the driver's side window of the Micra. He saw Hedges push back, as if startled. An arm appeared, grabbed Hedges' neck and pulled him towards the window. Hedges tried to peel the fingers back, but couldn't.

Dougan ran, ignoring the shouts of the people coming towards him, keeping his eyes on Hedges, who now appeared to be struggling with the driver of the car. His head and shoulders suddenly disappeared into the vehicle and he let out a howl of pain, before falling back. He hit the tarmac and pushed himself away, scuttling on his hands and heels.

"Watch it," he yelled, "Mike, watch it."

"Did you call it in?"

"Watch it."

"Andy, did you call it in?"

"Yes, of course, but watch it, for Christ's sake, watch it."

Dougan reached the Micra and was surprised at the amount of blood running down the door. The driver was right back in his seat, his face covered with blood. His head was tilted at an unnatural angle and there was a lump in the back of his neck, as if his spine had been broken. There was something in his mouth that Dougan couldn't quickly identify. The driver's nose was broken, mashed completely flat at the bridge, and that had obviously broken at least one cheekbone, since his left eye had partly slid down into the cavity. There was blood and matter on the steering wheel, the big shatter star on the windscreen was bloody. The seatbelt was clipped in.

Dougan looked at Hedges, who was now sitting cross-ledgged, his right arm pressed into his left armpit. "Watch out," he said. "Be careful."

There was a shout from the direction of the Vectra and Dougan stood up. Three people were standing around it and one, a tall, balding man in a crisp white shirt and sharply creased black trousers, was waving his hand.

"What is it?"

"The driver, he's moving, but he doesn't look good."

He had before, thought Dougan. "Why, what's wrong?"

"He's bringing up blood and more of it is coming out of his ears."

"Fuck," Dougan hissed and looked from the concerned citizen, to Hedges, and back. "Okay, don't move him and don't let him get out of the car. The ambulance will be here soon."

The man in his crisp white shirt stuck up his thumb, then turned his attention back to the Vectra.

Nothing about this scenario made any sense. Dougan leaned into the Micra, through the driver's window, to see if there was anyone else in the car who could have grabbed Hedges. As he did so, he caught movement from the corner of his eye. Startled, he pulled back and managed to evade the driver's grasp as he made it out of the window.

The driver was reaching for him, both hands grasping uselessly, the battered body restrained by the seat belt. The head wasn't moving of its own volition, only rocking with the body movement. Blood dripped from the fingers, the thumbs of both hands useless where—Dougan assumed—they'd been broken by the steering wheel as it span out of control.

"Holy shit." Dougan staggered backwards, the driver's arms reaching for him, and turned to Hedges, who was slowly getting to his feet. "What the fuck's that? He must be dead, his neck's broken and he's got major facial trauma, but he's grabbing for me."

Hedges didn't say anything as he stumbled towards Dougan. His right hand was down by his side now, blood running off it onto the tarmac. Dougan noticed that his first finger and a chunk of his thumb were missing.

"You're injured."

Hedges ignored him. There was a shout from behind and Dougan turned in time to see the man in the crisp white shirt staggering back into the road. Except that now, his shirt was dotted with blood and there was a gash on his cheek.

From somewhere in the distance came the sound of sirens.

The impact, as Hedges barged into him, took Dougan by

surprise and he fell against the Micra door. Instantly, the driver's hand was on his head, grabbing at his hair, fingers scratching his scalp. Dougan pushed himself away, onto all fours, keeping his eyes on Hedges. Or, at least, what had been Hedges. Whoever the person was, staring him down, it wasn't his partner any more. Beyond the violence, Hedges's eyes were dead, his face slack, as if every spark that had been Andy had been snuffed out.

There were more shouts and a few screams from behind and Dougan wondered if anyone else's pristine work clothes were now soiled.

Hedges lumbered towards him, his gait uncomfortable looking.

The sirens got louder, but they were still too far away.

Dougan kicked at Hedges legs and heard a kneecap pop. His partner went down without a sound. Dougan got to his feet quickly and looked around. It was carnage as far as he could see. There were so many people about and far too many of them appeared to have blood on them.

Worse, a group of them were coming towards him.

Off in the distance, over the tops of the parked cars, he could see the first blue flashes of the ambulance.

Hedges got to his feet, took a step and collapsed again.

The man whose crisp white shirt was now soaked red at the front staggered around the end of the Micra. His eyes were just like Andy's had been, pale and switched off. There was blood across his mouth and neck and a chunk of flesh from his cheek had been bitten away. He took another step forward.

The Micra driver grabbed Dougan's trouser, entwining his fingers in a belt loop.

Dougan hoped the ambulance arrived soon.

BLIND DATE

David Williamson

Norman Scrote wiped the palms of his sweaty hands down his corduroy trousers as he paced, impatiently, back and forth outside the Roxy Cinema, that fateful summer evening.

It was his first ever blind date and he was nervous as hell. He had arrived a full forty minutes early, and had regretted having all that extra time to fret over whether his date would indeed turn out to be the girl of his dreams.

In fact, it was some time before he realised that the gangly, greasy haired, spotty faced creature who was standing beside a lamp-post pulling the most horrendous faces, was in fact his date, at which stage, he began to wish that he actually was blind.

There was no doubt that Norman would have legged it there and then, had it not been for the fact that Barry King, the instigator of this rendezvous, had assured Norman that this girls' family were absolutely loaded. Her family were the Thrashlightlys, the fish and chip shop millionaires (surely you've heard of them?) and Norman, being the sponging, money grabbing, gold digging little rat that he was, was quite prepared to date Quasimodo's granny if he thought it could lead to him getting his greedy little hands on a load of loot.

So, with this aim in mind, he steeled himself and stepped forward to greet the apparition before him. Grim and greasy looking as she was, he was determined to sweep the young Miss Thrashlightly off her feet and claim his prize.

"Hello, are you the lovely Hilda?" he asked, a nano second before stepping on a neat spire of dog shit, which caused him to skid forwards and collapse in a heap at the girl's feet.

Hilda held out her hand, mechanically, and appeared not to notice that anything unusual had just occurred. A very red faced Norman scrambled to his feet, muttering something very unpleasant about dogs and their owners.

He pulled himself together as best he could, recalling the reason for being there in the first place, as a vision of sack-loads of fifty pound notes floated through his mind.

His 'date' still stood there, looking blank faced with her hand outstretched and not so much as the trace of a smile on her lips to show that Norman hadn't executed the most dashing of entrances.

Norman dusted himself down and took a closer look at the strange girl. She continued making the weirdest, uncontrolled facial expressions he had ever witnessed outside of a gurning competition. It was a blend somewhere between a leer, a snarl and a demented, manic grin and her mouth displayed two rows of uneven green tinged teeth, with what looked like every other tooth missing.

This, together with a disgusting cooing, bubbling noise that wheezed from somewhere in the back of her throat, gave Norman his only clue that Hilda Thrashlightly was attempting to smile at him.

He fought back the urge to shudder, gritted his teeth and placed her right hand in his before kissing it tenderly.

She had a faintly earthy smell and her hand had an odd almost slimy texture to it. 'Probably been helping her old man peel a few spuds?' thought Norman, resisting the overwhelming urge to snigger aloud.

No sooner had his lips left her unsavoury smelling skin, than she started making the most obnoxious mewing noise. She snatched her hand away and pressed it hard against her spotty, greasy cheek, stroking it as though it was a new pet kitten and continued making a sound very reminiscent of two pigs copulating.

In fact, so loud was the racket she was making, several passers-by gave her and Norman the oddest of looks. Norman merely shrugged his narrow shoulders and grinned sheepishly.

He could see where they were coming from though, they did look an odd couple, with the young good looking, well dressed man (Norman's thought's, not mine) standing beside an escapee from a Hammer Horror film set who was making a very unseemly fuss over it's own hand and uttering the most stomach churning noises this side of an army latrine.

Yes, as Norman watched the small crowd surrounding them grow, he had to admit that they had good cause to be there. He was pretty thick skinned, but even he was now embarrassed by the whole thing and with his limited imagination could think of only two things to do.

The first, and infinitely preferable to Norman's mind, was to run away as though the hounds of hell were snapping at his heels and seek refuge in the nearest pub. The second notion, was to stand his ground and take a deep bow to the assembled audience, and that, for reasons unknown to him, was what he did.

The crowd erupted into spontaneous applause and some even threw money at the odd looking duo. "Best street entertainers I've seen in a long time!" said one man.

"Must be an advert for a new movie?" said another.

"Brilliant make-up on the girl…she was absolutely horrendous!" marvelled a third.

Then, from nowhere appeared a light summer's breeze wafting the smell of dog shit, which was generously attached to Norman's trousers and shoe, throughout the crowd and they dispersed as quickly as they had arrived. Norman couldn't help but notice that there was another pretty unpleasant smell floating from the persona of Hilda as well, but reasoned that anyone who came from a long line of fishmongers was bound to be a bit whiffy?

Moments later, they were alone once more and Norman was pleased to notice that she had mercifully stopped all that billing and cooing over her own hand nonsense. Then, she made her first recognisable human gesture.

Hilda pointed at her incredibly flat chest and moved her mouth, emitting a sort of high pitched, bubbly-wheezy noise that sounded something like

'Meeee eeeeeennngar' and then 'Eeeeeeeegaaaaar.' It sounded as though she had the worst cold Norman had ever come across, or her vocal chords were bunged up with super glue, but as she finished making the weird sounds, she stood there, obviously waiting for some kind of response from a baffled Norman, that dreadful parody of a smile playing across her spotty, corpse-white face.

Norman, who had never been that bright, scratched his head and looked at her for a while. Then the penny finally dropped and he realised that the grease-thing was introducing herself.

"Ah...riiight...gotcha!" he replied "Your name is H I L D A!" he added, in a voice usually reserved for use on the mentally unwell or the hard of hearing. As he spoke, he couldn't bring himself to look her in the eye, not even for all the chips in her father's empire could he do that.

Hilda looked either excited or upset, Norman simply couldn't tell from the frightening expressions rippling across her face, but she 'spoke' once more.

"Neeeeeee! NeeeeeeeeeeeEEEEEEE!" she squealed like a pregnant banshee with terminally painful haemorrhoids.

"Yes... Hilda ...it's a very pretty name, for a very pretty girl." said Norman , ever the smooth talker as his date grimaced, shook her head from side to side and began making that strange mewing noise once again.

Norman considered whether it was actually a wise move to take her into the cinema. But at least no one would be able to see her in there? A courting couple smooched by and they reminded Norman of where his heart was. In his wallet. He decided to press on.

"My name is Norman...N O R M A N," he repeated, very slowly and looked for any sign that she understood this.

Hilda was still mewing and thrashing her head wildly from side to side, her short dark hair dripping with grease. "Neeeeeeoooooooooo!" she wailed, and for the very first time, Norman actually gazed into her eyes.

It was like looking into a vacant plot in a lonely, windswept cemetery, on a moonless night in the dead of winter. He shuddered involuntarily and looked quickly away.

"Noooorrrman" she managed to wheeze "Yooo Nooooorrrman...meeee eeeeeennnngaaaarrrrrr." she uttered in an almost intelligible voice. The problem being, thought Norman, now she'd started, the bloody loony won't shut up. And sure enough, Hilda repeated "Nooorrrman Eeeeeennngarrr Nooooorrrman Eeeeeeegarr" over and over, like a crazed minor bird on speed until Norman could stand it no longer.

"SHUT UP! SHUT UP! SHUT UP!" he screamed and she did so immediately, almost as if Norman had slapped her for being hysterical. Her head dropped to her chest and she stood there, staring at her feet, which Norman noticed, were filthy dirty and clad in a pair of sandals so old, they may well have been left behind by one of the first Romans to set foot on this island.

If it were at all possible for the girl's normally uncontrolled facial muscles to, just for once, work in unison, Norman would have been able to detect that Hilda was in fact sulking. As it was, Norman got the message when Hilda began to whimper like a starving puppy, only in her case, without any of a puppy's endearing ways.

"Now, now…" he tried to soothe the sulking girl, but carefully avoided actually touching her, until he relented and patted her on the arm, instantly regretted doing so .

She clasped his hand in an amazingly strong grip and pressed it firmly to her face.

"Oy!" spluttered a shocked Norman "Steady on, girl!" but Hilda was in raptures and bubbled, "Aaaaaaarrrrr….uuuuuummmmmm" while re-creating that frightening mating pigs sound. Norman just managed to snatch his hand back as she started licking and sucking at his fingers.

"GERROFF!" he screamed in a rather high pitched, shaky voice. He'd never been a man for what he considered 'kinky' stuff, and money or no money, even he had some scruples.

Hilda fell once again into sulking mode, and concentrating all his thoughts on the vast Thrashlightly fortune, Norman decided to make one last effort at winning her round … this time, without laying a hand anywhere near her.

"Come on, Hilda….let's go and see the movie, shall we?"

The film playing that evening was entitled *The Revenge of the Bone Crunchers*, an apparently scary little movie, that, had he been with anyone other than Hilda, would have ensured a lot of snogging in the back row of the cinema. But the very thought of doing anything like that with her, sent a shiver running down the length of Norman's puny spine.

While Norman went and bought the tickets, Hilda was engrossed in studying the stills in the foyer which showed graphic scenes from the film. As soon as Norman approached, she babbled "Maaaaaaamaaaa" in her strange wheezy voice and pointed at one of the stills in particular.

"Looooo" she said, as she dragged Norman closer by the sleeve of his faux leather jacket.

He studied the still briefly. "Yes… man… nasty man," he said, and managed to yank his sleeve free of her slimy grasp.

The main feature had already started, much to his relief, and he was more than grateful that they would soon be in a darkened cinema before anyone he knew could spot them .

Hilda finally managed to drag herself away from the preview stills in the foyer and was sauntering along behind Norman as he headed upstairs to the circle. She looked all about her as though this was the very first time she had ever been in a cinema, her strange piggy eyes lapping up the atmosphere as she walked up the red carpeted stairway.

The cinema was only half full and an enthralled Hilda dragged

Norman to a seat in the empty back row and sat there spellbound. She was instantly attracted to the action on screen, where the 'bone crunchers' were devouring their prey wholesale as Hilda sat drooling and making revolting sucking sounds with her mouth as she looked on, clearly awestruck by the whole experience.

When she started mewing once more, Norman considered that rich people seemed to have no idea of teaching their offspring how to behave in public places. Surely she should know that it's impolite to dribble like that? The seat in front of Hilda (fortunately it and the whole row was empty) was dripping with Hilda's saliva as she sat with her arms propped on it's back, oozing spit like a starving man looking at a steak dinner.

'No wonder her old man's never taken her to the movies before, if this is how she carries on?' mused Norman.

The horrible mangling on screen stopped for a while, due apparently, to a temporary shortage of 'good guys' to maim and Hilda sat back in her seat and looked vacant.

"Would you like some pop corn, a choc ice… anything?" he asked his date.

"Nooooormaan" she croaked, loud enough for a man four rows away to glare at them and say "Shhhhuuuush!" before tutting loudly. Norman held up a hand in apology. 'This is a bloody nightmare!' he thought 'Just you wait til I get my hands on you, Barry-friggin-King….I'll swing for you, lumbering me like this… money or no bleedin money!'

The killing had started once more on the big screen and Hilda sat transfixed and drooling. Norman stood up and determined to get himself a lolly to suck on, when he recalled the unfortunate episode of Hilda licking and sucking his fingers, and he suddenly went right off the idea.

He resumed his seat, half watching the boring film, half listening to Hilda drooling, grunting and squelching, when the dog shit on his trousers and shoe, now warmed by the heat of the cinema, started to hum with a vengeance, adding to the general nightmare quality of his evening.

Suddenly, Hilda began tugging feverishly at his sleeve and pointing excitedly at the on screen action.

"Loooo....Nooooooooorrrman.....meeeee maaaamaaaaaar!" she oozed, jabbing a filthy finger screen-wards.

It was a particularly stomach churning scene, involving a young catholic priest who was being eaten alive by a couple of bone crunching ghouls while he continued to scream for them to confess their sins and return to mother Church.

As the camera zoomed in to reveal one of the creatures stripping the living flesh from the priest's right arm, Hilda became even more animated.

"It's alright...calm down. That nasty thing won't hurt you, Hilda." He tried to calm her as her grunting reached fever pitch. Norman cast a quick look around the seats to see whether anyone was looking, for it sounded for all the world as though Hilda was in the middle of a mighty orgasm. He was amazed to see that the few people in the circle were actually as engrossed in the film as Hilda apparently was and far too busy to see where all the orgasmic racket was coming from.

Hilda was now beside herself with excitement. "NOOOOOOO!" she wailed "MII MAAAMAA!" and pointed wildly towards the screen as she clutched at Norman's right leg with her filthy, claw-like finger nails.

Norman let out a girly squeal of pain, before slapping her hand away as though it had been a tarantula crawling up his leg.

"For Christ's sake…calm down, you fucking loony!" he wailed "You hurt my leg with those bleedin claws of yours!"

By now, all thoughts of the vast Thrashlightly fortune had evaporated from his mind and he was unable to hide his revulsion of the girl for a moment longer.

"Just cos your old man's got a few quid, you seem to think you can carry on like some crazed Aardvark. Why…you can't even talk proper…you smelly bloody crackpot!" and with that, Norman got to his feet.

"I'm off, and your old man can stuff his money where the sun don't shine!"

She moved so fast, that Norman had no chance to react… even if he'd been strong enough.

Her hand darted out and clamped his throat in a grip of steel, dragging him back to his seat as though he was made of straw, and she held him there as he gasped for air.

Norman's eyes bulged from their sockets as Hilda struggled to summon up enough faculties for one last attempt at communication. She pointed once more at the on screen action, at one ghoul in particular, who was currently feasting on the remains of the priest's liver, and said in an amazingly clear voice;

"Tharts…mi…mummee…looook!" It was a command, not a request, and she emphasised the order by twisting Norman's head to face the screen. As he watched the action through bulging eyes, on the verge of passing out through lack of air, he spotted the family resemblance between Hilda and the blood streaked creature dining on the priest's internal organs.

All at once, and far too late, everything clicked into place. The smells of earth and things long dead which rose from the girl's clothing. The deathly whiteness of her pallor, the inability to speak properly via her dried up vocal chords. It all came together, and these thoughts were confirmed for Norman as Hilda roughly stretched his neck and took a huge bite which severed his jugular vein.

As his life ebbed quickly away, his last thought was,

'Shit....I've been on a date with a film star's daughter!'

No one noticed the crunching of bones amidst the screaming and carnage on the screen, or the revolting slurping, gnawing sounds coming from the back row of the cinema.

No body looked as the tall, greasy haired girl, left the cinema, covered in gore, through a side exit and slipped away into the gathering dusk. And when, the next morning, a cleaner discovered the cleanly picked bones stacked under a seat in the back row of the Roxy, a seat formerly occupied by one Norman Scrote, it was put down as a student prank and the bones disposed of in the recycling bin for composting.

Meanwhile, several hours earlier, a pretty blonde girl stood outside the Roxy Cinema and looked at her very expensive watch one last time, before heading off to catch a cab back to her apartment.

'That stupid bastard Barry King! I'll give him a piece of my mind the next time I see him!' thought Hilda Thrashlightly as she headed away from what should have been her very first blind date.

LONE AND LEVEL SANDS
Selina Lock

Egypt 1916

I DON'T KNOW WHAT'S WORSE, the heat, sand or flies. Each is a constant presence and you'd think we'd get used to them, but you don't. Heat like this is unimaginable in Blighty. I long for the gentler warmth of an English summer, breezes rippling through green leaves and feeling the sun kiss your cheeks. Not this interminable, damnable weather accompanied by droning flies and grains of sand in every conceivable orifice.

Routine sets in quickly. We are roused before five to dig trenches, a breakfast of tea and hard biscuits before more digging and the day's work done by eight am. After that the sun is too fierce and it is all we can do to lie in our tents.

This is not what we thought we were signing up for. Where is the fighting and the glory? I had visions of fighting the Germans in France, not slowly boiling to death in this Godforsaken land. Englishmen are not built for this climate. I am too tired and achy to write letters home or even read anything.

We are beset by the khamsin winds. They are heralded by lurid lights in the sky, but are followed by the stinging, biting hail of sand beating against the skin. I don goggles and tie a handkerchief over my mouth, but I only manage a few minutes outside, before the tornado of dust drives me back into my tent.

One day follows the next in a haze of heat, digging and discomfort. I have followed Kelly's advice and am lying naked in the tent. It is midday and I perspire from every pore of my body. It makes the heat slightly more tolerable. I close my eyes and try to sleep, though rest is nigh on impossible. Kelly has also hacked the sleeves from his uniform, but I dare not follow his example there.

I lie on my bunk and stare at the canvas above me. Night has caused the temperature to drop slightly, but it is still hotter than hell in here. I start to drop off, but am woken by tiny, sharp pains in my legs and arms. The sand flies are out in force tonight. I slap my limbs in an attempt to dislodge them, but they're persistent little blighters.

Kelly walks into the tent, his toothy grin cutting a line across the dust on his face. He waves a bundle of letters and a small parcel at me.

"Post's finally arrived. Nothing for you I'm afraid, but me Mum's sent a parcel."

I haven't heard from my sister in weeks, too busy writing to her husband. Last I heard he was stationed somewhere near Ypres. No other family left and no sweetheart waiting for me. Kelly, on the other hand, comes from a huge family and gets letters and parcels from his mother and numerous siblings. He's happy enough to share with me, ever since I shared my rations on the boat over.

He rips the parcel open and holds his prize aloft. A small pot of strawberry jam. Pure luxury compared to bully beef. Before I can say a word of congratulation, he produces a handful of dates from his pockets.

"There was some Gypos at the edge of camp, so I traded for some dates," he says.

We get out some of our ration of hard biscuits and reverently open the jam. Even as Kelly is lifting the lid, flies appear from nowhere, diving into the jam. They swarm round our mouths as we take little bites of biscuit and jam. I try to flick them off but they are not to be dissuaded. I've got used to eating flies along with my meals, but even they can't spoil the taste of sweet, sticky, strawberry jam.

Rumours are rife that we are to move out soon. Rumours are all we have to live on, as the officers remain tight-lipped as usual. Kelly reckons the Turks are preparing to attack and we'll either go up to the front lines, or across the desert to defend the Egyptian border. Anything rather than this interminable waiting. To fight an honourable enemy such as Johnny Turk, who's known to be brave and fights you face to face. Unlike the invisible perils that surround us here. The flies that give you sleeping sickness, the food that brings proud men low with dysentery and the heat that kills unexpectedly.

It's confirmed, we mobilise at dawn tomorrow. Part of an advance party to scout for Turks before the bulk of the battalion move out. The camp has swelled enormously over the last few weeks. We're inundated with members of the Camel Corps, who are needed to transport water and equipment. The men of the Camel Corps still look funny to me, with white clothes wound around their heads and their long tunics with trousers beneath. Most are pretty skinny and go barefoot. I find the Gypos so loud, always shouting something in Arabic, though the traders are far louder than the camel drivers. They do have a knack with those humpbacked beasts though, keeping them calm despite the bustle of troops. I heard the camels give a very nasty bite if they don't like the look of you.

There's an air of excitement in our tent tonight, as we're all eager to finally get to do something. I alternate between fidgeting on my bunk and pacing.

"Will you just relax," Kelly says.

"Can't help it," I reply.

"I know," Kelly says and then smiles. "Let's find out what our fate will be."

He scrabbles around in his pack and triumphantly produces his soothsayer chart. It's some strange native thing he picked up on his last leave to Cairo, though he's lucky that's all he picked up. Unlike Benson, who's been carted off to one of the hospitals, leaving us a man down.

Kelly smooths the chart out on the ground. It has letters on concentric circles and by choosing every fifth letter it will spell out the answer to a question. A couple of the other men give a little cheer at the sight of the chart and wander over to watch. Kelly looks at each of us gravely and then back at the chart.

"Oh mighty soothsayer, enlighten us with your truth. Are we in danger? Will the Turks attack tomorrow?"

"Don't be daft," I say. "If they see us they'll attack us. That's why we're here."

"Hush," he replies, waving me away.

He carefully counts out the answer, noting down each letter and finally looks up.

"The soothsayer says, 'you bring danger on yourselves.'"

"Of course we do," one of the other men says. "We're in the middle of a bloody war."

I think it's not worth getting worked up over a piece of paper. It's just a load of superstitious rot.

We are on the march, our feet sinking slightly into the sand with each step. Cairo is at our backs and the Sinai Desert stretches out before us. We were roused long before dawn and have been moving for a couple of hours, at least. Time becomes meaningless, as all we see is miles and miles of rolling sand, and simply strive to keep in step with the man in front of us.

The passage of time and distance is measured by our packs seeming heavier, our throats getting drier, and the temperature rising in line with the sun above us. I'm keenly aware of my water bottle bouncing off my back. If only I could just take a swig of the contents, but we are under orders not to drink until told to. I glance at Kelly beside me.

"At least it makes a change from digging trenches," he says.

I raise my eyebrows at him.

"Let's hope we get to stop soon," he continues.

I grunt in agreement.

Another hour passes and the sergeant finally calls for a rest break.

"Half your water rations only, lads," he shouts.

Most of the soldiers sink to the desert floor and gulp the water down gratefully. The Camel Corps arrive a few minutes later, and have to replenish the officer's water rations before they are allowed to take their break. I notice that the camel drivers only have a couple of water flasks between them, so must make do with a few sips each.

I try not to drink all my water but the temptation is strong; too strong for some of the others, earning them sharp words and the threat of a charge from the sergeant. I remain standing as the burning sand doesn't seem to offer much relief to my aching legs. I try to ease the muscle pains by stretching each leg out, one at a time. We wait for the order to make camp for the day. After all, the sun is already high enough to suggest it has gone nine am.

There is a disturbance among the officers, voices raised louder than normal, though not loud enough for us to hear. I doubt it's good news for us. It never is. The commander looks very red in the face and the sergeant makes one last remark to him before stomping towards us all. As he passes, I hear him mutter something about "a damn fool idiot."

"Fall in."

My own disbelief is mirrored on the faces of my comrades. Surely they weren't expecting us to continue marching in this heat; it was madness. We wouldn't be in any fit state to dig or fight or even defend ourselves if we went much further.

The camel drivers are initially reluctant to move, shouting in Arabic and pointing at their beasts. Not surprising, as I'd heard there were strict orders not to use the camels between nine and four. They were a much scarcer commodity than men and the army couldn't afford to lose any of them. We couldn't survive a march across the desert without those beasts to carry our water and equipment.

Kelly and I get back into position, shoulders slumped, sweat running down our faces and thirst parching our throats again already.

One foot in front of another, and another, and another. Each footstep brings a fresh stab of pain. The sand rubs between my clothing and skin leaving weeping furrows in its wake. Not even a drop of saliva to ease my burning throat. My tongue is swollen and furry. My lips are cracked and sore. All I can focus on are the heels of the man in front of me, moving to the same rhythm. The sounds of our movement dampened by the sand.

"We're surrounded!"

The shout startles me and I instinctively reach for my gun. It had come from a soldier several rows ahead. He runs out of the formation, several paces into the desert and stops. Looking panicked, head swinging wildly he surveys the empty horizon.

"Hundreds of them! The Turks are here to kill us all," he continues shouting.

Some of his squad rush towards him, but they seem to be moving so slowly to me. Too slowly to reach him before he loads a clip and swings his gun towards them.

"They're not gonna take me." He puts the gun under his chin and pulls the trigger.

The other soldiers slide to a halt as the blood fountains from the back of his head and his body falls backwards onto the sand.

I look away, knowing there is nothing to be done for him, and scan the opposite horizon. No sign of the enemy; nothing but miles and miles of sand.

Benson had succumbed to heat hallucinations back at base, before his current stay in hospital, but his visions had been centred on waterfalls and rivers. We'd found him attempting to swim in the sand, thinking he was back on Brighton beach. That seemed harmless and amusing now.

"Leave him for the vultures," the commander orders from the relative comfort of his horse. "Sergeant, get these men moving."

We stand in shock for a few seconds before the bellowing of the sergeant sets our feet moving again. One foot in front of the other, staring at the backpack of the man ahead. Minutes tick over into hours, sand grains rubbing between our skin and clothes, causing sores. One pain mingles with another and our bodies ache to stop.

A ripple of movement breaks through the waves of our marching, as ruins are spotted in the distance. Lump-like shapes through the heat haze on the horizon; hopefully our destination, or at least a rest stop with some meagre shade?

A couple of officers make their way down the column, reminding us to keep marching. The commander trots after them, his horse's head drooping before him. As he passes us, he whips his horse into a feeble trot, shouting "Get those men down! Imshi, imshi!"

We stumble to a halt to watch his antics, wondering if the sun has got to him too. He goes straight past the last line of soldiers and heads towards the camel train behind us. I can just see some of the camels and realise that some of the drivers have climbed aboard their animals. One or two slither down as the commander moves towards them. Others are slumped over the necks of their beasts, unconscious. Their legs dangling down, each ending in a cracked and bleeding foot.

The commander tugs his horse to a halt at the head of the camel train, gesturing with his whip. Those drivers who are still on their feet start to back away, and the camels start rolling their eyes. He stalks up to one of the unconscious drivers and yanks him to the ground. The man crashes to the sand, his arms flailing feebly. His eyes open, but he can barely focus as the commander leans over him.

Our legs are lead, anchoring us in place. We just stand and stare as the commander raises his whip. His face becomes a snarling mask of hatred as the whip comes down on the driver again and again. The man on the ground ceases to move and his eyes stare straight towards the burning sun.

The wailing of the other camel drivers breaks the spell and some of the officers start racing towards the camel train, their feet slipping in the sand. Before they arrive the commander has started on another half-dead driver, finishing the job just as one of the camels breaks free from the pack. Its eyes are rolling, and lips are drawn back to show its teeth. The commander whirls towards it, draws his pistol, and shoots it between the eyes. The camel's head lurches back and then its body topples sideways to the ground, crushing the containers it carried. For a few seconds, the precious water gushes onto the sand before being absorbed. The essence of life disappearing before our eyes galvanises the rest of us into action. We break rank and rush towards the camel drivers. I hardly know whether we mean to save them or kill them.

The camel drivers flee, some urging their camels with them, others on foot and one man trying to ride his away. An officer tackles the commander to the ground and disarms him. The commander bellows about insubordination and having him shot. Kelly and I are half stumbling and half running towards the nearest camel, whose driver is clinging to the camel's leash while being dragged through the sand.

There is a buzzing, droning noise in my ears. I think it's due to the blood pounding in my veins until I see the black shadow on the horizon. The noise gets louder and the shadow grows larger until we all grind to a halt to watch its approach. I become aware of a hot wind hitting my face and strange lights on the edge of my vision. The sensory overload and exhaustion drive me onto my knees.

The blackness resolves itself into a mass of insects. The sand starts to heave as hundreds of sand flies crawl from beneath, towards the bodies of the dead camel drivers. The insects converge on the bodies, flying into their open mouths, into their nostrils and ears, and crawling under their clothing. Eating through the soft jelly of their eyes, to take up residence in their heads. The bodies start to swell and bloat. Waves of motion beneath the skin make them jerk in a parody of life. They slowly shimmy into an upright position. Their movement is unlike anything I have seen. The cadavers undulate towards us. As they get closer, we see that their eye sockets are nothing but a crawling mass of darkness.

Kelly gasps. I tear my eyes away from the dead men to see that the same process has overcome the dead camel too. It looks like a badly stuffed specimen from the bazaar, bulging in the wrong places. It moves with an unnatural gait towards the commander, who is still lying on the burning sand. The officer who had tackled him scrambles to his feet, screaming with fear, and draws his pistol. A shot rings out and the sergeant barks the order for us to shoot at will. Training kicks in, and we rise to our feet, snatch up our guns, and start shooting at the insect-ridden corpses.

The dead Egyptians jerk as each bullet rips into them. The wounds spew out not blood but dead insects, and as each tiny body hits the ground, a new one crawls up from the sand to take its place. They move forward relentlessly, one foot in front of another, and another, and another. So many legs. The reanimated camel reaches the commander who is still prone with shock. It gnashes its teeth, rears up and smashes its front legs down on the commander's head. His skull bursts and stains the sand with his red life essence, before it, too, is sucked into the hungry ground.

We continue firing at the monstrous things, but it barely slows them down. During all the commotion, the rest of the Camel Corps have become distant specks, as they sensibly fled the scene. One of the insect men grabs the officer nearest the commander—Horshaw, I think his name was—and tears his arms off. Rips them off as easily as you might tear a chicken leg from a Sunday roast. Blood spurts from his armpits, as Horshaw topples to the ground.

I feel bile burning the back of my throat, to match the scorching heat on my hands and the stinging sand hitting my face.

I register the sergeant screaming for us to retreat, as Kelly grabs my arm and pulls me after him. We run towards the lumpen ruins we'd spotted earlier, the only shelter in sight. This is no orderly retreat as the rest of the troop scatter in all directions, fear and heat scrambling their senses. The occasional brief yell of pain tells us we have lost another comrade. All Kelly and I can do is focus on our destination and pray to God we make it.

Progress slows as our bodies start to seize up, pushed beyond their limits. The strange lights we saw earlier herald the arrival of a khamsin wind, whipping the sand up around us. Kelly stumbles and falls face-first onto the ground. I slide to a stop and turn back to help him. He rolls onto his back. A blood stained camel driver's corpse is bearing down on him. He glances back at me and shouts at me to run, before hauling his pack off his back. I assume he is going for a new clip. I fire my last remaining bullets into the lurching creature to give Kelly a chance to reload. Instead he pulls out his tiny jar of jam, and with faltering fingers, manages to unscrew the lid and he throws the jar towards the corpse's head. It bounces off the skull, but as it falls to the floor, a stream of insects fly out of the dead eye sockets. All unity abandoned, now they fight among themselves to be the first to taste the sticky nectar. The monster sags towards the ground and Kelly uses the chance to scramble up. He shoots me a fleeting grin and tells me to get a damn move on. I start running towards the ruins again.

The sand whirls about us as the sandstorm finally hits. I stagger as I try to shield my eyes from the sand, and bump into one of the stone walls of the ruin. Kelly had been a few paces behind me, but when I look back all I can see is a wall of dust and sand.

I slide to the base of the wall and do what I can to cover myself with the groundsheet from my pack. I keep thinking I hear Kelly calling for me, or the sergeant shouting for us to fall in.

I feel the sand pitter-pattering on my sheet, like a cool English rain shower. Perhaps I should throw back my covering and drink in the rainwater, to see if I can finally quench this thirst?

The sand flies start biting and the prickling on my legs reminds me where I am. Englishmen should never have been here at all.

This land does not want us. It has shown me what is worst… it's not the heat and it's not the sand. It's the flies.

And they are coming to claim me, one way or another.

WHITE LIGHT, BLACK FIRE

Stuart Young

I HAD BEEN WITH THE GROUP FOR NEARLY SIX WEEKS before any of them realised that I was more dangerous than the zombies.

They all thought I was a weak and feeble woman, too scared to get my hands dirty with shooting and stabbing, even if it was only on the undead. They never realised that was what I wanted them to think.

So it always surprised everyone whenever I volunteered to go on one of our scavenging raids. It endeared me to them too; everyone knew how much I hated leaving the safety of our camp, so they appreciated my making these occasional courageous efforts.

Morons.

The truth was that I needed to escape the confines of the camp every now and again or my frustration would boil over and I would reveal my true colours. And that would be the end of everything.

So I came into town and pushed a shopping trolley along the supermarket aisle, searching for any tinned food that hadn't already been looted. Terry stood watch by the supermarket doors, a double-barrelled shotgun in his hands, a van sitting outside, the engine idling. Seventeen years old, tooled up and looting shops; the apocalypse had made all his dreams come true. He didn't seem too happy about it.

I didn't really need the chaperone—the zombies had gone, everyone else was dead—but everyone knew how scared I was supposed to be. I had to keep playing the role.

The supermarket had lost its electricity the same time as every other building in town and the further I got from the windows the more the shadows got their claws into the sunlight, turning day into a grey facsimile of night.

"Don't go too far, Nicola." Terry's wispy adolescent beard was invisible from this distance. "I can't keep an eye on you and the van."

"There's some stuff I need to get on the other side of the store."

"All the food's down this end." Terry gestured with the shotgun. The sun blazed through the doors behind him; turning his lanky frame to a silhouette, making the gun barrels look like an extension of his body, a grotesque giant finger.

"These are personal items."

"What, you mean like booze and shit? Pick us up some fags, yeah?"

"I mean like sanitary towels."

"Oh." Even from twenty yards away I swear I could feel his testicles cringe. "You go get them, I'll guard the van."

"Good idea."

As I wheeled the trolley into the shadows Terry called after me. "Good job it's only zombies we got to worry about and not vampires otherwise once a month your sanitary towels would need to be armour-plated."

So witty and sophisticated. Hard to believe he was still a virgin.

I grabbed some sanitary towels and stuffed as many into the trolley as would fit. They weren't the real reason I wanted to get away from Terry but they were still handy to have.

I also grabbed a pack of rubber gloves and a plastic apron. Just in case.

Leaving the trolley by the emergency exit I slipped out into the back alley. Huge metal bins lined the walls. I flinched from the stench; fetid odours hit my nostrils so hard I thought my nose would turn inside out. Body odour had pretty much become a fact of life since the apocalypse and the lack of electricity meant the supermarket carried a nauseating blend of rotting meat and mouldy vegetables, but the bins had stunk even before the world turned to shit; by now their smell was something really special, bordering on the supernatural. Flies buzzed round in an excited dance, partying in an insect Mardi Gras.

Holding my breath I sneaked along the alley, hoping I would find what I so desperately needed.

No such luck.

My hands balled into little knots of frustration, the nails dug deep into my palms, gouging at the flesh, only the tiniest fraction of pressure away from drawing blood.

Then I heard something moving behind me.

Swinging round I dropped into a crouch, my entire body tensed to send me sprinting back towards the supermarket at the first sign of a zombie.

It wasn't a zombie. It was a man. A man with a bow and arrow. Pointed at me.

He was big, both in height and breadth. But from what I could make out beneath his dirty jumper and jeans his body was soft, squidgy. Beneath his beard his cheeks were sunken, the effects of a recently enforced crash diet. The bow was nothing special; it wasn't a compound bow with a complicated set of wires and pulleys that looked as if they had been designed by Heath Robinson. This was just a standard recurve bow; he had probably looted it from a leisure centre.

Most importantly, he looked scared. Not angry, not cold and emotionless the way some people got after they lost everything they cared about. Just scared. He didn't want to die but he didn't want to kill anyone either. So long as I didn't spook him I was safe.

I took the tension out of my crouch and turned on the waterworks. "Oh, thank God. I thought you were a zombie."

He kept the bowstring pulled tight. "They're in this area?"

"I've not seen any. Not for weeks. But I'm always scared they'll come back."

"When did you last see one? The exact date."

"About two weeks ago. Tuesday. A week last Tuesday."

He glanced around, trying to decide whether to believe me. Eventually he lowered the bow. Tiny tremors ran through his right hand; some of it probably came from the effort of having held the bowstring tight during our conversation but most of it was nerves. He was getting them under control now though; no zombies around and he had nothing to fear from a greasy-haired blonde who kept bawling her eyes out.

Taking a shuffling step towards him I put just the right

amount of desperation into my voice. "How many people in your group?"

Abruptly the hope that had been growing in his eyes vanished to be replaced by a terrible aching emptiness. "It's just me."

That was all I needed to hear. The knife I had been hiding in my hand plunged into his gut.

He jerked in surprise as I yanked the blade sideways, slicing from one love handle right over to the other. He dropped the bow and clutched feebly at my shoulder. I stepped back; his hand flopped down by his side. Blood gushed from the knife wound then the slit in his belly widened and part of his intestines slid out, a thick loop dangling down to his feet like a bloodstained skipping rope. The smell of his blood added to the alley's stench but it didn't make it any worse. I'm not sure if anything could.

He didn't cry out which was good. I was going to have to rush things as it was; I wasn't going to have time to do all the things I wanted. And if Terry heard anything I would have to rush even more. Every second was precious.

The bowman dropped to his knees with his hands clasped over his stomach. He looked like he was praying. Maybe he was.

Normally I liked using drugs to pacify my victims but I knew the stabbing had taken all the fight out of him. I just hoped he didn't die too soon. Under ideal conditions I could slice away for hours without causing a fatal wound but these weren't ideal conditions.

I stepped forward and kissed him on the lips. His tongue recoiled beneath mine. Then it was still.

I stepped over the corpse, drinking in the spectacle, the grandeur. I wanted it to last forever.

It didn't, of course. It ended when Terry came stumbling out the door and saw me standing over a dead body with a bloody knife in my hand.

"What the fuck?"

I suppose I could have told him about the thrill that killing gives me, about the ecstasy that spreads throughout my entire being. But I didn't think he would sympathise with that, so instead I turned on the waterworks again.

"He tried to rape me!"

Terry looked over at me, then over at the dead man. He spat on the corpse. "Sick cunt got what he deserved."

I'm not sure if he really believed me or if he just wanted to avoid shooting a woman. Not that it mattered. A quick kill wasn't enough for me anymore. It hadn't been for a long time.

I wanted to play.

Sidling towards Terry I slashed the knife across his right biceps; the shotgun dangled uselessly, his arm no longer able to lift it. Then I sliced his hamstring and he fell to the ground, screaming.

I stood over him. I was going to do to him all the things I had wanted to do to the bowman.

By the time I finished with him Terry wouldn't be a virgin anymore.

Ross's arm hugged my shoulders as I shivered inside the caravan. Outside I could hear other members of our group moving around as they made their way towards the four-foot deep trench that surrounded the camp. They planned to check the coils of barbed wire that lay at the bottom were still strong enough to trap any marauding zombies. As they marched along their voices drifted into the caravan as muted whispers, too faint to make out the words but with the emotions coming through all too clear.

Anger. Hatred. Fear.

Ross's voice carried none of those concerns. His tone was soft, comforting. It had to be, he was the leader: strong and capable and fearless. Besides, he was looking to get his leg over and he didn't want to ruin the mood.

His fingers stroked my hair, the blonde tresses in stark contrast to his black skin. "It's okay, Nicola. There was nothing you could have done."

Actually, I had done quite a lot. Hidden the bowman's body. Binned the plastic apron and gloves I had worn while working. Then loaded the supplies onto the van, along with Terry's corpse, and drove back to the camp with a story about a zombie attack.

Of course zombies use their teeth, not knives, but by the time I had finished with Terry no one was able to tell the difference. It helped that as the police were no longer around to do DNA testing I actually did use my teeth a couple times. All in all my fake zombie attack was so convincing that no one thought to look twice at Terry's corpse.

They didn't even ask what had happened to the rest of it.

They just stood screaming and crying and cursing until Ross took charge the way he always did. He ordered the supplies to be unloaded, Terry's body to be buried (the "zombie" had thoughtfully saved them the trouble of having to decapitate Terry) and then assembled a small squad to go into town and hunt down Terry's killer.

Not surprisingly this last part didn't go down too well. Especially with Roy and Matthew, two denim-clad petrolheads who defined masculinity through horsepower, not through collecting zombie scalps. They argued that it was just a lone zombie ; hunting it would be more trouble than it was worth. Hunting would put the women at risk, and the children. It made more sense to just stay out of the zombie's way.

"Tell that to Terry." Ross eyed the group sternly as he put on his best speechmaking voice. "We don't know how intelligent zombies are. If this one meets up with a large group then it might get it into its head to bring them here. Better to fight one zombie now than fifty later."

Reluctantly everyone agreed, although no one actually volunteered for the job. Except of course for Stevie. He was always looking for an excuse to go back into town. Maybe then he could find some drugs. Going cold turkey since the zombies arrived had cleaned out his system, but I could see in his hollowed out eyes that he wanted to feel the drugs coursing through his veins again, to experience that bliss just one more time. If he had any sense he would have OD'd as soon as he realised that zombies were real and not just a media hoax. Now he spent his entire existence dreaming of finding the one thing that made life bearable, if only for a fleeting instant.

I knew how he felt.

In a small group like this I couldn't satisfy my urges to kill without being discovered. I had gone months without killing and the strain was driving me insane. Every time someone laughed or cried or breathed too loud I wanted to suck out eyeballs, core out an anus like a big juicy apple, and drill holes into a trachea and then play it like a flute.

I kept a secret trophy bag filled with mementoes of my victims' bodies—a kneecap, a heart, a baby's skull—but it wasn't enough.

That's why I had gone into town. In the hope that I could find a dog, a cat, a fox—anything that I could vent my frustration upon. I hadn't dared hope that I would kill a human that day and yet I had been blessed with two of them.

But now it left me hollow. Empty. I could not survive in this small camp in the forest, sitting so quiet and empty with even the wildlife fled. I needed a city. I needed the hustle and bustle of crowds and honking motorcars and people yakking on their mobile phones and rotting their brains on reality TV. I needed somewhere to hide after a kill.

I had told Ross before that we should head out to London and I told him again now. That's where survivors would be gathering.

He wasn't convinced. "That's where the zombies will go too. It's safer out here." He started kissing my neck; his unkempt Afro tickled my neck. "Once society gets re-established they'll send patrols out looking for survivors. Until that happens we're better off staying on the fringes of a small town. The forest hides us from zombies and we're close enough to raid the shops for supplies."

"But the supplies are dwindling. And there's no livestock or game left to eat, there's no crops left to harvest."

"There's no zombies either." He unhooked my bra. "Stevie, Matthew, Roy and I couldn't find the one that killed Terry. He's gone. But we'll go out looking again tomorrow, just in case."

I caught the slight note of worry in his voice as he slid my underwear down my thighs. If he was concerned about my imaginary zombie leading a horde of the undead into camp perhaps I could use that to my advantage.

Ross lowered me onto the sleeping bag. As he entered me I

gave that little gasp of pleasure he always liked to hear. Then he was grinding away while I stared up at the ceiling making plans.

Even from my very first kill I had a sense of there being something more at work than merely physical pleasure.

Yes, the blood washed over me in an invigorating crimson rain. Yes, the filleting of bone and muscle made my clitoris throb and pulse. Yes, an excited tingle ran through me, my nerves dancing like ivory keys beneath the fingers of a gifted pianist. But there was something more.

As I gazed into the structure of the heart chambers, the architecture of the skeleton, the intricate network of veins and arteries, a feeling of joy came over me. And with it a faint spark of revelation.

Somehow the act of killing allowed me to see into my victim's soul.

"What you reckon?" Resting the barrels of his shotgun on his shoulder Stevie looked back at me. "Think we'll find anything worth eating?"

I picked my way through the forest, trying not to get my feet entangled in the undergrowth. "Probably not. The best we can hope to find are some berries that will give us diarrhoea and then a painful lingering death."

"Exactly. We should head into town, see what we can find there."

Stevie's lips twitched as he spoke and I knew it wasn't food he was worried about. He wanted to search every crack house he knew of, every hospital, every GP surgery and pharmacist, anywhere that might still have drugs.

I was tempted to agree with him. In town, away from the others, I could ease the frustration that gnawed at me. I could indulge myself.

Stevie had his addiction; I had mine.

Unfortunately we weren't alone. Behind us were two more pairs of survivors. We never left the camp in less than a pair. And with Ross believing there was a zombie roaming the local vicinity he was even more paranoid than usual, supplying half the foraging party with firearms so they could act as guards despite the reduction this would cause to our work rate. He also ordered each pair to keep twenty metres between us, working on the theory that if the zombie brought friends they would find it more difficult to surround us if we were spaced out.

Personally, I thought Ross was the one who was spaced out. Even though he had spent the last two days searching for my phantom zombie he still insisted on escorting the foraging party, despite being clearly exhausted. His skin used to look like onyx, now it looked like crumbling ashes. He said he was fine, that he used to work longer hours than that in the fire brigade, but back then he didn't survive on whatever road kill we managed to find or wake up in the middle of the night terrified that the tiniest sound warned of a zombie coming to bite his face off. But he pretended that none of this bothered him, that he could go on indefinitely.

I shrugged at Stevie. "Ross doesn't want us going into town. It's too dangerous unless it's either a small mobile unit or a group of a dozen or so."

"There's not even a dozen of us left in the entire camp. So, what, we're supposed to live on nuts and berries all because of one fucking zombie? That's bullshit."

"Be fair, we're living by a small town not a big city with larger numbers of survivors and more food and medical supplies and—"

Stevie took the bait, his eyes lit up at the mention of medical supplies. "Then maybe we should go to a fucking city."

"Maybe you should tell Ross that."

"I fucking will."

Stevie threw me a twitchy grin, his facial muscles failing to work in sync. Dappled sunlight broke through the dense foliage above us; spots of light peppered his body, revealing his form in illuminated pointillism. It created the illusion that the holes from all those needles he stuck in himself over the years had failed to heal up and now the sun shone right through him.

Or perhaps it wasn't sunlight. Perhaps it was the light of his soul.

I stood, transfixed, gazing at the light flowing through him, wishing I could give in to temptation and use my knife to turn it into the real thing.

Over the years each fresh kill had revealed more secrets to me, allowing me to delve deeper into the psyches of those I killed. That first fleeting sense of awe, that tiny spark of revelation had evolved into a steady flame into a fierce blaze into a glorious inferno. I bathed in my victims' souls, my entire being awash in ecstasy.

But each time it took more effort to reveal my victim's spirit. It hid from me, cowering deeper within its physical shell, the body becoming a labyrinth that I had to navigate with different forms of torture before I found the correct route to lead me to my prize.

Stevie would be a most exquisite maze to travel. He already wore his pain like a second skin; I wondered how many layers of skin and of suffering I would need to peel back to reveal what lay at his centre.

My hand closed around the handle of my knife.

Before I could strike I heard twigs snapping behind me and I remembered Ross and the others. They thought I carried the knife to use on myself if I ever got surrounded by zombies. Best not to reveal its true purpose. I would have to save Stevie for later.

More twigs snapped and popped. Leaves rustled violently in the trees. The sounds were too unguarded to be any of our group. Too loud, too conspicuous. And too close.

A zombie burst from the bushes, its decaying hands grabbed Stevie and knocked him to the ground. The shotgun flew from Stevie's grasp. He was too busy to use it anyway; his forearms crossed in front of him to form a bridge of bone and sinew, rammed up tight against the zombie's chest as its weight bore down on him, teeth snapping at his face. Stevie's arms trembled and began to give. As they folded a long moan of despair escaped his lips as though he were a human accordion playing his own agonised dirge.

A cold rage came upon me. Stevie was my kill. This zombie would not deny me my chance to ravage his soul.

Snatching up the shotgun, I jammed the barrels against the zombie's skull and yanked the trigger. Bone fragments and scraps of dead brain sprayed the air as the zombie's head exploded. Not content with that amount of violence the shotgun lashed out at me, the stock smashed into my shoulder and sent me flying. I lay on my back, staring at the zombie; the top of its head had disintegrated but the bottom half remained intact; its jaws still snapped away in a futile attempt to devour flesh one last time before falling still at last.

Stevie rolled about on the floor, screaming, his hands clutched to his face. The big girl was too busy wetting himself to notice that the zombie was dead. Then I caught a glimpse of his face and realised that he was screaming in pain, not fear. A shard of the zombie's exploding skull had struck him in the face, lodging itself deep in his eyeball.

Ross and the others had reached us by now. Some went to help Stevie, others helped me. They wrapped me in a coat and hugged me and talked softly and encouragingly, trying in vain to get me to answer them, thinking that I was in shock.

I wasn't in shock. I was overwhelmed by joy.

As I stared at the zombie I could see its soul escaping into the ether. It was the most beautiful thing I had ever seen.

The atmosphere in the camp was tense, nerves pulled as tight as the tripwires strung throughout the surrounding woods ready to warn of any zombies who came within twenty metres of the caravans. Any closer and the cans attached to the wires would jump and dance, the pebbles that weighed them down to prevent false alarms in case of a strong breeze rattling around like loose change in a washing machine.

But even with the early warning system in place, everyone slept with a loaded gun within easy reach.

It didn't help that Stevie's groans of pain could be heard throughout the camp as he lay awake, lamenting the loss of his eye.

Ross had spent all afternoon and all evening trying to reassure everyone that everything was all right, that the danger had passed, his voice becoming increasingly strained as he realised that no one believed him.

He lay awake beside me in the sleeping bag, going over the same points again and again.

"There's no way the zombie had enough time to meet up with any other zombies and then search around for our camp. The speed zombies travel it barely had time to reach our camp even if it came straight here. Besides, we've been scouting the area ever since you ran into him; if there was a large group of zombies nearby we would've found them by now. Breaking camp just makes us vulnerable; if we're mobile we don't have our early warning system or the trench. We're safest staying put."

He was right. But staying put didn't fit in with my plans. Already I could feel the bloodlust reawakening within me. I needed more victims. And not just human victims. I needed zombies.

I had never killed a zombie before that day. There had never been any reason to. Whenever I encountered a large group of them I either ran or I hid; fighting them would be suicide. An abandoned lockup in the centre of town served as my hiding place until Ross and the others found me and invited me into their group. And while a lone zombie is not much of a threat if handled correctly there seemed little point killing something that felt no pain, which had no soul.

But now I knew better.

The light that spiralled up from the zombie's corpse had a purity that no human soul could match. It possessed a negative illumination that stretched far beyond the accepted spectrum of light, that reached deep into the darkness of realms unknown. It was like staring into the sun: it burned so brightly that it left black spots burned into the viewer's eyes. Killing a human revealed an individual soul; killing a zombie revealed a view of infinity. The black fire spoke of things that link us all, that bind us to the cosmos: death, rot, entropy. All the things that permeate the universe. It went beyond the luminous and into the numinous.

The fact that I saw all this without even having to go to the trouble of dismembering the zombie was just a bonus.

After the others buried the zombie I sneaked back and took its jawbone to add to my trophy bag. But even as I hid it among my other keepsakes I knew it wouldn't be enough.

I had to find more zombies. No one would mind if I killed the walking dead, I could slaughter as many as I liked and no one would care. And I would still have the protection of the group if I ran into more zombies than I could handle.

All I had to do now was convince Ross to stop playing it safe and instead go out hunting for prey.

"What do you mean the zombie that attacked Stevie wasn't the same one that killed Terry?"

To say Ross was unhappy about this revelation was akin to saying that King Herod had been mildly perturbed to hear about the birth of Jesus. Ross scowled so hard his brow nearly reached his downturned mouth.

I shrugged. "It was a different zombie. There must have been two of them."

Ross paced up and down between the barrels of water that hid us from view of the rest of the group. He ran a hand through his untidy Afro; the vest he wore in the autumn sun showed off the agitated ripple of muscle beneath his ebony skin.

"How can you be sure it was a different zombie? Its head exploded into a thousand different pieces. The only way you can identify it for sure is if you're really good at jigsaw puzzles."

"It was wearing different clothes."

He stopped pacing. "What?"

"The zombie that killed Terry wore a T-shirt and shorts; the one that attacked Stevie wore a suit and tie. So unless the zombie decided to dress for dinner…"

Ross's shoulders slumped. "Shit."

I stood beside him and stroked his arm, made him think I was on his side. When I first joined the group I thought Ross was in charge because his fire brigade training made him pragmatic and emotionally tough; qualities essential in a leader. But I quickly discovered that he totally misunderstood his role in the new world. He still thought like a fireman; he wanted to extinguish burning buildings and rescue cats from trees, whereas any sane person could tell you that since the zombies took over you did what you had to do to survive; you skinned the cat and cooked it with the flames from the burning building. Ross couldn't quite accept this; he wanted to keep everyone alive and unhurt, and with each new decision that could jeopardise that outcome came endless self-examination as he weighed up which parts of himself he valued most and which he was willing to discard.

Trying to relieve my boredom as Ross contemplated his navel I glanced over to the other side of camp where Roy and Matthew did battle with the engine of one of the caravans. Motor oil left black marks smudged over their denims. Matthew's bald head glistened in the sunshine while Roy wore an annoying grey ponytail that I wanted to cut nearly as bad as I wanted to cut his throat.

When enough time had passed for Ross to have finished his namby-pamby soul-searching I asked the question.

"What are you going to do?"

He shook his head, speechless.

A cloud drifted slowly overhead; streaks of vapour trailed from around its edges. They reminded me of spilled entrails.

I squeezed Ross's hand. "How many zombies do you think are out there?"

His voice sounded small, defeated. "I don't know."

"You don't think there's a group of them hiding somewhere?" I let my eyes go wide, my lip tremble. The damsel in distress act usually persuaded Ross to do what I wanted. "If there's enough of them the trench wouldn't stop them. They'd swarm over the top of the ones who got stuck and march into the camp. We'd be helpless."

He closed his eyes. Breathed in deeply through his nose.

"Ross, what are you going to do?"

He didn't answer.

"Ross?"

He opened his eyes.

"I don't know."

Taking my hand from his arm he walked over to the edge of the camp. He stood there, staring at the trees and the bushes and the choice that he didn't want to have to make.

Stevie's screams were getting worse.

For a while he had quietened down, drifting off into a fitful sleep, but now he was awake and giving voice to his pain. His throat was raw; his howls of agony had turned hoarse and raspy like a heavy metal singer recovering from a tracheotomy.

The door to his caravan opened and out stepped Laura, the closest thing we had to a doctor – she had worked as a receptionist for a GP.

Her hands clutched at a first aid kit while her face clutched at despair.

I wandered over to her and smiled shyly. "How's Stevie doing?"

Laura shuddered before answering. She used to answer phones and file prescriptions; the worst medical condition she ever witnessed directly was a bad case of chickenpox. "I gave him some paracetamol and rebandaged his wound. I don't even know how long I can keep doing that; we're low on bandages and paracetamol. Ross says the hospitals and pharmacies were all ransacked for drugs months ago. Even if we found some morphine I don't know what the correct dose would be. Besides, Stevie …"

She trailed off, letting me make the connection between morphine and Stevie's drug dependency by myself. That was how Laura worked; she never actually spread gossip herself, she just took a conversation to the point where you had no choice but to fill in the blanks in order to understand what she was talking about. It left her with the satisfaction of dishing the dirt while allowing her to believe that her conscience was still clean.

But nothing about her was clean. Not her conscience. Not her ragged dress or her greasy skin, all sprinkled with blackheads. And certainly not her soul.

I had always looked upon humans with contempt. They were ugly, noisy, repulsive creatures. Their only redeeming feature was the light of their souls. But even that paled beside the negative light of a zombie's soul, that glorious glimpse into infinity. I knew my own soul could not be as feeble as Laura's and the others. When I finally pass away, many years from now, my soul will be a beautiful soothing vision. It sickened me to spend time with

Ross and Laura and the rest of the mindless drones. If I didn't need the group for protection I would slaughter the lot of them just to be rid of them.

But I did need their protection.

So I hid my disgust and nodded knowingly while Laura looked all coy and innocent because certainly no slander had escaped her lips.

Laura tucked the first aid box under her arm. "I think that Ross might know how to administer morphine—he had first aid training in the fire brigade. But even if we found some morphine…"

Ross had not been to see Stevie since applying first aid after the zombie attack. Stevie's injury was a reminder of how Ross had failed the group and how he needed to decide whether to strike camp or stay put. Laura obviously thought that Ross needed to rummage around inside his underwear and see if he could find a pair of testicles.

I agreed. In fact I was going to help him out of his paralysed indecision.

Looking as sympathetic as possible I nodded to Stevie's caravan. "Do you think he'll get any more sleep?"

"Maybe. He's exhausted and the paracetamol will kick in after a while so hopefully he'll take a nap. It'll give his throat a rest and, you know…"

"Give our ears a rest too."

Laura gave me a surprised smile as though shocked that I could say such a thing; then she turned and trotted off across the camp.

Sitting on the step of the caravan I looked out across the camp. Ross stood by the trench, checking the metal sheet we used as a drawbridge could be hauled up quickly enough on its pulley and chains if we were attacked. I hoped he was also considering how quickly it could be lowered. He would be soon anyway.

In the centre of the camp the children played. Tara, Ben and Sanjay. I say played, they just tossed a ball back and forth between them in a desultory fashion, their faces blank and drooping. I was on my break so Beverly watched over them, offering half-hearted encouragement to their games. Beverly kept glancing over at Ross—she had been in local government before she retired and felt more comfortable making plans and strategies than minding a group of snot-nosed kids. Whatever maternal instincts she possessed died at the same time as her grandchildren. Small, sad twitches pulled at her mouth and she looked ready to gnaw her own arm off if it meant a break from babysitting.

Normally I would have cut my rest period short and gone back to tending the kids in order to ingratiate myself with Beverly. Apart from Ross she was the main voice of authority in the group and it was always best to stay on her good side. This wasn't easy as, being plump and plain, she had the tendency to view all women younger and prettier than her as scheming bimbos. The fact that Beverly knew I was sleeping with Ross didn't help. She could tolerate Laura thanks to Laura's cellulite and the blackheads that made her face look like it had been constructed from a dot-the-dot picture, but in this zombie-ravaged world my own rather average looks had acquired supermodel status. Consequently, appeasing for my attractiveness was a full-time job.

But I had something to do that took priority over sucking up to Beverly. I stayed on the step.

Eventually Stevie's screams died down from within the caravan and I stood, stretched, then stepped inside the caravan.

"Stevie?"

He didn't answer. I called him again. I had visited him earlier but he had still been awake. For what I had planned he needed to be asleep.

He still didn't answer, so I crept across the caravan and gently peeled the bandage away from his eye. A tiny black hole peered out from his skull, the edges of the eyelids crusted with dried blood.

After the zombie attack left the bone fragment embedded in Stevie's eye Ross had tried to remove the foreign body. This totally contradicted all his first aid training, but with no prospect of ever finding a living ocular surgeon it seemed the only option. Gripping the bone with a pair of pliers he tugged on it; gently at first then gradually harder and harder. The bone started to shift and then Stevie's entire eyeball popped out, dangling on the end of the optic nerve. If we had yanked out his other eye we could have played conkers. Ross still couldn't get the bone loose, so in the end he severed the optic nerve, cringing as he did so. Neither Ross nor Laura could bring themselves to root around in the eye socket to tidy up this piece of improvised optical surgery, so now the remaining end of the nerve poked out of Stevie's eye socket like a worm burrowing up out of the earth.

Of course I could have dealt with the nerve, I had an intimate understanding of human anatomy, but as I had stood watching Ross butchering Stevie's eye I felt the bloodlust build within me. I wanted to slice open Stevie's chest to reveal his heart and watch it throb and pulse faster and faster as I went to work on the rest of his body. Fighting back the urge caused me physical pain; tears flooded my cheeks. Everyone thought I was upset about what was happening to Stevie. I was, but not in the way they thought.

The only thing that saved me was the fact that I had just seen the zombie's soul. I clung to that glorious vision as I fought the desire to rip open Stevie's torso and use his floating ribs as a dildo.

I didn't have that to help me now as I prepared to carry out my plan. Once I started to desecrate Stevie's sleeping body the bloodlust would be upon me and the only thing to stop me killing him was my own strength of will.

Taking deep breaths I reached down far inside myself, searching for clarity, for sense of purpose. Stevie's soul was unclean; it was beneath me. The dark purity of a zombie's soul was the only prize worthy of me. Compared to that terrible black flame a human soul would be as unsatisfying to me as methadone would be to Stevie's heroin-addled body.

Yes. Now I was ready.

Reaching into my trophy bag I produced the zombie's jawbone. I placed it over Stevie's eye socket and pushed the jaws together so that the teeth nibbled gently at the flesh, drawing forth a trickle of blood.

Shoving the jawbone back in my pocket I replaced Stevie's bandage and exited the caravan. As I left Stevie uttered a small moan. He was waking up; soon he would be screaming again.

If the zombie bite worked he wouldn't be the only one.

Gunshots.

Unintelligible snarls.

Frantic footsteps.

More gunshots.

A window shattered, fragmenting into a constellation of cracks and fissures.

Frightened yells.

Yet more gunshots.
Silence.

Stevie's body barely had time to hit the ground after getting its head blown off before everyone demanded that we abandon the camp and head for London. Ross had to bow to group pressure.

As we left the camp I saw Beverly and Laura hunched over the steering wheels of their respective vehicles. They both looked tense: Beverly with her driving glasses balanced on her fat face and Laura with her mouth hanging open as though waiting for someone to complete one last piece of gossip for her.

Personally, I was excited. We were finally heading off to find some zombies. If I had had time I would have packed a picnic. As it was I had managed to pack my trophy bag, stowing it beneath the driver's seat. It might be some time before we ran into any zombies and I would need something to keep my bloodlust at bay.

I was still disappointed that I hadn't been the one to kill Stevie. His soul had tantalised me when he was human and as a zombie it would have been even more delicious. I suspected that the black flame would burn even brighter in him than in other zombies, his pain and addiction adding to the intensity of the fire. But I never got the chance to find out if this was actually the case. Roy took out one of Stevie's knees (while aiming for his head) which slowed Stevie down enough for Matthew to shoot him in the head (while aiming for the other knee in an attempt to slow Stevie down even more). Now they had finally killed a zombie macho posturing mingled with their fear; Matthew sucked in his gut and Roy preened with his irritating ponytail as they declared themselves authorities on slaying the undead. Of course it was their expert opinion that we should run away before any more zombies showed up.

Still, I couldn't complain. My plan had worked, we were out of the camp and soon I would get the chance to kill as many zombies as I desired. Even better, the kids were in the other caravan so I didn't have to put up with their vacant stares and off-putting smells.

The van and the two caravans trundled along the road in a bedraggled convoy. One driver and one guard to each vehicle. That's all we had left. Ross wanted to just take a single caravan, allowing us to concentrate our firepower if we were attacked, but he was shouted down. Everyone decided it would take too long to redistribute our supplies and cram them into one vehicle.

We travelled at a crawl, not the breakneck speeds everyone had hoped for. The first two vehicles ran fine but the second caravan limped along, belching out smoke like a bonfire mounted on wheels.

Sitting beside me in the passenger seat Ross frowned. "I still don't understand how Stevie got turned. The zombie never bit him."

"Maybe its teeth only nicked him. He had plenty of scratches from rolling around on the ground so it would've been easy to miss a small bite."

"But zombie bites are pretty much instantaneous. How come it took so long to affect him?"

I shrugged. "Maybe smaller bites take longer to infect the victim?"

"Maybe." He didn't sound convinced.

It didn't matter that Ross thought there was something fishy. Stevie's bandage stopped anyone from seeing that he had been bitten after the zombie was already dead.

The dual carriageway was blocked with abandoned cars: some sitting empty with their doors hanging open; some burnt-out husks; some crushed chunks of metal and broken glass as the result of high-speed collisions. Cutting through town was the quickest route to the motorway. We didn't have to worry about the one-way system anymore.

We passed the deserted shops without even pausing; we had already decided that stopping to look for extra supplies would slow us down too much. We drove past the town hall and the sports centre and the lockup where I used to hide from zombies before the group found me.

I was just negotiating a double-decker bus that had overturned on a roundabout when I saw the zombies.

There were barely a half dozen of them; with the whole town to hide in it was no wonder our scouting parties had missed them.

"Fuck!" Ross gripped his shotgun. "Go right! We can be on the motorway before they even reach the roundabout!"

I went left.

After it was all over I could cook up some excuse about not wanting them to trail the smoke from the caravan—it probably really was how they had found us—but right then all I cared about was bathing in the radiance of zombie souls.

Laura was behind us and the sudden turn must have confused her, because she misjudged the distance needed to get round the bus. Her front wheel clipped the back of the bus and the caravan spun around, smashing into the crash barriers. This left Beverly nowhere to go in the van and tyres screeched as she crashed into the bus. Metal crunched and glass tinkled but there wasn't any real damage. Except that the smoke spewing from the caravan now had a flame at its centre.

"Back up!" Ross's voice was a screech. "Back up! We have to get them out!"

My foot hovered over the accelerator. Blood pumped through my body. I wanted to mow down the zombies and watch their souls glow through the windscreen.

But I needed the group in order to survive.

My foot twitched, undecided.

Flames spread from the caravan, licking at the bus and reaching for the van.

Ross leaned over and threw the caravan into reverse, then stamped my foot down onto the accelerator. We sped backwards, both of us fighting for control of the steering wheel.

We smashed into the other caravan. Balls of flames splashed onto our vehicle; bubbles of blistering paint dotted the chassis.

Ross and I wrestled each other to put the caravan into drive but the engine had stalled. I twisted the ignition key; nothing but a pained metallic cough.

More flames spilled upon our caravan.

"Come on!" Grabbing my hand, Ross kicked open the passenger door and dragged me out onto the road. He reached back inside for the small fire extinguisher stashed beneath the seat, but came away with something else.

My trophy bag.

The contents spilled over the tarmac: Terry's fingers, the bowman's tongue, the zombie's jawbone. Ross stared at them for a second, stunned, then snapped back into rescue mode. "Get the kids out of the caravan. Use your jacket to cover your hands when you open the door."

I had no idea why the hell he thought I would risk my life to save those snot-nosed brats, especially after what he had just seen. But he kept yelling instructions to me as he grabbed the fire extinguisher from our caravan.

The flames spread across the other caravan. Through the windscreen I could see Matthew and Laura screaming, but I couldn't tell if they were words or just cries of terror. Then Matthew raised his shotgun to blow out the windscreen so they could crawl out that way, and the crack of the gunshot was joined by a huge whoosh as the muzzle flash ignited the petrol fumes.

The blast hit Roy and Beverly just as they climbed out of their van. The shockwave hurled Beverly backwards; her flight came to an abrupt halt as her legs slammed against the van's wheel arch but her upper body kept going, doubling over backwards across the bonnet; vertebrae snapped under the force of the whiplash. Meanwhile a shard of glass from the exploding windscreen decapitated Roy; he finally got that awful ponytail cut.

Ross and I stared at the blazing wreck of the caravan. Through a broken window I could see little Tara, blood covering her unconscious face and her hair on fire. At least now she wouldn't have to worry about the men fighting over who got to rape her first once she hit puberty.

Heat rolled off the caravan, along with the smell of petrol and burning rubber. I wondered how long it would take for the aroma of burning flesh to add to the mix.

Ross screamed at the flames in impotent fury. The tiny extinguisher in his hand was useless against such a blaze. He might as well try to put the fire out by spitting on it. Snarling with frustration, he hurled the fire extinguisher into the blaze.

Looking round I saw the zombies had been shuffling closer the whole time. They were nearly upon us.

Every fibre of my being told me to kill them, but it was six against two and I didn't even have a gun.

I ran.

We had passed my old lockup on the way here; if I could just reach it I would be safe. Shouldn't be too difficult, it was only a couple of blocks away and zombies weren't exactly renowned for their speed. Even so my heart raced and I could feel the cold sweat of fear upon my skin.

This must be how my victims felt.

Glancing back over my shoulder I saw Ross sprinting after me. More importantly, the zombies were shuffling towards me. They didn't even stop to look at the bodies in the caravans. I'm not sure if that was because they were afraid of the flames or if they just didn't like barbecue.

I raced along the pavement, past deserted shops and empty petrol stations. My lungs wheezed; I didn't know if I could make it. Forcing myself to keep going, I ducked down a weed-infested alley.

Reaching my old lockup I dashed inside and slammed the door shut. I was safe.

Slowly the door swung back open. The lock was busted.

I stared about me, terrified. There was nowhere else to hide. The alley was a dead end.

Behind me I heard shots. Spinning round, I saw Ross turn the corner into the alley and race towards me. Behind him lurched a pair of zombies; each of the walking corpses sporting a spread of ragged black dots where the buckshot had hit. The wounds didn't even slow them down.

Ross caught up with me and practically collapsed against the doorframe. Gasping for breath, he looked at the broken lock and then back at the advancing zombies. Something passed across his face. Something dark. Something terrible.

Straightening up, he shoved me into the lockup. He slammed the door shut and I heard him slot something through the door handles. Whatever it was it held the door shut when I tried to open it.

Staring out the tiny gap around the doorframe, I saw Ross turn to face the zombies. His hands were empty. The thing he used to bar the door was his shotgun.

It was double-barrelled; too slow to reload against multiple attackers. He had decided to put it to better use.

He waved the zombies on. "Come on, you fuckers! Come on!"

He didn't fool me. He didn't care about killing. All he cared about was saving people. Even me. It was his obsession, the only thing that mattered. I almost respected him, even as I despised him.

I wondered what he felt when he saved someone. Whether it was as beautiful as the gift my obsession gave to me.

The zombies swarmed over him. He didn't even try to fight back.

I can't get out.

The shotgun is wedged too tight. I can't get the door open.

That wouldn't be such a problem, but it's the only exit.

Food is becoming an issue. Water even more so.

But the biggest problem is what I saw as the zombies killed Ross. The look in their eyes. I always thought zombies didn't feel emotion, but they do.

They feel joy. Every time they eat.

And not just joy. Ecstatic, transcendent joy; the kind that only killing brings. I should know.

But what they feel far surpasses anything I have ever felt. It stands to reason. They are not hindered by fear or guilt or doubt. They are not bothered by thought at all. They experience everything as pure sensation, including killing. Especially killing.

I see it now. Their black flame blends with the light of their victim's soul. They experience everything. Next to them my own glimpses of the infinite are pitiful.

I should have become one of them.

All this time I've been running from them when I should have welcomed their dead embrace.

And now I'm trapped in here, unable to partake in their glory.

But I'm still hopeful. They can still smell me; they clamour about outside, waiting to feast. Eventually one of them will figure out how to remove the shotgun.

In the meantime I have to satisfy my bloodlust, and as I am the only one here I turn my knife on myself, avoiding veins and arteries but collecting a new stash of trophies: a tongue, two ears, two eyelids, ten fingernails, ten toenails.

I have even unravelled the secret of my own labyrinth. I have seen my soul.

I wish I hadn't. It isn't beautiful at all.

I lie here weeping, wishing someone would rid me of the hideous thing.

Please let them figure out how to open the door.

BUGGING OUT

Joe McKinney

GREG SUTTON SAT WATCHING THE NEWS, a smile tugging at the corners his mouth. On the TV a rookie newswoman struggled to make sense of the jumbled and, in some cases, contradictory updates she'd just been handed. Her composure was fading fast. Behind her was a map of the United States, and on the map, overlapping red circles were spreading like bloodstains. Greg knew it wasn't right to be happy about this, but he couldn't help it. He watched the red circles growing bigger, listened to the fear and trembling in the pretty newscaster's voice, and all he could think was: Hell yeah, baby!

Because he had this.

He was ready for it.

Zombies. He shook his head. That was some crazy shit. He had expected some sort of pandemic. The flu, probably. Maybe some airborne variety of mad cow disease or something like that. Zombies hadn't even made his list of top five most likely world-enders. But zombies would do.

On the couch beside him was a Glock. He had dozens of high capacity magazines for the pistol, plus enough ammunition to turn his little hometown of Gatling, Ohio into his own version of the Chinese New Year. And he had MREs and water and extra clothing and first aid supplies and matches and camping gear and water purification tablets and sturdy shoes.

Yeah, he had this.

Everything was gonna be just fine.

Hell yeah, baby!

Her mother wasn't screaming anymore, but that didn't make it any better. The things were still eating her. Rose Sherman flinched each time they tore away another piece of flesh; every time one of them snarled and snapped at another for getting in its way; or slipped on the pooling blood; or lifted her mother's corpse and then let it thud back to the hardwood floor like a bag of rocks. All this was taking place less than ten feet from her. Rose could have seen it all through the slats in the louvered closet door of her spare bedroom, if she'd had the stomach for it. Instead, she kept her eyes closed and her hands clapped over her ears.

Rose had no idea how long she sat there, terror squeezing her chest, the tears running down her cheeks, the sounds of the feeding frenzy tearing at her nerves, but eventually the noises stopped.

She opened her eyes—and wished she hadn't.

Mr. Masello, her across-the-street neighbor, had been mowing his lawn when the ghouls first descended on their street. He hadn't heard the dead man stumbling up behind him over the roar of his mower, and Rose's own cries and frantic arm waving had gone unheeded. He still had little blades of grass stuck to his socks and shoes. The rest of him was black with her mother's blood and viscera.

He stood up from her mother's body and staggered off.

The others followed.

Rose heard them bumping around in the hallway, the living room, then out onto the front patio.

Her mother's dead eyes were staring at her across a vast pool of blood. Rose stared back, angry at the woman. Her mother had had no reason to come over today except to bitch at her about the Fourth of July. Rose's brother's wife had gone into some kind of meltdown because the dinner was at Rose's house, and not their new place over on Katy Street. Her brother and his bat-shit crazy wife had skipped the party, which was fine by Rose because she'd never liked that woman anyway; but somehow, because Rose's mother was the craziest of them all, the whole thing had turned into Rose's fault. Here it was two weeks later and her mother was still finding excuses to call or come over and start up the argument all over again. She wouldn't let it go. She had to keep picking at it, refusing to let the issue go away. The needless stupidity of all that drama made Rose furious, and not only at her mother—who might still be alive if she'd just been able to leave well enough alone—but at herself, because here she was feeling angry when her mother was dead and what she should be feeling instead was sorrow and a great, soul-numbing emptiness. Rose nearly kicked the closet doors in her frustration. Even in death her mother made her crazy.

But she knew she couldn't stay in the closet forever. Already she was thirsty. Hunger would follow soon after. And she would have to go to the bathroom eventually. The idea of doing that in here, being closed up with the smell, was the deciding factor. She stood up, listened carefully, and not hearing anything but the distant warble of a receding police siren, slowly and quietly pushed the door open.

An afghan pulled from the foot of the bed had soaked up a lot of her mother's blood, giving Rose a straight shot to the door. At least she wouldn't have to walk through it, even if she couldn't exactly help looking at it.

She turned her head and walked toward the door.

She was almost through to the hallway when she caught movement out of the corner of her eye.

Mr. Harris, the creepy Gulf War vet who lived two doors down, was kneeling between her mother's knees, his face buried in a massive gash a few inches from her groin. He was tearing at the flesh there, ripping it away, when suddenly the leg separated and hit the floor with a dull, heavy thud.

Rose sucked on her teeth, a whimper escaping her throat.

Mr. Harris looked up. Half of his face was torn away, and what was left of the eye in the ruined socket twitched and jumped constantly, like a moth caught in a jar. He climbed to his feet, and to Rose's horror picked up her mother's severed leg before stumbling after her.

Rose ran screaming from the room.

She tore through the hallway, the living room and out the front door, tumbling down the front steps and landing face-first in the grass. When she looked back at the house, the front door was yawning open. Mr. Harris was standing there, holding her mother's leg by the ankle, letting it drag behind him.

It was getting dark. Gloom pooled beneath the trees and in the spaces between the houses. But there was still enough light to see the dead gathering in the street, turning their heads as one in her direction. They began to moan, and one by one started toward her.

Mr. Harris dragged the leg down the stairs. The next instant, he was standing over her, his damaged eye jumping madly in its socket.

Rose turned and ran. She had no plan, no idea where she was going. All around her huge columns of smoke climbed to the darkening sky. Dogs were barking wildly. Here and there a gunshot. A siren. Screams.

And then, several streets over, she stumbled out from between two houses and found herself facing Greg Sutton's house.

She'd gone out with him a few times during her junior year, but had told him—quite publicly, in fact—to go cram it when she found out he was telling the whole school they were fucking.

All that drama seemed like a million years ago. She'd forgotten he lived so close.

Looking past the lies that they'd been intimate (he hadn't even gotten under her bra, the bastard), she remembered that he was a survival nut, always talking about what he was going to do when the big one hit. She didn't know if he was still into all that survivalist stuff, but the tall brick wall that surrounded his yard certainly looked better than standing out here in the street.

She went to the wrought iron gate at the front and found it chained and locked.

"Damn it," she said.

A low, stuttering moan behind her caused her to whirl around. Mr. Harris was there, still dragging her mother's leg.

She turned to the gate and rattled the bars, calling for Greg to come open them.

A moment later, Greg opened his front door. He stared at her, then his eyes went wide with recognition.

He hustled down the front walk.

Greg Sutton had gained a little weight since high school, but it had only served to fill him out. In his flannel shirt with the rolled up sleeves and faded jeans he actually looked better than Rose remembered.

"What are you doing out there?" he asked.

"Greg, open the door. Hurry please!"

He looked over her shoulder to where Mr. Harris was staggering into the street, the severed leg leaving a gory trail across the pavement to mark his progress.

Greg nodded. "I got the key here somewhere," he said, and pulled a large carabiner key chain from his pocket and started flipping through the keys.

"Jesus, Greg, hurry!"

"This is it," he said.

The lock sprang open and Greg pulled the chain free from the bars. Rose pushed past him, into the yard. "Close it up," she said. She was out of breath, the blood pounding in her ears. "Hurry!"

She started babbling, telling him about the zombie that had attacked Mr. Masello while he was mowing the lawn and how they had gotten into her house and how her mother had pushed her into the closet and closed the door and tried to fight the dead men who had managed to get inside the house and how her mother had died and was eaten.

Greg grabbed her shoulders and shook her until she stopped. She closed her eyes and breathed deeply, collecting herself.

"We have to get inside," she said.

"Uh," he said.

He looked terrified, though Rose hardly noticed. She thought it was because Mr. Harris had finally made it to the gate. He still held her mother's leg in his right hand, but now he was beating on the metal bars with his other hand.

And he was starting to draw a crowd.

"We have to get inside," Rose said again.

"Uh, yeah." He looked like a man steeling himself against bad news. "Come on. It's easier if we go in through the kitchen around back." He led her around to the back, where a short, covered walkway connected the back door to the garage. "Watch your step," he said, and opened the door onto a mudroom. There were boxes stacked along the walls, most of them showing pictures of police and hiking boots on the lids. Stacks of coats were piled high on the washer and dryer.

At first Rose thought it was some hasty attempt to barricade the door, but then she saw the kitchen and the living room beyond that, and she gasped. Everywhere she looked there were piles upon piles of boxes, stacks of clothes, plastic storage bins, clutter everywhere. But not just clutter, she saw. The clutter was made of tents, backpacks, portable camping stoves, sleeping bags, jackets, medical first aid kits, plastic buckets marked 72 hour disaster kit, jumper cables, more backpacks, machetes and knives and pistols and ammunition, nearly all of it still in the original boxes and stacked three or four feet deep in a jumbled mess that resembled a junkyard after a tornado. It was everywhere. There weren't even lanes through the clutter. It was simply one large amorphous mound of stuff. Greg Sutton, the guy she had once dated, was a hoarder.

"Greg," she said hesitantly. "What…is all this?"

"Watch your step," he said. "It gets a little tricky. Here, come on, there's a spot on the couch where I sit."

He offered to take her hand, but when she didn't take it he climbed onto a pile of boxes and crawled over the clutter toward the living room.

"Hey, Mom! Somebody's here!"

His sudden scream jolted her loose from her thoughts. She blinked at him as he climbed over the piles of survival gear, testing his footing before putting his weight down, one hand out to steady himself on a teetering stack of plastic storage bins.

She had seen this on TV, on those reality intervention shows, but seeing it now, like this…for the moment, the zombies were forgotten. Even her dead and mangled mother was forgotten.

Her nose crinkled in sudden disgust. There was a rotten food smell in the air that she was only now noticing. Greg didn't seem to notice, though. He had made it to the couch and was giving her a wounded, apologetic smile.

"You're the first person I've let in here in four years," he said.

She didn't know what to say. She tried to speak, but couldn't find her voice.

"I'm sorry about your mother," he said. "I remember her. She was nice."

Rose guffawed. It was a crazy, hysterical sound.

Greg frowned.

He tried again. "I've got some water, if you're thirsty. Food, too. Some of those MREs, you know, the Meals Ready to Eat? They have like thirty-five hundred calories each. Enough for one meal to last all day."

Greg slid down the side of a stack of boxes and shifted some ponchos and rain-proof tarpaulins to one side. He lifted a cardboard box labeled ASSORTED MEALS - READY TO EAT and dropped it onto another stack of boxes. The bottom of the box was wet and it split open when it was dropped. A brown, sludgy goo ran down the side of the stack, giving off a vile, rotten smell.

Rose gagged and pushed the heel of her hand against her nostrils, trying in vain to block out the smell.

"Oh, man," Greg said.

He peeled away the side of the box, lifted a ruptured bag of something rotten between his index finger and thumb and dropped it off to one side.

Rose saw flies buzzing around his head.

"Some of this stuff is probably still good," Greg said. "Yeah, I can save some of this."

Rose gagged and nearly vomited.

"You can't eat that, Greg. Oh God."

"No, no, it's okay. This is military stuff. It's made to keep the food inside safe. Really, it's okay."

She shook her head.

"We should leave here," she said. "This isn't safe."

"Yeah, those things out there," he said.

"Do you have a car?"

He nodded. "A '74 Bronco. Four wheel drive."

"Has it got gas?"

"Yeah," he said, the word coming out as a part chuckle. "I got plenty of gas. I've got gas cans and spare tires and enough gear to rebuild that thing three times over if we need to."

"That's good. Maybe we could, uh, pack up some of this stuff in the Bronco and leave. I don't know, go out to the country someplace, away from the big cities. I heard it was happening everywhere, but that it was really bad in the big cities."

She was nearly babbling again, but something about the look on his face made her pause. He was horror-stricken. He looked as frightened by what she was saying as she had been when Mr. Harris stood up from her mother's groin, blood running down his chin, strips of flesh hanging from his teeth.

"What?" she said.

He shook his head. "No, you don't understand."

"Huh?"

"I can't leave…here. I can't leave this stuff. It's my stuff. I need it."

"Your stuff? Greg, most of this is trash."

"Trash?" He laughed. It was a whiny, delirious sound. "No, it's my stuff. I have lots of stuff. I'm protected."

She didn't like the look on his face, the way he was looking at her. It was all wrong. She felt suddenly nauseous.

"I have stuff," he said. His tone was becoming defensive, angry. "Do you have stuff? You don't, do you? That's why you came here. You're not prepared, are you? But I am. I have all this stuff. You may think it's trash, but it's not. It makes me feel safe. I am safe. Are you safe?"

She stared at him, utterly dismayed. For the first time she noticed the TV was on, some news show, the same spreading red circles on the map she'd been seeing since earlier that morning. The light from the image cast half of his face in a flickering yellow glow. It made his skin look sallow in the dimness of the living room.

"Greg, what happened?" She gestured at the piles of crap all around them. "How did it get like this?"

"This is the way I like it."

"Yeah, but, what purpose does all this serve? How could you possibly expect to use all of this stuff?"

He seemed honestly perplexed by the question. He pointed toward the street. "You just came from out there. How can you not see that all of this stuff has value? Those zombies can swarm for years out there. I can hold out. I have all this stuff. And if things get really bad, I can bug out."

"But that's just the thing. You won't bug out. You're so tied to this stuff you can't leave it behind, even when it's the right thing to do."

"Stop trying to get me to leave my stuff!" he said. The sudden fury of his words shocked her. He looked savage and cruel, like she had just threatened something he held sacred. It scared her. She wanted to leave. Or least not be around him.

"Greg, I...I need to use the bathroom."

Gradually, the heat left his eyes.

"Yeah," he said. "Yeah, okay. Um, it's through there. Down that hallway. Can you get through there?"

She climbed onto a pile of boxes and worked her way back to the hall that led to the rest of the house. Boxes were stacked floor to ceiling down the length of the hallway, though a narrow lane had been left to allow access. If she turned her shoulders sideways and shuffle-stepped she could make it.

She came to the end of the hallway and looked around. The power was out or the lights didn't work, Rose wasn't sure which. Either way she was standing in the dark, wondering why in the hell she was doing this. It was ridiculous for her to be groping her way around this horrible house, but she was doing it just the same, going deeper and deeper into the outward manifestation of Greg's insanity. Anything to be out of his presence.

There were several doors back here and any one of them could have been the bathroom. Each one was nearly blocked by trash and for a moment she thought of the hoarder shows she'd seen on the TV, the way some of those bathrooms looked. She didn't know if she could handle something that disgusting. Clothes and junk—that was one thing. Even the spoiled, oozing food she could sort of deal with. But to walk in on a bathroom spilling over with mold and human waste, that would put her over the edge.

She opened a door next to her and coughed. The smell of rotten food was even stronger in here than it had been when Greg busted that box up front. Rose was closing the door when she heard a faint rustling, like a chain smoker breathing.

Something moved in the darkness.

"Hello?" she said. "Mrs. Sutton?"

She put a hand over her mouth and stepped as far into the room as the stacks of survival gear allowed.

"Mrs. Sutton?"

Again, something shifted in the darkness. The smell was awful. Rose turned her head to one side in a grimace and saw a flashlight poking out from beneath a pile of coats. She picked it up, turned it on, and pointed it through the stacks of the boxes.

A desiccated woman, long, long dead, nearly mummified, was staring back at her through a bird's nest tangle of gray hair. She looked brittle, dusty, and when she moved, a swarm of flies moved with her. She opened her blackened mouth and a gravel-rough gurgle escaped her throat. A gnarled bony hand shot out at her through a gap in the stacks and Rose stumbled backwards, tripping over something and landing on her butt in a box of medical supplies.

Mrs. Sutton was really struggling now, raging against the boxes that trapped her in the far corner of the room. Rose stared at the woman's leathery arm, the sliver of her face visible through the crack, and then she turned toward front of the house, contemplating Greg Sutton. This was his mother, for God's sake. How long had she been back here, dead? Was this some weird "A Rose for Emily" type of thing, or did he even know she had died? Rose couldn't decide which alternative was worse.

The boxes toppled. They crashed down at Rose's feet and Mrs. Sutton stumbled forward, the gurgle in her throat going up an octave, becoming urgent.

Rose scrambled out of the room, tripping over boxes, groping along the wall as she found the hallway in the dark. Mrs. Sutton was right behind her, the flies murmuring angrily around the gummy pits that had been her eyes and the blackness of her mouth. Rose pulled boxes down behind her, hoping they'd prove a barricade against the woman.

Then she was out in the living room and Greg Sutton was there, standing exactly where she'd left him in front of the TV, staring after her.

"Gonna head out on my own," she said to him. "Thanks for taking me in."

"You're gonna what…?"

He crawled onto the boxes and tried to go after her, but she was already dropping down into the kitchen.

"Rose, wait."

She didn't slow down. She waved once over her shoulder without turning around and headed for the mud room. She had her hand on the back door when she heard him say, "Mom, what are you—"

His screams were cut off by the slamming of the door.

She crossed the yard to the driveway, not bothering with the front gate. She didn't have the key, after all; and besides, there were plenty of those things out there, hovering around the front of the house. Better to jump the side fence and slink off into the darkness, unseen.

She was impressed by how calmly she decided all of this. All things considered, she had every right to behave like a stark raving lunatic right about now. But she wasn't going to do that.

Rose reached the brick wall and climbed over it, taking her time to make sure she landed safely. There was no point in rushing this. Rushing would get her hurt, and a sprained ankle right about now would be as almost as deadly as a bite from one of the walking dead roaming the streets.

But being careful wasn't the same thing as being quiet, and she ended up making a lot of noise. She turned the flashlight she'd taken from Greg Sutton's back room on the front corner of the house and was not surprised to see Mr. Harris rounding the corner, still dragging her mother's severed leg. It was the kind of day, after all, when mothers kept coming back for more.

THE RHYME OF ALBERT GREENTREE

Zach Black

IT WAS JUST AN OLD CEMETERY. At least, that's how Samuel Doyle, Brayhurst Graveyard's only living resident described it; just an old cemetery... to them, but to Doyle, it was his home.

The lofty attendant's house sat neatly in the corner of the cemetery as it had done for years. It was an heirloom, occupied by generations of Doyle's who had passed on the family trade to their successors. Samuel Doyle could not imagine himself living anywhere else.

From a young age, Doyle had helped his father attend to the cemetery, frequently acting as sexton and caretaker. It was more than just a graveyard to Samuel Doyle back then too. It was a place of exquisite and exaggerated emotion, filled with darkness and pain for some, but not for Doyle. For him, the cemetery was overflowing with delights everywhere he looked, leading his young, fertile imagination down every possible avenue, where it would flourish.

He would wander the rows of headstones, and memorials reading the numerous epitaphs and imagining what the people resting beneath the ground had been like in life. Every slab bore a story, sometimes of despair but just as often of inspiration. First regiment second battalion, Sgt. Gareth Hippock, loving husband and son, fought valiantly and died for his country Sept. 21st 1916 aged thirty-five. The young Samuel Doyle had imagined a tall, square jawed soldier with bulging forearms and a severe look of determination in his eyes, a real, old fashioned hero.

Some of the dates reached all the way back to the late 1700's. Doyle's favourite was positioned in a focal point between two, sturdy oak trees at the rear of the cemetery. The grave was that of Albert Greentree, once mayor of Kingshire.

1790 – 1861
Betwixt these boughs, whom seeds he did sow,
Lies Albert Greentree, to a debt we owe,
Once mayor of Kingshire, now heaven bound,
Lest threat should befall this hallowed ground.

The rhyme had caused young Doyle many a sleepless night in his youth. There were nights where he would awake screaming in terror from horrifying nightmares of Mayor Greentree pulling his long dead, skeletal form out of his grave. That is, until his father forbade him to attend to that particular site again.

The last known burial was that of Wendaline Finnarton back in nineteen sixty-five. Wendaline was the caring mother of James and Erica Finnarton and the loving wife of Joseph Finnarton; so her epitaph claimed.

By that time, Doyle had taken over his sickly father's duties in the cemetery. After his father died, Samuel continued those duties, keeping the grass mown, the flowers fresh and the gravestones clean all year round despite the cemetery's lack of visitors. Even after the cemetery had run out of plots, as a captain remains faithful to his sinking ship, he continued his service to the dead, for one day he himself would be amongst them.

The local council had made plans to exhume the corpses and flatten the land to make way for a development project that would see Brayhurst, with current population of little over two thousand people become a booming retail centre.

Doyle couldn't allow it—for one thing, Elspeth, his wife lay in her eternal resting place in the Doyle family private burial ground out back along with his mother and father. The notion of her still being so close to him had convinced the old man that Brayhurst was where he belonged, 'til his final breath and beyond.

Brayhurst was a little forgotten seaside village with more sea than side. Doyle could look out of his bedroom window over the craggy coastline and meagre bay on a clear day and watch the beacon of the lighthouse on Horse Island puncture the night intermittently. That's where he was standing on the evening he saw the ominous black BMW roll through the front gates of the cemetery like a panther stalking its prey.

Old Doyle had invited Glen Hutchinson and the tall, looming Kyle Jackson, legal representatives of Kingshire council into his humble abode at the very corner of Brayhurst cemetery and served them two steaming mugs of his finest instant coffee. Doyle had seen the plans and spoke to the men long enough to realise that eventually, the powers that be would have their way; whether he was alive and kicking, or occupied the one remaining plot his father had reserved for him back when business was in full swing. And if that was the way things would pan out, Doyle wasn't about to make it easy for them.

"Mr Doyle; I'm afraid don't understand your stance on this. We would make every provision for you and our offer is more than generous- others would have been offered a fraction of what my client has put on the table so to speak." Hutchinson sniffed and shook his head pityingly.

"I don't give a damn what those bastards are offering, you can tell them to shove the whole lot up their tight backsides!" Doyle growled, frowning angrily.

"But your neighbours have accepted a price that…"

"That, sir is not my business," the old man snapped. "Have some bloody respect for the dead for Christ's sake— Let them rest in peace. Would you stand by and watch your families graves desecrated to make way for a flamin' shopping centre?"

"Actually, Mr Doyle, most of the relatives of the more recent passed in Brayhurst have been contacted and have given their permission to have the bodies…relocated." Hutchinson raised an eyebrow as he accentuated 'passed', this only served in enraging Doyle further.

"Relocated?" Doyle drawled, mimicking the solicitor's pomposity. "Exhumed then burned to cinders and posted to a distant relative in a jar no doubt. If they have given their consent, so be it. However, I have not given my permission for anything and I shan't be. So, if you would be so kind as to remove your ghoulish backsides from my couch and make your way to the exit, please."

Hutchinson stood up and snapped his briefcase closed. Then, as an afterthought, lifted the contract and held it out to Doyle. "If you should change your mind—"

"I won't," the old man snapped, holding the solicitor's gaze in stubborn refusal of the document.

"I am disappointed to find you so resolute Mr Doyle. Maybe you should consider making use of that secure looking padlock fixed on the entrance of your property." Hutchinson pointed a long, tapered finger in the direction of the open gate, "I was most sorry to hear about Mr Akhtar, the proprietor of Brayhurst convenience store. Burned to death while he slept in the flat above his business I believe. Shame, he was such a likeable fellow too. He shared the same views on the council's enterprise plans as you."

Hutchinson stood for a long moment, as though searching for a micro-expression of vague understanding on the old man's countenance. Doyle stared back into the solicitor's cold, sunken eyes and his sharp features impassively. Doyle could feel the eyes of the big man—Jackson—boring into the back of his skull like two burning pinpricks. Finally, Hutchinson broke his gaze, jerked his head at Jackson who lumbered past, dwarfing Doyle as he exited the house.

"Goodbye, Mr Doyle, take ca—" Doyle slammed the door shut, muting the end of the solicitor's farewell.

Of course he had heard about Akhtar. News travels fast in small villages and bad news travels twice as fast. Doyle doubted that his death was an accident and he knew that Hutchinson's advice was not that of a concerned acquaintance. The solicitor was anything but that, and his colleague's silent stare disturbed Doyle deeply. There was violence behind that seemingly neutral gaze. Although a simple, uncomplicated man, free from the burdens of high intellect, Doyle was not stupid. He knew a threat when he heard one and he also knew Hutchinson had implicated himself in Akhtar's death. There would be no point in calling Sergeant Denholm as the pair would only deny it.

He leaned with his back against the door for a time until he heard the growling engine of the BMW fade as it made its retreat out of the cemetery.

Doyle ran a damp cloth over the fascia of the modest headstone, taking special care to avoid the fading gold paint in the shallow, carved indents spelling Elspeth's name. He had spent the past hour or so explaining the situation to his deceased wife. He had to keep her in the loop. After all, it was her home too and he was determined that no one was going to take it from them.

Sometimes he imagined her sitting by the fireplace, a roaring heat in the hearth and her knitting needles clacking erratically, slowly churning out yards upon yards of woollen items. Crocheted throws and woollen plaids adorned their furniture and Doyle was never short of sweaters and cardigans. The image was so poignant, that he swore he could hear her rolling out one of her favourite and often uttered sayings. It's the way of the world no Samuel. No one respects us old biddies anymore.

A smattering of rain began to descend and the temperature dropped further. Doyle shivered involuntarily and pulled himself to his feet, grunting at the stiffness in his back and legs. He hobbled to the back door of the house and let himself in, locking and bolting the door behind him. This was something he was not in the habit of doing but under the circumstances, he felt it wise to take precautions. He had even heeded Hutchinson's advice by fastening the padlock to the entrance of the premises earlier in the evening. Although, if he were to fall prey to foul play, Doyle doubted whether lock or bolt would keep the duo from trespassing. That is, if they did their own dirty work. Regardless, if they arrived, Doyle would be ready.

He had hefted the long-handled wooden axe he had retrieved from the hut shortly after Hutchinson and Jackson's departure and creaked upstairs to the master bedroom, turning out the lights as he went. He propped the axe by the side of his bed and crawled onto the soft mattress still fully clothed. He was convinced that sleep would evade him after the day's events, but after a few minutes' idle contemplation, he drifted into a serene state beyond consciousness.

It was around three in the morning before Doyle woke. He was sure he had heard the crunch of gravel under foot below his bedroom window. He was about to dismiss it as the waking effects of his dream, but as he lay, now fully awake, the blazing outdoor security light blinked on. Something or someone had tripped the sensor.

Doyle swung his legs out of bed and sat there for a moment to collect his thoughts. The security light was sensitive, it wasn't unusual for a stray cat, fox or even a hedgehog to trip the sensor, but the events of the day had made him wary, even more than usual. His unwanted visitors had given him the willies and he had every right to be cautious.

He pulled on his boots, not relishing the prospect of even so much as a brief foray out into the cold, damp night, especially if the trespassers turned out to be Hutchinson and Jackson. What would he do then? He was an old man he stood no chance against those two. If he wandered outside into the darkness, he would just be falling into their trap. But Doyle wasn't going to give up that easily, he would still put up a fight for what little he had left; his land and his dignity.

He gripped the axe, testing its weight to ensure that he had enough strength to wield it should circumstance require him to use force to defend himself before quietly descending the staircase. Then, he pulled the door open cautiously, reaching blindly for the torch he kept on the alcove, and ventured into the night, pulling the door closed behind him.

He gazed into the still syrupy blackness for a long moment before stepping into the night and immediately, the dazzling glare of the security light tripped on again revealing a vast portion of ground, almost blinding him.

Doyle gazed around at the familiar myriad shapes of surrounding headstones and monuments. When nothing moved, he trudged across the soft ground, away from the glare of the outdoor light, sweeping the torch beam in wide arcs. Doyle wandered the circumference of the house in this fashion, but he found no evidence of trespassers.

He was about to head back inside when a sharp crack carried across the cemetery, followed by another. Doyle gripped the axe tight and stepped off the gravel path, on to the turf, where his footsteps would not be heard.

Further up the graveyard, he caught sight of two figures. He knew immediately who they were. He didn't need to see their faces. The largest of the pair, who Doyle assumed was Kyle Jackson, swung a hefty sledgehammer, smashing a nearby headstone to pieces. Doyle dashed forward, crying out.

Hutchinson slowly turned to face the old man, bringing the beam of his torch in line with Doyle's face. "Good evening, Mr Doyle."

"Get out of here, now, before I call the police."

Jackson gazed at him distractedly for a second before hefting the sledgehammer again, breaking another stone in half.

"The police will not help you Mr Doyle. Only you can help yourself." Hutchinson removed a neatly folded piece of paper from his suit jacket.

Doyle glowered at the man. He trembled with anger and as the adrenaline began to soar through his veins, he grew braver. Shoving the torch carelessly into his pocket, he brandished the axe before him in both hands.

"Last chance, I'm warning you," he growled.

Hutchinson merely smiled, unperturbed. He seemed to know that Doyle barely had the strength, let alone the will to use the weapon. He proffered the contract, smiling steadily.

Meanwhile, Jackson had dropped the hammer and was striding towards Doyle. Doyle shook the axe menacingly, but the big man easily plucked the weapon from his grip and with one hand on the grip, buried the blade almost completely into a nearby oak tree.

Hutchinson's smile diminished, he raised his leg, aiming a well placed kick to Doyle's abdomen. The old man crumpled, collapsing on to his knees and sucking great lung-fuls of frigid air.

"I've tried being nice to you, Mr Doyle, and it's clear that you don't respond well to courtesy. Now, I am beginning to lose my temper with you, so, SIGN-THE-FUCKING-PAPER, you old BUGGER!"

Doyle finally accepted the page with a trembling hand. While Hutchinson reached into his pocket for a pen, Doyle tore the paper in half and squeezing it into a ball he threw it at the solicitor's face.

Hutchinson's eyes bulged. He replaced the pen, balled his fist and swung it with surprising velocity, connecting with Doyle's jaw. Doyle's vision blurred and sparks danced before his eyes as he collapsed to the ground, burying his fingers into the cold earth as the pain in his face set in.

Hutchinson aimed the light from his torch towards Jackson, casting an orange hue upon the fascia of Albert Greentree's headstone between two oak trees. The handle of Doyle's axe protruded from the thick trunk of one, Jackson shifted his position to avoid colliding with it.

"Now, Mr Doyle, I believe your late wife resides in the plot to the rear of your home. Mr Jackson will now demonstrate what we plan to do to her grave."

Jackson nodded. He swung the sledgehammer once again. The headstone exploded as the hammer made contact. A shower of fragments scattered around the circumference of the plot and a cloud of dust drifted away eerily on a gentle breeze as though the spirit of the dead had finally escaped the confines of its grave.

"Please…" Doyle moaned.

"Please what? Did you listen to me when I said please, Mr Doyle? The time has passed for pleading. You were war—" Hutchinson's oratory was cut short by a high pitched wail from Jackson.

Doyle spun. At first he thought his companion's leg had been severed at the knee, but then he noticed the mound of earth pulsing around the limb.

"Stop mucking around Kyle," Hutchinson barked, but Jackson was struggling, scrabbling at the ground for purchase to pull himself out of the hole. "Christ, man. What is the problem?"

Hutchinson stepped forward to help the other man when Jackson grunted and yanked his leg from the hole in the ground. The mound of earth grew as he pulled his foot free, and a skeletal, clawed hand emerged from the recess.

Hutchinson froze and Doyle pushed himself from the ground, horrified by the scene unfolding before him. His eyes flitted between the axe wedged in the tree and the bony arm protruding from the earth, still grasping at the air blindly, in search of Jackson.

Then, the mound of soil in front of the grave began to shift again and another hand emerged, raking deep welts in the turf, hauling a rotting, emaciated corpse from the ground. Jackson yelped and scuttled back like an injured crab.

"Mr Doyle, what the hell is going on here?" Hutchinson hazarded a glance at Doyle, who shook his head, his mouth hung open as he tried utter words which were not forthcoming.

The resurrected skeletal remains of Albert Greentree unfolded and rose to his full height gazing at Jackson through empty eye sockets. The corpse's mouth opened and a clod of dirt flopped out, impacting the ground with an audible smack in the silent graveyard. The dead mayor lunged with surprising speed and agility, grabbing the terrified Jackson and sinking his teeth into the stocky man's shoulder.

Jackson screamed and flailed, throwing the skeleton off, but Greentree would not be deterred so easily and rose again for another attempt.

Doyle backed away, clutching the sides of his head in disbelief. He looked around him and with a jolt, realised that Mayor Greentree was not the only reanimated corpse. Most of the graves in the cemetery were bulging. The wasted bodies of the dead were emerging right, left and centre some already shuffling, limping or dragging their shattered forms towards the source of the commotion. They passed Doyle with indifference, as though they hadn't even noticed his presence.

Descending upon Jackson, they brought him to the ground kicking and screaming. A crimson mist ascended around the ragged gathering of un-dead surrounding Jackson. In no time, mercifully, the man's wails had ceased, but an equally harrowing tearing sound supplanted the cacophony.

Doyle turned away from the scene, still too afraid to make his escape as a hoard of corpses ambled to and fro between headstones as though browsing the isles of a supermarket. At the moment they had little interest in him, he prayed that would remain the case.

"Oh, *fuck*," Hutchinson wailed as he turned to flee, leaving his silenced companion behind.

The solicitor had barely taken a few steps before being knocked to the ground. A tall cadaver stood before him, clad in decorated, yet tattered army regalia. The dead man's head was swollen with fungi, a mass of green moss from which numerous tiny spores protruded. Loose flesh hung in ribbons around his throat like a morbid cravat.

The zombie stooped with a series of rapid ratchety jerks, grasping Hutchinson by the upper arm with an elongated claw of a hand before the solicitor could make his escape. Hutchinson uttered a series of terrified breathless swearwords as the dead soldier's angular, gap toothed maw swung open, spilling forth a writhing mass of black beetles before plunging his rotting teeth into Hutchinson's face.

The spell was broken. Doyle ran as fast as his arthritic legs could take him, propelled by Hutchinson's short lived screams. He weaved between masses of wandering un-dead, towards the safety of his house. Horrifying apparitions ambled listlessly before him. Corpses in various stages of decomposition, lacking all but the minimum of basic motor skills and balance veered into each other.

Doyle cried out in panic, attempting to quicken his pace. He barely halted when he cannon-balled through the front door, flicking the catch on the lever lock which issued a heavy clunk and fastening the chain for added security.

He sank to his knees, panting heavily, rasping breaths. Wasting no time, he crawled across the floor of the darkened living room, snatched the telephone from the cradle before pausing. Who would he call and what would he say? He didn't have a hope in hell of convincing Sergeant Denholm or his colleagues of this particular danger.

A sharp, clattering cacophony emanating from the kitchen caused Doyle to jump, and his slowing heart skipped a beat before thrashing a frantic tattoo against his ribcage again. He dropped the phone and staggered to his feet, stepping tentatively through the kitchen doorway, preparing for the worst, preparing to come face to face with one of those things.

The kitchen was empty however the back door lay ajar. He was sure he had locked it upon retiring earlier that evening. Slowly, he crept to the back door, pushing it closed and turning the key clockwise with as little noise a possible.

He considered turning on the kitchen light before quickly deciding against it. He was suddenly overcome with the urge to remain hidden and unnoticed.

Considering the consequences of drawing attention to the house, Doyle shuddered equally with revulsion and fear. Concealing himself in a dark corner away from the cold lifeless gaze of the dead until the nightmare had abated seemed the most appealing option.

That's when he heard it; a deep, bubbling fluidic sound, rising in pitch, becoming the unmistakable sound of boiling water. Puzzled, he strained to detect the origin of the sound. His head snapped round to the electric hob of the cooker, just as the old kettle let out a noisy, high-pitched whine.

Doyle had been in the kitchen preparing tea when the doorbell rang. He started, almost spilling scalding water on himself. For a brief moment, he considered ignoring it as he wasn't expecting anyone, but decided that would be folly. He didn't want to raise any suspicions.

He had been out in the cemetery, tending plots and re-burying corpses. In fact, he had just finished that particular task earlier that very morning. It had taken him two whole days to put the cemetery back to its original state. As dawn arrived, the morning after the dead had risen, they had shuffled back to their own graves as though returning home from a long, hard slog on the nightshift, leaving Doyle to pick up the pieces, literally. Not that there were many pieces of Hutchinson and Jackson left.

He sat the kettle back on the hob and marched through the living room, trailing mud from his caked wellington boots, gazing through the front window.

A police car sat parked out front. But he was expecting this; it was only a matter of time before the authorities started asking questions.

Doyle composed himself before yanking the front door open, feigning the grumpiest expression he could muster.

Sergeant Denhholm grinned when Doyle opened the door. Another police officer whom Doyle did not recognise stood poised at the bottom of the porch with his left foot placed firmly on the bottom step as though coiled and ready to take action should Sergeant Denholm require his assistance. Doyle wondered vaguely if the game was up.

"Afternoon, Sammy," the sergeant said nodding.

"Afternoon, Ron. What can I do you for?"

"We're investigating a missing persons report, coupla' bigwig solicitors from the city. Glen Hutchinson and Kyle Jackson… know 'em?"

Doyle's face remained impassive. "Yes, they were here a few days ago trying to convince me to sign over the house so the council could build some mall or shopping centre over the cemetery. I sent 'em packing."

Sergeant Denholm nodded carefully, placing his hand on the door frame and shifting his weight. Doyle stepped back a little, opening the door wider.

"You boys want to come in? I've not long put the kettle on."

"Thanks, Sammy, but no, we've got to keep moving with this one," Denholm replied, nodding towards Doyle's caked boots. "Besides, we don't want to hold you back,"

"Okay, Ron, hope you find your men," Doyle lied, closing the door gently.

When the policemen had exited the cemetery, Doyle let out a sigh of relief. He swatted a blowfly, buzzing around his ear with an irritating, high pitched whine and entered the living room, throwing himself down into his chair. He plucked a framed photograph of Elspeth from the mantle and held it before him close enough for his poor eyesight to make out her features and sighed.

"I didn't like those men one bit, dear," he said. "They were crooked as the branches on old Greentree's oaks, and dangerous to boot. Imagine, trying to take an old man's home from him."

Doyle shook his head as he switched his gaze from the photograph, calmly to the rotting husk on the settee, slowly stroking a knitted plaid which covered its knees with narrow, withered fingers.

The corpse of Elspeth Doyle regarded her husband with sightless eyes which had been glued shut with putrefaction. Her narrow neck crackled as she raised her head, opening her mouth impossibly wide and letting out a dry, broken peel of almost inaudible groans. But Doyle understood every word his wife uttered.

It's the way of the world now, Samuel. No one respects us old biddies anymore.

In the kitchen, the kettle began to whistle.

'TIL DEATH DO US PART

Shaun Jeffrey

"It's her, Dad, I swear it is. Over there, it's Mum."

I exhaled slowly and looked at my fourteen year old son as he excitedly pointed across the street. Before he could say anymore, I took hold of his shoulder and turned him towards me. "You know it isn't her, Tim. She's dead. We buried her. You know that."

Tim twisted out of my hands. "I'm not making it up, she's alive. I just saw her."

Before I could stop him, Tim bolted across the road, a car horn blaring in response as the driver of a Honda Civic slammed on his brakes to avoid sending my son to see his mother in a more literal sense, which would have been an ironic twist of fate if he'd died in the same way.

"Come back," I shouted before giving chase.

I couldn't be too angry with him. His mother's death had hit him hard. Probably harder than it had me if I'm honest, but saying he'd seen her in the street, well, it was sad and rather unnerving.

Sure I shed bucketfuls of tears when Joanna died, spent days questioning why God was so cruel to take her away from us in the prime of her life; but Tim and his mother, they'd shared a special bond, one that only mothers and sons can share.

I dodged shoppers wandering along the high street and gulped deep breaths, my knees cracking. Although only in my mid thirties, I was out of shape.

Tim was about forty feet ahead and running like a gazelle, his gangly frame almost as thin as the shadow that trailed in his wake. He got his willowy stature from his mum. Not that I was obese, but my trouser size had outgrown my age by a couple of numbers, giving me a paunch—much of which was a direct result of the alcohol I'd drowned myself in after the funeral. Tim had been my lifeline. When I realised how destructive my drinking had become, I stopped. Had to be strong.

I still hadn't adjusted fully and had taken for granted all that Joanna did around the house. I didn't have a clue how the washing machine worked, couldn't iron to save my life; but I'd had to go on a steep learning curve, if not for my sake, then for Tim's. The house had become a shit hole. I didn't wash or clean for days at a time. Dishes piled up in the sink and once the cupboards were empty we'd relied on takeaway food. The local Chinese restaurant was on speed dial.

For a while Tim became the adult and me the child. But now I was back in control. I'd gone back to work at the bank and Tim had settled back in at school. He'd fallen behind on his work, but he was catching up and the teachers were understanding and weren't on his back about it.

I realised that Tim had stopped running and he was standing in front of a dishevelled looking figure that, from behind, looked like a homeless person; one of the dispossessed as I liked to think of them.

As I caught him up I could feel a pain in my side and I stood wheezing for a couple of seconds. "Come on, Tim. Let's go home."

"I told you. I told you it was her," Tim said, a smile on his face that I never thought I'd see again.

Confused, I shook my head. "Come on, stop being stupid."

"Look. Look at her." He pointed at the homeless person.

I glanced towards the figure, not really wanting to make eye contact in case I got drawn into conversation with them, but I felt that I should apologise. Instead I stared open-mouthed. Despite the grey skin with the sores and welts, the lopsided mouth and the dead, glassy eyes, there was no mistaking the face. Impossible as it seemed, it was Joanna.

"Mum, it's me. Tim."

I listened to my son as though he was speaking from the end of a tunnel; couldn't take my eyes off Joanna. Her skin looked papery and dry, tendons protruding from the back of her hands where the skin had sunken in. Her fingernails were torn and there was dirt around them, as though she had been clawing through the earth.

Joanna didn't respond. She started walking, although it was more of a shuffle.

"Mum. Talk to me, Mum." Tim barred her path and Joanna bumped into him, rocking back on her heels.

She was wearing the dress we'd buried her in. Tim had chosen it, saying it was her favourite. I guess he knew her better than me as I didn't have a clue what her favourite piece of clothing had been.

Sunlight glared from the shop window behind Joanna, making me squint. When I looked back it had given her head a halo effect, like that of an angel.

I gulped, my tongue a thick slug stuck to the roof of my mouth.

"Jo, is it really you?" I asked, the words coming out in a rush.

Joanna didn't reply.

I cleared my throat and said, "How? I don't understand. You…you were dead. They buried you."

Still no response.

Afraid that I may have been caught up in Tim's delusion, I reached out and touched Jo's hand. She was real but her skin was cold and leathery to the touch and I recoiled slightly.

After a moment I realised there was an aroma in the air that originated from Joanna. It was cloying, like spoiled meat that had gone past its sell-by date.

"Dad, why isn't she answering?"

I looked at Tim and shook my head. "I don't know." Truth was I didn't know anything anymore. Joanna was dead, and yet here she was, walking.

It just wasn't possible.

"We need to get her home," Tim said.

I watched Joanna continuing her attempt to walk forwards, but Tim kept holding her back. She was like an insistent fly butting into a window and seemed to have no concept of what was happening.

Swallowing to moisten my throat, I tried to think what to do. I noticed a few people staring at us as they walked past and knew I had to get us off the street to somewhere where we could work this out.

"Okay, give me hand to help her," I said as I grabbed her arm. Tim took hold of her on the other side and we walked her towards the car park where I'd left the car.

Once we arrived, I opened the door and bent her joints to allow us to sit her on the front seat. Then I fastened the seat belt, more to secure her in position than for any form of safety, as deep in my heart I knew she was dead.

Once we were all inside the car the smell was more pungent and it clung to the back of my throat, making me feel a little sick, so I lowered the window to let some fresh air in then started the engine.

Joanna sat there, rocking backwards and forwards like a nodding car novelty.

I glanced in the rear view mirror. Tim was still smiling.

Before going home I drove to the cemetery.

"What are we doing here?" Tim asked.

"I need to check that it's really her."

"Of course it's her."

I exhaled slowly. "Well, I just need to check." I exited the vehicle and Tim followed. He grabbed the door handle to help his mother out, but I said, "She'll be better off staying in the car." Tim looked at me for a moment and then nodded.

We followed the path among the gravestones. I tried to swallow as I walked, but couldn't produce any saliva. Dappled sunlight flickered through the surrounding trees. I was hoping to see the grave was undisturbed so that I could say it wasn't Joanna, but even from a distance I noticed a mound of earth—like a giant mole had burrowed its way out from below.

I stood before the mound and stared down into the hole,

trying to imagine Joanna clawing at the coffin lid, scraping away for weeks on end until she scratched her way through.

I parked in the driveway and then made sure the coast was clear before leading Joanna out of the car. I didn't want to explain what was going on to the neighbours as I didn't have a clue myself and wouldn't know where to begin. All I knew was that impossible as it seemed, my wife had returned from the grave.

Tim and I ushered her into the house and I closed the door. Joanna hadn't said a word all the way home. I wondered whether she recognised us. Wondered whether she was cognizant.

"We need to get her cleaned up and then get some fresh clothes on her," Tim said.

I nodded dumbly, happy to let Tim take control of the situation while I tried to think about what the hell was going on. We led Joanna upstairs to the bathroom and I started to undress her while Tim went to fetch some fresh clothes from the ones we hadn't yet been able to throw away. Joanna stood stock still as I unbuttoned her dress at the back, letting it drop to the floor, and I realised she was staring at her reflection in the mirror. Did she recognise herself?

There were signs on her body where the car had struck, deep lesions that had been sewn shut. I tried not to look at them as I removed her bra, her once full breasts now flaps of skin that made me feel a little repulsed to look at.

Tim hurried into the bathroom as I was removing her underwear and I felt a little embarrassed both for Jo and myself, but Tim seemed unfazed and took it all perfectly in his stride. He got his practicality from his mother.

"I've got her another dress," he said. "It'll be easier to get on and off. I didn't bother with underwear. Do you think she'll need any?"

I shook my head. "I guess not."

Tim had selected a pale blue knee-length dress with large white flowers that he put on the edge of the bath. "She needs a shower," he said.

I ushered her into the shower stall and switched on the spray. Hot steaming water shot out and I tested the temperature before remembering she was dead so probably wouldn't know how hot it was anyway. Once she was underneath the spray she kept walking forwards into the wall, water bouncing off her head. Tim leaned in and grabbed a bottle of shampoo.

"Soon have you looking like your old self," he said as he washed her hair.

I lowered the toilet seat and sat down to watch as Tim lovingly washed his mother like it was the most natural thing in the world. Bits of skin and hair came away in his hands but he didn't seem concerned.

Once he had finished we guided her out of the shower, towelled her dry and then I sprayed her with some of my antiperspirant to mask the smell that still emanated from her. Then I raised her arms to allow Tim to pull the dress over them and then over her head. Tim then combed her tresses, ignoring the fact that he was pulling more out than he was straightening.

While he did this I stared into her eyes. They had once been bright blue. Now they looked dead and lifeless. Could she still see? If she did, could she recognise anything?

I felt myself choking up so I swallowed and rubbed my eyes. Steam drifted around the room and I felt hot but didn't know if it was due to the temperature or the circumstances.

"Now what are we going to do?" I asked as I wiped perspiration from my brow.

Tim looked at me. "Well, me and Mum are going to go watch telly," he said before leading Joanna away. As he reached the door, Tim turned and looked at me. "I love you, Dad." Then he left the room. A tear rolled down my cheek and I wiped it away. Seconds later I heard the television downstairs and the sound of Tim laughing at something.

I knew I had to find out how she had returned from the grave, so I walked through to the spare bedroom where the computer was and switched it on. If more people had come back to life, surely there would be news of it. After ten minutes of searching I came up with nothing. Perhaps if it had happened to other people, whoever found them wouldn't say anything. Perhaps they were just glad to have their loved ones back. Or perhaps they were afraid that someone would come and take their nearest and dearest away to experiment on them to find out how it had occurred and what was making them tick.

Unable to find out whether it had happened elsewhere, my next course of action was to see if I could discern why or how it happened.

After an hour's searching I discovered that zombification, for want of a better word, can supposedly result from parasitic bites like one from a single cell organism called toxoplasmosa gondii that infects rats but can only breed inside a cat's intestines. So it takes over the rat's brain and basically programs itself to get eaten by a cat. Then there were neurotoxins, or certain kinds of poisons that slow your bodily functions to the point that you'll be considered dead even though you're not. Or perhaps a virus of some kind. Finally there was neurogenesis, or the method by which scientists can re-grow dead brain tissue.

None of them helped me discover how Joanna had come back, just that it wasn't outside the realms of possibility that she could have done so. And the woman downstairs was proof enough if any were ever needed that it certainly was possible.

I switched the computer off and then went downstairs to join my family.

The knock at the door made me jump. I stared across at Tim as he sat reading to his mum. She paid no attention as she staggered around the room. Despite having had her in the house for a couple of days, I still hadn't gotten used to having my wife back.

The knock came again, more insistent, joined by the ringing of the doorbell. I jumped up and walked to see who was there. "Keep quiet," I said as I shut the living room door behind me.

I opened the front door and my jaw dropped when I saw the acne-scarred police officer standing there.

"Mr White?"

I nodded dumbly, my pulse racing.

"I'm afraid I have some disturbing news for you. There's no easy way to say this, but your wife's grave has been desecrated and her body removed."

I swallowed the lump in my throat. "Desecrated?"

"Don't worry sir, we're going to do our best to find her body."

I glanced along the hallway before turning back. "Who would do something like that?"

The police officer shrugged and stared at his feet. "I don't know sir. I really don't."

The next few days were spent in a kind of haze as I learned to accept that Joanna was back in our lives. We didn't tell anybody.

She was our secret. While I went to work and Tim went to school, we kept her locked in the cupboard under the stairs.

Tim seemed to believe that everything was back to normal, and that we should just carry on as though nothing had happened. He even expected me to accept her back into my bed, but certainly for now, that wasn't going to happen and I wrapped her in a sleeping bag at night, pulling the toggle on it tight enough to cocoon her. Not that she slept and I could hear her bumping around, shuffling like a giant caterpillar. Even though she was my wife, I still didn't know exactly how I felt about having a dead woman in the house, never mind in my bed. Necrophilia wasn't something I wanted any part of. Not that Joanna would be in the least bit able to reciprocate. She ambled around the house like a robot, bumping into walls and falling over things as though she couldn't see too well. Perhaps that's why she walked along with her arms raised most of the time, sort of like feelers.

She certainly didn't cost much to look after. She didn't eat and she didn't go to the toilet and once you got used to her being around you could almost believe she wasn't dead. I even started talking to her and although she didn't reply, I found her presence comforting.

I will admit that for the first few days I was nervous, as zombies had a reputation for biting people and making them one of the undead, but Joanna didn't seem to have any interest in biting, so I eventually accepted that she wasn't going to eat us.

Tim doted on her. He took over all the chores involved with looking after his mum. Bathing, dressing and generally taking care of her as though she was an invalid. I gradually accepted the situation.

My main fear—aside from being eaten—had been that Joanna

would slowly rot away and we'd lose her all over again, but after a few days she stopped decomposing and reached a point of stasis.

Now I was no artist, but with the use of liberal amounts of makeup my wife could be made to look almost normal (this was the only thing Tim didn't do for her as he accepted Joanna for what she looked like, but he was happy for me to apply foundation, blusher and rouge as I saw fit). When all of her hair dropped out I bought her a wig and glued it in place. And even though she stopped smelling of decay, I sprayed Jo with her favourite perfume so I could smell her as she shuffled around the room, the scent conjuring a host of memories.

To all intents and purposes we were one big happy family.

Now I was still wondering how Joanna had come back to life, never mind how she'd escaped her coffin under the ground, and I did consider that perhaps she had been the result of some form of experiment. But if that was the case, how had she escaped?

On a regular basis, I sat her down and, for want of a better word, interrogated her with a barrage of questions about what had happened, but she never replied and her dead eyes grew more and more blank, the blue eyeballs now covered by a white film. All she wanted to do was wander around in an aimless daze.

But our secret couldn't last forever and the next thing we knew, a neighbour spotted Joanna through the window. When he recovered from his faint he called the police. At that point he may as well have called the army, navy and the air force because everyone and his mother descended on our detached house. Reporters set up camp outside and then scientists came. As I'd feared, they wanted to experiment on her to see how she had risen from the dead, even offering vast sums of money, but I declined. Although dead, she was still my wife. In sickness and in health and all that (I didn't like to think about the 'til death do us part' as that had already happened.)

Next came the zealots. The religious nutters who claimed that like Jesus, Joanna had risen from the grave, so she must be the new messiah. Well, she didn't die for anyone's sins. She died in an accident when hit by a car, but they didn't want to hear the truth. All they wanted was to see their messiah. To be touched by her as she obviously had special powers and could cure all their ailments.

As a result of all this attention we became prisoners in our own house.

I peered through a gap in the curtain. It was like a riot out there. People kept knocking at the door and I'd already taken the batteries out of the doorbell and unplugged the telephone.

Someone banged on the window and I recoiled and backed away.

"What are we going to do?" Tim asked.

I collapsed onto the settee and cupped my face in my hands.

Tim sat next to me. "We can't stay in here for ever. We've already run out of food."

Across the room, Joanna bumped into the wall. I stared at her.

Despite what Tim thought, the person opposite wasn't his mother anymore. It was just an animated shell. We were holding onto a memory of who she once was. But I knew what I had to do. Tim would probably hate me for doing it, but I had no other choice.

"Tim, I want you to go upstairs and pack."

My son looked at me and frowned. "Pack for what?"

"We're leaving."

Tim hesitated as though he sensed something in my words, but after a moment he turned and ran up the stairs. A moment later I heard drawers opening and cupboard doors banging.

With no time to lose I stood and ran into the kitchen and picked up a large kitchen knife with a serrated edge. Then I returned to the living room. I turned Joanna to face me and briefly kissed her on the lips. Words were not necessary, but I had to be strong, both physically and mentally.

I placed the serrated edge against her throat and a tear rolled down my cheek. Hopefully the other information I'd learned about zombies and decapitation were true.

If so, Joanna would live forever, at least in our memories.

CHECKING OUT

Richard Farren Farber

This time it took them four weeks to find him. Four weeks when Joe Pugliano flinched at every movement at the edge of his vision. Four weeks when the dark nights seemed to ache with their low murmurs. In the end it was almost a relief when he realised they had arrived.

He was sitting on the bed, reading a paperback he'd picked up in the lobby, when the screams started. He dropped the book and started packing, shoving what he could into the small bag. There was nothing that couldn't be replaced—nothing except the money. And there was so little of that left it was hardly worth worrying about.

He finished piling his toiletries into the bag and opened the door. He looked out onto an empty corridor—pale yellow walls, scratched along the bottom with rubber-black marks from the maids' trolleys. The screaming had stopped for now.

His room was tucked away. Always a ground floor room. Always at the back of the building. Sometimes he received strange looks from the receptionist when he made the request, but it was the reason he was still alive six months after De Ladro had set them after him.

On the opposite side of the corridor was the fire exit. Five quick steps and he would be in the alley behind the hotel.

Their low murmuring rushed through the hotel corridors like rising flood water. Joe paused in the open door for a moment, trying to determine how far away they were, how many of them were left, but it was futile.

He launched himself at the fire door and started running. The door slammed open against an outer wall. The alley was filled with industrial bins, overflowing with broken-down cardboard boxes and rotting vegetables. The ground was slick and the stink of rot came at him in waves, turning his stomach.

Joe ran close to the wall, tripping over debris as he snatched quick glances behind him. He ploughed through the rubbish, stumbling his way along the narrow alley until he reached the junction with South Parade. Ahead he looked out onto a sea view; fat gulls twisting in the air, the promenade bordered with Victorian wrought iron railings. He looked along the street to his right.

There was a crowd gathered at the front of the hotel, a surge of them trying to force their way through the hotel lobby. They were never going to give up. A wave of desperation broke over him. There were more of them now. Fucking De Ladro. The gift that just kept on giving.

Their low murmurs rolled down the street. Voices joined together, a rumble of discontent. "Puuuug," they moaned. "Puugluno."

His name. They were trying to say his name.

One of them turned and saw him. The buzz of voices rose a notch, like a disturbed swarm of bees. First one head and then another creaked slowly around to look at him. The chunter of voices increased: were they talking to each other, actually talking? And then the first one turned round and started to stumble towards him.

They lurched along the footpath, pushing against each other. One staggered onto the road and was side-swiped by the wing of a Ford Mondeo. He went down and the others stomped over him in their desperate need to get to Joe. The last thing Joe saw of the body were purple-black hands stretching out, fingers almost reaching him.

They weren't fast. They stumbled and rolled and juddered their way along and he could easily outrun them, but they had almost hypnotised him. Could that happen? How many of their victims had simply given up? How many had just watched the pack flow towards them like a wave?

In the end it was the smell that released Joe. The smell of the undead; their organs turning to black jelly and rotting inside their bodies. The stench broke over Joe and caused him to retch, but he turned away from the horde that De Ladro had set on him and started to run.

The car was parked across the street. As he ran towards it he checked his pocket for his keys. The tank was full - the tank was always full. For Joe every day was about preparation. Everything in his life was geared to surviving the next few minutes, to putting distance between himself and De Ladro's horde each time they found him. Because they always found him.

His pocket was empty. Joe almost stopped in shock. His fucking pocket was empty. Where were the keys?

He looked up to check on the progress of the crowd. They were still a good distance back, rolling side to side along the pavement, spilling out onto the road. The front of the hotel was clear now, except for a prone body. Joe thought it might be the doorman. As he watched, the man staggered to his feet. He looked to the right, looked to the left, and put one foot carefully forward. The right side of his head was caved in.

Joe watched. He already knew De Ladro's original band had grown to a crowd of twenty, but to witness one of the horde's victims get up and join the chase for him was enough to make him cry.

They would never tire. Never give in. Never stop.

All because he had taken a few thousand from the pot before he handed it over.

"Fuck you, De Ladro. If I'd known this would happen I'd have taken a hundred thousand, a million. All this for a few fucking pounds?" Joe screamed at the horde, but it made no difference. They lumbered towards him. Unaware.

They were closer. Always closer. Joe checked his pockets a third time, a fourth time, but there were no keys. He'd known this day would come, it had been inevitable. Despite the constant preparation, he'd known that one day he would slip up, and the mistake would probably kill him.

He reached round and pulled the bag from his shoulders, plunged his hand to the bottom and surfed down through layers of dirty clothes. He felt the metal edge of the gun's butt and seized it, dragged it back up. He didn't even take the time to check: the gun was loaded, just like the keys were in his pocket. He couldn't be wrong twice.

The pistol bucked in his hand and the thunderclap rang

around the street. The first body stumbled as a chunk of shoulder muscle sheared away.

Joe fired again, this time aiming for the head. The face of the man at the front dissolved into a mist of blood and bones. Joe thought it was the one who had first spotted him on the steps of the hotel reception.

"Got you, you bastard."

The zombie fell to the floor and the others stomped him into the pavement, his fingers still twitching, his legs still moving forwards in an attempt to reach Joe.

For a moment there was a gap at the head of the column where the man had been, and then the horde closed in and the pack was whole again.

Joe fired again.

And again.

They fell and stomped and thrashed and he took some pleasure in watching them die, but it didn't matter how many he killed; there would always be more. De Ladro had known what he was doing when he had selected this particular vengeance for Joe's theft.

The trigger clicked loud and dry. Empty.

Joe stuffed the gun into his bag. He tried his pockets one last time, in case he had somehow missed the keys. No such luck. He checked his watch. There was a train in fifteen minutes. He'd memorised the timetable.

A train would get him out of here quickly. It was the safest option; boosting a car would just bring the police down on his head like the wrath of God.

It was ten minutes to the train station. He had walked the route every day since he had arrived. He wasn't going to have a repeat of Brighton where he had got lost and tracked a horde of brain-eating zombies through the town for half an hour before finally finding his way to the railway. The police had almost done De Ladro's work for him, came close to putting a bullet in Joe's head before the encounter was over.

He started to run. If he could put enough space between him and the pack he could make the train and get out before they caught up with him.

He knew he didn't have the time, but Joe couldn't stop himself from watching the pack as he ran away. They broke around his car and reformed on the other side. Some of the group clambered over the vehicle; he heard the breaking of glass and a metallic crunch as the roof buckled under the weight.

He turned left onto the Attenborough Road and started to run. For a moment the street behind him was empty, and there was a false relief because he knew they were still following him; but for that one brief moment he could almost believe he was safe.

And then the first of the pack turned the corner and began to stagger up the road after him. When De Ladro had first set them onto him there had only been four. In hindsight if he had attacked instead of running from them then he could have defeated them. But there were a number of things he would have done differently with hindsight. Not stealing from De Ladro was high on that list.

Before him the road emptied. Shop doors slammed and faces peered out through display windows. Joe could see pity in those faces but no hint that anyone would come to his rescue. If he stumbled, if he fell, those people would watch as the pack dropped on him and consumed him.

Behind the horde he saw the flash of a police siren, but knew better than to look to them for help. At first they'd tried to intervene, but once the authorities understood the nature of the zombies they didn't get involved. It was too risky. Much better to stand back and wait for them to pass through like a forest fire. They'd lost too many men in the early days. Now everyone knew: stay out of their way, and as long as they didn't have your scent you were safe.

Joe tripped over the kerb and nearly clattered to the ground, arms pin-wheeling off balance for a moment. Somehow he regained his balance without crashing to the floor and kept on running.

The station was at the edge of town, amongst derelict factories and barren land, where the nubs of old warehouses rose up through clumps of brown grass. A lone taxi was parked in the circle in front of the entrance. As Joe got closer he saw the driver reading a copy of The *Sun*, the paper spread over the steering wheel. He looked like he'd been sitting there for the last five hours.

Joe crossed under the eaves and onto the platform. A huddle of passengers gathered together at the far end. The clock over the A dot matrix sign hung over the platform said that the 10:42 was delayed by fifteen minutes.

"Shit." Joe whirled around on the platform. "I can't wait fifteen minutes," he muttered. He paced the platform. He was aware that the group of passengers had seen him.

"Shit. Shit, shit, *shit*," he shouted. A woman drew out a hand and pulled a young boy closer to her. Joe wanted to shout at her. She shouldn't be worrying about him, he wasn't going to harm the kid.

He ran out of the station and stood beside the bus stop. No escape. Part of him had always known that this moment would arrive. That one day they would find him with nowhere left to run. He'd known it but he could never accept it.

"I should have taken more. I should have wiped De Ladro out," he said. The idea raised a laugh, even at this terrible moment.

There was a telephone box in the station's atrium. An old-time red kiosk. Joe wasn't sure the phone inside would even work. He squeezed inside and dialled De Ladro's number from memory.

The call was answered on the second ring.

"*Si?*"

"Call them off. Call off your dogs."

The old Italian laughed. "Joe. So nice to hear from you. I have not heard your voice in many months."

"Call them off, De Ladro."

The laughter stopped abruptly. "Nobody steals from me, Pugliano. Nobody. Are they close now, Joseph? Can you smell them?"

"I get it," Joe said. He could hear the desperation in his own voice.

"No you don't. This isn't about you. It was never about you. This is about everyone else. You are my warning to them: nobody steals from De Ladro. They see what happened to you and they understand that."

Joe hung up and then dialled a second number. A number that had cost him most of the money he had stolen from De Ladro. Thousands just to find out how De Ladro had set the pack after him, who he had used. And even then he'd only learned that there was no answer – no way to call them off. Once they had his scent they were locked in until... well, until it was over.

His call was answered with silence.

"It's Pugliano," Joe said. Still silence. He could hear breathing at the other end of the line.

"We have a deal?"

Silence.

"We have a deal?" He heard the desperation in his own voice. "If I don't get away this time, we have a deal?"

"*Si.*" The line went dead. Joe stood in the kiosk a moment longer. He tried to tell himself he hadn't given up, not yet. That he was just preparing for all possibilities.

He ran from the kiosk onto the station's forecourt. The taxi still sat, silent before the station. Joe plunged a hand into the bag. He pulled open the door, pushed the gun into the driver's face. From his expression, he thought the guy was going to drop dead from a heart attack.

"Get out," Joe ordered.

The driver's face was as grey as those of the undead. He reached over the dashboard and for a moment Joe thought he was going to pull out his own gun; if he'd had any bullets left Joe would probably have emptied them into the driver. Instead, the man held out a leather wallet as large as a filofax.

"Take it," he said. The wallet shook. "I ain't got much, but take it. It ain't worth dying for."

Joe waved the gun. "I don't want your money, get out of the fucking car. Now!"

The driver reached for the ignition to remove his keys—pure instinct—but Joe laughed at the stupidity. "Leave the keys. What do you think I'm going to do, push it out of here?" The man looked embarrassed, angry and confused. He clambered out of the car and stood on the tarmac.

"What you...?" he started to ask and then he looked up. Joe heard it too.

They were coming. The low moans. The scrape of worn shoe heels on concrete. The murmur of the pack. They were coming.

"Oh, God," the driver said. Realisation flooded his face. Maybe it was Joe's imagination, but he thought he saw sympathy bloom in the taxi driver's features. Just for a moment. And then it was replaced with terror.

"Don't worry, they're not after you," Joe said. He didn't know if the driver would understand, if he was capable of understanding any more.

They rolled around the corner. At the front was the original pack, their slack faces showing signs of wear. They strung out in a line across the approach road to the station. No way out.

Joe twisted the ignition key and the engine fired; sloppy and irregular. The air filled with the stink of exhaust fumes. It was a welcome change to the tang of rotting bodies that seemed to hang around him all the time.

He gunned the engine, the whine rising and falling.

The pack moved closer. He wondered if they even understood what he was doing; he didn't imagine so. He didn't think they understood anything more than walking and the deep-seated lust for the scent that had been given to them. Joe Pugliano's scent.

Joe stamped down on the pedal; the fanbelt screamed like a dying man.

Closer. Joe could now see their blood-red eyes and their blue lips. He could see the green, grave-mould growing on their cheeks. He thought he recognised the man at the front and wondered if he was one of the original four that De Ladro had set upon him.

Closer. Now their moaning could be heard over the taxi's engine. *"Puuug. Puuugluno."* His name. It had been the only thing he had heard them say in the six months they had been following him.

Closer.

Joe dropped the clutch and the car lurched forwards. For one heart-stopping moment he was sure he'd stalled it, but then the taxi struck the first of the pack. The windscreen cracked as the body rolled across the bonnet. He pushed down harder on the pedal, as though attempting to press it through the floor of the vehicle.

The car bucked and rolled. "Got you," Joe screamed. His voice echoed within the car, unable to escape. The taxi jolted as he ran over another one. There were no shouts, no screams, just the constant low moaning from the rest of the pack.

He felt the impact as the car rocked with each body he struck. The windows were blocked with flesh. A face pressed up against the side window, but then it was gone and a bloodied fist was punching at the glass. Joe saw flesh slough from the bones until white knuckles scraped against the pane. A large crack spread from top to bottom. He actually heard the glass snap and then a moment later the window collapsed inwards and fingertips brushed against his throat.

He tried to push them away. He felt raw bone scratch against his face. The smell of hot blood filled the car. *His* blood.

"No," Joe tried to cry but the words were wrenched from his mouth.

A green car pulled up outside the railway station. The driver stepped out and pushed his way through the milling crowd of zombies. There was a casual confidence in the man's movements, like a dog trainer passing through the cage. It didn't take him long to find Pugliano and pull the remains of the man from the taxi. Joe's hands pawed ineffectively at the driver's sharp suit and left bloodstain tracks on the lapels.

"Bite this," the driver said, but Pugliano was beyond understanding. The driver pushed a rag into Joe's face.

"This was what you wanted, wasn't it? This was the deal." The driver stared into Pugliano's face. There was nothing alive in those eyes—just pupils which flared in the light.

"De Ladro," Joe muttered. The word was low and slurred and almost nothing. "De Ladro," he said again, and started walking.

SOUL FOOD

Alison Littlewood

A NEW YOU IN EVERY BITE. No one ever noticed the advertising in here: it was preaching to the converted, and no one cared anyway. They were too intent on the experience. No one ever listened to the constant audio track about this burger or that, either: the jingle was just background to the ever-constant chewing.

Jake, the supervisor, he told me what to do. "You feed the patties in here," he said, "so they pass under the teeth." He fed a raw pink patty, semi-liquid, like paste, into the machine. The machine never stopped, not for anything.

"If they start to back up, don't poke them through. They might not be cooked enough. Food poisoning."

At the other end, brown bubbling burgers appeared. They never stopped, not for anything.

"One every twenty seconds."

I nodded.

Soul Food

"I need hardly remind you," Jake continued, "about your fingers." He waggled one gloved hand in the air. It looked like each of his fingers was sealed in a condom: size small.

"Don't get them near the teeth." He nodded towards Oswald. Oz was the resident burger zomb. "It happened to him," he said. "One day, the patties backed up. It kept pulling them through, but nothing was coming out the other side. So Ozzie there, he smells burning. And he decides to pull them out."

He pointed again at the shining teeth.

"They point inward," he said. "So once you're caught…"

He waved at Ozzie, and Ozzie waved slowly back. One of his hands was made of steel. The other bore only the shiny stumps of two fingers and a thumb.

"He tried to pull his hand free. Using his other hand." Jake leaned in, conspiratorial now, being pally with the new guy. "The machine doesn't stop for anything. It's self-maintained, self-cleaning, self-fixing. No downtime. Any hour of the day or night, we sell all we can make."

He straightened and pulled the peak of his Soul Food hat to a jaunty angle. He nodded at Oz, towards his blank, empty eyes. "We had to lock him in the back," he said cheerily, "so they wouldn't hear him screaming, as a piece of his soul went down." He paused. "It didn't make any difference to the burgers."

I remember the first time I tasted a soul burger: I think everybody can. There's the initial reluctance, the first taste—you can tell when it's someone's first time because of the way they flinch. It's the richness of it, too real somehow, as if everything they've eaten up to now was only pretending to be food.

Teresa didn't want me to do it. She asked me not to. "I had one once," she said, and gave me a dubious look. It irritated me. How could she ask me not to do something she'd done herself? But then, if she hadn't tried it, I suppose I wouldn't have listened anyway, because how would she know? It was a lose-lose situation.

I remember I had to step over the addicts at the door. I saw them and thought, just one. Teresa had followed me, but showed her reluctance in the way she lagged behind. She was frowning, and she gave the addicts the same look she'd given me when I'd insisted on coming. They were all ages, sitting outside—young men and old, too enraptured to work, too poor to pay.

Up until I bought the burger, peeled back the wrapper, Teresa had been silent. Now she started talking; it was like she couldn't stop. There was Teresa's mouth moving and moving and I didn't hear a word. I only remember biting into the burger—that, and the way I suddenly felt someone. At first, I thought it was that odd feeling you get when someone's watching you from across the room: then it became more than that. I realised I could feel her inside my mind. Contact.

Sometimes, back in the good days, I sometimes found I knew what Teresa was about to say. Or she'd say the words and they weren't quite what she meant, only I understood anyway. It was like that.

The girl in my mind had known sorrow, I felt it. Especially at the end, I think. She'd grieved for someone, someone she'd lost. She was more present with every moment I chewed, while Teresa went further and further away.

The soul burger, I realised, that's all it was: it was working. It was like some kind of communion, her soul and mine.

No one knows how they do it. Fix the soul, right in there with the meat. A trade secret, I guess.

Teresa's lips kept on moving. After a while it looked silly, them moving like that and meaning nothing. I finished it, and I still wasn't listening; but I saw the question in her eyes.

I licked the grease off the bottom of the paper. I asked Teresa to go and buy some drinks, so she wouldn't see me do it. Even while we drank them, she was still there; deep inside, in that place Teresa could never be.

"A soul burger and a cola."

I took the credit card from the blank-eyed teen, scooped the parcel from the chute and passed it over. The soul burgers came out in the middle, between the chicken burgers and the fish burgers—at the moment, those chutes were empty. Hardly anyone ate chicken or beef or fish here any longer; we had to make those special. They used to sell a lot of them, until the soul burgers; some hung on, the anti-cannibalism brigade and the sandal-wearers, but then they stopped coming in altogether, or they got converted and quietly dropped the protests.

A lot of people were like that, until the First Contamination gave them a taste. They each got a little piece of human soul mixed in with their beef. Some said Soul Food did it on purpose, mixed the people in with the cows: anyway, it stopped a lot of complaining.

Now the huddle of addicts at the door was growing. Sometimes they'd sneak in to lick the empty wrappers; we had to watch out for it. Sometimes they'd follow people who got take-out and snatch or beat or stab. Not many people got take-out. We'd fooled the addicts at first by wrapping the burgers in green for chicken or blue for beef or yellow for fish, but no one fell for that any more: no one came in here for chicken or beef or fish.

At break-time, I got my staff burger. I didn't wait to get to a seat, just bit into it there and then. This time it tasted of loss. There had been too many of those lately. The meat was juicy, liquid coursing to the surface, but it was full of that deep melancholy; I could almost see dark eyes staring into mine, their sadness.

So few of the burgers tasted of joy. Those ones were special. But then, I shouldn't have been surprised; if Jake got wind of a batch like that, he'd take them. Sometimes he sold the special ones at the door, cash in hand, no questions asked, as long as the price was right.

I shivered and finished the burger, tearing the paper apart to reach the last drop of ichor. I licked shamelessly, lapping on the grease and the grief.

It wasn't bad, working in Soul Food. Not a bit.

In one day I could feel anxiety, pride, and contentment and pain, and none of it my own. When Jake wasn't looking, I could sneak a taste of whatever came through the machine. The other staff did it too; it was almost expected. You had to test the wares.

This was one of the few jobs, Jake said, where you could give it your heart and soul: literally. I mean, when I'm gone, I'm guaranteed a place. There's nothing left to chance, when you're staff: there's only one place left to go. Especially for someone like Oz, who was halfway there already.

I asked him what it was like being a zomb, but he just turned those cow eyes on me, nothing inside them. Sometimes I had to tell him to close his mouth to stop him drooling into the burgers.

It must have hurt.

Still, when he died, it was guaranteed: it was the same for all the zombs. It was in the contract. Most people have no idea if their soul will carry on when they die. They fret about it, pray about it, scare themselves stupid. It's a matter of faith, but with us, it's concrete: we know. We've tasted it.

That's why so many people want to work here. I miss my old job, sometimes. The law paid well, but the prospects…well, they weren't so long term as at Soul Food.

Teresa didn't like it when I told her I'd got on the staff. "Have you heard about that guy who ate a soul burger," she said, all casual, "and lost all his own memories? It was like the soul possessed him." She waited for a reaction. When she didn't get one, she came out with more horror stories: the burger that had cancer. The one made from the guy with steel pins in his leg that never got taken out. The one made from a serial killer.

I nodded, but I wasn't really listening.

"You've heard about the soul who was cursed. The one who was insane. You know what that did to the person who ate it."

I just carried on writing out my resignation. Urban legends, the lot of them; amazing they still made this stuff up.

Ozzie slept in the quarters behind Soul Food. They built them special and painted them green. He wore green overalls when he wasn't in uniform. He looked like he belonged, day and night. His meals were provided.

Ozzie fried the fries, fizzle, fizzle, all day long.

Sometimes he tossed the salad. It's good even for a zomb to have some variety in life—or death, depending on how you look at it. He tossed the salad in the oil that dripped out of the soul burgers, to give it extra zing.

Ozzie went from the burger bar to the sleeping quarters every night at eleven. He watched TV, his blank eyes staring, and sometimes with a line of drool joining his chin to his chest, because Ozzie's fingers went into the fixer. No one fixes the fixer. It's self-maintaining, self-cleaning, so no one looks inside: no one knows how it works. We just know it does.

Once, in a reversal of what they did with the Contamination, someone fed beef patties into the soul food machine. They did it so they could watch the dull expressions on customers' faces when they tasted cow soul; sometimes, they said, the customers went out mooing. They said this was hilarious.

I told Teresa about it, feeding people on cow soul, and I laughed, but she didn't.

Later that night, she came to see me in the restaurant. I was surprised; I started to take a burger from the chute, I would have sneaked it to her for free, but she shook her head and told me it was over.

In the end it was Teresa who moved out. She said she couldn't stand the way I looked at her any longer, like I was somewhere else in my mind. Then she started appearing at Soul Food.

She said she missed me. I told her I was right there.

It's funny how Teresa always said I was the one who went away, when I was steady as a rock: I lived in our house, slept in our bed, went to work, came home. And all the time she'd started to revolve around me like a moon, moving a little further away before some force drew her back.

I'd see her sometimes while I served, her face looking in at the window. Sometimes the glass would be steamed up, if we were busy, and she'd be streaked between drops of condensed sweat or tears or grease.

I don't know why she didn't just come in.

"They're given injections," Teresa said one night. She'd waited for me outside the entrance, didn't even say hello before she began. "The people. They're given lethal injections, so they don't feel anything. There are busloads of them carted in, and they just roll up their sleeves and line up. They say the processing's so quick, the drugs don't have time to get into the meat."

I kept walking. I didn't know where this was coming from.

"But how could it not? There's not much they won't put in burgers. Which bit is left behind, with the drugs inside?"

I walked. Teresa still trotted behind me.

"I'm pregnant," she said.

After that, Teresa said she wanted to come home. And it was fine, I spent most of the time at Soul Food anyway. Ozzie, he wasn't such bad company when it came down to it.

Jake had a new boy. Danny had light brown hair that fell across his eyes. Jake told him to cut it, but the new boy just laughed and clapped him on the back.

Danny spent some of the time on the fixer, some on the farmyard, some out front. He didn't talk to me much; he saved his energy for the Super. He'd talk about Teresa, though, if he saw her at the window: "Who's the babe?" he'd ask, every time, as if he never listened to the answer.

One day, Teresa was there and she was crying. She came inside and told me she was leaving, which was weird, because I'd thought she was just coming back.

"Steady as a rock," I said. "Why are you like the moon?"

She stopped crying and looked at me as though I'd gone mad.

As soon as I got to Soul Food I could hear screaming, somewhere out back. Someone with a takeaway, maybe: we found the addicts round the back more and more, waiting around, just in case.

I went to the counter and saw Oz, which was weird. Oz never worked the counter.

"What is it?" I asked him.

He just looked at me, his eyes bovine.

Danny stuck his head around the side. "Some nutter sneaked in," he said, "put their hand in the fixer." There was something in the way he looked at me. I started to go through, but then Jake was there, and he blocked my way. He held something out.

"It's all taken care of," he said. "Here, take your staff burger. Eat it out front."

It was too soon, I shouldn't have had my staff burger for another four hours, but I didn't question it: I could smell it already. So I went out front and I started to eat. And I found myself, for the first time in a long time, really thinking about Teresa.

I could see the colour of her hair. It was like long, shining pieces of stretched-out toffee. I saw myself running my fingers through it.

I pushed the thought aside and kept eating.

She was sad; I could see it in her eyes. There were tears in them, my face reflected in each little globe.

It was back in the good old days. Walking along, her arm in mine, laughing. She'd wanted to kick leaves like a child and I wouldn't let her, but she pulled her arm free and did it anyway. Her cheeks were flushed pink, her mouth open in a laugh, her eyes flashing back little pieces of sky.

Then she was crying again. Why always crying?

I saw her standing and turning in a long mirror, smoothing down her dress. Then she was really crying again, out of control, because it was gone; our baby, mine and hers, it wasn't happening any more.

The sorrow hit me. I tasted the grief, black ashes in my mouth. I forced myself to swallow.

And then I knew exactly who it was out back.

I bolted through the seating area, past the impatient queue, past the counter, past Oz who was frying fries, past the fixer, out of the door. Outside was a pastel afternoon, the sky all pink and blue.

Danny and Jake were there, their backs turned.

Danny was trying to stifle the blood that was dripping from her arm. He had a whole-limb dressing wrapped around it; it was supposed to stem the flow instantly, but it hadn't worked, the blood was still coming through.

Her toffee-coloured hair was streaked with it. It was all over her front. Her face was white.

I took hold of her shoulder, feeling the bones inside, how small they were. "Teresa," I said.

Her eyes were already blank.

I stepped away, found I couldn't look at her. I realised I was still holding the soul burger. It dripped grease onto the ground. There was an addict standing by the bins, he'd been going through them, and now he'd turned and his eyes were fixed on it: drip, drip. After we'd gone, he'd be over here licking the asphalt.

I wasn't hungry anymore. I felt like I never wanted to eat again.

I stared at it, the thing in my hands. If I left it, threw it away, what then? What would happen to her? The addict was an old man with straggle-grey hair. I knew the look Teresa would have given him, if she'd still been able; the same look she gave all of them once, the hopeless, all the lost causes. The same look she'd given me.

I raised it to my mouth and I took a bite. Just like that, just like all of the others.

And this one, too, tasted of loss.

IMAGINARY KINGDOM

Jay Eales

Man goes to the doctor. He says "What's the first sign of madness, doc?" The doctor says, "Looking for hair on the palms of your hands." "Hairy palms is a sign of madness?" he says. "No," the doctor replies, "Looking for it." Bit of a shit joke, I know, but I'm a bit rusty these days.

I'm not sure what tipped me off that I'd gone tonto. Was it that I was seeing the walking dead everywhere? Friends and family dropping like flies and getting up with a taste for more than ketchup? Was that it, or was that really happening? Maybe it was when I started hearing voices in my head.

When I was a kid, I had this friend, Billybones. Best mate a growing boy could have. We did everything together. He stayed with me when I fell out of the tree in Old Man Woody's Orchard. Saying that, he's the one who got me to climb the bloody thing in the first place, but still. Billybones taught me to ride a Chopper.

Well, I say a Chopper, but it was actually a Vindec High Riser. My Dad wouldn't stump up for a Raleigh. He showed me how to turn sticks into catapults, boomerangs and all kinds of weapons. Only thing was, nobody else could see him but me.

After me and Billybones did over the school chemistry lab, Mum and Dad started to take notice of him. Sent me to all kinds of headshrinkers. I didn't understand much of what they said, but old Billybones, he didn't like it. The shrinks' jibber-jabber was like his Kryptonite, or a garlic sausage sandwich to Dracula. Still, it made things easier at home. Mum stopped crying all the time, and Dad bought me a Cobblers season ticket. That must have hurt him, having to put his hand in his pocket for something. It was such a novelty to have him show an interest in me, that I couldn't face telling him I was only into the footy for the Panini sticker albums. I had to change schools, and along with all my other friends, Billybones quietly went away too. I hadn't given him a thought in years.

Then, the big WTF happened. I call it the WTF because nobody really figured out what the fuck happened. One day, everyone's watching *I'm A Nonentity, Get Me Out of Here*, and eating Pot Noodles. The next, people start to get sick. I mean, *really* sick. And not from the Pot Noodles, either. Temperatures off the scale with no warning. Blood vessels busting left, right and centre and people chucking up guts everywhere. It took a few days before anyone really took it seriously. I think it was when that famous newsreader, you know the one – the one with the jumpers – brought up a kidney right at the camera on breakfast telly, that people shat themselves. Too late, by then.

The government fell apart immediately, of course. Not that they were exactly together before the WTF, but it's like they were almost relieved to have something to take people's minds off the economy. To start with, the Prime Minister's on the News telling people to stay calm, "we're all in this together" and so on, and days later, he and most of the cabinet are just gone. Flying abroad for urgent talks about the Euro, they said. Only nobody says where they were going. Dev down the corner shop reckoned they'd done a runner, because they knew what was coming. Whatever, they obviously didn't tell the poor sod given the job of filling in for them. Do you know what, I can't even remember his name... If there was still a *Guinness Book of Records*, he'd be in there as shortest serving PM in history. Plus, first one to have his face bitten off by a zombie. Beat that, McWhirters!

Personally, I like to imagine the plane full of cabinet ministers cracking open the champers, congratulating themselves for giving the country one final shaft, when cuddly Ken Clarke vamps out and suddenly, the 757 is just another tin of canned food; an all Ken can eat buffet.

Fast forward a few months and it's all gone to shit. Everyone out for themselves, killing for cans of tuna, and a trip to Tesco always seems to end with having to smack a pop-up flesh-eater with whatever household appliance is closest to hand. You'd think with all those zombie films, there'd be people banding together to hold off the ravening hordes, but it just isn't like that. Knowing my luck, it'd be just like at school, always picked last for sports. What was it Thatcher said about there being no such thing as society? Well, welcome to your world, Maggie. Welcome to it.

I'd been living rough, moving camp every few days after I was nearly caught in my own house. My own damn house, for fuck's sake. Not by the zoms. Way too stupid to live, as long as you don't let yourself get boxed in and make sure you're not followed. Most of all, don't do what Dev did, and try to fill up the silence by blasting out Led Zep on a battery-operated CD player at all hours. Might as well put out the welcome mat, cos' you'll bring those suckers in from all over town. On the plus side, Dev managed to pull in most of the shamblers from hiding, along with a few survivors like me, blinking out in the sunlight. We were a bit wary at first, but grateful to see another living breathing face, so once we'd done the necessary, the town was pretty quiet overall. That's probably why I got cocky. This guy Grant, who was pretty tasty with a cricket bat, seemed to be a stand-up individual. We'd stood and broken heads together. When Dev took a nasty nip trying to protect his shop, Grant did what had to be done. I let slip about my stash of beef jerky sticks and Peperami, grabbed on my first Tesco take-out, before the place got a bit too hairy with zoms and I had to torch it. School all over again. Earned myself a cracked skull for my misplaced trust, but got a valuable lesson out of it. Trust no fucker. So that's me, keeping myself to myself. Nobody gets in, and nobody lets you down. You want my cans? Come get some. I've got a 9 iron waiting for you, and I've been working on my handicap.

I'd not spoken to a living soul for over two months when Billybones came calling for a school reunion. Freaked me right out he did, since I was sitting on a roof, watching a stray shambler swaying aimlessly in my direction. Had to have been a local, walking down the middle of the road like that. Known for it, we are. I'd just decided to call him Dodger on account of his clothes being all 'jammy', when old BB pipes up, clear as a bell. Thought for a minute that Dodger was replying to me. Good job I was on a flat roof. If I'd been perched on a slope, I'd probably have pitched off the front into the street, like manna from Heaven for the Dodger. As it was, Billybones was tipping me off about the crawling zom I hadn't spotted behind me.

After that, things seemed better again. No longer alone, it was like the good old days: Butch and Sundance, Ben and Billybones—the team supreme. With BB watching my back, I could take a few more chances. His eyes were way better than mine, or maybe it was his nose. He could sniff out a stash of hidden food better than anyone I ever met. And those eyes, he must have them in the back of his head. No zombie ever got by him. With him urging me on, we were going further and further out of my comfort zone. I'd never had risked going into the city. Too many bodies, too many variables. Not knowing the streets like the back of my hand, there was too much chance of running down a blind alley. But as Billybones put it to me, how long would the food last in this little town? We weren't the only survivors, and between us, we'd pretty much picked the bones from the place.

Billybones made me feel safe, so when he said jump, I'd do it, even if it was out of a tall tree. Wouldn't be the first time, after all. And if BB started taking me to other places, to pick up things other than canned goods, well, you do favours for mates, don't you? Even if it makes your backpacks weigh a ton, what's a few electronic components between friends?

Whatever he was planning, he didn't feel the need to let me in on it. I started hearing another voice around then, much fainter though, and this one sounded like me. It started to sow doubts in my mind. What would Billybones want with a bunch of radio odds and sods? He didn't really sound that much like Billybones, did he? I'd argue with my inner voice that BB had grown up. It's not like I hadn't changed myself after all those years. But the voice kept on, at times threatening to blot out Billybones' voice in my head.

I'd forgotten the big rule. Trust no fucker. Least of all a fucker I couldn't even see. Had to admit to myself, I had a point.

The next time BB piped up, I confronted him – brought up the Woody's Orchard story, and caught him in a lie. He didn't remember it at all. That's about when it hit me how screwed up I was. Bad enough to have invented an imaginary friend, but to come up with someone only pretending to be that friend? That… that's pretty fucked up.

I said some things. He tried to explain himself, but I wasn't listening. I told him I never wanted to hear from him again. End of.

Billybones, or whatever name he wanted to call himself, said fine, and all the voices went away, leaving me alone. Alone, and in a city I barely knew. Maybe not the smartest move of all time.

"Wake up!" I was jolted out of sleep by the voice of Billybones, not really clear on where the voice was coming from, or even where it was I was holed up for the night. I'd picked one of those World of Leather type superstores, where the place was divvied up into room settings, and I'd spied what looked to be a comfy pull out sofa bed as I passed by. I found a way in easily enough, and blocked up my entry point, to be sure that no zoms could accidentally stumble into my hideout while I slept. The sofa bed I'd had my eye on turned out to be lumpy as hell, but in a side room, I found a much better offer. An actual bed, no less. Been a while since I'd had one of those.

Blinking furiously in the darkness to wipe away the firework explosions before my eyes, I remembered my anger, "Thought I told you to sling your hook."

"Stay exactly where you are," BB said calmly, ignoring my complaint completely. "Don't panic at what's about to happen." Before I could think of some kind of comeback, there was the sound of breaking glass from above me, and something hit the ground in front of me.

"Cover your eyes for a minute," he continued. I did as he said, and glad I did when I heard a momentary crackle and whatever it was that had been tossed into the room detonated and the room flared artificially into daylight. Fanning my hand in front of my face to diffuse the light, as though that would have made any difference, I then saw what it was that Billybones wanted me to remain calm about. Shuffling about, bumping into each other constantly, I was pretty much surrounded by shamblers. I groped for my golf club, close-by as always, and pull on my backpack, ready to make a break for it. Even armed, I had nowhere to go, and nothing to do but go down fighting.

"Keep your head down," he barked. Before I could protest, semi-automatic gunfire sent the remaining glass exploding out of the window frame, and the front rank of shuffling dead danced their final spastic dance, and their torn-up corpses formed a barrier, albeit a minor one, that would not stop the zombies for long. All that gunfire in a confined space left me deafened to all but a high-pitched whine, and feeling more vulnerable than ever. At least I didn't have to listen to the moans of the dead.

"Look up now," Billybones' voice cut through my tinnitus, and I was no longer questioning him. There was some kind of masked special forces soldier leaning through the destroyed window, arm outstretched towards me, and gesturing for me to do the same. I needed no further hints, and scrambled up to take his hand. Not quite close enough, I had to clamber up on the headboard to get a bit more height. Shrugging the heavy backpack from my shoulder, I stretch for my life. Still tantalisingly out of reach.

"Jump!" Billybones screamed in my head, and I was back in Woody's Orchard again. I launched myself from the precariously thin headboard, trusting that the man in black would grab me, and that he was strong enough to hold and pull me up. If I was wrong, I'd be throwing myself to the shambling mass, closing in once again, now that they had overcome the wall of dead meat between us. He grunted, but luckily for me, the soldier was as good as his promise. Probably picked first for sports at school, and for the first time, I felt no stab of envy towards him and his kind. Another soldier was bracing him against the wall as he reached forward with his other hand and hauled me up and away from the grasping hands below, and out into the night.

I fell heavily, but got to my feet immediately, and was clutching at my rescuers, seeing the van they had arrived in, urging them to move, to get to the van, to do it now! Why were they delaying? Muffled by their masks, the soldiers spoke, their voices crashing over each other, the urgency obvious, "Were you bitten? Are you unharmed? Where is the backpack? Are you infected?"

All the time, they paw at me, checking me for any obvious wounds or broken skin. My clothes are unceremoniously yanked up and down, but I don't protest. I know what scares them, and it scares me too. They seem to be satisfied, and I'm allowed to recover my dignity and hustled over to the waiting van, where more armed men help me inside, along with my rescuers. We all sit on wooden benches facing each other, and saying nothing at all.

They take me into a compound—they call it Stormfort—typical squaddies, always making up dramatic names for things, and they keep us all together until they're sure none of us have been compromised. One by one, everyone is taken out for debriefing. Out of their stormtrooper masks, they're not as intimidating, but still not all that talkative. One of them has a dig at the guy who hauled me out of the window for picking me over the backpack.

"Get your priorities straight," he bellows right in his face, but my rescuer doesn't sweat it.

"Will you listen to yourself?" he says with a calming Irish brogue. "We'll get it as part of the clean-up in the morning. It's not like the skels will eat it, unlike yer man there." He indicates towards me, and I shuffle uncomfortably as Mr Touchy sends me daggers.

When it's my go under the lights, I expect it to be like the cop shows, where they interrogate the suspect in the box, trying to catch them in a lie, but it's nothing like that. They just ask about the situation out on the streets, what my experiences have been like. It's the fine detail they're after, but they seem to know pretty much all of it already. I catch a glimpse of a logo on the door as I go in. It's some kind of stylised military insignia, with the words *Operation* and *Invulnerable* stencilled above and below the crest. I expect my hosts to be all Secret Squirrel about telling me anything, but they seem pretty open. They tell me that Operation Invulnerable is a specialist field unit, conducting a feasibility study on the viability of something called Remote Viewing. They use a load more big words that make my head hurt, but as far as I can tell, they get their Viewer, someone who's got some sort of psychic gift, to sit and think himself somewhere, and he can see and report back on what he sees. It all sounds like a load of bollocks to me, and they freely admit it's never been officially accepted scientifically. But they're sold on it, you can see it in their eyes.

"Do you know how they get those pictures from Broadcasting House into your TV set?" they ask. I mumble something vague about signals and transmitters, but confess beyond that, I haven't really thought about it.

"Doesn't stop you from enjoying *Top Gear* though, does it?"

"No, the end of the world made a good job of that, given the grid went down just a few days after the WTF happened." I could see where he was coming from, though. End of the day, it doesn't matter how it works as long as it does work. Don't look a gift horse in the mouth, and all that.

The Director explains to me that they are hoping that Remote Viewing will be an invaluable resource in protecting their men when they go out on sorties to scavenge for food and supplies. They're operating on a scale way bigger than mine. In comparison, I was stumbling blindly in the dark, hoping to find somewhere that hadn't been looted long ago, without running into a pack of zoms. Needle in a haystack time. Imagine if you could send out a scout to find whatever it is you need; a scout that can cover hundreds of miles in a day; one who can zoom in on cans of soup, batteries or I don't know… toilet rolls, and all of it with no chance of being touched by a shambler. It's like the WTF is the perfect playground to test Operation Invulnerable.

It was a pure fluke they found me. The Remote Viewer was out hunting for electronic components they were running short of at Stormfort, and I pinged on his psychic radar. They decided to kill two birds with one stone, and let me be their personal shopper to pick up all the goodies they needed, and keep me safe all the way back to base. It's a win-win situation, for them and for me. That's when the last pieces of the puzzle fell into place for me, and I realised who their Viewer is. Never said I was that quick on the uptake, did I?

When they decide they've answered enough of my questions for the night, the Director walks me out into the hall, on the way to the mess to get some hot food inside me. We pass by another nondescript office, pretty much like all the rest, except this one has tinted windows. I spot my reflection in the shiny black surface, and do I look a state. A few months back, if I'd passed me on the street, I'd expect to be tapped up for spare change, if I didn't cross to the other side quickly enough.

"Oh, where are my manners," the Director said, "There's someone you'll be wanting to meet." He tapped quietly on the door, etched with a variation of the Operation Invulnerable logo, and with one of those sliding plates divided into green and red sections to tell if the occupant was free or busy. Right now, green was the colour. The Director didn't wait for confirmation, but opened the door. Inside, a young guy, probably one of the soldiers by his army fatigues, sat up from the leather couch he was stretched out on, and ran a hand through his hair. He got to his feet and came towards me, rubbing his hand on his trouser leg before offering it for me to shake. His broad smile took me off guard, given we'd never met before. And yet…

"Ben! So good that you're here," He pumped my arm vigorously, "I'm Sergeant…" I stopped him in mid-flow. By now, I was smiling too. "You'll always be Billybones to me."

THE THIRD DAY

Adrian Chamberlin

And there shall be a resurrection of the dead, both of the just and unjust. - Acts 24:15

But those mine enemies, which would not that I should reign over them, bring hither, and slay them before me. – Luke 19.27

THE BASTARDS were even playing dice. He closed his eyes with despair at this, the final insult. He couldn't bring his head back up to the sky, so weak was he with the loss of blood; but the strain on his crucified arms sent fresh waves of agony through his body, and increased the suffocating pressure on his chest.

With an effort that had him biting his lower lip, causing fresh blood to run down his chin, he pushed his head back against the upright. The pine felt damp and greasy, slick with his sweat and blood. Then more pain flared, this time in the back of his skull. The thorns were driven deeper into his scalp. Stars cartwheeled across the curtain of his closed eyelids and he felt his head spin.

Above the dry murmur of the desert wind he heard laughter. Familiar laughing from two of the four soldiers who guarded him.

It was forced, false. He knew this. Just as he knew they would never admit their fear or doubt. He allowed himself a small smile of triumph, hoped they saw it as that, and not the rictus grin of one approaching death and obscene rebirth.

He waited for the gust of wind to pass before opening his eyelids; preventing more of the radioactive ash and grit from further scouring his dried eyes.

The two soldiers stared up at him, the laughter dead on their lips. Blinking away the tears and blood did little to make them visible; their faces remained fleshy blurs. Their desert fatigue uniforms blended them into the hilltop, making them one with the desolation, and their Kevlar helmeted heads appeared as misshapen boulders in the dust that clung to every unprotected surface like a second skin.

The furthest guard wiped gloved fingers through the coating on his goggles. Wide, panicked eyes stared up at him through the clear shield—no need for tints or UV protection in a world that suffered perpetual twilight—and the crucified man wondered if the guard's expression was one of guilt or fear. Probably both.

Where have I seen him before? He knows me, he recognised me—but who... another spasm of pain shot up from his abdomen and wiped the question from his mind. The cramps were getting stronger. He cried out.

The dice were forgotten. The troopers had gotten to their feet, AR-15s clutched to their chests. The spasm passed and his smile broadened at the sight.

They're more frightened of me than the Empty Ones. They'd even forgotten their training. Granted, any marauders would have to pass the gauntlet of the two battalions stationed at each end of the valley, and that stretched a distance of twelve miles; but even so, this was an exposed hilltop. Who could say that nothing had slipped through the fortifications? Who could say that those things had all succumbed to the Cleansing Fires? After all, the Elders had not stayed the duration of the execution. Just enough to see the nails driven into wrists and ankles and the crosspiece raised to the sky. Then they had gone, their robes billowing in the desert breeze as they descended the hill, and hastened towards the waiting helicopter.

Sentence carried out and witnessed. No reason to stay and watch the condemned expire. After all, they have four armed soldiers to bear witness. In addition, four FloatCams formed their own cross, hovering at his eye line and streaming every second of his death to churches and the now-Christianised mosques and synagogues in the surviving parts of the globe. That would be the Elders' official reason for leaving.

But he knew better.

A rumbling from his throat jerked his chest into spasms of agony. He didn't recognise the sound that accompanied it, but the panicked retreat of the soldiers told him it was his own laughter.

You're scared of me. I defied The Appointed and that's why you're terrified. Because you always suspected the truth, I merely put it into words.

He no longer had the strength or energy to shake with fury as he had done when the sentence of crucifixion had been passed. The scourging, the beating, being goaded through the settlement where the inhabitants were forced to throw rocks in his path – a recreation of the Passion, but merely the beginning of his sentence. A sentence born of love, The Appointed insisted. *Your suffering will return Christ to us. From apostate to saviour. From heretic to hero.*

Hero. His followers had called him that once. The same

followers who cast stones at him as he stumbled through the rubbish-strewn streets of the village under the weight of the crosspiece. Oh, they had done so with averted eyes and forced, false shouts of hatred; fear of retribution from The Appointed had demanded this, to save their own skins.

Was it worth it? Not one of them spoke in my defence. Not one. How many Peters denied me?

His smile vanished, his lips pulled back into a grimace of pain. The soldiers appeared to relax. Fingers moved from trigger bar to trigger guard. Shoulders became less tense. Eyes moved from the dying man on the cross to the distant horizon. The four members of the armed execution detail began to relax.

All but one. His eyes returned to the nervous soldier, then narrowed in recognition.

Wilson? Good God, it is you! What the hell are you doing here?

Each time Private Wilson looked upon the horizon the view seemed to change. He tried to tell himself it was just a trick of the light, the scarlet bleeding of the Earth mingled with the radioactive dust to create an eternal sunset. Perhaps it was the shortage of food and the insufficient sleep they had all endured since being assigned to the Execution Detail. Maybe the antiRad medication had not been strong enough?

This was certainly not the easy posting he had expected it to be. The Appointed had called it a Holy Task: not just the execution of a heretic and traitor, but ensuring the return of the Messiah.

Now the full meaning of his command settled over him. To walk in the shadow of history was one thing. To recreate history was something else.

Even Simms and Pearson felt it. He watched the corporal and private surreptitiously; noted their well-fed bellies that bulged against the webbing of their utility packs, the alertness of their posture gradually succumbing to the sloth that came with inaction. They kicked shale down the slope on odd moments, picked up pieces of flint and threw them into the darkness. Wilson had seen it all before. A challenge to the Empty Ones: *Come on, you undead bastards, come and get what's coming to you!*

They didn't want to admit to each other that the Empty Ones had indeed been all destroyed. No more zombies to kill, so what was there to fight against?

Heretics? No, the last heretic was dying before their eyes. No one would rise against The Appointed after this, no one.

Wilson kept his eyes on the shifting horizon, unwilling to face the crucified man once more. Not because of what they had done to him—Wilson had seen, and indeed done, far worse in his three years in the Army of Light—but because of the way the condemned looked at him.

He'd been recognised. Was he expected to act? What could he do? He fingered the trigger guard of his automatic rifle. *One against three, and then what? The FloatCams will signal my actions to the Chapter House, and I'll never get out of the Holy Land alive.* A sense of powerlessness settled over him. Then doubt.

What if his former leader was wrong after all? What if The Appointed was correct in interpreting the Will of God? Would he, a lowly private, be able to bear the burden of condemning the remainder of humanity?

No. Doubt is good. If we question, demand answers, we're truly human. That is the true gift of God: to understand that we are on our own, that the future of humanity rests in our own hands, not prayer. That's what will help us to survive, to rebuild our shattered world. A simple message, one that had been so easily dismissed by The Appointed and his Elders.

He had seen the proof with his own eyes. It was real, undeniable. But the discs and the books had been seized by the Elders, consigned to the flames and forgeries issued and hastily distributed.

Were they really forgeries? Perhaps it was fakes we were shown by our former leader. It was the easier version to believe. Truth is pain. The masses fear that.

Not that the masses would admit to it, of course. Despite all suggestion to the contrary, they swallowed the lies told by The Appointed. They needed the lies. They needed to believe that the fate of the Earth was in divine hands, that it was subject to the conflict between God and the Dark One. You were more likely to remain sane if you knew humanity had no control over its destiny.

It was easy enough to believe that in the settlements, with constant reminders of the infallibility of The Appointed. Out here, surrounded by the abomination of desolation – *man-made* desolation, he reminded himself, *not* Satanic – it was harder to accept that God still had a plan for His children.

Thunder clouds neared from the east; a shroud for the dying planet. The blackness was punctuated by the occasional flare of orange and scarlet, as the wounded Earth shrieked its pain to the heavens.

The newest Rupture had increased in size. This close to what had once been the Holy Land. Wilson remembered the cries of the locals, the chilling welcome as the Hercules disgorged the four man Execution Detail onto the Meggido Plain.

A new Rupture. More of the Empty Ones will spill forth— Satan holds power in the Holy Land. We truly are the Damned, and nothing holy remains for us.

The soldiers had mumbled platitudes and blessings to the crowd while waiting for the armoured personnel carrier, trying not to notice the weeping sores on skeletal limbs that poked through ragged shifts and tunics, the hairless scalps, the jaundiced skin and toothless grimaces. There was little life to distinguish them from the Empty Ones.

It was not the welcome they'd been expecting. The Army of Light had made good on their promise of deliverance from the plagues that scourged the Holy Land, and now they brought a new blessing. Had The Appointed not sent this detail to the ruins of Jerusalem to deliver a new Messiah? In his divine wisdom, had he not decreed that the last heretic be the instrument of Christ's return? So why was the greeting so sullen?

A new moon after the spring equinox. Friday, the day of execution. The Appointed had wisely judged the date. A new Easter, a new resurrection. Yet even that had failed to rouse them. One, a shrivelled man who Wilson learned later from the death warrant was two weeks past his thirtieth birthday, uttered blasphemy.

A resurrection of the dead, both of the just and the unjust, the bible promised. But to slay the living? The Elders tell us the Evil One has usurped God's power of resurrection. God? God abandoned us a long time ago, trooper! The Empty Ones are proof of that. Empty Ones? Why do we shy from speaking of their true nature? They are no demons from Hell. They are man-made, just as the apocalypse was. Nuclear weaponry and biological warfare destroyed the world and raised the dead, not God!

Man-made. The word that defied The Appointed's decree that the resurrected dead were empty shells possessed by the Dark One. That speech earned the man a swift passage to the Breaking Wheel. While the rest of his troop had gone to lay down Cleansing Fire upon the Empty Ones spilling forth from the

Rupture. Wilson's first task in the Holy Land had been to hoist the cartwheel with its braiding of broken human limbs onto the pole and lift it into the scorching desert sun. It had been too easy. The man was light as a feather. Corporal Simms had grinned a little too broadly at Wilson's discomfort. *Welcome to Jerusalem. Nice little warm-up for you, chap.*

Yes, corp. Fuck you as well.

Warm-up, he thought with a shiver. He stared at the blood that had turned to gritty black jelly on the cross's upright, the insects and flies feasting on the faeces that dripped from the condemned's evacuated bowels; tried hard not to raise his eyes and meet those of the crucified man.

Wilson turned back to the cracked and ruptured landscape that had once bloomed with palm trees and olive groves. It was bad enough in Britain—the Ruptures that broke the land after the ascension of the Righteous had turned Wilson's homeland into a volcanic nightmare, but at least it had been spared the nuclear rage that had swept this part of the Earth.

The last heretic's blood will make the Holy Land bloom anew. As he is drained, and becomes an Empty One, Christ will answer the call and take his body. The blood spilled will be a balm to the wounded land, will seal the ulcers that spill forth abominations from Satan's realm. The Tribulation will be complete, and the Millennium will begin. Thus is the will of God.

It will take time, though. The Tribulation has many years to go... Wilson shuddered. Who could really believe that this was the will of God? To crucify a heretic, and then inject him with the essence of the Empty Ones; to condemn him to writhe in undead torment until the Son of Man returned. And what place for him and his companions? How many years would it be before Christ returned—if he returned?

How many years will we be guarding this man, watching his zombified body writhe in agony on the cross? Have you bastards even given that any thought?

Wilson glared at his comrades, busily rattling dice in chipped plastic beakers.

He envied them; for their ignorance, their blind faith and fanatical obedience to Scripture. He wished he could blind himself to the truth.

What's the point of a truth that offers no hope?

None would admit the world was changing, that what The Appointed preached was flawed logic. None but the man on the cross behind him. Wilson felt a chill and told himself it was the breeze. Not the piercing eyes of the heretic condemned to be a saviour. Eyes that burned with recognition.

What do you want from me? There's nothing I can do now!

He glanced at the mess tent with envious eyes. What he'd give for shelter from the elements, a lie-down and a sleep…

No!

He wasn't the only one to have nightmares, he was certain. The army psychologist had warned them that by being bivouacked on the site of the original Passion their minds would play tricks on them, but entreated them to put their trust into God to give them the strength to prevail. Golgotha had seen many more deaths since the Holy Land was enveloped in nuclear rage, but no crucifixions. Until now.

The wind abated, allowing the harsh croak of the heretic's laughter to settle on him, as thick and cloying as the desert dust. He shuddered, felt his finger tighten involuntarily on the trigger guard of his automatic rifle.

Why won't you just fucking die? Why spin this out? Wilson took a deep breath and forced himself to relax, but the stench of scorched earth and roasted meat made him gag. Two days and still the stench was fresh to his nostrils.

Two days had passed and still the heretic lived.

Sergeant Banks turned towards him. He inclined his head towards the field tent and then glanced warily at the two soldiers behind them. The message was clear.

A private chat, soldier. Wilson felt a mixture of relief and fear. Relief because he had seen the momentary doubt in their platoon leader's eyes, the quickly hidden sense of revulsion as he hammered the ancient iron spikes into the prisoner; fear because he suspected the sergeant recognised his own weakness of faith, and would cover it by reporting Wilson to the Army Council when they were safely evac'd to the Chapter House.

So what does he want from me?

The waves of pain were constant, but fading. Like the ebbing tide, the sound of the waves scraping across shingle and rocky coastline remained, but became distant. The end was near.

What now? Despite his light-headedness, the verses of the Gospels came with total recall, briefly wiping out the solid Truth he had memorised. Would they pierce his side with a spear? Would they break his legs with a club?

The clouds should darken for three hours ... but they've been dark for the last twelve years, ever since the Rapture. He wondered if the Chapter House would undergo an earthquake. *Now that would be something. A new Rupture, striking the temple of The Appointed. Explain that as the will of God!*

He felt nothing below his legs, and wondered if that was due to the injection they had given him. No, the essence of the Empty Ones would only activate once death had occurred. He remembered that much.

He couldn't work out why he wasn't dead. It was true that his years in the Army of Light—before he had seen the real light—had fortified him. The best rations and the finest medical care were reserved for God's warriors, and although it had been three years since he had deserted and formed his own army, his knowledge of the supply depots and transport routes ensured he and his men remained in top physical condition. But the scourging and crucifixion …

This is the third day on the cross. I should be dead.

He had judged the passing of time by the shift changes of the four troopers. He remembered all too well his own time in the Army of Light, and his own shifts on Execution Detail. Four hours on, four hours off, two men on each watch. It hadn't changed, unlike the method of killing.

Executions followed the ancient method of breaking on the wheel, the shattered limbs braided around the spokes of old cartwheels before hoisting onto six foot high poles, then left to die through exposure to the elements, dehydration and the ravages of the carrion crows.

God, to think it was a duty I once enjoyed. That I believed the condemned deserved their fate. It hadn't taken long for the novelty to wear off. Guarding the dying wasn't to prevent attempted rescue from family members and loved ones.

Pest control, that's all it was. Standing guard to ensure the Empty Ones didn't get near enough to add them to their ranks. Just pest control. The thought made him aware of the buzzing sound that had failed to penetrate his hearing. Now he heard them he could feel them, crawling over his dehydrated skin, following the dried trails of crusted jelly that had once flowed through his veins. He didn't need to open his eyes to know how large they were. Inch-thick bodies with wings that would have shamed dragonflies, would have been greeted with alarm and horror before Judgement Day; now were seen as normal, expected, just like the dog-sized rats that prowled the graveyards, and the vultures that stalked the dead air like pterodactyls from a pre-human past. The only creatures that thrived in the post-Rapture world were those that fed on the dead.

That applies to human beings as well. You know I'm right, Appointed. Your flock knows it as well. When the dead walk the Earth you know God has abandoned us. 'Cast ye the unprofitable servant into the outer darkness,' Matthew wrote. Well, the outer darkness is here, and your lies, your lust for dominion brought it here!

That was what had led him to this. He closed his eyes and played back the scene that had been the culmination of his life's struggle, and the means by which he signed his own death warrant. His destiny.

The assault in the Chapter House, the ornate tapestries and drapes that belonged to an even older world soaked in blood and cut through with bullet holes; the Holy Guard overpowered, held at bay by the ancient, pre-Rapture rifles of the heretic's rag-tag army; the monitor screens covered with images of The Appointed's terrified, far from holy face; the FloatCams zooming in on the man who held the false prophet at gunpoint, his steel grey eyes turning to face the camera lenses and meeting the audience of the world, his words calm but authoritative as he reeled off the list of lies and crimes The Appointed had inflicted upon a stunned world emerging from nuclear catastrophe and geological calamity. The proof of the ancient discs slowly changing the mind of the world—witnessing the doubt and then hatred in the eyes of the Elders had been the crowning achievement. Then speaking the words of Luke 19.27, which he had thought would change the world for ever.

"But those mine enemies, which would not that I should reign over them, bring hither, and slay them before me." Your credo, Appointed. It's all about power, isn't it? That's all it's ever about. Throwing the weeping, pleading man to the floor as he spoke the words into the FloatCams...and then discarding his own weapon.

We're free. All of you, you've now seen the proof with your own eyes. I won't reign, neither will I kill. Now it's time for you to take control. It is for you to decide.

The world did decide. The years of lies had taken their toll, and were not to be overruled by a five minute replay of some ancient video footage. The world wanted to believe the easier truth.

He had wept then. Knew the world was truly damned, that the survivors were no better than the zombies they begged the Army of Light protection from. He knew then who the real Empty Ones were.

And yet...here was Wilson, who had enabled access to the Chapter House. How had he slipped through the round-up of the heretic's followers? *Perhaps...perhaps there's hope after all.*

But why was he just standing there, unwilling to meet his former leader's eyes? He had nothing to lose now, just had to turn the rifle on the slack pair playing dice and that sergeant...

Bloody hell, Wilson. You're taking your time. Why?

His vision grew faint. Already impaired by the dried blood from his thorn-prickled forehead, the narrow gap afforded by his gummed eyelids became cloudy, less distinct. Each inhalation was fresh agony, each exhalation a new torture. The air seemed thicker, heavy and oppressive; like the build-up before a thunderstorm. He stared into the distance, into the approaching cloud of blackness that swallowed up what passed for the landscape here.

Land and sky became indivisible, save for the occasional flare of scarlet from the Rupture.

Another wound in the Earth, another portal to Hell. But there would be no more Empty Ones. The Cleansing Fire of the Army of Light had destroyed them all.

And now they'll create them anew. A zombie of man's own creation, in his own likeness. God Almighty, they really don't know what they're doing. But I can't ask forgiveness for them. I hate them. I want them dead, all dead.

His head slumped. The pressure in his chest increased, but the pain in his arms no longer forced him to raise his head. He felt cold.

Is this right? To do with hatred in my heart and a desire for revenge, rather than forgiveness? Or is that the virus beginning to work, the essence of the Empty Ones?

It was always rage that fuelled the resurrected dead. He could feel it now, as the blood ran cold and slow in his veins and his flesh began to mortify. He felt the stirrings of a new pain now. He saw two soldiers approaching. One had fixed a bayonet to his AR-15.

The spear, he thought. *Wondered how they were going to do that.*

Any desire Private Wilson had had to return to the sanctuary of the mess hut vanished when his superior officer removed his helmet. Sergeant Banks sealed the tent flaps, and Wilson noted his gloved hands shook as he pulled the zipper.

Banks's face was paler than usual, sickly white with bloodshot eyes blinking from within black pits, but there was no weakness in the calm, appraising gaze. Wilson followed his superior's lead and removed his own goggles and helmet. He tossed them onto his camp bed, frowning at the ash that fell away like soot.

Banks stepped forward and placed his hands on Wilson's shoulders. The private recoiled; those hands were soaked with sweat and the fingers trembled as the nails dug into the bony hollows of Wilson's sternum.

"Private," Banks said in as low a voice as he could manage. "Spill it." His accent was strange to Wilson's ear. It spoke of a land across the ocean, on the western seaboard of what used to be known as America. The tan had faded, was nothing like his fellow countryman's orange hue. It had often been asked of Banks how The Appointed had maintained such a healthy glow, when no-one else from what was once California had seen decent sunshine since Armageddon darkened its skies.

But Banks' voice was different to The Appointed's. The sergeant's voice was firm, commanding; crude at times, but the no-nonsense tone didn't hide a fondness and respect for his men. The Appointed, however … if the heretic hadn't shown him the recorded disks of their leader's former career, a loud-mouthed evangelist beseeching the audience to send something called "dollars" to a numbered account, Wilson would never have believed it. But it fitted. Greasy, over-confident. Too smooth.

Insincere. Even with that telemessage following the assault on the Chapter House, the denial of the filmed footage the heretic had shown the world and the replacement images … all delivered too smoothly. Too slick.

But that's what the masses want, he reminded himself.

"The guy on the cross – he knows you. You got something to say to me, soldier?"

Wilson took a deep breath, but didn't answer.

Banks glanced over his shoulder as the tent flaps ruffled. It was a breeze, nothing more. Yet the sound of boots crunching on gravel kept the private tense until they passed by.

"They ain't snooping. Just bored. You better be grateful they didn't see the look you two shared."

Endless minutes passed. The canvas flapped and fluttered on the poles, the wind murmured a lifeless lament and the lights swayed on their mountings. Shadows lengthened and advanced.

"I don't know what you're talking about, sarge." *Shit. Said that too quickly.*

Banks smiled. "You come from the northern territories, right? Dear ol' Blighty?"

Wilson's eyes narrowed. "It used to be called England, yes. Before The Appointed renamed it New Jerusalem—"

"Exactly. Jolly old England. Same place the heretic came from. He had military training, came from the same battalion you did. So, what's the story, mister?"

"You've lost me, sarge." Wilson failed to keep the quaver in his throat. Sweat began to bead on his forehead. He felt it trickle down his back.

"Goddamn it. That's twice. Your first name Peter?"

"Sarge?"

"Make it three. Go on, Wilson. No cocks to crow round here, but everything else is as it should be."

Shit. "When did you realise?" Now it was Wilson's turn to eye the sealed flaps of the mess tent. They looked decidedly flimsy.

"After you drove the foot nail in. You had to take your goggles off to clean the blood away—he almost stopped screaming then. I saw the look that passed between you.

"So tell me. How'd you escape the identification? The rest of his army were thrown into the Rupture after being broken on the wheel. Why weren't you amongst them?"

"They...the Elders don't know."

"Bullshit, soldier! The Elders know. They always know. They must've seen that look, but they didn't say anything. Here's something else for you to think about. Why d'you think you were sequestered to Execution Detail?"

Wilson shrugged, making an effort to appear nonchalant. "The Empty Ones are all gone. I believe The Appointed granted me this honour as reward for my servitude to the One Faith, and—"

"Cut the shit, Wilson. The Appointed isn't here. Don'tcha think he'd be here in attendance for such an event?" Banks raised his arm and wiped dried blood and ash from his chronograph. "The heretic was injected with the essence of the Empty Ones at 15.00 hours, Friday. *Three days ago.*" He indicated the radio transmitter "Soon as the third day came they stopped asking for hourly status reports. Fact is, they ain't dialled through at all on my watches. Only when Simms is on watch. So why d'you reckon that is?"

Over two days on the cross. With the desert heat, shock and blood loss from the scourging, dehydration and muscle cramps—there's no way he should still be alive. Unless...

"You got a brain, mister. You try to hide it, just like the rest of us."

Rest of us?

"He ain't the last heretic. Neither are you." Banks growled. "Pearson—hell, he's a damn sight more convincing as loyal follower of the Faith than you, but even he's been compromised. The Elders know. That's why we're all here."

"And why The Appointed isn't," Wilson muttered. "So, what're they going to do to us? Why did they let us carry on believing we were undiscovered?"

"I don't know, Wilson." Banks turned and spat on the R/T. The hot metal hissed in reply.

They let us nail up our leader, but didn't stay to watch him die. Instead, they seemed in rather a hurry to get off...they left Simms, though. Kept in comms with him, but not us. Shit, that explains it.

"We're the last," he said suddenly. "His last followers. We're here to bear witness."

"Say what?"

"To bear witness to his death and rebirth. Three days on the cross and he's still alive. Don't you see? Good God, even he didn't realise his own destiny! He is the Second Coming. *We've crucified our new Messiah!*"

And we're here to bear witness to his death and...rebirth. But reborn as what?

"Goddamn it. There's still time to stop it. If we—" Banks's words were swallowed by the desert wind that snapped open the flaps of the tent.

Banks brought his rifle up. Wilson reached for his own rifle rather than his goggles and regretted his choice.

The wind was hotter than before, and the ash it carried burned his skin. A sirocco that carried screams of the damned, a blast from Hell.

Then the screams became cries of pleading. A man's voice, one that had been so mocking as its owner watched the outspoken blasphemer die on the Breaking Wheel, now became childlike and pleading. The roars of an Empty One swallowed the screams, denied the pleas.

No, Wilson thought as he released the safety on his rifle, knowing bullets would do no good. *This can't be. He's nailed to the cross, how can he—*

Splintering of wood, cracking of bone. Thudding of bullets

striking dead flesh and solid pine, with shouts of denial from Pearson.

The desert wind softened momentarily, just enough for Wilson to hear the words, "you can't be ... can't be. The Appointed is the Antichrist, not you. You are... *you were our only hope. In the name of God, WHAT ARE YOU NOW?*"

Pearson's cries ended in a wet choking, gurgling sound and then faded into the fury of the desert wind. Wilson sighed, remembering all too well the voice of the people when sentence was passed against the last heretic. *No one will rise against The Appointed after this, no one.*

"No," he whispered. "They won't Not *against*, anyway…"

There would be no Millennium. Golgotha had claimed two Messiahs, but this time the Temple wouldn't be struck in two. The Tribulation would be eternal.

Wilson discarded his goggles and braced himself. He would rather be blinded by the desert ash than see what his former leader had become. He nodded curtly towards Banks, allowed him to exit the tent first. It was only right; he was the squad leader after all.

He waited for Banks's rifle magazine to empty and his screams to fade, then he pulled the tent flaps apart and stepped forth to bear witness.

MIDNIGHT TWILIGHT

Jan Edwards

Land of the Midnight Sun? Not quite how Ellie would have put it. Even though that sultry, red-gold light source hanging heavy on the horizon really was the sun and it really was midnight.

Her editor had said "If your eyesight's good enough you can read a book outdoors at one in the morning." Intriguing, maybe, but Ellie couldn't help feeling it wasn't much of a pitch. She could do that back home if the moon was full enough. She had envisaged more than this tinted gloom.

Ellie could have coped with the light levels for the single month she'd be here to research the researchers. It was the dammed sled dogs waking her just after twelve each "night" that exhausted her. Tonight she had managed just two hours before the howling had begun.

She pulled the quilt past her nose and revelled in the sudden heat of her trapped breath.

"You want to go tramping around in the ice?" her boss had told her. "We're into silly season and we've got another Global Emissions summit coming up. I want a 'climate research stations paid for by oil conglomerates' expose. Or anything else you can dig up. That's your brief. You want to do this Sasquatch thing while you are at it? Fine. But make your expense account pay for once."

After begging for an assignment that was more challenging, this was starting to feel more punishment than prize. Except that her Modern Myths of the World by-line couldn't afford to pass up this new spate of whispered reports once they were out there in the conspiracy universe. The "Sasquatch of the Arctic" rumour needed looking into if only because no one else had yet done so. She had wondered why that had been. Now she knew. "Because nobody else was this stupid," she muttered, breathing out heavily to raise the temperature another nano-degree. The howling rose a notch. Ellie waited for any signs that the "residents" were going to go and check it out. Nothing stirred, which was weird. That Apsel guy was usually so manic over his precious dogs.

"Fuck it." She twitched back the quilts and slid from the bunk's clinging warmth to peer through the window. Nothing out of place, but as she could see little beyond the cabin opposite that proved nothing. She looked at her watch. Almost 1.00 a.m. Ellie hauled on her parka, boots and gloves, remembering to grab the every–present rifle from its hooks by the main door, and went outside. The tethered dog team was the best indicator of any intrusion, and the animals were not bothered by anything within the camp perimeter. Their attention was riveted on the tundra and, as always, no ordering from Ellie would quieten them. She walked past the dogs to the edge of the camp, watching the horizon with its deeply tinted dawn-dusk light.

"It's downright bloody unnerving, is what it is," she called back to them, the only ears to hear her. Several members of the pack looked in her direction without missing either howl or yip. "Six stocky, stiff-legged, Spitzen sled-dogs," she said, "salivating savagely at the sun." She wandered back to make soothing noises at them, though being careful to keep out of their reach.

The Research Head, Dr Hiegel, had been very clear on that. "These are not pets, my dear," he'd assured her when she arrived. "They're one step away from the wolf, and every team is a pack. If Apsel is not here don't touch them. In fact, don't touch them if he is here. The man's almost as savage as his beasts."

It didn't inspire confidence. And was a gross exaggeration as it turned out because the dogs were not unfriendly toward her, merely indifferent. Not the ravening hell hounds that Hiegel had inferred.

Apsel was a different matter.

"What in hell these people want you lot here for is beyond me," she said to the nearest dog. It stopped barking long enough to snarl, making Ellie take a rapid step back. "I've read the figures. More sled dogs in Finnmark than humans. Except these guys here have skidoos. They've got radios and mobile phones and internet. They could call for a rescue team anytime. Plus it's heading toward high summer. What in hell do they need you guys for?"

The shaggy, grey-coated Spitz glanced toward her, tail wafting, before pointing its snout towards the ice flow. The snarl gave way to a quiet whine.

"What is it, girl? Bears?" Ellie said, and snorted back a quick laugh. "This place is getting to me. I'm starting to sound like a Lassie repeat." The dog looked back at her, licking nervously at its lips. The gesture was out of character for such a stoic matriarch which, Apsel had assured Ellie, was the best lead dog he'd ever had. As befitted its role, the dog's ice-blue eyes showed only disdain for the camp and everyone in it.

Ellie peered across the open expanse and sighed. "We've got to stop meeting this way. People will talk."

The dog whined, paddled its front feet, and uttered a few short yips.

"What's that, girl? You say a little girl fell down a mine shaft? Or just more bears?" She wrapped her arms around herself, fighting against a sudden shudder. "Bears. God, I hope not." She remembered last week's bear visit all too vividly. When the storeroom door was ripped up and scattered across the ice, before Apsel could send the beast on its way with a volley of rifle fire.

Away in the half-light she could swear something moved; way, way off where the hills opened into an icy plateau. Without field glasses she couldn't be certain. It was unsettling, because the only things of that size out there were polar bears. And those she could do without. Whatever it was had seemingly moved on because the dogs were returning to their rest; quiet now but for the odd snarl as the lead dog claimed priority.

The almost-silence that followed was as unnerving as the almost-dark, with just the tink and crack of distant ice, and the occasion whirring of wind between the cabins.

Once, she thought, the ice wouldn't have melted this far north. Once, this tiny valley, risen way about sea level, would never have bared its rocky face to the sky, but would remain secreted within its permanent, blue-white ice shell.

"But that's why I'm here,' she said. "The Big Meltdown. Anything else is gravy."

She let herself back into the cabin, racked the gun, and entered the galley in search of coffee; lighting the propane stove and settling the kettle as quietly as she could.

"Maybe coffee's not the best thing for the sleepless." Apsel leaned against the doorjamb, tousled and bleary, his quilt wrapped around him in place of his parka.

"And yet here we are," Ellie replied. She smiled at him, over-cheery perhaps, but he was a hard man to nail for an interview. This might be her only chance. All of the research team had been more than happy to talk, mostly to debunk everything she asked them, and she expected no less. These were scientists—measurers of rocks and winds and ice temperatures—and scientists who were reluctant to make a public statement on their funding—let alone anything Fortean—whatever their private thoughts. Apsel's reluctance was totally different, and Ellie could not work out if it was personal or just antipathy toward strangers in general. She pulled another mug toward the kettle. "Want some?"

He nodded. "You fixing to go out again, miss?"

"Something disturbed the dogs. I went out to see."

"They do that sometimes, this time of year. They don't like when they can't see the moonlight." He frowned, scratching at his bird's-nest beard.

Ellie smiled at his fractured English. It was something she found hard to get used to. "Don't they get used to the twilight?" she said.

He shrugged, not quite meeting her eye. She wasn't buying it. "They saw something out there. I know they did." She poured water on the dried coffee grains, slowly to give herself thinking space. "And I saw something out there. It was moving north. A sled, I think." She watched his face carefully for the merest hint of expression in those weather-worn features, but there was nothing. "You do know why I'm here?" she said. 'There've been rumours.'

He nodded. Sharp yet reluctant. There it was. The chink in Apsel's defence.

"So what do you think? Is there something in it? Do we have an Arctic Sasquatch?"

"Stallo?" he grinned, his flat features suddenly animated. "You want a story for the young ones? You tell them about them Stallo. Big things. Fierce."

"Stallo are some kind of Troll, right?" She shook her head. "I'm not talking old folk tales. I'm talking of genuine sightings going back over the past fifty years or more."

"You think maybe those tales only come from the old days? Like we don't get new ones?"

"Good point," Ellie said. "So what do you think about these sightings? Have you seen anything? You're out here more than most."

Apsel's smile snapped off, his face shifting back to the inscrutable blank that seemed to be his default setting. "I think maybe bears," he said finally. "We got bears. Plenty of bears, you know? Like last week." He waved in the general direction of the storage shack across the camp. "Don't go outside without that gun, lady. Or better, don't go out on your own at all in the dark."

"That gives me plenty of time. The sun's always up." She pushed a mug of black coffee across the table and watched him spoon in mounds of whitener and sugar.

"Lady, just about anything up here is a hunter. And hunters, they know a straggler when they see one. Stragglers are weak. They're the prey. Just saying. My job's keeping you people safe.

Cold in here," he added. "Going to get some sleep now." He picked up the mug and headed for his bunk without another word.

Ellie slapped her fingers against the edge of the counter. She knew she'd handled that badly, half asleep and too eager for answers. Somehow she didn't think Apsel was ever going to give up the things he knew easily. Instead he patronised her.

"Moron. His sodding dogs keep me awake and it's nothing to do with him? I'll leave them for the bloody bears next time." She shovelled sugar into her coffee and stirred until it slopped. She hadn't been a journo this long without getting to spot a lie. She paused, watching the brown vortex swirl a few tiny bubbles around the epicentre. "Well, maybe I'll get that story after all."

The next night, at 12.30 sharp when the Spitzen began their yammering, Ellie was prepared. Fully dressed, she only had to put on her boots and collect the gun before she slipped out into the crepuscular night.

The dogs barely acknowledged her as she emerged. She knew it was no use trying to shush them. A stranger such as herself, once deemed harmless, was ignored.

Ellie crossed the cleared paths to the edge of the camp and scanned the snow covered slopes and dips, adjusting her binoculars time and again, but she saw nothing. Maybe Apsel had it. Those stupid mutts could just be barking at the sun.

A noise from the cabin made her glance back, expecting one of the team to come after her. No-one emerged, though the dogs' noise was cut short.

Looking back to the horizon she spotted that same fleeting shadow from the previous night. Through her glasses it took form.

"Not a bear," she said. "Not unless they've mastered sledding without the world's notice. Okay, so what is some guy doing driving a sled across the wastes this far out? There's nothing out there but the cold." She watched until the sled vanished into the shadows of distance before she retreated to the cabin for the inevitable coffee.

For two more nights she was woken in that same hour between twelve and one by the dogs; and each night she saw the same sled, moving along the same trail.

When she asked who else had seen it the scientific team were, in turn, amused, exasperated, and as downright patronising as the taciturn Apsel. Ellie wasn't surprised. If she'd heard someone claiming to see the same sledder heading across the tundra at the same time every night, she would probably have laughed with them. She might have toyed with the idea of a story, but she'd have laughed. MYSTERY SLEDDER ON MIDNIGHT TUNDRA. It was a real Sunday Sport headline.

Apsel gave her one of "those" looks and left the room before she could get around to him.

"Which makes me wonder one thing," she told Hiegel, "if it's the same guy every night how come he's always going in the same direction? He has to come back, unless he's got some weird kind of arctic circuit training thing going?"

Hiegel had laughed her off and demanded she kept to her brief.

"We deal in facts Miss Levin. If you wanted fairy tales there are any number of Father Christmas camps in the region. Perhaps it's Santa out on a practice run?"

Taking his lead, she was met with that same derision from the rest of his team. She was used to that. An interest in unknown phenomenon came with that baggage. She tried a few more runs at Apsel and was systematically blanked every time. That just clinched it. There was something here, and she could not—would not—ignore it.

At just past midnight she was waiting, kitted up in all weather gear and short-skis. Right on cue the dogs began to twitch and moan, padding back and forth, licking nervously at each others' muzzles and sending anxious glances towards the horizon. It was only a minute or two before they began to point noses to the sky and howl. She pushed off in the general direction of the sled's path.

It took her a few minutes to get into stride. Langrenn - cross-country skiing - was not a sport she knew well, but it wasn't so hard once she got the rhythm. Distances, she knew, were deceptive in deserts, whether they were made of sand or ice; and she had travelled for a quarter of an hour, legs and arms pumping in unison whilst keeping her breathing slow and even, before she stopped to ensure her target was on the same trail as on previous nights.

He was. He seemed to be so sure of himself, skirting the edges of the vanishing ice, urging his team occasionally to "Gee" and "Haw", but mostly to "Hike! Hike!" in a bellowing roar. These words she picked out across the expanse because she knew them. Now and then other words that she could not catch drifted in. Names, maybe?

Another few minutes and she stopped; glancing back to make sure the base station was still in sight. Getting lost out here was not an option.

Her target sledder was close enough to see each dog clearly. She could pick out their colours and sizes, and hear the steady scrape of the sled's runners knocking across cracks and ridges in the ice crust.

The sled had not slowed, nor changed course, other than to make a few detours around rocky outcrops in the ice. As he came nearer she could see that his face was all but obscured by a fur hood, protection against the cold winds that came with the sled's speed. It could explain why he had apparently not spotted her yet.

She altered course to put herself directly in his path, but as the sled came nearer Ellie began to seriously doubt the sanity of what she was doing. There was no reason to expect him to be hostile, yet she found herself swinging the rifle from her back to rest against her hip, ready and waiting. Being in sight of the camp was all very sensible, but line of sight out here was measured in kilometres. If she got into trouble this far out there was no help. Even if someone back at camp saw her they would not be able to do much.

The sled was pulled not by the usual six or eight dogs but twelve, and as they saw her their noise became deafening. No wonder Apsel's crew were getting so nervous, she thought. She fiddled with the webbing gun strap, and began to measure the distance back. Too late now to change her mind.

Roaring expletives at the dogs in a mixture of Sámi, German and English, he veered slightly to his left, coming between her and the camp; cutting off her escape as he slewed to a halt. He leaned forward from the back of the sled and cracked his whip above the howling canine chaos, separating skirmishes and restoring calm.

Ellie wondered again what in hell she was doing out here, and whether she could get past him without that whip coming in her direction.

He was a big man, towering above the laden sled. She estimated his height at close on two and half metres, far larger than even the local Nordics. He was swathed in traditional Sámi garb rather than contemporary Arctic gear. He turned his attention towards her. There was little of his face to be seen between the furred hood and high collar of his reindeer-hide parka, but she had the impression he was not a young man. Ellie stifled her impulse to whimper like a whipped puppy.

In silence he stepped from the footboard and crunched the gang line's brake hook into the ice, an automatic sequence that spoke of long years behind the runners. He wound the reins across the handlebar, and stomped across the half dozen paces separating him from Ellie, halting just beyond arms reach.

With his whip still clutched in one huge, mitten-cased paw, he pushed his hood back and stared down at her. Ellie realised now he was not just a big man; he was huge. A neck-creaking hugeness that forced her to look upwards into cold eyes of slate grey, their whites now coloured a dull, vein-threaded yellow, the skin around them creased and wind-burnt. He pawed at his face mask, pulling it down just far enough to reveal a wide mouth with thin dark lips and startlingly white teeth. Amongst those leathery creases, which covered his whole face, she could not avoid noticing a series of faded white scars. They ran around his jaw line and neck and across his brows.

He wasn't angry as she had expected, or even faintly hostile. Not a fleck of aggression in him—provided she ignored that whip.

"Hi." She wondered what language he spoke by habit. Her Norwegian was miniscule and her Sámi non-existent. And that wasn't even considering the other possibilities up here like

German or Russian or—heaven forbid—the throat-grinding Finnish tongue. She was sure he had used English commands to his dogs; she could only hope the rest of his English was good.

Sometimes hopes exceed expectations. "Good evening, Miss," he said. His voice was deep as she had anticipated, but equally soft, which she definitely hadn't. Cultured "Richard Burton" vowels, with the slightest edge; some tiny hint of accent that was out of place here. His English was cultured, yes, but not his native tongue. "You come from there?" He waved the whip's haft at the camp and she could only nod by way of reply. "Hmmmm." The sound he made was not so much a word as a deep rumble of acceptance. His nod was slow, almost a bow. "You should not be out here alone, Miss. There are bears—and other things."

Ellie had the impression of amusement in those eyes, though the voice remained politely passive. "I was told that. I couldn't sleep, though. Then I heard the dogs. And I saw you out here -" She halted, aware she was babbling. Something she never did; cool was her default setting. It was her infallible ability to charm that had got her this far in the trade.

She exhaled, glancing at her ski tips before she raised her gaze back to his face and held out her hand. "My name is Ellie Levin. You may have read some of my articles?"

That face was blank, and no name was offered in return, which didn't match up. That voice spoke of manners and elegance. And in Ellie's experience any man with a voice like that would keep to the social niceties.

"Elizabeth," she said, "Elizabeth Le—"

"No!"

She flinched from his bark, and flinched again as the dogs released a fresh chorus of yips. The sledder stumbled a few paces away and stood motionless for a moment with his back toward her and his head bowed. As if sensing their driver's mood the dogs began to yammer, heads thrown back in sharp, mist-wreathed jerks with each sound.

Ellie grasped the rifle, swinging it to the ready, and wondered for a split moment if her best option wouldn't be to just run.

It was several long seconds before the sledder straightened and turned to face her, rapping out a sharp command to the dogs to hush. The silence that followed was broken by a few tiny whimpers. The sledder advanced the few steps he had given way and she renewed her grip on the gunstock, the barrel snouting toward him unsteadily.

He glanced at it, then reached out to gently turn it away. "Forgive me," he murmured. "You took me by surprise. I had no intention of causing you anguish. I speak so seldom with anyone now. If indeed I ever did speak often."

She lowered the weapon, embarrassed at her actions. "Apology accepted. I wanted to talk with you, if that's all right?" She tucked the rifle under her right arm and reached into her pocket for her tiny cam-recorder, holding it up and flicking it to record. "Do you mind?"

"What does it do?"

"It makes sure that I have what you say exactly right. Nothing to worry about." She took his lack of reply as an acceptance. It was already running in any case. "Just speak clearly and naturally..." I am here in the Arctic researching world myths," she said into the recorder, smiling at him. "Following up on recent rumours of the Arctic Sasquatch, or Yeti. And quite by chance I have come across a wanderer of the inland wastes of Finnmark. Land of ice and the midnight sun. Can I ask you, sir, have you ever seen things up here that cannot be explained?"

He didn't answer for a moment, regarding her with sad resignation. "Sasquatch? I have heard nothing of that thing. What is it?"

"Never heard of a Yeti either?"

He shook his head. "You must forgive my ignorance. I have not been in contact with the civilised world for some time."

"You must have heard of the Yeti at least? It's basic Cryptozoology," she said. "Creatures of mystery? Monsters to some."

His dark lips jerked into what was obviously an unfamiliar upward posture, the merest shadow of a smile. "I have heard of many monsters. I have seen but two."

"You've seen the monster?" She struggled to maintain her calm, aware this was probably her only chance at this one. "Tell me more…please."

He sighed and walked back to his sled, retrieving his ice brake with a practised flick of his wrist. "You seek monsters? Look around you. The world exists for them."

"But you said you had seen two, right here. Can you give me details?"

The sledder laughed sharply and unhitched his reins. "One died, and I vowed once to burn the other. Hey up, team! Hike! Hike!" He flicked the leather strapping and his lead dog renewed her howling command to her underlings. The team lurched eagerly into their harness.

Ellie jumped back. Already the sled was slipping past.

"Be safe, Elizabeth," he shouted at her "There are more kinds of monsters than you can ever capture on a page." His hand snaked out and whipped the recorder from her.

She had a brief notion of its movement as it arced into the air and then crashed ice ward.

And then he was gone. Vanished, somewhere in the red-gold haze.

She waited, listening for any hint of the singing of dogs or the deep booming of that dark voice. She should have caught some echo. The smallest sounds travelled far beyond normal ranges out here. But there was nothing to be heard except the wind and the creaking thaw; and, eventually, her own shuddering body as immobility permitted cold breezes to penetrate the fabrics of her parka and all that lay beneath to her very heart.

Ellie skittered toward the recorder's last visible point, raggedly, stiff from the chill, but revitalising as her blood ran faster with her physical efforts. A couple of sweeps didn't come up with that precious machine and its unique recording. What had transpired between her and him was lost to all but the two of them. Nothing left to do but head back to the camp, her return slower than her exit.

Apsel's dogs didn't bark at her return. Which was puzzling until she noticed Apsel lurking in the lee of the stores shack, rifle cradled across the crook of his left arm.

"Told you not to go out alone," he said, turning toward their cabin. "One day you're going to get dead, lady."

"Probably." She unlatched her skis and followed him inside, homing in on the coffee.

As she heated water and retrieved mugs she sensed Apsel watching her, waiting for her. Vapour drifting from the kettle spout matched her own head of steam. "What?" she snapped. "You got something else to say?"

"Stallo," he said. "That's what you saw. That was Stallo."

"You were watching me? You stood back here and watched?"

He shrugged. "You're no child. You go out chasing shadows? Your business."

"But you saw." She handed him a mug, coming close up to smile into his face in an attempt to appeal to the man in him. "You can verify the sighting. This would be huge, Apsel. Make you famous."

"The Big One don't want to know so much. We respect that. While he travels we are good. Safe. They say when the Big One finds his place, when he finds his peace and he burns…the world will end."

"Who says? I've never heard this legend."

"Not a legend," Apsel replied. "When I was small, my grandma would talk of this. She remembers her mother telling her 'bout when the Big One came a long time ago. He came looking for his maker. She says when the Big One finds him, he'll go to the end of the world to burn. Until then the Big One comes and he goes, and always he travels north. That is the story my grandma told me. We leave him alone. He needs nothing from us. It's what I always said. The Stallo is a Troll." He turned to walk away. "You know what that means?" he said from the doorway. "This Troll?"

"It's a mythical being that…"

"Stallo is Troll…" he vanished from view, only his voice left for a parting shot. "But Troll in your words is The Monster."

DED END JOBZ

Stuart Hughes

"You need to sort your garden out."

George glanced through the kitchen window at his overgrown and out of control back garden.

"For starters, you need to get that great big hole where the pond used to be filled in."

He looked back at his daughter. He loved her unconditionally, but at times like this Cheryl sounded just like her mother Elaine. Exasperatingly so.

"And I'm surprised you haven't got lions and tigers roaming around that jungle you call a lawn."

"Oh, we have." George smiled.

"It must be up to your knees," Cheryl said. She wore her stern face. Her mother's stern face.

"Your knees, my waist. It's all relative."

"Seriously, Dad. It needs sorting." Stern face, but George could tell she was trying hard not to laugh.

"I know." Every time he saw his daughter these days—and it wasn't often enough, nowhere near often enough—it reminded him how old he was getting. Cheryl was in her mid-thirties and he no longer towered over her. Now Cheryl was a good two inches taller than him. "I'm shrinking, you know."

"Dad …" Her face broke out into a smile and then Cheryl laughed. She always came alive when she laughed. His daughter looked just like her mother but, when she laughed, she was all Cheryl. Her green eyes sparkled, her lips parted showing the perfect teeth of a retired dentist's daughter, her bouncy brown hair floated in the air as her head moved from side to side. He loved his daughter most of all when she was laughing.

He laughed too.

"Give your daughter a hug."

George spread his arms and wrapped them around Cheryl. She held him tight for a moment—a long, delightful moment—and then pulled away. She kissed him lightly on the cheek.

"Cup of tea?" George asked.

"That'd be nice."

He filled the kettle and switched it on. He turned back to his daughter, who was staring out at the garden.

"I'll get around to it, you know."

Cheryl smiled. George knew he was biased but he had a beautiful daughter. When she smiled, Cheryl became the most beautiful woman in the world.

"Why don't you get someone in?"

He shook his head. His pension wasn't keeping up with inflation or the cost of living these days, and things were tighter financially than they used to be.

"If it's a case of money…"

"No," he said, shaking his head, amazed at how in tune Cheryl always seemed to be with him.

"Rachel and I can pay for it if you like."

"It's not that." A small lie, but he wouldn't take charity from his own daughter. He was too proud to take money off Cheryl and her…partner. "Not that at all."

"Rachel won't mind, if that's what you're worried about."

George shook his head again, firmly this time. He still felt guilty about the way he had reacted when Cheryl first told him she was gay. But he'd soon come around to the idea, particularly after he'd met Rachel and saw how happy she made Cheryl. His daughter had gone out with a number of men, but none of them had made her happy, and some of them had made her downright miserable. No doubt about it, Rachel made Cheryl far happier than any man ever had.

"No, I'll get to it," he said. "I would've done it by now if I wasn't so worried about your mother."

"How is she?"

"Better than she was. Why don't you go through while I make the tea?"

Elaine and Cheryl were deep in conversation when George carried the teas into the living room. Elaine was sitting in his high backed chair, the chair they'd bought because of his bad back, the chair that only really came into its own after his replacement knee was fitted. He didn't mind, though. He loved Elaine and right now his wife's need was greater than his.

Cheryl sat on the far end of the settee, leaning forward, her hands on her knees. Occasionally Cheryl would reach out as she spoke and pat Elaine on the knee.

He sat down in the armchair next to his wife. Her two walking sticks lay on the floor by her feet.

"Mum tells me you nearly cancelled the medical insurance, Dad."

"Yeah, kept seeing the payment on the bank statements and…"

"Good job you didn't," Elaine said.

"I bet you're glad you kept it going now. Mum looks and sounds much better."

"Yeah," George said, thinking about the monthly payments and wondering, not for the first time, how much the premiums would go up now they'd made a claim.? And, more to the point, how much they'd go up again if, as seemed likely, Elaine needed a new hip? "I know. We were getting nowhere under the NHS and your Mum couldn't have gone on like that."

"I was in so much pain…" Elaine said.

"Let me tell it, Elaine. You rest."

"Dad," Cheryl said, protesting at his put-down of her mother. She was probably right but the way his wife would interrupt him when he'd started telling a story irritated him. Not this time.

"I don't think the GP…what was his name?"

"Dr Davies."

"That's it. Dr Davies. I don't think he had a clue what was wrong with your mother and he wouldn't put himself out to find out."

"Probably didn't have any money left in the budget," Cheryl said.

"Maybe," George said. "He kept telling Mum to rest, to take anti-inflammatories, and that it was probably arthritis. As soon as I asked about going private he couldn't do enough for us."

"Mr Cresswell was brilliant, though," Elaine said.

"Yeah, he was," George said. "Mr Cresswell organised an X-ray and some scans and identified the problem with your mother's hip."

"It was a relief just to know what was wrong with me."

"I bet it was," Cheryl said.

"So, to cut a long story short, your mother probably needs a hip replacement."

"I hope not," Elaine said.

"We'll do what Mr Cresswell thinks best, love."

Elaine reached across and picked up her tea, wincing slightly with the effort.

"But he suggested trying an injection first. He said sometimes it works and sometimes it doesn't. Sometimes it takes permanently, and sometimes it doesn't."

"So far so good," Cheryl said.

"Yes. Your mother's in far less pain now and walking about the house with only one stick. Hopefully it's taken permanently."

"I do hope so," Elaine said, putting her cup back in its saucer. "Tea's drinkable."

Cheryl smiled, patted her mother's knee, and picked up her own tea.

George took a sip and tried hard not to pull a face. He'd let it stew too long in the pot and he hated stewed tea. He glanced at Elaine and Cheryl but his wife and daughter didn't appear to have noticed.

"I see you've spent some more of my inheritance."

George looked at his daughter without comprehending what she was talking about. His expression must've given him away.

"The TV," Cheryl said, indicating the new television set with a gesture of her head.

"Oh, yeah. The picture was getting so bad on the old one we could hardly watch it."

"And this one's a good size. Not like the old one, might as well have been a portable."

"This one's too big," Elaine said.

"No it's not. It's only a 42 inch."

"It's too big."

"We needed a bigger one. Our eyesight's not as good as it once was, love."

"I still say it's too big."

Cheryl laughed. Elaine could be pig-headed and embarrassing sometimes . He wished she wouldn't show him up as often as she did, especially not in front of their daughter.

George drank the rest of his stewed tea.

"I've been thinking," Cheryl said. "You should get an alternate in."

"Sorry, thinking about what?" George said.

"The garden. You should get an alternate in?"

"A what?"

"Alternate workers. You must've heard of them."

George shook his head. Elaine's frown suggested she didn't have a clue what their daughter was talking about, either.

"Alternate workers. Rachel's boss at Rolls Royce swears by them. He told Rachel he was sceptical at first but now he'd have them back any day of the week. Said they were efficient, did a great job, and didn't charge much either. Hang on…" Cheryl fished her mobile out of her pocket. "I think I've got the details in here."

George stared at his daughter as she pressed seemingly random buttons on her phone, her fingers darting about in a frenzy.

"Alternate workers?" Elaine said.

He could vaguely remember hearing something about them on the news a month or so ago. Now he thought about it, he remembered thinking how gimmicky it had all sounded. "I thought it wouldn't catch on."

"They're all the rage right now. Here we are." Cheryl looked up from the phone and her face beamed with that special excited look she sometimes got. "Dead End Jobs. I'll write the number down for you."

"Dead End Jobs," he said. "What sort of a name is that?"

Cheryl grabbed a notebook and pen and scribbled something down. She ripped off the bit of paper, got to her feet, and handed it to him.

"Rachel's boss speaks very highly of them."

He took the piece of paper and looked at it. The name Cheryl had scribbled wasn't 'Dead End Jobs' as he'd heard but 'Ded End Jobz.' He hated this new craze for incorrect spellings.

At least the number was a freephone one.

"When did she tell you that?"

"When you were making tea," Elaine said. "I thought she'd told you in the kitchen."

"No," George said. "You should know by now that Cheryl always tells you and leaves you to drop the bombshell."

"At least she gets to see the world, dear." Elaine smiled at him but it looked somewhat forced. "That's more than we ever did."

Cheryl's bombshell was that she was moving overseas again. Singapore this time. Rachel had got a three-year work placement out there. Elaine hadn't understood what but Rachel would be working out of Singapore airport. Cheryl would be giving up her job as a secretary and going out to Singapore to be with Rachel. Rolls Royce would pay for their accommodation and they'd rent out their house in Belper until they got back.

"Did she say when they'd be going?"

"Next week."

"That's quick."

"Are you surprised?"

George shook his head. This would be Rachel's fourth work placement abroad…or was it five? Germany, Denmark, Japan, California…and now Singapore. Five. This would be the fifth time.

"They're going to have a month's holiday in Australia and then go on to Singapore so Rachel can start work. It was stewed, by the way."

"What was?"

"The tea. Maybe I should make it in future?"

"No you won't, love. You need to rest."

Elaine muttered something under her breath. George didn't quite catch what but decided to let it go.

He passed the TV remote to Elaine and got up.

"Where are you going?"

"To call that number Cheryl gave us."

"Can we afford it?"

George shrugged. "No harm in getting a quote, is there?"

George and Elaine were watching daytime TV when the knock came at the front door.

"I'll go," Elaine said, and reached for her walking sticks.

Ded End Jobz

"No," George said with slightly more alarm than he'd realised. "It'll be the guy about the garden."

Elaine needed to rest. Even if she went to answer the door, shuffling slowly, stooped over her two walking sticks, she'd only call him eventually as she wouldn't be able to deal with the garden man.

George slowly got to his feet, automatically stretched out for his own walking stick, then stopped with his fingers a couple of inches away from it. He didn't really need the stick any more. His metal knee gave him little pain these days, but he had lost some feeling and sensation in his right foot and had become accident-prone, frequently catching his foot and nearly tripping himself up. Three times he'd fallen full length, somewhat fortunate not to break anything, but he'd had many more narrow escapes.

The knocking came again. Louder, more insistent.

George grabbed his walking stick.

"Shall I make a cup of tea?" Elaine asked.

"No." George headed towards the kitchen. "I'll do it."

George turned the key in the lock, removed the security chain, and opened the back door to reveal a young man in his early twenties. He wore a red and white checked shirt, denim jeans, and Doc Martin's boots. Greasy, ginger hair poked out from under a Derby County baseball cap. He carried a clipboard and a couple of biros poked out his shirt pocket.

"Are ya Mr Rushton?" the young man asked. He grinned, revealing a mouth full of fillings and caps.

"Yeah. That's me."

"Cool," the young man said. "How ya doin'? I'm Thomas Ward. From Ded End Jobz, ya know. We spoke yesterday."

"That's right, Mr...sorry, what was your name?"

The young man laughed, nervously. "Just call me Tommy, Mr Rushton. Tommy's fine. Fine and dandy." The young man held out his hand.

George switched his walking stick from right to left and grabbed Tommy's hand. They shook. Tommy's grip was firm and strong. "Then you'd better call me George."

"Cool. Wanna show me the job, George?"

"Sure." George stepped outside and switched the stick back to his right hand. He led the way around the corner of the bungalow and Tommy followed. He stopped on the unevenly paved patio outside the kitchen. Weeds poked through the gaps between the slabs.

"I'm afraid I've rather let it go over the last year or so."

"Ayuh," Tommy said, nodding. His eyes took in the overgrown and unkempt garden. "Dunna worry, George. We'll sort it for ya."

"Well, for starters, there's that hole there that needs filling in." George pointed with his stick at the huge crater where their lovely fish pond had once been.

"Ayuh." Tommy nodded.

George went on, pointing at the long grass that needed to be got under control, the weeds that needed pulling out, and the trees that needed their branches cutting back. Each time George pointed with his stick, Tommy would nod and say "Ayuh."

"What about ya fence, George?" Tommy said. "Some treatment wouldna hurt before the bad weather kicks in ya know."

George thought for a moment, staring at the fence. "I guess it is looking a bit worse for wear."

"Ayuh. Anything else?"

He looked over the garden, dismayed by the bad state it had fallen into. He used to be a proud and keen gardener but he wasn't as young as he once was. "No, that's it."

"So that's the hole, the grass, the fence, and the trees."

"Yeah, that's it."

"Cool. We's should only need a day for that and a four worker team should get it done. How's that sound, George?"

"Fine, I guess. How much—"

"Aww, stupid me," Tommy said and slapped the side of his head with the flat of his hand. "You gonna wanna know how much?" Tommy smiled. "One day, four workers. How's a hundred sound to ya?"

George had a long think about that. Normally a hundred quid would be no problem, but with the new TV they'd only just purchased, and the new washing machine for Elaine before that, funds were a little depleted. Mentally he ran through the bills still to be paid that month and deducted them from the balance.

"That's fine," George said. "Is a cheque all right?"

"Of course, though I'll have to charge ya tax for cheque. So that'll be another twenty."

George nodded.

"Cool." Tommy took a pen from his pocket and started writing on the papers on his clipboard. "One last thing for ya. I hate this legal stuff, but under the Health and Safety at Work Act I have to tell ya that we use alternate workers. Is that okay?"

George nodded.

"Ya knows what alternate workers are, George, don't ya? You comfortable with them being on ya property, working on ya property?"

"Sure." George wasn't sure at all. It was all very well for Rachel's boss to swear by them, but the only reason he was agreeing to this was because they were cheap.

"Dunna ya worry yaself," Tommy said. "We only use the dociles and I'll go through it with ya tomorrow."

"Tomorrow?"

"Ayuh, we's can start tomorrow if that's a-okay with ya, George?"

"Sure," George said, a little taken aback by the speed of it all. "The sooner the better."

"Just need ya to sign this." Tommy offered the clipboard to George. He took it, accepted the pen, and started to read. The job was recorded accurately: fill in pond, cut down grass, prune tree branches, treat fence. One day. Four worker team. £100.00 plus £20.00 tax. Payment by cheque on completion of the job. Then there was a lot of small print that he couldn't read without his glasses.

"What's all this?"

"Nothin' to worry yaself about. Just the standard stuff. Our service level agreement, our environmental and recycling policies, our debt recovery procedures, stuff like that. Nothin' a fine upstanding citizen like you need worry about. I just needs ya to sign, George."

George signed and dated the form and handed the clipboard back. Tommy looked down, nodded, tore off the top copy, and handed it to him.

"See ya tomorrow, George." Tommy turned his back and walked briskly away. "Bright and breezy," Tommy said as he turned the corner. "We've loads of satisfied customers, George, ya won't be disappointed."

And then Tommy disappeared round the corner of the house and was gone.

"They're here already."

The noise had woken George the next morning and he'd struggled out of bed to investigate. Struggled because his replacement knee always seized up over night, his back hurt like buggery, and most of his other joints ached and didn't work properly. As he grabbed his walking stick to help him out of bed he noticed the alarm clock read 6:05.

Looking through the curtains he saw a large truck depositing a skip at the bottom of his drive. He saw Tommy in the driver's seat and a couple of other fellers milling about around the skip.

"They're here," George repeated. Elaine didn't stir and he decided to leave her be. She hadn't been sleeping well for months and she needed all the sleep she could get.

Leaning heavily on his walking stick, George made his way towards the bathroom.

By the time George had deactivated the alarm, washed, dressed, and unlocked the back door, Tommy had organised the other fellers and they were hard at work. There were four of them. The alternates, he supposed.

At first glance they looked just like ordinary people to George—one was filling in the hole, another was cutting back the tree branches, a third was strimming the lawn, and the fourth one appeared to be clearing up after the other three—but when he looked more closely George could tell they definitely weren't ordinary people.

The three of them doing the more intensive work didn't look too bad. They all wore red and white checked shirts, denim jeans, and heavy duty boots caked in mud; but their skin was pale and grey and they looked almost sightlessly out from eyes that appeared cloudy with cataracts. Their stiff limbs moved awkwardly as they went about their work.

The one tidying up after the other three was in a bad way, though. He was dressed the same way as the others, but his clothes were torn and hung in rags. Beneath the tattered clothes, he was nothing more than skin and bones. Literally, skin and bones with the skin peeling off his skeleton to reveal the bones underneath. His mouth was full of gaps and the remaining rotten teeth—brown and whittled away to sharp points—were the worst George had ever seen in a dentistry career that spanned over forty years.

"Howdy, George."

George broke away from the alternates and saw Tommy walking towards him with his right hand raised in a wave.

"Bright and breezy I said, George." Tommy grinned. "And bright and breezy here we are."

"You are," George said. "But they don't look so bright and breezy."

"Dunna worry about them, George. They gonna do a good job for you and tomorrow you wunna know they've been here."

George looked from the bright and breezy Tommy to the far from bright and breezy alternates and back again. He wasn't convinced.

"Aw, come on George," Tommy said. "I told ya we used alternates yesterday and ya were fine with it."

"I hadn't seen them then."

"Just one day, George. Not even a full day, really. I'm gonna have them gone and out your hair by half-six. And you dunna have to look at them. Just stay inside ya house and let them work. They gonna do a grand job for ya."

George wasn't sure. He couldn't stand looking at them, but found he was drawn to the alternates by some invisible force. "Are they…?"

"Dead?"

George nodded.

"Yeah, we think so. Although some scientists still think it's some kinda infection. Anyways, whatever it is, they ain't human no more. They ain't like me and you, George."

"So I see."

"You okay, George?"

He continued to stare at the alternates as they went about their work in that awkward, stiff way of theirs. He had to admit they had made considerable progress in the short time he'd been watching.

"Ya want me to call 'em off, George? I can get regular workers in if ya want, but ya's have to wait a month or so and it'll cost three or four times as much."

George shook his head. "They're here now, aren't they?"

"Yeah, they are."

"Okay."

"There's nothin' to worry about, George. These are dociles so they wunna hurt ya but, nevertheless, I'd recommend ya stay inside and keep out of their way. You dunna need to do anything. I'll be back at lunch for feeding time. Just keep out of their way, dunna let them touch ya; definitely dunna let them bite ya."

George nodded.

"Ya got me phone number, ain't ya?"

"Yeah."

"You wunna need to, but call me if ya have any problems."

"Sure."

"Cool." Tommy held out his hand and George shook it. "See ya at lunchtime, George."

"Come away from the window."

"In a minute," George said. "I'm just checking how they're getting on."

"They give me the creeps."

"I know, love. Me, too."

Grudgingly George had to admit that his daughter's recommendation, albeit based on hearsay from Rachel's boss, had been a good one. He'd had his reservations, particularly when he first saw the alternates, but in their slow and cumbersome way they were doing a great job. The big hole that used to be a pond was already half filled in, the grass had been cut back to a manageable level and almost resembled a lawn again, and the tree branches no longer encroached or overhung the neighbours' properties.

The alternates might be slow, he thought, but unlike regular workers they didn't take tea breaks, they didn't take cigarette breaks, they didn't spend time talking to each other, and they didn't down tools every time their mobile phone rang or bleeped with a text message.

Then he saw Tommy walk around the corner of the bungalow carrying a mallet. Behind him shuffled another alternate.

"Now what?" George said, moving purposefully away from the window.

"George?" Elaine said, concern in her voice. She reached for her sticks.

"Don't get up, love." He had crossed the living room and opened the door into the hall.

"What is it?"

Something in her voice made him stop and he looked back over his shoulder at her. She was reaching for her sticks again.

"Tommy's back."

"It'll be lunchtime," she said and George observed her visibly relax as she settled back into the chair.

Tommy being back didn't concern him; after all, he'd said he would be back at lunch. How had he put it? Oh yes, for feeding time. He was surprised by the presence of the fifth alternate, though.

He'd better not charge us for an extra alternate, George thought. It's their fault, not mine, if they're behind schedule.

He closed the door behind him, leaving Elaine watching TV, and headed into the kitchen. He was halfway across the tiled kitchen floor, the question he was going to ask Tommy already forming in his head, when a loud, shrill whistle brought him to an abrupt stop.

Through the kitchen window he saw that Tommy held a whistle to his lips. The fifth alternate—a female, George noticed—shuffled up to Tommy and stood by his side.

The whistle sounded again, louder and even more shrill, and the other alternates stopped what they were doing and began shuffling towards Tommy.

As if summoned by the whistle, George also shuffled across the kitchen, opened the back door, and made his way towards Tommy. By the time he'd turned the corner of the bungalow, the alternates were standing in a loose approximation of a half circle facing Tommy. None of them moved.

"Tommy!" George called out.

Tommy turned his head and spotted George.

"Stop!" Tommy called out. "Stop right there! Ya wunna want to get too close. Be with ya in a minute."

George took another step.

"George, stay there!"

There was a tone to Tommy's voice that George hadn't heard before, an edginess that brought him to a stop. He leant on his walking stick and watched.

The alternates were shuffling even closer to Tommy. Tommy quickly raised the whistle to his lips and blew. Outside the bungalow, the shrill sound pierced George's ears and he winced. The alternates instantly halted in their shuffling tracks.

Tommy grabbed the torn collar of the raggedy alternate who had been clearing up after the others and pulled it forward. Releasing its collar, Tommy stepped back, raised the mallet, and swung it into the alternate's skull. George heard a loud, crunching sound and the alternate fell to the ground. Tommy skipped back two or three steps as the other alternates shuffled forward, crouching down as they did so, and threw themselves on top their co-worker. Suddenly the slow, shambling alternates were a blur of motion as they tore flesh from bone and ravenously fed.

Disturbed and disgusted by what he was observing, George was unable to tear his gaze away from the feeding frenzy taking place in his own back garden.

Then his view was blocked as Tommy stepped in front of him. "Sorry ya had to see that, George."

George opened his mouth to speak but no words came out. He didn't know what to say or where to start.

"I said I'd be back at lunch to feed them."

"Feeding time," George said quietly. He noticed the blood and other stuff stuck to the head of the mallet.

"Yeah. That's right. Feeding time."

"But…but they ate one of their own."

Tommy laughed. "Yeah, but he wasn't much of a worker anymore. And I brought another alternate to bring the team back up to four. I told you we take our recycling responsibilities seriously."

"Recycling," George repeated, slowly.

Tommy nodded. "It's all covered in the contract I left ya with yesterday."

"It is?"

"Ayuh. I'll just wait here until they've finished feeding and set them to work again. The new alternate will do the fence and the others will carry on with what they were doing before. Okay, George?"

He nodded. He was still disgusted by what he had just seen, and the ripping and slurping noises coming from behind Tommy turned his stomach, but he thought it better to simply let Tommy and his alternate workers complete the job. It would only take five or six more hours and then it would all be over. Between now and then all he had to do was hide inside the bungalow with Elaine and wait for it all to be over.

"Cool," Tommy said. "Now go back inside and I'll get them working for ya again. I'll see ya later…about six thirty. Okay?"

George nodded and headed back to the safety of his own home.

George spent most of the afternoon staring out of the living room window, watching the alternates work. He had to admit that they were doing a fantastic job. The hole was not only completely filled in, but the ground levelled so well that George couldn't tell exactly where the pond had once been. The long grass was not only cut back to manageable levels, but mown into neatly manicured stripes. The trees were cut and pruned immaculately.

Perhaps the best job of all, George thought, was done by the new worker, the female alternate. In half the time her co-workers had spent she had treated the full length of the fence.

George had spent most of the afternoon watching her and, at times, even forgot that she was an alternate. Her movements were nowhere near as awkward and stiff as those of her colleagues and her long, red hair still had a lightness and glow to it. Only when she turned and he caught sight of her grey skin and cloudy eyes did George remember she was an alternate.

That she was dead.

That she was no longer human.

And then the memory of the lunchtime feeding frenzy returned and nausea rushed up on him. Twice, he had to rush to the bathroom and throw up in the sink.

Bright and breezy this morning, Tommy returned at 6.30 PM as good as his word. By then the alternates had finished and it took twenty minutes for Tommy to load the skip onto the back of truck and chain the alternates securely inside the truck.

"That's us done then, George," Tommy said.

"Yes. Thank you."

"What d'ya think?"

George smiled. "I have to admit it's a fantastic job. I'm surprised, genuinely surprised, but I'm impressed too."

"Cool. Now if I can just have that cheque, I'll be on my way."

"Of course." George handed over the cheque he had written earlier that afternoon.

Tommy looked at it for a moment.

"Thank ya," Tommy said. "I sure hate saying this to such a fine upstanding citizen as yaself but I has to remind ya that our debt recovery procedures are documented on the contract I gave ya."

George nodded. He hadn't read the small print but was sure it contained the standard legalese.

"Not that ya need worry about that, George."

George extended his hand and Tommy shook it.

"Thank you," George said.

"You're welcome, George."

"Well, what do you think?" George asked later that evening during a commercial break.

"It's great to have our garden back again. Even better not to have to worry about falling into the pond."

George smiled.

"I didn't like those things, though." Elaine gave a pretend shiver and winced slightly. "They gave me the heebie-jeebies."

"I agree." He hadn't discussed what he'd seen during feeding time with Elaine and had no way of telling whether she'd witnessed it as well. He hoped she hadn't, although she must've heard the shrill sound of the whistle. "The alternates were creepy."

"Alternates," Elaine repeated and tutted, making a loud, wet sound with her lips that always irritated George. "How politically correct. Why don't people call them what they really are?"

"Which is?" George asked, although he knew very well what his wife was going to say.

"Zombies," Elaine said, confirming his own thoughts. "They are zombies, pure and simple. But nobody calls them that, do they?"

"No, love."

"Not politically correct enough."

"They did a good job, though."

"Yes, but they still give me the creeps."

They both fell silent as Coronation Street came back on.

"I bet Cheryl will be impressed," George said some ten minutes or so later when the credits started to roll. "We'll have to think of an excuse to invite her round."

"That won't be for some time now."

"Oh?"

"Yes, I forgot to tell you, she rang earlier while you were out with those zombie things –"

"Alternates, love."

"Whatever. Anyway, Cheryl and Rachel fly out to Australia tomorrow."

"Well that's that, then," George said. "Cup of tea, love?"

The letter from the bank arrived a week later. The postman delivered it with a postcard from Cheryl.

On one side of the postcard was a beautiful photo of the Sydney Opera House and on the reverse, opposite their name and address, Cheryl had written: "Dear Mum and Dad, Having a wonderful time in Australia. Missing you loads. Love to you both, Cheryl and Rachel X X X"

That was Cheryl, all right. Concise and to the point. He loved his daughter unconditionally. He just wished he got to see her more often.

Walking into the living room, he casually handed the postcard to Elaine. He sat down in his chair and opened the envelope that contained the letter from the bank.

"Aah, that's nice," Elaine said but George didn't hear her. His mind was pre-occupied with the contents of the letter.

"Bloody hell," George said and got to his feet. "Bloody hell!"

"Well?" Elaine asked as soon as he put down the telephone.

George had been on the telephone for over an hour and felt exhausted. Mentally he ran through each of the conversations he'd had, making sure he understood everything and knew what was going to happen.

"Well?"

He ran through it again, confirming in his own mind that he was done and didn't need to make any more calls. He'd spoken to the bank—well, a few different departments at the bank; he'd talked to the electronics store who'd sold him the TV and given them a piece of his mind; and he'd left messages on the main number for Ded End Jobz and also on Tommy's personal mobile. He would have liked to have spoken to Tommy personally but had done all he could.

"Well?" Elaine asked again. "What did they say?"

"Let me sit down a minute, love, and catch my breath." George sat down in his favourite chair and took a few deep breaths.

"Tell me, George. Was it a mistake?"

"No, unfortunately. Well, it was a mistake, but not the bank's fault. They were right to bounce the cheque, although given that we're such long-standing loyal customers I would've thought they could've honoured it."

"Banks don't care about loyalty, just the bottom line. Who's fault is it, then?"

"The TV place. You know that extended warranty we took out?"

"Yes."

"Did they say it was a monthly premium or an annual premium?"

Elaine thought for a moment. Her eyes rolled towards the ceiling as they always did when she was thinking. George thought about saying I can hear the cogs whirring, but this was neither the time nor the place to roll out that worn old joke one more time.

"Monthly," Elaine said at last. "Wasn't it?"

"That's right. Well guess what?" He didn't allow her time to answer. "They claimed an annual premium, not a monthly premium. So the bank honoured it, apparently that's how direct debits work, 'variable amounts on variable dates' and that left our account short. So when Ded End Jobz paid the cheque in there wasn't enough to cover it and the cheque bounced."

"Unbelievable." Elaine shook her head. "Can nobody get anything right these days?"

"Apparently not."

"It's every time we go to do something it goes wrong." Elaine looked like she was going to cry.

"Don't worry," he said. "It's all sorted, love."

"How? What are they going to do?"

"The TV place will reimburse the annual premium and set up a monthly debit instead. And I've left messages telling Ded End Jobz what happened and told them to re-present the cheque and it'll get paid."

Elaine still looked like she was going to cry.

"There's nothing to worry about, love. It's all sorted."

"I hope so," Elaine said, dabbing at her eyes with a handkerchief. "Should we ring Cheryl?"

"No," George said, shaking his head. "Everything's sorted now. No need to concern Cheryl. We don't want to disturb her holiday, do we?"

Elaine dabbed her eyes again. "I suppose not."

"Good, let's say no more about it." George got to his feet. "Cup of tea, love?"

"What was that?"

George felt a sharp, stabbing pain in his ribs and slowly began to surface from the depths of a dark, deep sleep. Disorientated momentarily, he didn't know where he was, who was talking, or why his ribs were hurting.?

"George?" Another stabbing pain to his ribs. "Did you hear that?"

He opened his eyes and vaguely made out the familiar surroundings of his bedroom. The lights were off but the room wasn't totally dark, which suggested it was early morning. Very early morning.

"George!" And now he was rocking from side to side.

"Whoa," George said. "Whoa there. I'm awake."

The rocking stopped and he rolled over to look at his wife, aching more than usual due to the rough treatment he'd just received.

"What is it?"

Elaine was sitting up in bed, looking down at him, frown and worry lines etched across her face.

"I heard something."

"What?" George said with more irritation in his voice than he'd intended. "What did you hear?"

"I don't know." Elaine looked towards the bedroom door. "Something."

George sighed and rolled over onto his comfortable side, the side that presented his back to his wife. He closed his eyes. "You probably dreamt it."

"No, I didn't."

"Or imagined it."

"No."

George could feel the cold. He grabbed the quilt and tugged it hard, much harder than he would have done if he was playing with her. But he wasn't playing with her, he was annoyed because she'd woken him for nothing in the middle of the night and he was cold.

"Hey!" Elaine said. George smiled and tugged the quilt again, even harder this time.

"I didn't imagine it," Elaine repeated emphatically and jabbed him in the ribs.

He opened his eyes and read the alarm clock display.

"Do you know what time it is?"

"I heard something."

"It's two o'clock in the bloody morning." George pulled the quilt again.

"Stop it. I definitely heard—"

And then George heard something too. He used his arms to lever himself up and looked at Elaine. There was fear in her eyes now.

"Did you hear that?" she said.

"Yes."

He heard it again. Breaking glass. This time, undeniably, the sound of breaking glass.

"George?"

"I heard it, love." He threw the quilt off and rolled himself out of bed, wincing as the pain in his back kicked in. His replacement knee wouldn't work properly and his body ached all over.

More breaking glass.

"What is it?"

"I don't know."

A thud. Another thud. Followed by another thud. Then a metallic clanging sound, like pots and pans falling off the draining board onto the tiled kitchen floor.

"I'm scared, George."

"Me, too." He grabbed his walking stick and inched his way around the bed, using not just the stick, but the bed itself to support his weight. His bad knee painfully protested and he wasn't sure he trusted it. Elaine lifted the quilt on her side of the bed.

"No," George said. "You stay there. I'll go."

And then a screaming siren rang out. Behind him, Elaine mouthed something but he couldn't hear her over the house alarm.

Ignoring the pain in his knee, he took a deep breath and stepped away from the bed. He'd expected his knee to give out, sending him sprawling face down, but it held. It screamed at him in silent pain, but didn't give out. Using the walking stick for support he made his way towards the door. He could hear nothing other than the alarm.

At the door he stopped and looked back at his wife. Elaine was sitting up in bed, her knees raised up to her chin, the quilt pulled up to her eyes.

George opened the bedroom door, stepped into the hall, and saw them shuffling towards him.

Alternates.

Zombies.

It didn't matter what you called them because they were inside his house and shuffling towards him, their arms outstretched, fingers extended, long nails pointing towards him.

For a moment he simply stood there, frozen in time and space, his mouth wide open and gaping at the sight before him. He didn't count them—he was unable to count them—because there were too many of them.

They were half-way down the hall now, approximately four feet away from him, getting closer. They stood three abreast, completely filling the hallway, and behind the first row there was another row, then another row, then another.

He stood frozen—not because he was paralysed with fear like characters in the horror novels he used to read—but because he couldn't decide what to do. Should he step out into the hallway and fight them off? But what with? His walking stick was all he had.

And they kept coming, shuffling closer to him: three feet away now.

Should he attempt to get past them? He was an old man, and didn't rate his chances, but he might be able to force his way through and past them and…and then what?

The alarm reverberated inside his head and he couldn't think, couldn't think straight. What to do? What to do?

Should he retreat back into the bedroom and barricade the door? But with what? There was no time.

The alternates, the zombies, shuffled even closer.

The alarm bounced around inside his head.

Elaine? He had to protect Elaine.

George retreated back into the bedroom, closing the door behind him. No time to barricade it, so he threw himself to the floor and pushed backwards towards the door. When he felt his buttocks contact the door's hard surface he sat up and put all his weight against it.

Elaine hadn't moved. She still sat on the bed with her knees drawn up, only her eyes, forehead, and grey hair showing above the quilt.

That was when the handle rattled and the first blow thumped into the door. He felt the door opening behind him and threw all his weight at it, forcing it back and closing it again.

He thought Elaine screamed but he couldn't hear anything above the wailing siren of the house alarm.

The door thudded again and pushed him forward with more force this time. Again he threw his weight at it and held it back.

"Ring the police!" George shouted. With his right hand he made a phone with his thumb and little finger and held it to his ear. Elaine didn't move. He could see the telephone on the bedside table and waved his hand-phone in her direction.

And then she got it. Elaine slid herself up the bed and grabbed the phone. She began pressing buttons as the door thudded behind him again with even more force. He realised that with each attempt to get in more and more alternates, zombies, or whatever were adding their weight to the task.

On the bed, Elaine spoke into the phone. Her mouth moved in an agitated fashion but he could neither hear nor lip-read what she was saying.

Another thud, and this time the door shoved him forward and away. He scrambled back and pushed the door with all his weight but it wouldn't shift. There was too much weight on the other side.

There was a gap of about two inches between the door and

the jamb. Hands reached through, fingers clawing the air with long nails. Some of the fingers were still fleshy—although the skin was grey and decomposing—but the others were little more than naked bones.

The door inched forward again and he dug his heels against the floor, trying to gain as much purchase as he could. Using his walking stick, he swung at the hands reaching through the gap, but he did not have a good angle and had to swing the stick with his right hand across his body. The end of the stick struck his targets with insufficient force.

He looked at Elaine who was screaming into the phone. Above the alarm he thought he could make out the occasional word— "Help." "Please." "Zombies." —but he couldn't be sure.

A cold draught of wind blew across him and took him by surprise. He looked towards the windows and saw the curtains billowing inwards.

Behind him the door thudded again, but with less force this time, and he was not thrown forward.

And then they were in the bedroom. Not through the door, but through the broken bedroom window. They landed awkwardly as they jumped in, stumbling and crumpling to the floor, but one by one they got to their feet. They were hideous to look at. Their eyes were clouded and devoid of colour, their flesh grey and blotched with green and white rot.

The door thudded behind him and his bottom slid along the floor. He scrambled backwards but the door had opened further. Arms reached through, bent at the elbows, and clawed at him with rotting fingers and sharp nails.

Inside the bedroom, the first zombies to land now shambled awkwardly towards him, reaching out for him.

The house alarm wailed on, its siren drowning out all other sounds.

On the bed Elaine continued to scream into the telephone.

Looking directly at his wife George slowly mouthed the words "I love you," then struggled to his feet. The door swung open and the zombies poured into the bedroom, tripping and falling over each other.

PYRAMID POWER

Katherine Tomlinson

Man fears time; time fears the pyramids...
—Herodotus

Tarik had been born in the shadow of the pyramids. His parents lived on the outskirts of Cairo, their apartment facing southwest into the desert where the great monuments of the Giza necropolis stood in photogenic splendor just twenty-five kilometers away.

His mother had worked in a tea shop serving refreshments to the people who came from all over the world; his father had been a tout, working the hotels and the places where foreigners gathered.

When Tarik was five, he was sent out into the streets to sell cheap souvenirs, most of them made in China.

He was a beautiful boy, with long-lashed, big brown eyes. The tourists, especially the Americans, were a soft touch. They almost always let him keep the change.

Some days he made more than his parents combined.

His mother died of breast cancer when Tarik was fourteen. His father had been killed, along with the driver, when a bus struck the taxi they were in. The two tourists in the back survived.

Tarik had paid his way through university working as a tour guide. He spoke three languages—his own and two of the colonial tongues, English and French—which trebled his chances of employment.

He'd grown into a good-looking man, and the English ladies in particular tipped him well after his five-hour tour of the pyramids and surrounding area.

Tarik hated the tourists.

But he hated the pyramids more; hated what they stood for, symbols of his country's godless past, the focus for an idolatry that spanned millennia.

"The Great Pyramid is the world's oldest structure," he would say as part of his spiel, which was actually not true. The megalithic temples in Malta were older by a thousand years, but tourists didn't want to hear that.

But they liked hearing that you could see the Great Pyramid from space.

Tarik rarely referred to the "Great Pyramid" as the "Pyramid of Khufu" because he'd found tourists generally had no idea who Khufu was.

The only pharaohs they could name were Tutankhamen and Ramses. It amused him that "Ramses" had once been the brand name of a popular kind of condom in America. As far as Tarik was concerned, everything about the pharaohs and their miserable culture was filthy, so the association was fitting.

Tourists were always surprised by how large the pyramids were, particularly the Great Pyramid. It wasn't the height so much as the sheer bulk of the thing—its massive base, its cavernous internal dimensions.

Tourists always wanted to know the numbers. They needed to quantify their experience.

The figures rolled off Tarik's tongue as easily as his daily prayers. "The Great Pyramid stands 145.5 meters high," he would say.

He always had to add, "That's 480.6 feet," for the Americans.

He could always tell when the tourists were doing the mental math, comparing the statistics to something familiar. They were impressed, but they also wanted to feel a little superior.

The Brits always went away disappointed-upset that the Great Pyramid dwarfed the Big Ben Tower (96 meters) and the London Eye (135 meters).

The French and the Americans, though, they were smug.

Yes, the Great Pyramid was 146.5 meters high but what was that next to the 324 meters of the Eiffel Tower? Or the 417 meters of the World Trade Center?

Well, the World Trade Center wasn't there any more, was it?

After University, Tarik had been unable to find a job in his field, so he'd continued working as a tour guide.

His loathing of tourists deepened. And he learned that he was not the only one who despised them for their love of the pyramids, those monuments to a dark age of false idols and death-worship.

And he was not alone in his fantasies of destroying the great piles of limestone that pockmarked the desert like smallpox scars.

When the hated regime of Hosni Mubarak was deposed by the people's will, Tarik's heart was gladdened.

When the elections began and others raised their concerns about the visible reminders of the country's misbegotten past, suggesting they should be leveled or at least covered in wax, Tarik realized it was a sign.

Not that he was superstitious, for to be superstitious is to walk a path of ignorance. And did not the Prophet (peace and blessings of Allah be upon him) say, "There is no such thing as superstition?"

So it was with the spirit of scientific inquiry that Tarik began to explore certain possibilities with his like-minded friends as they talked for long hours over coffee and cigarettes and snacks of sweet, plump dates.

It was Babu who first mentioned that he had a friend who had a brother in the Army; a brother who had access to certain… materials.

This brother was not a believer but he was a man with too many children and too little money, and so it was easy enough to persuade him to procure a quantity of explosives, along with the timers and detonators to set them off.

And so a plan was put into motion.

For the next month, as he shuttled tourists in and out of the Great Pyramid by way of the Robber's Tunnel, Tarik planted explosives and set his devices.

To distract the tourists he would spin stories of lost tombs and purloined treasure and fateful curses. Tourists were always surprised to discover there had been no mummies found in the chambers of the Great Pyramid and disappointed by the lack of treasure, also.

His fairy tales set their childish imaginations ablaze as they looked upon the desert sites of the surrounding Necropolis and wondered if the sands hid a king's ransom in gold and silver and lapis lazuli.

History didn't interest them; fables did.

Tarik might have chosen any hour for his act but he had no wish to shed innocent blood, so he waited until midnight. If he'd had a sense of irony, he might have waited another hour but he was unaware that midnight holds a special significance for Jews, that the time is twice mentioned in the Book of Exodus in connection with the massacre of Egyptian first-born celebrated as Passover.

At midnight the only living souls in the area were the military guards posted at the site to keep the tourist attractions safe.

Tarik had no compunction about killing any of them. As far as he was concerned they were kafirs, of no more consequence to him than a fly on a pile of steaming dog shit.

Tarik had no regrets about his own martyrdom and no hesitation either.

He had been born in the shadow of the pyramid; he would die in the same place.

Like the pharaohs of old, Tarik did not enter the afterlife alone, but brought three unwilling companions with him.

The linked explosions collapsed the roof of the Queen's chamber and partially filled it with rubble, but other than that, the Great Pyramid was unscathed. However, the shockwaves radiating out into the desert shifted the sands so significantly that the tombs of twenty-five long-dead kings were exposed, and with them, their occupants.

The ancient Egyptians had used powerful magic to guard these tombs. Tarik's actions had broken those spells.

The first to emerge from his resting place was a man unknown to history who had been feared and hated by his subjects and also by his sister-wife, who'd had him poisoned.

Other figures soon stood beside him in the cold moonlight, and though some had been far more powerful in life, they deferred to his command for he had been the first to wake.

With the unnamed pharaoh at the head of the procession, the undead turned toward the lights of Cairo, twenty-five kilometers to the northeast and began to walk. And as they walked, their funeral finery-amulets and scarabs of carnelian and blue faience, necklaces of gold and jewels-fell from their bodies like so much dandruff.

Some stumbled over their unwinding bandages, for the undead were clumsy after so many centuries of sleep.

They were also hungry.

They reached the outskirts of Cairo just as the call for the dawn prayers faded from the air.

ULTIMATE ANA
R.J. Gaulding

My "first impressions" radar is usually spot one. Even voided by copious amounts of vodka or bedazzled by the features of some pretty boy or gal, I know what a client, person or creep is going to be like within ten seconds.

Now the guy I'm facing across his desk, in his Long Island work threads and his minimalist nihilist top floor office the size of my whole apartment is a grade A fucking cocksucker.

He was fifty trying to look forty, and they way he was chatting me up just because I had tits and hole down below made me wanna vomit, cry and throw the overly tanner SOB out of this office window—all twenty-five storeys high.

The guy was hitting on me, while trying to hire me to find his goddamn missing troubled teenager daughter. I know, not my usual fare; but the money was too good to turn down and Detective Di Livio said it would be good for my soul and help keep my ass outta jail.

So here I am listening to his spiel as he sits on the edge of the desk, his eyes glued to my boob gulley like miniature dinosaurs were going to pop out of the dark confines of my bra and do a hot shoe shuffle. All the while he's laying it on thick about how he loves his daughter and how his bitch is an ex or something like that. How his little girl is so troubled after the divorce, never got over catching him in bed with two of his wife's college friends' daughters on his yacht yadda...yadda, but I digress.

I won't bore you with the rest of the meeting; the bare facts were his part-time daughter left a note in her bedroom of her mom's huge divorce mansion. Saying the usual teen stuff that she was ashamed of them both, they did not understand her and she was going off to find another way; live the life she craved.

Not much to go on and not even a ghastly wraith in sight to spur me on to any enthusiasm for the job, except the bumper six months' rent pay check if I pulled this off. Mr Steinman had given me a photo of his girl from two years ago, all blonde long locks, braces and eyes full of hope and not yet seen the fallible side to her parents.

A call to Di Livio got me inside the mom's huge white wooden boarded house, where the streets had verges and trees, not fire hydrants and ten dollar whores like my neighbourhood. Di Livio flashed his sparkling Italian pearly whites and eyes at the girl's mother, letting me slip off to examine the missing girl's room.

The near hysterical mother's voice echoed up the stairs as I tried not to stain the cream carpet with my dirty boots. "I gave that girl everything—everything! Ponies, the love her father didn't, Botox, rhinoplasty and still it wasn't enough."

To a male eye it would look just like a perfectly normal teenage girl's room: posters, pics of friends making fish-lips to arm-length camera cell phones were Blu-Tacked along the head board of her pink trimmed bed.

Yet I'm neither guy nor much of a lady most of the time and something didn't feel right. Posters of the trendiest Indie bands were fixed next to two or three large pictures of Kate Middleton, looking so thin I could vomit. I patted my womanly hips and vowed to cut out bacon and eggs again, but even if I converted to Judaism that sin would still happen.

I sat on the edge of the missing girl's bed and frowned, gazing from the blinds, past the drapes to a mirror sat on a busy looking dresser that reflected my image. I pulled at the dark rings under my eyes: too much night work in this game and, sadly, not of the sex kind.

No, something was bugging me big time; the pictures of this teen were, all it seemed, two years old; nothing new—not in her dad's office or downstairs in mummy's place. Not a single picture up here either. Had this girl suddenly got hit with an ugly stick, or was there a deeper story here?

Di Livio said that no diary had been found and her blog and Facebook page mentioned nothing past the odd spot problem, guy she liked or trouble with the latest trig assignment. Her laptop revealed nothing sinister either, so what was the breaker deal here, why was my macabre radar going nutsoid?

I pushed myself off the bed and walked over to the dresser and pulled it two inches out from the right hand side. Something like card or paper skidded down the back behind the mirror and got stuck at the dresser table level. I reached into the thin gap, the back of my hand plucked at by old sticky tape. With my top pearly whites on my bottom lip in concentration as I delved, my fingers finally grabbed the prize.

My dusty hand came back holding an old Polaroid picture and I brought it up to my face. A badly lit picture of the girl, skinny as a rake. She wore nothing but panties that hung off her protruding hips, her arms crossed over her withered chest area, her ribs exposed. The light gave the missing girl's skin a sallow tint, adding to the image of the hollow-cheeked, bag of bones she had become.

Her once bouncy blonde hair looked dank and lifeless, and her eyes had sunken back into brown rimmed sockets that reminded me of a four day old banana skin. This missing girl had been fucked up royally by her douche-bag parents, had given up on life and been starved or traumatised into an eating disorder.

I flicked the photograph over to ease my eyes and see if it was dated. There were no dates, but some words. It read Ultimate-Ana in purple Sharpie and underneath was the word *Mildred77*: it looked it a password.

I slipped the pic in the back pocket of my jeans and made my way into the on-suite bathroom to see if any more evidence produced itself. There were no physical signs or evidence of diet pills, but I did notice something unusual. Inside the cabinet was a toothbrush holder, with two brushes in situ. A quick sniff told me everything I wanted to know: the first smelt of peppermint and the second like the inside of a fast-food restaurant's trashcan.

"One for puking, one for best," I muttered and wandered out of the bathroom and over to the bed once more. I fished my cell phone out of my back jeans' pocket and snapped close-ups of the three friends Jessica Steinman had put on her headrest.

Seeing nothing else that would give me any clues, I trotted downstairs, all full of ponderous frowns for the mother, but my mind going overdrive on what my next step would be.

"So find anything, Mel?" was Di Livio's first question when we were safely outside in the warm, sunny, formal garden only the rich could afford.

"Mel, eh? Why we are being informal today, Detective Di Livio? What's the matter, the wife not putting out this month?"

"Fuck you Montrose," he replied gruffly and pulled open the driver's side door of his car. "I forgot you don't need no help, do you?"

Then he was off, into the car lickety-split, before I could say shut-your-big-damn-stupid-mouth-Melantha. His wheels spinning, the car shot off, leaving me outside the house with only the sting of driveway stones on my shins for company.

"Jeez, everyone is so touchy these days," I said to myself, and pulled a carton of smokes from my other back pocket. I lit up as I trudged down the long drive to the security gate.

I needed help and a ride and both came in the form of a guy listed in my cell phone as Jimmy the Filth.

I was on my fourth smoke, absorbing all the glares and stress of the rich pseudo healthy types that frequented this part of Richville. They lost weight with the help of personal trainers, crunched ice cubes trying not to break their fake white teeth, caused by years of stomach acid erosion from barfing up their lunches since they were twelve years old. Maybe this was Jessica's problem. All the evidence pointed to that fact: skinny celeb pics on the walls, puking toothbrush and one for cleaning afterwards.

My ride turned up in the form of a beat-up van: matt black livery, with gloss spray paint covering some company logo or advertisement on the sides. It was some European shit, because the driver's side was on the right, which only meant I didn't have to walk far to get inside.

"Hey, I thought the parole board said you could own or hire a car no more, only motorbikes that couldn't carry more than one passenger?" was the first thing I asked as I slid inside, brush an empty chips packet off the seat, before my butt hit the fake leather upholstery.

Mötley Crüe was playing on a tape-deck of all things. Jimmy the Filth lived up to his name, with his Kid Rock skanky beard and greasy over-his-ears blond locks.

"This belongs to one of my bitches," Jimmy replied not looking at me, but in his wing mirrors before pulling off down the well tended roads, back to the greasy side of town where we both lived.

"You have a girlfriend that's old enough to drive, Jimmy?"

"Funny," Jimmy sneered. "So what you got for me, then?"

"A name, probably a website and a password to find for me." I put one boot up on the van's dash.

"Okay, but that plus the ride is gonna cost ya."

"I have money," I replied, "for a change."

"Oh, I don't want your money Montrose." Jimmy winked at me and I fully well knew what the creep meant. *Least I get to keep my money*, was how I tried to console myself on the ride to his place.

"Do your stuff, man," I said, offering the picture to Jimmy as we sat in his super air conditioned den of computers, screens and DVD to DVD recording equipment. I handed it to him writing-side up, but he instantly flicked it over with his fingers to show the scrawny, ill-looking posing pic of Jessica Steinman.

"Bit thin for my liking. Couple-a trips to Burger King and I'd do her," Jimmy said, and licked his lips in a salacious manner.

"Just find me the site this password relates to, ya sick fuck," I said, kicking the side of his swivel chair.

"Jeez Montrose, how about a bit of professional curtsey, huh?"

"Just do it Jimmy you greasy fuck, before I tell your parole officer about the van." I wanted to get on with this and what followed after quickly as possible.

"Well, Ana is one of those eating disorder sites I bet, like anorexic chicks got on and tell each other how fat they look—when they look fine to me—but let's see what we turn up." Jimmy flexed his fingers and went to work on his keyboard. His first search brought up no matching results.

"Dead end from the start," I said, downhearted, wanting this to go easy for once.

"Hey, that's just our first port of call; these sites get banned worse than my shit, and it might take some digging. The searches I use go six levels deep, and will find any sick shit however much it's protected and hidden away. Take about an hour, though, so we might as well get down to business, Montrose." Jimmy leant back in his chair, licked his lips again and rubbed at the crotch of his jeans.

"Where?" I asked, resigned to indulge this convicted paedophile's pleasures to get the information I wanted.

"Through that door there, last outfit on the left rail." He winked and pointed to a door in the right hand wall behind him. I got up quickly, wanting this to be over and to get back home with the information and soak in a shower for a day or two.

I emerged ten minutes later, my hair in two pigtail bunches, wearing a white school blouse tied up to show my flat midriff, with a tiny yellow and blue tie to match. My outfit was finished off with a tight grey cardy, frilly bobby-socks and a skirt so short and pleated I could almost see my butt cheeks as I walked.

"Nice," Jimmy said from his chair. "Now walk up and down a little".

I did, feeling foolish. I'd done this stuff for other guys and gals I liked, but none of them looked like Jimmy the Filth.

"Now bend over the chair real slowly."

I did as I was asked; getting goose bumps on my ass and legs from the cold air-con in the room.

"Now pull those frilly panties down to half-mast," he said in a thicker voice, getting up from his chair to unzip his fly.

I obeyed his request, bored as hell until I noticed a magazine open on the desk open to a page about the shitty lives of one of my favourite female film stars. I read on, as Jimmy whacked his pork sword and grunted behind me. I continued to read an article from some B-listed actress who said earning money, though fun, wasn't the recipe for a great life. *Tell me about it*, I thought as something wet and ropey hit my bare left butt cheek and began to run down the back of my thigh.

"Please tell me you have something now," I said twenty-five minutes later, wiped down and dressed back in my normal clothes.

"Just come up," Jimmy took a slug of Dr Pepper and a near blank screen appeared on his large monitor. "Took a hellava lot of digging. These guys make this like a knight's quest to find this site, a real Holy Grail for anorexics."

The screen wasn't blank as I first thought, there was an inner—almost black—grey screen, with a white text box and the word PASSWORD next to it.

"You sure this is it, it could be anything?" I hated the internet, even more than hunting Necro-Chefs on wet and cold December evenings.

"Let's put in the password then." Jimmy typed *Mildred77* into the white box that just showed up as ********* and pressed return on his keyboard.

The white box vanished and in purple the words *Ultimate Ana* grew on the screen flashing small to large like it was coming towards us.

Then underneath words in light grey appeared, saying: *Welcome back to the Ultimate Ana site! Please choose from one of our latest movies below.* It was followed by a rolling list of thirty or so movies, with no pictures or thumbnails behind just titles like:

Randy movie 1: Just interned
Kelly movie 3: Proving her Ultimate Ana status
Rebecca movie 10: Snuffed out
Jessica movie 4: The ultimate flat stomach.

"Shit, what is this site?" Jimmy murmured, feeling uncomfortable about the titles. Even this sicko had his limits.

There were four Jessica movies in total and each seemed to have the same titles and stages. My heart sank and my stomach felt sicker than when Jimmy had jazzed over my pale ass.

"Click on Jessica Four," I said in a weak tone and cleared my throat.

"Okay," Jimmy replied in a dubious voice and doubled clicked that title.

A film started, showing a brick wall in a small room that looked like someone's basement. On the floor were two long benches like the ones we used to do bunny hop jumps on in gym glasses at school. They were placed in a T-shape and the thinnest naked girl you'd ever seen was tied in a sick parody of the crucifixion to the benches. Metal handcuffs kept her wrists and ankles in place, a rope tied over the sunken flats that had once been her bust and across her all bony legs. She had one of those ball-gags strapped into her mouth, over her sunken sallow cheeks and under her dark, greasy, long blonde hair.

"Is that her?" I asked out loud to myself in disgust and disbelief.

"She looks dead, Montrose," Jimmy said and swallowed hard.

Then it got worse. Two guys with ski masks came into shot carrying baseball bats and suddenly the corpse-thing on the benches became animated and thrashed within her bonds, trying to reach for the nearest guy, the veins on her neck and body standing out like steel wires.

Without warning the two heavy-set men began to take it in turns to pound their baseball bats into the stomach of the thrashing girl. Heavy came the blows, flattening her sallow-skinned stomach until you could see her spine showing in the concave pit beneath her ribs.

Yet that was not the most shocking part: the girl did not seem to feel any of the blows that would have killed any other human, she just struggled at her bonds, trying to get to her attackers, not flinching once: and then the film ended and the movie menu came up again.

"What the hell did we just watch?" Jimmy asked, taking a slug of his soda and breathing hard through his nose.

"The Ultimate Ana," I whispered, heartburn rising in my ribs and a vile idea of what was going on forming in my brain.

"Nobody could still live after such a pummelling, they'd bleed to death inside."

"I don't think she's still alive, Jimmy," I said gently, "now play the rest of her movies, will you?"

I puked in the side alley of the warehouse where Jimmy had his studio apartment, though I doubted he paid any rent. My vented breakfast didn't seem out of place in the grimy trash-strewn alley, as out of nowhere the grey skies above began to spit on me.

I had to walk two blocks to find a cab to take me home, a flash drive in my pocket containing copies of Jessica's films—for evidence purposes only. Jimmy would call me if any more movies of her popped up on the site.

The back of the cab smelt worse than the puke taste in my mouth. I fished a couple of mints out of a deep pocket and breathed through my nose.

"Where to?"

"To…" I was gonna say my home address and then had a change of heart. "Scared Hearts Girls School, Upper East side."

"Twenty minutes," the driver replied and we set off into the mid-afternoon traffic, the sidewalks soon slick with oily puddles from the rain.

The rain had stopped by the time we got to where the rich and the affluent wannabies sent their kids to talk better than them and grow up to be tight-assed little resentful bitches. The sun came out as I paid the cabbie and I walked the perimeter of the school exits, the sun now hot on my head and shoulders: the rich even got the better weather, it seemed. The sidewalks smelt dank and humid as the sun steamed them dry.

I found what I wanted, a small park next to the right hand side of the school entrance. I popped into a nearby liquor store, bought a paper from a vending machine and put it on top of a park bench to stop my ass getting sodden. I only had half an hour to wait; with my jacket off next to me, and a smoke clamped between my perfect lips—hey, a girl knows where good and bad parts, my lips were awesome and many a guy and girl had enjoyed their soft pleasures.

This might be a colossal waste of my time, but that was the usual territory whether I was investigating ghostly entities to more normal human scum. Girls in blue jumpers, white blouses and tartan shorter-than-shit pleated skirts soon began to walk by and I was really glad Jimmy wasn't with me.

Past they went: the ugly ones on their own, the less popular in twos and the pretty and thin girl goddesses in group of four plus. Then I saw one of the girls from Jessica's picture collection.

"Hey, you fancy a smoke?" I offered the half-empty packet of Lucky Strikes in the group's direction, hoping I had enough dirty-cool chic for them to accept.

The girls stopped and giggled, not sure about the strange woman in the park offering them free cancer sticks.

"Or do you prefer vodka?" I fished out the half-bottle from the pocket of my coat draped over the back of bench my ass was parked on and it was the deal clincher. So putting my newspaper down on the bench, two sat girls sat and two stood and partook of my free smokes and vodka.

"So any of you fine ladies know a Jessica Steinman?" The money shot question asked, I watched the eyes dart around the foursome and settle on the girl from the photo in Jessica's bedroom.

"Why do you want to know about her? You a cop or a private investigator?" Pouty Lips and Blonde Locks asked me, trying to look hard, but only rating just above jellyfish on my scales.

"I'm a Capricorn," I replied and took a swig of the vodka and winked at the other girls to undermine my target. "Also, I want to know your theories on her abduction."

"Abduction? They said she ran away, left a note," squeaked a pretty brunette like she was gonna wet herself or something.

"I'll see you girls later," Pouty Blonde said, standing up and walked off across the wet grass with no regard for her two hundred dollar flats or her ever-so-white socks.

"Have fun," I said, thrusting the vodka bottle into the brunette's hand and jumped down from my perch to follow her.

"Call me," the brunette said with a bashful smile and thrust a pink business card into my hand with her name and cell number on it.

With raised eyebrows I pocketed the card. Even hard-assed Melantha Keegan Montrose can be surprised now and again. The youth of today, eh? Go figure. Leaving the jailbait-crush brunette and her friends behind, I soon caught up with Pouty Blonde as she walked through a roughly spread-apart line of trees sets in five rows.

"What do you want?" she sneered over her shoulder as I approached.

"An explanation of your reaction to the word abduction," I panted. Running wasn't good for me. "It didn't look as much as a shock to you as your girlfriends."

"Look, Jessica was my best friend for seven years, but after her parents divorced—well, it messed her up pretty bad. She lost too much weight, her breath always stank of puke after meals and like Kate Middleton and Keira Knightly were her new goddesses. I lost weight with her for a while, but I like burgers and steak, it took too much to bring it all back up, but she ate diet pills like Pez and started looking at sick fucking sites." Pouty Blonde's lips were quivering now; she had lost her friend and even I—the callous bitch, even I—could see the hurt in her eyes.

"What's your name?"

"Abigail," she replied, her eyes rimmed with tears, looking her age now and not the pouty near-adult.

"Abigail, what were these sites? Did she ever show them to you?"

"Yes, first it was Ana sites— you know, stick-thin girls looking like those African staving kids. Then one time—not so long ago, when we were a little high, she showed me a really sick one, it was fucking evil, you know?" Abigail's shoulders were shaking now and I did something unusual and hugged the girl, I knew exactly what she had seen.

"Hey, I've seen them too. Tell me everything, there's still hope we can save her life." I pretty much lied out my ass to her and wiped a tear from the corner of her left eye.

"Those girls on the site looked half-dead and the things they did to them…Jesus. But Jess wanted to be one of them, to be thin forever she said, the Ultimate Ana. God, she always was a spoilt bitch—her mother gave in and indulged her every whim."

"What about her father?"

"He had his secretary to fuck, She only saw him birthdays and holidays. She couldn't wrap him around her little finger like her mother."

"When did you see her last, and what frame of mind was she in?" I pressed, glad this girl had more self-respect for herself.

"Well, she was on a bummer for like two weeks, hardly at school as she got every cold going. Then the day before she went missing, she was all smiles and the old Jess again. I asked what had changed and she said her dreams were soon to become true…and that was the last I saw of her."

"Was anyone following her the days before she disappeared?

How did she normally get home?"

"Not that I knew, but there's something I never told anyone, not even the cops," Abigail stared at the wet grass, kicking with her toe at a fallen branch.

"Tell me, Abi."

"Well, Ellie and I," she pointed back to where her friends were disappearing off down a path.

"The pretty brunette?"

"Yeah, well we had borrowed her brother's car, like without permission, the night she vanished to smoke some dope and we scored near Jess's place and parked up in this secluded wood across the way from her house. I rang Jess's cell but got only voicemail. Then I dialled her home number, her mother answered and said that she was feeling sick and they were both going to settle down and watch a movie together in their pyjamas. We were enjoying ourselves, so we stay in the wood and smoked our gear. Ellie was busy, erm… doing stuff, when I saw the gates open and Jess's mom drove out with a guy I'd never seen before in the front seat next to her and I'm sure there was someone else in the back, but the car was gone in a second."

"And you never told the cops because of the dope and the borrowed car," I added.

"Yeah," she nodded. "But it might not mean anything."

"I'll find out," I replied, scratching a spot on the back of my shoulder.

"What do we do now?"

"You go home, Abi, smoke less dope and have Ellie as a best friend." I patted her shoulder and moved off under the cover of the dappled sunlight coming through the trees.

"What about Jess?"

"Jess is dead," I replied and walked away from the weeping schoolgirl.

"Another one just popped up, Montrose," Jimmy the Filth informed me as I took another cab up the heights to Mrs Steinman's mansion.

"What does it show, dare I ask?" I sucked in my breath; I really could've done with a burger and smoke right then.

"Liposuction, with a fully awake patient," Jimmy made a sucking sound like even he was sickened. "But made a little progress with the site: it's run by some Haitian crime boss, somewhere in the 'burbs. I'll get the address from one of my contacts, but this guy scares the shit outta people—so it's gonna cost ya."

"Don't worry about that, Jimmy, her dad's loaded. Look, I'm going to get some more information, call me the second you know anymore."

"Roger-dodge," Jimmy said before I ended the call. Fifteen minutes later the cab pulled up outside Jessica mother's big old gates, I paid the cabbie and went up and thumbed the buzzer.

"Who is it?" Mrs Steinman finally answered after what felt like five minutes, but was probably only one.

"It's Mel Montrose, Detective Di Livio's partner. I was wondering if I could have a quick word with you." A simple lie, but it seemed to do the trick.

"Erm, okay, I'll buzz you in," she said grudgingly, sounding like she'd knocked back more than one glass of Merlot with her dinner tonight.

The gates up to the drive powered inwards and I walked through; she'd obviously expected me to be in a police car. Luckily the drive was long and wound round trees and scrubs so the gates was out of sight from the front door as I rang the doorbell.

"You don't look like a police detective." Her thin lips were pursed, and I could smell wine on her breath from where I was standing.

"Undercover," I winked at her and moved forward to get inside, causing her to stagger back a little too much for a sober person. "I left my car at the gate; need to stretch my legs, you know."

"Hmmn," she replied, breathing through her nose, her eyes trying hard to focus on me as she shut the door behind us. "Let's go into the living room and sit down."

Fall down in her case, I thought, but I went along with the ride; watching her try to walk sober as I followed behind was kinda amusing really. Hey, I gotta get my kicks where I can, with my crapola lifestyle.

Mrs Steinman ushered me into a very cream-looking living room, big and airy and stinking of money, from the pictures on the walls to the crystal chandelier. I looked down the room to see a white piano on a raised area of floor and wondered if Liberace was coming back from the dead to twinkle the ivories again.

"What can I do for you, Detective Montrose? I thought I'd answered all the questions Detective Di Livio asked of me."

"Just like to be thorough, just in case we missed anything that can help locate your missing daughter, alive," I said, sitting on the same couch as her. She had to turn her body at an uncomfortable angle to talk to me.

"Is there any news?" Her question felt like an afterthought, her eyes darting toward the glass table nearby where sat her empty glass and a bottle of wine with only a few last dregs inside.

"Mrs Steinman, on the night before your daughter went missing, you stated that you and she stayed in and watched a movie for a couple of hours, before you both retired to bed at the same time."

"Yes about half-ten. She was feeling off-colour so we watched Ghost in our pyjamas and then said goodnight, nothing seemed wrong at all. When I went up to see why she hadn't come down for breakfast the next morning I found her bed unslept in and the note your detective friend took with him." Mrs Steinman added a sob and a few wet tears for show, hoping I was giving out mother-of-the-year Oscars.

"Anyone call that night or come to the house at all?" I pressed, watching the bitch's every move.

"No," she shook her head. "Wait a moment. Her friend Abi called to see if she wanted to come out, but Jess was feeling a little sick so I said she was staying in and watching a movie with her mother." Mrs Steinman spoke the word mother like she had just found out the chocolate chips in her cookie were really rat's droppings.

"Wish I'd had a mom half as caring as you Mrs Steinman; you gave that girl everything she ever wanted, but the ungrateful little cunt still ran away didn't she?" The C-U-Next-Tuesday bad swear shocked her and she blinked way too much for the safety of her fake eyelashes, and asked for a recount, as she was sure her half-cut ears had heard incorrectly.

"Pardon?"

"Or did she run away? Because I have an eye witness that saw you, a man and your daughter in an unknown vehicle, leave this very house after dark and way before the movie finished at half-ten." I sat back in the sofa and crossed my legs in a very relaxed manner.

"You're—they are mistaken then, I didn't leave the house all night." She moved forward to grab her glass, missed it by an inch and knocked it onto the carpet. To my surprise she left it there - well, I'm sure she had people to clean up after her.

"Jess was a very troubled girl after the split wasn't she, Mrs Steinman? Lost a load of weight, took up puking in her on-suite as her new hobby; why didn't you try and help her?"

"I did," Jess's mother suddenly screeched in reply, tears rolling down her foundation like snowy steam after a thaw. "I got the best life-coaches and shrinks money could buy but no one could help her, she was stupid stubborn girl, she got that from her fucking father."

Now that was more like it, ranting and raving and on the emotional edge I was pushing her closer to. Now for the coup d'grace.

"But she just wanted to be thin, right? The ultimate of all the thin chicks around the globe: Miss Anorexic Pageant Queen. Something her dad couldn't help her with, but you could; you had half his money now, you were the good parent that gave in to her every whim, you loved her more."

"Too fucking right, her father was too busy fucking around to care about anyone or anything but his ego. I held her in my arms as she begged me to help her, I was one that knew her the best. He didn't understand how Jessica's mind worked at all, she showed me the websites and how she wanted to look. She pleaded for weeks for help and finally I gave in." The poor stupid rich bitch had really done it and now she was sobbing her heart out, her words slurred with booze and some sort of emotion that could've been remorse.

"So you contacted the Haitian guy who ran the websites and

then arranged for her to be taken," I said, slowly—so she understood every word and syllable.

"Yes, yes, yes," Mrs Steinman shouted, pulled at her hair and shaking her head so fast from left to right her tears splashed down on the glass table.

"Where did they take you when they picked you up that night?" I pressed, hoping she could still answer my questions coherently.

"I don't know, we drove to a vacant car lot… it—it was dark and there were more men and I said goodbye to my only child and she thanked me and told me she loved me for doing this. Jessica was taken into a van and that was the last I saw of her. I hope she's happy now, I hope they gave her what she wanted."

I stood up, feeling sick to my stomach that a mother could give her only child to such sicko crime creeps, knowing the depraved abuse the men would inflict upon her young body and would film for a selected audience.

"Mrs Steinman, one last thing: what's your full maiden name, please?" My left hand was in my short leather jacket, gripping something hard and plastic inside.

"Angela Mildred Taylor," she dutifully replied, knowing the game was up. "Why do you ask?"

"Tying up loose ends," I said, pulled a plastic bottle full of horse-tranquilisers from my jacket pocket and threw them at her. Give the sobbing wreck of a bad-mother her due, she caught them in both hands and then stared up at me; her face calm now, but questioning.

"What are these for?"

"I'll give you two hours before I call Detective Di Livio and tell him all about your confession I recorded on my cell phone," was my only reply, and I left the woman staring at the plastic bottle as I left the room and made for the exit.

I heard the lid pop just before I opened her front door and, with a smile, walked out into the night air and pulled out my cell. Even if it did have a way to record people, I wouldn't have a clue how to use it.

I called Jimmy the Filth, but got no answer so phoned up Johnny the Nose's cab firm to get Herb or one of his other schmucks to pick me up pronto. Twenty minutes later, a new guy called Praveed was taking me over to Jimmy's place and I hoped that he was finding out where this Haitian scumbag was doing his unnatural web shows from, or Jess would stay there in limbo until they reached Movie Ten.

Praveed was new so the tip was minimal and I rushed up to the warehouse where Jimmy lived and hoped the reason he wasn't answering wasn't 'cos he was attempting statutory rape with one of his groomed under-aged teen girlfriends.

When I got to his place the door was wide open and as I made my way cautiously inside, with my SIG handgun drawn, I swore that Jimmy the Filth wouldn't fuck another fourteen year old cheerleader ever again, not with his dick cut off and stuffed down his throat until he either choked to death or died through blood loss.

"Jimmy," was all I could say, as I stood shaking my brown locks at the man who was helping me, sat in his swivel chair in front of his many screens, murdered.

I saw a dim reflection in one of the monitors and turned to fire, just as something hit the side of my neck and hung down with an external weight rather than blow my throat out. I fired off one shot into the ceiling and remembered dust and debris falling like snow as my vision darkened. Two burly men came rushing into my dimming view, one holding a tranquiller gun, I felt them catch my arms as I sank groggily to my knees and then I felt, saw and heard nothing.

Luckily for me, or some could argue unluckily, I'd had my share of enforced blackouts—tranquilisations, Siren Sounds, whacks to the cranium, swamp sleep venom and the ilk—in my short but eventful life to recover a lot quicker from such experiences of unconsciousness.

I awoke just as van doors opened. I saw it was still night outside and the edge of an unlit building, before I closed them shut again and played possum. The voices and the crunch of three sets of shoes on gravel told me the three people in Jimmy's last resting place hadn't multiplied. The heavies grabbed me under each armpit and dragged me out of the back of the van; my head face down and covered by my hair, my nose hitting every rough bit of peeling paint on the dusty floor.

My feet hit the gravel and I was dragged easily; my hands were tied behind my back, but I was otherwise unencumbered. I had to hand it to these fellas, they were old time professionals with the Indian burns from the rope binding my wrists, no plastic ties or handcuffs with these schmucks, they were the real nuts-cutlets.

My head bowed, I let my eyes open to slits, seeing and feeling them heft me down five stone steps to an iron-clad door that wouldn't have been out of place on a battleship. Moving in front of me and my minders were a pair of sharp looking shoes, maybe snakeskin: I couldn't tell because of the dark, but the trousers were from not from some off-the-rack suit.

I heard a metal grille slide open and after several bolts later, the iron door opened inwards, sending out no light at all and another pair of less expensive black shoes steps back into an alcove, as Snakeskin and his goons dragged me in down a corridor that smelt of moist limestone and graveyard turf a day after a wet funeral.

Snakeskin lead the way up to a dead end, pulled out something from a right trousers pocket and inserted it into something unseen on the wall. I heard a click, a turn and a rumble as the wall slid to the left. Like something outta *Scooby-Doo*.

I was dragged once more into another corridor, still no lights: Jeez, these guys must have had cat's eyes or something. The wall ground shut behind us and then we went down a wide set of chipped stones steps again, twenty steps I counted, wondering if there would be any wear left on the toes of my boots by the time this was all over. Down along another corridor which smelled like the cleaning products from under my kitchen sink, then and only then did we reach another wooden door.

Snakeskin got out what I must assumed was another key, and opened the door to reveal light at last. I squeezed my eyes shut, trying not to move my head or show any signs of life b. This was one heavy duty secret hideout and these guys were professional grave-fillers and even a cocky cunt like me was wishing I hadn't cashed in my life policies to buy my latest motorbike.

No words had been uttered since I had - unbeknownst to my captors - awoken, which added to my worries about these guys. They knew their jobs, probably believed in that "loose talk costs lives" mantra folk used to say during the Second World War.

Wipe-clean and recently disinfected linoleum covered the floor as I was dragged, by toes squeaking so badly even I wanted to give up the game and walk, rather than endure the torturous noise. The professionals dragging me didn't seem to mind, nor Snakeskin; hell they hadn't even bothered to feel up my rack.

Talking of suited and booted, he opened a magnolia painted door which led down to a grey walled corridor with another lino covered floor, past two doors on either side up to a T-junction ahead. Then the smell hit me, the smell of rotting flesh and farts and gases and of blood. I was dragged left down another corridor where the lighting was duller by choice and then stopped outside a barred-shut, reinforced steel door.

Snakeskin unbarred the door and laid the metal bar down against the wall. There was an electric buzz from within the wall and an audible click as the door was released and Snakeskin pulled the door back, missing the top of my bowed head by a hair's breadth.

I nearly retched as I was bundled sidewards through the doorway, so bad was the smell of putrid flesh and decay. Something jumped and moved to my right; my eyes darted open for a second to see a steel bed, on which lay strapped and gagged the twitching, emaciated body of Jessica Steinman.

I had found my girl and her captors, but me getting out and claiming my money off her dad felt less likely than winning the lottery.

"Jessica, don't fret. I've bought a nosey little friend for you to play with," Snakeskin purred with a soothing, yet slimy, heavily-accented voice.

"Shall I start filming now, boss?" One of the heavies holding me up asked.

"It ain't viewing time on the live feeds for another twenty minutes, and anyway we need to go fetch the ski masks. I think I want to feed Jessica myself tonight. Shame the bitch isn't awake, but if Jess bites off that nosey beak of hers, that might snap her into the world of the living, for a while leastways."

I tried not to tense as Snakeskin walked over to stand in front of my hung head, his large, rough, chilled hands reached up my top and into my black bra to give my nipples a twist and a turn, like the bastard was trying to tune in an old car radio. Luckily my hair hanging down hid my grimace of pain, but I had endured worse during my underage porno part of my teenage life, memories usually duct-taped to a brick, covered in a bin liner and dumped into the Atlantic Ocean of my submerged, scarred subconscious.

"Leave her here," muttered Snakeskin and I could hear the scratch of his manicured nails down the stubble of his cheek and chin, "but lock the door behind you just in case."

I was unceremoniously dropped to the floor, all cold, hard concrete. My head landed on the crook of his right shoulder and upper arm and it was my right hip that took the impact, ending fibre-optic flashes of pain down my thigh and up my side. The three men exited the room and shut and bolted the door after me, one of the heavies asking Snakeskin's permission to ass-rape me before the show began.

I let out a low hiss of breath and pain and turned my head to gaze back at the looked door. The hatch was shut and apart from the video camera on a tripod before the metal bed, the room was empty. I rolled over, my hands under my back and onto my front from my pain-free other side. I was quickly into a kneeling position, then leaning on the wall with my right elbow to steady myself, I pushed myself shakily to my feet.

This caused the gaunt, naked thing that was once a pretty rich girl, who wanted for nothing except the love she so badly craved, to thrash about in her restraints. I looked at her teeth, the white enamel exposed because her lips and gums had withered into her emaciated, skull-like countenance. I stumbled, then walked more upright, not wanting to fall anywhere near her air-biting teeth.

"Jessica, what the fuck did you do to yourself?" I whispered, bending over her face, with a good margin of safety for my tender flesh. Her eyes darted towards me, but her irises were no longer blue, just covered in milky cataracts.

But I had no time to morn this lost youth, I moved behind her head and turned around, my arms extended behind me to breaking point. Looking over my right shoulder, I pulled my tied wrists apart as far as they could go and waited. Every time I lowered my bound wrists, she rose up with snapping teeth like a half-starved junkyard dog. With time running out before the three men returned, I took a chance and pushed the gap in the rope my pulling and sweat had extended, down into the jaws of walking death itself.

I was back on the floor when the three stooges came back in, my wrists tender, slightly bitten, but the ropes now lay coiled, untied around my wrist and held loosely in my hands.

"Time for the show bitch!" A kick to my left shin took the pain temporarily away from my chewed wrists.

I played dead again as one heavy picked me easily from the floor, the other manning the video camera, while Snakeskin stood on the other side of the metal table next to Jessica's head.

The heavy dragged me over and held me up on the opposite side of Jessica's thrashing head, the rest of her body strapped down in place.

"Tonight, my Bocor ancestors would be proud," Snakeskin began to speak in accented American English, slightly muffled by the ski mask he wore. "I have brought a sacrifice to feed pretty little Jessica here, as she has been a good girl: the Ultimate Ana."

I felt the thug put one arm around my waist; the other grabbed a large knot of my dark hair and pushed me over the snapping and foaming teeth of what was left of the soulless Jessica Steinman.

It was now or never: my right hand slipped out of the loose loop of rope, down into the belt of the henchman's pants, found my SIG handgun and pulled the trigger with all my might. The slug took off his left nut, sliced through his thick thigh and blew off his kneecap, sending him howling with pain to the floor.

Then I whipped around and slam-dunked Snakeskin's masked face—with the butt of my handgun striking the nape of his neck—down into the waiting jaws of Jessica Steinman, his client and victim.

I held his face to hers as she bit the crap out of him, my eyes only on the cameraman, who finally realised take one was not going according to script, fumbling at the back of his waistband for his handgun.

I clonked Snakeskin on the back of the head with my SIG liberated from the uni-testicalled guy screaming and writhing on the blood splattered floor, then raised my gun and shot the cameraman twice in the forehead, before his Berretta was even out of his slacks.

Snakeskin the Bocor Witchdoctor crime boss tried to raise his bloodied face and torn ski mask from Jessica's ravenous teeth, but another crack to the cranium was the last thing he felt in this life as Jess bit off the cocksucker's nose. He slid to the floor on the other side of the metal bed frame.

Two more rounds ended One-nuts's wailing and Bocor Snakeskin's miserable lives. Then I set Jessica free, pushing her in front of me with a broom I found and let her wander the corridors of the underground complex, finishing off Snakeskin's other men, while my trusty SIG and I gave final endings to the lives of the other residents of the cells.

I waited in Jessica's cell, for her bullet-holed, naked, stick-like frame to totter home, to hunger after me, as I was the last bit of living flesh alive in the place now. I waited at the far end of the bed frame for her to get into camera shot before I put an end to her torturous half-life.

"Shows over, you sick fucks," I said in an exhausted voice—not my best delivery ever as I shot the shit out of the video camera.

The outside guard had long since high-tailed it back to mamma's home for rice and peas and with my cell taken from the cameraman's corpse I called for a taxi and then Di Livio. I waited across the street in a dark alley and watched as Detective Di Livio and his squad cars found the place.

It was not hard to miss, as the flames from the building were already several storeys high.

THE SILENT DEAD
William Meikle

Augustus Seton still felt woozy from the ale he'd been consuming when the summons came, and would much have preferred to be back in the tavern with a wench or two on his lap. But the King had called, and that was one request you did not refuse if you wanted to keep your head.

It was a typical winter night in Stirling. Sleety rain lashed straight down the Castle Wynd into his face as he trudged uphill against the wind, regretting with every step ever having left the tavern. By the time he arrived at the main gate of the old castle he felt like a dog that had been swimming in a river.

And I probably smell just as rank.

The guards were obviously expecting him. He was allowed entrance with no fuss or over-zealous questioning and soon was in the relative comfort of the main quadrangle. He expected to be received in the Great Hall, but instead he was shown to a small chamber with a view looking out over the esplanade to the driving rain and the flickering lights of the town below. A small man swaddled in heavy furs sat hunched forward to get some heat from a large fire. It took Seton several seconds to recognise the King, for he had never seen the man without his pomp and finery.

I am just glad I did not open my mouth without thinking.

"You sent for me, sire?" Seton said.

The King waved him over to a trestle on the other side of the fireplace.

"Sit with me, Seton. I have a favour to ask of you."

The King poured Seton a flagon of hot mulled wine from a pot by the fire.

Served by a King. They will never believe me back in the taverns.

He forced himself to concentrate. When a King asked rather than commanded it usually meant trouble ahead. As if to reinforce that thought the sword at his waist chose that moment to thrum and send a blast of warmth along that side of Seton's body. He put a hand on the hilt to quieten it.

The King saw the movement and nodded.

"It knows that I must send you into danger?"

Seton had a long swig of the wine before replying—it might be his last for some time.

"Aye sire," he replied after wiping off his moustache and beard with a damp sleeve. "It kens. But you know I have forsworn myself against its use?"

"After you sold your very soul to acquire the weapon?"

Seton finished off the wine in one gulp. Some memories were not to be borne sober; especially the thought of the night he met the Wee Man and traded twenty innocents for his own desires.

"And I will pay for it dearly," Seton finally replied. "I can attempt to atone, but I will do so without the accursed weapon… if I can."

The King sipped at his own wine.

"That may not be possible in the place I must send you," he said. "Have you heard of Loch Leven?"

Seton did not quite know how to reply without being indelicate; the King's family history was involved here. The King himself came to Seton's aid.

"Aye, I can see you have," the smaller man said. "My mother was an unwilling guest there for a time. But that is not what has brought you here tonight. For the past ten years the castle has been given over to the Church and all has been calm. But tonight I have heard tales of despair and carnage from the neighbouring township of Kinross. There is talk of demons and black arts. The Sheriff of Kinross has pleaded for my help."

"And you would send me, sire? What can I do?"

The King laughed, but with little humour.

"I think it might be more a matter of what you cannot do," he said. "Your reputation precedes you, Seton. I have heard all the tales that are told in the town, and if only a quarter of them are true then I could write a damnable fine book of it. No…I am convinced you are the only man for the job. My man outside will ensure you get everything you need. If you leave now you can be there by sunrise."

Seton knew a dismissal, and a command, when he heard one. He put down the tankard and rose.

"As always, I am your man, sire," he said. The King waved him away with a tired movement of his right hand.

Less than an hour later Seton rode out of Stirling into the night.

The journey to Kinross proved uneventful. He took the old cattle-droving road through Tillicoultry and Dollar along the base of the Ochils. The horse knew this road well. Seton was able to sleep in the saddle for long parts of the trip, and when he wasn't dozing he watched the night sky overhead. The rain had ceased for a time and Seton enjoyed the play of moonlight in the trees. The sword stayed quiet at his side; there was no danger here.

The first sign of anything untoward come as they crested the last hill. Seton looked over a mist-shrouded Loch Leven as a red dawn came up over the Kingdom of Fife. The air was still and all was quiet. But the thing that drew his attention was the tall plume of black smoke that rose almost straight up into the air from a point near the centre of town. By the time he rode through the Cowgate and down to the origin of the smoke he started to smell it, and taste it in his throat; the unmistakable tang of burning meat.

And cows are too precious to be burning in these parts.

He dreaded what he was heading into, but the sword stayed quiet at his side, so it seemed that there was no immediate danger. Nevertheless he kept one hand on the weapon's hilt, and a close eye out for any sudden movement in the road ahead. His suspicions as to the nature of the smoke were confirmed when he reached a small square opposite the coaching inn. What looked enough folk to be the full population of the town stood around a fiercely burning pyre, and Seton had arrived just in time to see them toss a body into the flames, sending a shower of sparks and ash high into the air.

Seton stopped beside a small group of women who looked at the fire with despair in their faces and tears running down their cheeks.

"What has happened here?" he asked. At first he did not think he would get a reply but one, bolder than the rest, came over and looked up at him.

"Ride on, sir," she said. "This is no place for good Christian men. We are cursed; the Devil is here and we are cursed."

At that she started to wail; a piteous thing, like a child in pain. Seton did not know what to do in the face of such anguish, and was relieved when the other women gathered round and shepherded the first one away from him. Ashamed at his own sense of relief he rode over to the inn, hoping to garner more information there. As he made his way across the square the townspeople started to disperse. It was obvious that whatever had transpired was finished, for now. But by the look on the folk's faces it was clear that despair and fear had taken deep roots among them.

After he had seen that the horse would be stabled, watered and fed he headed for the bar. The innkeeper was just setting up for the day, and indeed seemed surprised to see a traveller of any kind, but quickly remembered his position and offered Seton the uisque. Seton reluctantly declined. Tempting as it would be to lose himself in hard liquor for a while, he was on the King's business. A clear head was what was required.

But a beer or two would nae harm anything.

He ordered ale and started what would prove to be a long process of discovering what ailed this town. The innkeeper himself was one of the tight-mouthed reticent type, but several of the locals, once they learned that Seton had come at the behest of the King himself, were only too keen to tell the tale. The trouble was they insisted on all speaking at once, and it seemed there were numerous ideas as to what the truth of the matter might be.

"There's a witch out on yon castle, I tell you. Has to be…"

"No. It's the deadly shade of the auld queen, come to punish us for her getting her heid chopped aff…"

"It was the Wee Man that did it. I saw him with my own eyes, all bent and twisted he was and..."

Only two facts seemed constant through the tales. Over the last month an affliction had hit this town. Many people had gone missing, and over a dozen others—the ones whose burning he had witnessed—seemed to have lost their very souls, becoming languid, their senses dulled, with only an appetite for raw meat left to show they were alive. At first they had been placid, but in recent days their appetites had grown stronger. First dogs, then sheep, then townspeople themselves started to fall prey to clawing hands and tearing teeth. A burning had become necessary.

The other thing the villagers all agreed on was the source of this contagion. They may have disagreed on the manner of delivery, but all knew that the evil came from the squat castle that sat out in the loch to the east of the town.

"And why have you not done anything about this for yourselves?" Seton asked.

"We did," a small man replied. "Six men went over in a boat yesterday. They have not returned."

Ten minutes later Seton was at the oars of a small boat and rowing hard. Some of the villagers stood on a small jetty watching him but none had offered to accompany him on the quarter of a mile trip to the island on which the castle sat. The sword chose that moment to warn him of impending trouble.

I ken already that this is a very bad idea.

He had to stop for a rest at the approximate halfway point. The villagers were still on the jetty watching him. The waters below the boat sat flat and calm, looking like a mirror on which a very thin layer of water had been poured. He took the opportunity of the stop to take a closer look at his destination.

The island was no more than a hundred yards long and half again as wide. A fortified wall ran around the perimeter and the thatched roofs of several outbuildings could be seen, clustered around the dominating structure—a tall square keep. There was no sign of activity; no kitchen fires burned and no sound at all carried across the water. Even the local crows, usually so vociferous in warning of any approach, seemed to have abandoned the place. The King's mother Mary had been held prisoner here for a time during her long incarceration. That and the fact that it had been turned over to a monastic order some years ago totalled the sum of his knowledge.

Seton took up the oars again and the splash they made as they cut through the water was the only sound as he approached the stone jetty; the only obvious access to the island.

No one was there to welcome him. He tied the boat up, making sure the oars were positioned such that he could make a rapid getaway if the need arose. The sword thrummed at his thigh, eager to be free. He gave in to the inevitable and drew the weapon. In truth, despite his antipathy to the sword and his disgust with himself over the bargain he made so many years ago, the feel of the weapon in his hand gave him a sense of security he would not have otherwise.

Seton walked off the jetty onto the island itself, ready for whatever might come.

He didn't know what to expect, given the range of stories told in the tavern. What he hadn't counted on was that the place seemed to be completely empty. It looked like somewhere in the region of fifty monks lived—had lived—in the enclosure, but they were not here now. There was no sign at all of any recent activity; all the hearths he investigated were stone cold, all the cooking pots empty. Once he was satisfied that there was no danger lurking in the outbuildings he made his way to the main keep.

Here he found his first signs of anything untoward, but even then it was only a row of knocked-over pews in the small chapel that had been set up inside the main chamber of the keep. He switched the sword to his left hand and made the sign of the cross with his right as he walked down the main aisle, as ever feeling slightly guilty as he did so. The sword showed no such qualms; it thrummed ever harder as he approached the block of stone that marked the altar itself. It was only as he got closer he saw that the stone had been moved off-centre, showing a passageway beneath leading down into the bedrock of the island. The sword sent a burst of heat up through his palm and wrist as he returned it to his right hand.

Whatever ails this place, it seems it is down there.

Seton wanted more than anything to leave, to row away and never look back, but he was bondsman to the King, and sworn to obey. He had done enough forswearing of vows for this lifetime. Grasping the sword tighter he headed down.

A set of heavily worn stone steps led into darkness below. The air smelled dank and putrid with something he took a second to identify before recognizing—the nauseous tang of corruption. He covered his mouth with his free hand and sent a finding spell down ahead of him, its dim blue flicker just enough to show him the way.

There was no sound save his breathing and the shuffle of the soles of his boots on the stone steps. The air got heavier still, and more foul than anything he'd previously encountered. Just as he was about to concede defeat and retreat up to cleaner air, the steps reached bottom and the passageway opened out into a wider chamber, a natural cave. He sent his finding spell up to the roof and called out.

Dhumna Ort!

The flickering spell brightened, lighting up the whole chamber. Seton wished he had not bothered. Twelve robed figures stood in a tight circle facing inward, cowls pulled forward such that their faces were obscured in deep shadows. And the smell was worse than ever in this place. The light was not quite bright enough for Seton to see past the monks; for surely that is who they must be—but there was a darker patch in the shadows over there that seemed to be the main source of the foulness. The sword bucked in his hand every time he looked that way, confirming his suspicions.

He started to call out, then thought better of it.

I really do not wish to see what is under those cowls.

Instead he walked slowly across the chamber. There was no movement from any of the hooded figures. The light spell started to dim so he sent another up in its place, feeling heat at his wrist from the sword as it passed the power through to him.

Dhumna Ort!

The light flared and, now that he was closer, Seton could see part of what sat in the darker shadow beyond the monks. It seemed to be an altar of sorts, but a debased blasphemous form. A flat shelf of rock had been hewn into the shape of a woman's body, one sitting on what might be a throne had it not been carved too crudely to be certain. The upper part of the idol was in deeper shadow so he could not yet see any facial features.

And I am not sure that I wish to.

At the foot of the statue lay what he at first took for bundles of clothing, but as he stepped closer he saw they were people—or rather, parts of what had once been people. The clothes indicated that the dead had come from monks and commoners alike; probably missing townspeople or local farmers. Whoever they might once have been, they were now little more than a jumble of torsos and limbs, all torn or hewn into pieces, white bone showing clearly through bloody flesh. To his horror he saw that some of the parts looked as if they had been gnawed on and partially eaten. The floor of the cavern was awash with gore and Seton realized with dismay that he had been walking in it for several seconds now without realizing.

The sword sent a pulse of almost unbearable heat up his arm as he took another step towards the bloody altar. He turned just in time to see one of the hooded monks leave the circle and come straight for him. The monk's robe reached all the way to the floor and was so voluminous it gave the illusion that the monk was floating just above the ground, an illusion that was almost immediately shattered as the cloth trailed in the gore and started to turn red.

"Keep away," Seton said. "I have no desire to hurt a man of the cloth."

Even as he said it he knew that these monks had long renounced any Christian values they might once have avowed. Still, Seton hesitated slightly as the hooded figure approached, loath to use the weapon he had come to dread.

The matter was quickly taken out of his hands. The sword twitched and leapt forward. Before he could stop it, the point tore through the monk's hood, lifting the remaining material away to reveal the head below.

Seton stared into the face of a dead man.

What remained of the skin was green and mottled, damp patches gleaming where corruption seeped to the surface. White bone showed where flesh had sloughed off around the jaw and maggots crawled in the weeping ruin that had once been an eyeball.

What fresh hell is this?

The thing that had once been a monk kept coming. It raised an arm and reached out a hand that was more bone than flesh. Seton acted on instinct—he was not about to allow himself to be touched by such filth. The sword came up and went down and a new limb joined the others strewn on the floor of the cavern.

But the monk did not even flinch, and continued to come forward. Seton just had time to note that no blood flowed from the shoulder socket where he had cleaved off the arm, then he was too busy defending himself for further reflection. Even as he engaged the monk at close quarters he saw over its shoulder that the circle had broken and the rest of the assembled group were heading in his direction.

The spell he'd used for lighting chose that moment to dim, just as the monk reached for him with its remaining hand.

Dhumna Ort!

He called out, but the sword did not give him any power for the spell. Instead it helped him with the momentum of a swinging backhand chop that took the monk in the chest and kept going, cleaving the man in two parts that fell wetly away.

Dhumna Ort!

Seton called out again as the light dimmed even further, just as the rest of the monks floated towards him.

He made his next sword-stroke in total darkness.

Cold bodies crowded around him, clammy flesh pressing against his. He hacked and hewed, trying to stay on the move for he knew that if he was, even once, borne to the floor of the chamber, there was only a slim chance of him ever regaining his feet. The monks fought without a sound, relying only on the press of their bodies and the bite of their teeth as attack. Seton felt cloth tear in his jerkin. It was only a matter of time before their teeth found his flesh.

He struck out with his free hand. His fist, more by luck than judgement, hit a monk full in the face. Bones cracked, flesh caved and Seton felt the cold slime of brain tissue in his palm.

Dhumna Ort, he called out again, but the sword was too busy to lend him any light. It sliced through flesh and bone as effectively as any butcher, and for the first time in many a month Seton was glad for its presence, for without it he would already have been just another victim.

The fight seemed to go on forever, a dance of death there in the dark. Seton's left foot slid away from him in a patch of gore and he stumbled, almost fell. A cold body leapt on him. Legs gripped him at the waist and arms locked around his neck. He sensed more than felt a face approach his own. What he did feel was the cold tongue that probed at his lips in an obscene attempt at a kiss.

Seton cried out in disgust and did the only thing he could think of. He threw himself forward to the ground with all his strength. They hit the rocky floor with a solid thud and Seton smiled grimly as his passenger came apart in a splash of thick liquid and bone.

The smell was suddenly much worse, and he had to force back a sudden rush of nausea as he rose, swinging the blade and traversing a full circle as fast as he was able. He felt flesh slice from bone and sinew with every cut, every thrust. He hacked and swung until his sword arm grew too heavy to lift, and only then did he stop.

His breath came in great heaving gulps and all he could do was stand and wait for his fate, wait for the cold embrace of any monks left standing to take him down into death.

But there was no attack, no sound save his breathing, already returning to something approaching normal.

Dhumna Ort! he said, barely able to manage much more than a whisper. But this time the sword complied, lending him a burst of heat and sending a dancing blue following spell high overhead.

It lit a scene of carnage the like of which Seton could not have imagined. Bodies, and body parts, lay strewn the length and breadth of the chamber where the sword had cut its swathe through the monks. Heads had been hewn from bodies, legs and arms lay in tangled heaps and the stench of corruption hung heavy in the air.

There was almost no blood.

And some of the body parts seemed to still retain some semblance of life. Even now a bony hand tried to crawl at Seton's feet. He brought his heel down, hard, and smiled as the bones crushed underfoot.

He made sure no attack was going to be forthcoming before turning his attention to the tall stone altar and the object of the monks' devotion. It was only when he looked up at the head that he understood what had happened here.

Ten minutes later he was back in the rowboat. The keep burned behind him—he hoped the fire would be enough for the present to keep the evil at bay—he'd used every scrap of straw and every jar of oil he could find. On his return to Stirling he would ensure that the King would have the place razed, consecrated and salted.

But there was one part of the story the King must never know.

He glanced again at the thing he had taken from the top of the carving on the altar.

He'd heard the stories—every Scotsman had—tales of the rightful heir being denied the throne, of an order of execution, and of a dark curse muttered in the pre-dawn of the final day; a curse that had been working its deviltry on this town until Seton came to break it.

He stopped at what he considered must be the deepest part of the loch, reached over, and, ensuring the crown was still firmly in place dropped the head over the side.

It went in with barely a splash and immediately sank. He watched for a time; staying there long after the dead features of Mary, Queen of Scots, had gone from view.

ASCENSION?

Dave Jeffery

The Sickness re-wrote the rules about death. In fact, it affectively killed over sixty million people before the ink was dry on the first draft. Not bad for a disease with no name.

First we knew of it was a small bulletin on the local news. One minute and ten seconds if you're a stickler for the detail. But that's as good as it got for a while, Bob Warman's narrative of a group of ramblers 'assaulted' by an escapee inmate of nearby HMP Hewell was low key, sedate even. The show had won 'Best Regional Television News Programme' two years running. The camera never lies, just the people rammed in front of them, it seems. So we ate what they served up as truth. For a time the fare was good enough. Then public hunger was to grow in oh-so-many ways.

Who was to know the speed at which *The Sickness* liked to travel? Someone did, of course. Someone with an MSc in bureaucracy when they needed a Doctorate in disaster management.

Because, disaster did come to our world. Disaster borne of *The Sickness*, with its raging fever, boiling blood, turning veins into fierce, red tributaries; forcing them to the surface of the skin until the body became a road map with all routes leading to Hell. Then the cramps came, so severe the screams of the infected were in competition with the sound of cracking bones.

Death would come. Bodies contorted into such implausible, rigid shapes it was difficult to cover them with a soiled sheet or slide them into a body bag.

Death, the small mercy, may have come to visit, but it had only paid for short stay. It was no longer the eternal host. It got cheap. Try an hour.

Tops.

One hour before a loved one would begin to move a finger, or flutter an eyelid. One hour before those around them lifted their heads in rapture thinking that, for once, the Dear Sweet Lord had answered their prayers, only to find that when the sheet was pulled back 'Big G' really did have a shitty sense of humour.

The things returning from their brief stint with the Reaper were just masquerading meat suits wearing the masks of people we once knew. People to whom we gave our love and, if we were lucky, gave it back.

No giving back any more. Not in the early days. Their arms may have been reaching out, but their embrace came at a cost, teeth tearing wads of flesh from anyone blinded by this miracle of faux resurrection.

But lessons were learned fast, even for those who initially hadn't put in the study time. The population who survived the early stages of *The Sickness*—that is, those who managed to avoid being eaten alive by the reanimated corpses of their loved ones—were pretty much on their own. All semblance of government appeared to have disappeared; panic the new politic, lawlessness dangerously close to becoming the New World Order.

Society is a fragile creature, humanity equally as tenuous. *The Sickness* showed us this very early on, the terrible images spilling out of the TV, flooding our living rooms with carnage and despair, numbing us all. Somehow it was kind of a relief the day the TV died. It meant that we could take stock, deal with what was to come; to limit its impact through strength in numbers, strength in a united purpose.

Instead, the horizon became our window on events. First, the explosions—from the cities—concrete skyscrapers turning to towers of flame, reaching into the skin like incandescent fingers pointing their accusations to any deity who cared to take the rap. Then, the smoke; black and belching, a dirty smudge against the skyline. And, as days passed, the smoke gave way to other dark, yet sinister, clouds: swarms of fat bloated flies taking to the air fresh from blown bodies, putrid parental pedestrians shuffling in congested cities around the country.

I'm under no illusion that it was our sense of community that got us through those early days. The Blakewell Spirit we called it, our small but potent stand against potential chaos. It was a doctrine that had been in situ even before the dark times; neighbours looking out for each other, taking care of each other. A haven from 21st Century ills, our lofty aspirations keeping house prices high; keeping things exclusive.

Decent?

Yes, perhaps that played a part in the ethic—the ethos—of Blakewell Village, community synonymous with family.

Newcomers keen on planting roots as welcome as those who had made good on aged foundations.

The village of Blakewell wasn't a village in the true sense of the word, but those of us who lived there thought it so. There was a small shop that had once doubled as a post office until it was robbed twice in three months and the Postmaster tenure was terminated. There was a Blakewell Social Club, where seasonal events were hosted to the 500 strong community. And finally Blakewell First School which had a total of 30 pupils and six teachers.

That was it, Blakewell Village in a nutshell. But what we had went deeper than brick and mortar, tile and thatch. We had The Blakewell Spirit, the glue holding us together. And yes, it got tacky when The Sickness first turned up the heat, but it did not yield because we decided it would not, could not, falter. It stood for too much, our commitment to our families, to our community. All hail The Blakewell Spirit, the new euphemism for a little Isle of stability in the ever growing floods of unrest.

We used our parish council as the mechanism to evoke village order and structure. We walled ourselves in using cars and trucks to bar the four roads into our town.

We looked after our own, taking care of those that were touched by *The Sickness*; The Blakewell Spirit extended to those who wanted to cause us ill. It was the heritage of humanity we intended to keep in our quiet corner of an increasingly quietened world.

No matter what.

The landscape defied the horror of the past twelve months. Given time, nature has a habit of erasing man's dirty deeds, doesn't it?

Well, that's how I saw it.

Especially in the viewfinder of the binoculars jammed to my eyes. The rolling fields and hillsides were more than distant, they felt detached, as though they were not part of the here and now, but the then and when. But while it was easy to dupe the senses towards the cordial, the view would occasionally yield a hint of the bitterness. The blackened, gutted shell of a 4x4, for example, lying on its side and dumped in a ditch. Then there was the horizon, once a symbol of hopes and dreams and adventure - the shape of things to come - now a jagged line you had to keep in sight just in case the dreams turned bad and came looking for someone to blame. Today, the tail fin of a downed 747—cutting a dog-legged silhouette against the cobalt sky—is testament to this; the huge gash in the terrain marking its final destination had been carpeted by new grass but this is a simple dressing, like using Band Aid to treat gangrene.

And that analogy isn't there by chance; it highlights something the binoculars cannot, the pervading stink of decay on the breeze.

The corpses, of course. Always, the corpses; shuffling, shambolic and—despite their varied and increasing state of decomposition—aimless and ambulant. There were several in the viewfinder, ambling across the open fields ahead like an ill-fated Sunday morning rambler's club. At once I was consumed with sadness and revulsion; emotions that blended into a toxic mix of duty.

I watched one of them now; the shell of a man struggling to walk up a hill. His right leg was shaped as an ugly "Z," impeding his progress, his face sloppy, slack and impassive; his left cheek slapped against his shoulder as his mouth discharged ropes of purple-black goo down the front of his dishevelled business suit.

And in his right hand, oblivious to him, he clutched a brief case; the black leather wet with his over-ripe juices and lichen-green grime. The hand clutching the case betrayed his pre-existence, a wedding band glimmering in the noon sun; once a husband, a father, now a lost, hapless soulless soul struggling to assail an embankment. Its efforts were as relentless as they were pitiful. My heart scudded in my chest. Not fear, never at this distance; but breaking for his loss, his family's loss. No Blakewell Spirit here. It is a rare thing. I know this with a gnawing certainty.

The distant shape shivered mildly in the viewfinder, my hands shuddering as shoulders shrugged and shimmied in time with my sobs.

"Poor bastard."

I brought the binoculars away and stowed them in their sheath at my hip. I mopped my eyes on my sleeve. Shit. I was sentimental before all of this stuff happened. A while back most of my friends would tease that I should've been born a girl. Some went as far as to ask when the gender reassignment appointment was due. Office life was dull but a blast once you had a good team around you. I made a living selling insurance; the irony was plain to see when the apocalypse took a stroll across the world. I'd laughed so hard I almost messed myself. There was a lot of madness mixed in with the mirth.

No joking now, of course. No office either, just last offices for those who were shot in the head to make sure that they stayed still for good.

"See much?"

Annie Kane was at my side, all 5' 4" of her; buried in swathes of combat fabric and the SA80 assault rifle huge in her grasp.

She looked like a kid playing "army." I'd told her that once and it earned me an oversized boot to the shin.

"The usual."

"Shit. You okay?" she said. The "smiley" badge on her Alice band appeared to conflict with her grim countenance.

"Yeah," I said. "We're lucky. Sometimes it makes the guilt bite harder."

She nodded and the movement made a strand of mousy hair fall from its cordon of fabric and onto her cheek. She scanned the vista and put the errant lock back in place, clucking her tongue in tune to "iCarly."

"You thinking of the recon or the kids?" I sniffed.

"Can't think of one without the other," Annie said. "That's why we're up here and the world below has gone to shit, right?"

That was The Blakewell Spirit talking, the family—the community—our bedrock. It was who we were and all we fought to maintain. The recons were part of this, excursions into what had become known as The Wilderness, to see the lay of the land, gather information and find other survivors.

So here we were, Annie and I, trawling the Worcestershire countryside for those who were walking but still had life in their eyes and air in their lungs.

"Guess we'd best move on," Annie said, slinging the rifle over her right shoulder and heading towards our ride: a black Range Rover sporting a skirt of mud and chopped grass.

In the Range Rover, our third team member sat manning the short wave. Tom Bramwell was a small man with a big heart. Before The Sickness he was in real estate yet these days he was the one who made sure that things were just kept real.

"You guys giving up that easily?" Tom said from the driver's seat. "You've only been on lookout for a few minutes." He placed the cup of a set of headphones to his left ear like some urban DJ, his blonde crew cut adding to the affect.

"You can't see what isn't there, Tom," I said as I climbed into the passenger seat. "You hearing anything?"

Tom shook his head, his fingers slowly twisting the dial of the scanner sitting on the dash, a hyphened line of red lights responding to his touch. The hi-tech equipment wasn't alone on the dash. It shared the plastic shelf with several photographs, images of Blakewell and our community, group shots, all smiles and hugs, and family portraits; portable slices of home for the journey.

Julia, my wife of twenty years, was amongst them, her hair dark and bobbed and a smile that warmed my post-apocalypse soul; and Maddie, my beautiful six year old angel was standing on her mother's lap, face bright with life; a testament to all we aimed to protect. I thought of them both chilling out back in Blakewell and sighed a little. They were my world, after all.

"You planning on coming back to us some point soon?" Annie laughed.

"Sorry," I said.

"Hold up!" Tom said, his voice enthusiastic. "I think I got something."

"Put it on speaker," I said. Not an order, that's not the way we do things.

Tom disconnected the headphone jack as Annie leaned forward from the back seat, her face so close to mine that I could smell the soap on her skin. I thought about the first time we'd had sex and it settled me. Monogamy was Old Skool in Blakewell. Share and share alike, no need for societal breakdown and lawlessness. The Blakewell Spirit, extending beyond rhetoric for the good of all. It shouldn't have worked, but it did; it kept us in control, kept us focused on what was important: survival. Hope as bastion against a futile future.

"I don't hear any—" I began but Tom interjected.

"No one is going to hear anything if you carry on jabbering. Listen!"

The scanner fizzed, an incessant hiss that filled the car, reminding me of the sound of a summer rain shower hitting the windscreen of my MG back in the days before the dead ate the living.

Just when I thought that it would yield nothing, a low discordant murmur emerged through the white noise, an unintelligible whisper that slowly morphed into chatter in the scanner's grill.

"You seeing 'em, Eddie?" A female voice but harsh, hardened.

"Yeah, I got 'em, Alex," the man who would be Eddie replied. "Three marks at two o'clock."

"How we playin' this?" Alex said in between bursts of hiss and fizz.

"Treat as hostile until proven otherwise," Eddie shot back.

"Sounds like these guys are on recon," Tom whispered as though the people on the scanner could hear. "They mean business."

"Yeah," I said. Three marks at two o'clock. "That pretty much sums it up."

"Us?" Annie said whimsically. The smile on her face was in fierce competition with her "smiley" badge. "Guess we'd better show 'em we're not bad guys, then, eh?"

But before I could answer, there was the sharp rap of metal on glass to my left. I turned toward the sound and found myself staring out of my window, and down the ditch dark barrel of an AK47.

"Get out!" said the guy with the gun. "And keep your hands where I can see them." I raised my hands and continued to stare at the muzzle. It was stock-still, no sign of confusion or hesitation; the hallmarks of experience.

"We don't mean any harm," Tom said as he opened his door.

"I'll be the judge of that," our captor said gruffly. "And it's too damn early in the game to make that call. Now, leave all weapons in the cab."

I finally saw past the gun jammed in our direction. It would be overstating things if I referred to him as a 'man', he was more a teenager with dark, shoulder length hair resting on broad shoulders. He was lean and mean, I saw the latter in his green eyes; eyes that had seen too much, too young as the song goes.

His Judas Priest T-shirt said that he was "Screaming for Vengeance" and he probably was in so many ways. Given his familiarity with the rifle I guessed he was well on the road to retribution. I hoped he could determine the signs that differentiated friend from foe along the way.

We each exited the car, our weapons abandoned on the seats and in foot wells. It mattered not. We had other defences, strength of spirit and a will to perpetuate community to name a few. Not much against a bullet, but a bullet is the end game, isn't it? You had to defend early, communicate. It was the finger on the trigger and the inclination to pull on it that ultimately ended you. None of us had any need of a full metal jacket being added to our outfits, so we learned to suss not shoot very early on in this game of survival.

And, so far, we'd failed to lose a game.

"What you got there, Carl?"

Another voice now; from behind us. Female; the tone of the question from someone older.

No one turned. Carl's AK47 holding us firm. We waited patiently for the woman to materialise.

"Not sure, sis," he said.

Sis came into view; tall and majestic, she commanded our attention even without the Beretta she had trained on us.

"Then I guess we'll have to wait for Eddie to come and have a pow-wow," the woman said.

She looked directly at me, her eyes—blue as ice—sparkled in the sunlight; unruly blonde hair framing a face as stern as it was beautiful. She had fine lines under her eyes and in the corners of her mouth, laughter lines—as they were once called—though I figured that it had been some time since this woman had much to laugh over. I knew the look instantly, family determined to protect her kin. I respected that even though the care ethic came at the end of a Beretta. She had the weapon drawn and aimed at us, finger outside the guard and pointing down the barrel, pointing at me. Safety first, safety off, I presumed.

"If you're going to shoot us, can we at least know your names?" Annie said to the woman. She was going to work early, trying to establish the social order in play. Psychology had become the new master in a world gone insane.

"Alex," the woman said without hesitation. "And I'm not calling the shots on who gets shot, get me?"

"I guess so."

"No point trying to sweet talk her, Annie," I said. "Alex, here, doesn't carry any weight in the decision making."

"I carry enough," Alex said in a caustic tone. "Especially if someone chooses to get smart. We clear on that?"

She was tough, but it was by proxy. It never went all the way to her eyes.

"Crystal," I conceded all the same.

She seemed satisfied with that, the token assertion putting me in my place, putting her back on top. I figured she liked being on top. Oddly, I wondered if that was how she liked to make love.

The sound of a vehicle grabbed my attention. At first it was a low hum, like a bumble bee cruising low as it targeted a patch of flora. Then the noise thinned out, easily distinguished in the silent world about us. A van, a Ford Transit by my estimation. This time I did risk turning and watching the van growing in size as it sped towards us, leaving a thick blue smoke trail in its wake.

"That thing is blowing oil," I said. "You guys will be lucky if it gets here."

"It'll get here," Alex said. Even if she didn't feel it, her tone was confident. I admired the bluff.

"That damn thing is going to get us noticed," Tom said looking at the smoke. "The world's a goddamn car showroom and you take that?"

"You're already on the radar, mister," Carl said. "And we were raised right, you don't take what's not your own."

"The world's changed some, son," Tom said. "All bets are off."

"I ain't your son," Carl shot back, defiantly.

"No," Tom said with sorrow, "my son is- " his sentence faded.

"Easy, Tom." Annie reached over and squeezed her friend's arm. "It'll be okay."

I watched the van coming towards us, not sharing Annie's assessment one little bit.

The van pulled up behind the Range Rover, the doors flying open as soon as the engine cut out a swirling cloud of dust pumped skywards where it mingled with the blue smoke to create a dark, dirty smudge on the air.

The person who came forward snapped off the safety catch, the staccato click loud in the silence. He was a big man with an even bigger beard, carrying a machine pistol; his hulking, muscular shape swathed in a green combat jacket and cargo pants.

"You got 'em, Alex," the big man said. I saw his grin emerge from beneath his beard like a beast from the undergrowth.

"You bet, Eddie," Alex said. I noticed that she appeared tenser now that Eddie was here. This wasn't good news. It meant she knew something we didn't. Nothing like not being in the loop; especially when there were loaded guns in the mix; guns with the safeties off. Suddenly I didn't want to be in the loop for fear it turned out to be a noose.

"Why are you doing this?" Tom said to the approaching man. I was grateful, it saved me the job.

"I'm doin' the askin' from here on in," Eddie said. "Got that?"

"What do you want?" I said regardless.

Yeah, I was pushing buttons, dipping an infected toe in the dirty waters, some might say. But the world already had *The Sickness*, it needed no other god. Human or otherwise.

"What I want," Eddie said as he aimed his machine pistol towards Annie, "is her."

Overhead a large crow let go a squawk, putting a dent in the wall of silence Eddie's comment had built around the moment.

"You want me?" Annie said, bemused. "As in sex?"

"Yes," Eddie said. "And I want you now. In the van."

"Smooth talk a speciality of yours, is it?" I said.

"No," Eddie said patting the gun in his mitts. "I got other talents."

"Well I'll be the judge of that," Annie said removing the webbing from her fatigues. The material spooled at her feet like discarded intestines.

"What?" Eddie's face went through several expressions until it settled on confusion. But it was on the raggedy edge, a chasm of suspicion lay waiting below.

"I'm sorry," Annie said. "I thought you said you wanted me?"

Eddie's steely demeanour buckled for a moment. His power play had backfired. In making a clear statement of group domination, he'd been outflanked and driven into a corner from which there wasn't any coming back. I saw something in him that may have been relief briefly surfacing. Then it was sucked beneath waves of suspicion.

"You saying that you'd do that willingly?"

"If you take it as proof that we mean no harm, then yes I will."

The surprise on his face told us that he wasn't used to such candour. How could he be? He'd never been exposed to The Blakewell Spirit, didn't know the level of determination fuelling it.

I looked over at Alex; saw those blue eyes and what was in them.

Not me today, they said. Today I get a break from having him inside me. I couldn't figure if there was envy or relief in such injunction.

"What about these guys?" Eddie said jerking his head towards

Tom and me. "They going to behave while we get it on?"

"Sunday best," Tom said evenly.

"What about you?" Alex said, the Beretta in her hand wavering slightly. There was hope in her eyes, hope I wasn't going to be a proverbial boil on the buttocks.

"Its Annie's call, not ours," I said.

"He's got that right," Annie said. She stepped up to Eddie and ran her fingers across the machine pistol. "You won't need your toys for a while." Her eyes were coy, her voice husky with seduction. A 5' 4" siren melting the man mountain that was Eddie.

Eddie switched on the safety and allowed the weapon to hang on the strap about his shoulder. He put a big arm about Annie and steered her towards the van.

"No peeking," Annie called to us as Eddie pulled open the back doors and lifted her inside. The doors slammed shut seconds later.

"What say I just keep a lookout so nothing bites us on the ass whilst people procreate?"

"Look the other way, you mean?" Alex said. It was a small comment, but the wind brought it to me. Contempt fell from her lips like bitter spittle.

"You don't get us," I said. "But you will. In time."

"What's not to get?" Alex said. "You'd let a stranger take your woman."

"Annie belongs to no one," Tom said. "She makes her choices for the good of our community. As do we all. We will all benefit from her actions here."

I reached for the pack on my hip and Alex brought up the Beretta again.

"What are you doing?"

"Binoculars," I said. "Remember the keeping a lookout part?"

She bobbed her head, but the pistol stayed steady. Carl was watching me intently, his face twitching with confusion.

"Where you from?" he said, the suddenness of it made me jump slightly.

"South east of Birmingham," Tom said. By this time he'd taken to sitting on the grass, his legs a "V" of camouflaged fabric against the blades and daisies.

"You're some way out," Carl said. "What brings you this far?"

"People," I said simply, the world now pulled close by the artificial vista in the viewfinder. The zombified businessman continued his uphill struggle; death possibly mirroring his lifestyle.

"You on a quest or something?" Carl mused. "Like King Arthur?"

I smiled. I guess there was still some of the kid left in him. It was buried deep beneath layers of anxiety and trauma, but it still wanted out, like a bright light finding the chink in the blackout curtains. It made me sad for him. And it made me think of Maddie, curls and frills and full of life. My smile broadened so much my cheeks ached.

"If you mean are we always looking for people to become part of our community, perpetuate the family, then yes, I guess you could call it a quest."

I returned the binoculars to the pouch, their job done. The world hadn't changed since our guests had arrived; an ambiguous mix of life and lifelessness.

"So how about you guys. Where are you from?" I said.

"Nowhere," Alex said. At first I thought she was being defiant, guarded. But the sadness in her voice hinted at something more than simple vanguard politics. They weren't part of a colony, they were nomads, rudderless souls drifting through a blighted landscape known to us as The Wilderness, a place to pass through on our way to Blakewell. But to these folks it was a way of life.

"That must be awful," Tom spoke my thoughts out loud. "You mean you have no home? No community?"

"Community is overrated, as I remember it," Alex sniped. But it was a cheap shot from someone craving the high life. And the neutered tone in her voice, the lack of conviction, gave her away like a school snitch.

"You may be right," Tom said. "But family isn't overrated, right? You guys must realise that above all others."

I saw Alex and Carl exchange glances, a brief, unspoken accord between brother and sister.

"You could come with us," I said. "Be part of something bigger."

"Bigger than what?" she said.

I looked about me, indicating the still, sullen landscape. The emptiness. "This?"

She appeared genuinely surprised. "I got a gun in your face and you're waving an olive branch?"

"The Blakewell Spirit transcends all, Alex," I offered, noting how her shoulders sagged a little when I said her name. Resignation that maybe—just maybe—we weren't bad guys after all.

"It's not my call," she said. Her eyes flitted to my left, towards the van. A dirty white hunk of metal inside which a new kind of parley was in force. Two groups becoming one in the ultimate act of unity.

"Eddie will make the right choice," I said. "You'll see."

Alex's gun was no longer trained on us. Even the muzzle of Carl's rifle pointed at the grass, redundant.

Then the rhythmic squeak of the van's aged chassis augmented the moment, punctuated by muted cries, not of pain, but ecstasy; the impasse pushed aside by passion.

The transit stopped its jig as two huge sighs faded away to nothing. In the quiet that followed I looked over at Tom who was busy plucking grass and allowing the southern breeze to play with the blades. The scene was sedate. Only the faint stink of decay betrayed the reality, that and the ease in which sex was now given as commodity.

After a few minutes the doors of the transit creaked open and Annie and Eddie jumped down onto the grass.

As they walked towards us I noticed that Annie's neck and cheeks sported an isle of red flush. I'd seen it before and I knew what it meant. Eddie had done the do; Eddie had taken her to a place where for an instant the horror of The Sickness was shut down; Little Death turning its back on its much bigger brother. Even now he had an arm about her; his new found lover, his saviour in a world sinking in sin.

The warmth in my belly reflected the radiance on the faces of the post-coitus couple. The deed was done, the decision made. All would be well.

"Alex," Eddie said, his voice smooth and at ease.

"Yes?"

"These people are our family," he said.

Carl and Alex nodded and stowed their weapons; the Beretta went into the waistband of Alex's cargo pants, the AK47 slung over Carl's shoulder.

Annie smiled as she stopped a few feet from me.

"Have fun?" I said.

She squeezed Eddie's waist. "You betcha."

"Now what?" Eddie said. His eyes had lost their doubts, suspicion now a ghost lost in the ether.

"We go home," I replied.

We left the van behind, the transit now a ghost on the green landscape. Our Range Rover absorbed the new members of our community with ease. They brought little with them. A few packs and sleeping rolls, all unkempt; evidence of life on the move.

Eddie told us that they'd travelled light, making them less likely to be caught off guard. We were saddened to learn that in the East, at least, there were few still walking with a pulse. Most had perished at the clamouring, gnarled hands of the undead. There were other communities but they were closed to outsiders, paranoia the new politic in this awful era. Most were shooting people out of fear.

Better safe than bitten was the new mandate, it seemed.

"The world has gone to Hell," Eddie said. The man who had waved a machine pistol was gone; calmness had come to him like a lover in the night. Or maybe a Ford Transit.

"You're going to a better place," Tom said, his eyes flitting from the terrain ahead and the rear view mirror. "The residents of Blakewell welcome you."

Alex was sitting next to me, the hands in her lap—redundant now that she had holstered the weapon—fidgeted, fingers interlacing and unfurling rhythmically.

"Penny for those thoughts of yours," I said.

"Money is dead, haven't you heard?" she said smiling. Her face was a mask of fatigue but it didn't blight her beauty. Or her strength. She was stoic and resilient and honest.

And I wanted her. I could not deny it, the thought of being inside her, feeling her skin—slick and salted—on my tongue was too much to bear.

"When we get to Blakewell," she said quietly, "maybe you could show me around?"

One of her hands moved from her lap and found mine, squeezing gently.

"I'd like that," I said.

"This idea of sharing each other, the good of one for all," she said quietly, "does that extend to you?"

"You mean us?"

"Yes," she said.

I nodded and allowed my eyes to play on hers for a while.

"Good," she whispered.

As was usual, the journey back to Blakewell was indistinct. When survivors were found there was no stopping, we travelled, we ate, without respite. There was too much to lose in stopping. Jerry cans strapped to the 4x4 meant we didn't need to risk pulling over to siphon petrol pumps of long abandoned fuel stations.

We took turns in driving, even Eddie and Alex doing their share under our instruction. The roads were a chicane of wrecks and abandoned vehicles, yet we were able to navigate with authority; this was *The Wilderness*, after all. A place full of shells; buildings, vehicles, people— the living and the dead—everything empty, broken.

And amongst it all: Blakewell, our home, our Bastion against the barbaric. I sighed as the sign leading the way came into view, iconic and beautiful, and announced that we had a mile before we could see our own again, a mile before I could be with my wife and daughter and fill my heart with the mere sight of them.

"Here we are," Annie said from behind the wheel. Through the windscreen I could see two trucks blocking the road. Not by chance this time, but by design. A gateway in the shape of a skip wagon and a three quarter truck, parked alongside each other. As we approached, figures appeared in the cabs; and the heavy chug of diesel engines coming to life filled the air.

Carl appeared restless, his fingers drumming against the butt of the rifle lying across his lap.

"Nearly there," Tom said quietly.

Carl nodded, but his fingers continued their tiny tattoo on the weapon's wooden stock.

The trucks moved aside, allowing us through. Beyond, there was a narrow access road that climbed to a one quarter gradient. Before *The Sickness* had left its stain, it was known locally as Rose Hill. These days we called it Ascension, an incline that lifted us from the hell that was *The Wilderness*, and into the haven of home.

Rose Hill had changed in other ways. Once, trees arched over the road, creating a rough green canopy that let in little light, whilst hedgerows of honeysuckle made the air heavy with its thick, sweet perfume.

But now Ascension was enclosed, the trees and the hedgerows barred by a rectangular structure constructed from bricks, mortar and concrete that gave the impression of driving into an underground car park. At intermittent points, lights threw dim, creamy splashes on the dull walls, and Annie activated the headlights to help her out a little.

"What is this place?" Eddie said thickly. I noted that his voice had lost its gruff tone, especially when addressing Annie.

"Don't worry," Annie said softly. "This just makes it more difficult for outsiders to get inside."

I watched Eddie bob his head.

"What's at the end of it?" Alex said.

"A decontamination suite," I said. "Just to make sure."

"Make sure of what?" Carl said.

"That we only bring back what we intend to bring back," I explained. "Seems to work, too. We've had no further outbreaks since the early days."

"How many did you lose?" Alex said, her face wan with experience.

"Enough to make a difference; to change things, forever," Annie sighed as the concrete corridor ahead swallowed the light.

"We lost some of our community, but we found them again, in each other, in the people we return from *The Wilderness*. It gives us all hope."

"Hope? It's been a while since I heard that word said with conviction," Eddie said. He stared ahead, his persona suddenly melancholy.

"Hope is alive and well in Blakewell," Tom said brightly. "You'll see."

We all drifted off to our own quiet corners for a while, six people each with their own stories to tell. But at that moment we were relishing them in private. I had a sated heart, we had brought new blood to the village of Blakewell, and that could never be a bad thing. It meant that life could go on, the past, present and a future maintained as one. It felt good.

I felt good.

The Range Rover stopped at a large, gated archway. As Annie hit the horn twice, the big doors eased inwards giving out to a compound hewn into a neat square and walled with a green, mesh fence.

Two adjacent rectangular buildings took up space in the centre; both prefab portacabins that had once served a building site before migrating to Blakewell.

At the opposite end of the compound lay another gate, guarded by two Blakewell villagers, each armed with high powered rifles.

I saw Alex watching them, her face impassive. I imagined what life must've been like for her, all those months in *The Wilderness*. The experiences that she carried with her, the trauma that made the presence of gun toting guards appear totally normal. My heart ached for her loss, whatever that may have been.

"What now?" Eddie said as Annie killed the engine.

"We decontaminate," Tom said. "You go to the building on the right, we go left."

"Why?" Carl said.

"Only the pure get into heaven," I said winking at him. "Such is Ascension."

"Yeah, I get the decontamination part," he said flatly. "But why we splittin' up?"

"The stations only take three at a time, Carl," Tom said softly. "I guess us Blakewell folk are used to getting down to our bare skins in front of each other and presumed you may not be as bold."

"But if you're happy to get buck naked in front of Annie here then let's mix n match," I offered. I watched Alex shuffle on the spot.

"I see what you mean,," Alex said, her pale cheeks no mask for the slight flush blossoming there. "It'll be okay, Carl. Let's you and me go with Eddie and meet up with these guys on the other side."

"If you say so," the boy replied sullenly.

"She does," Eddie said.

Decision made.

I entered the prefab building and stepped up to a bank of lockers in the small ante chamber beyond. Shrugging off my wilderness gear I pulled a pack of cigarettes from my combat pants and sparked up, much to Annie's disgust.

"You told me you'd quit," she said.

"I lied."

"Well we all do that from time to time," Tom said unloading his own gear.

Annie nodded wistfully. I thought at that moment she was the most beautiful woman in the world.

"Yes we do," I replied. "But we lie for our community, don't we? We lie to maintain the Blakewell Spirit?"

"Yes," she said. "You with your cigarettes. And me with my love."

"You are a siren," Tom said. "No doubt about that."

She was a siren. Today she was Eddie's siren. His muse, his false promise. He was the strongest in the team and Annie made him weak, pliable. That was her role in all this, of course. Find the chinks in the armour, before setting out the stall and selling hard. And the deal? Blakewell and the safe haven it provided to those lost in The Wilderness. The comfort of company, sanctuary from the insanity. A silken path from The Wilderness to the car and finally to Blakewell and the decontamination building.

No decontamination facility in our building, of course. Just an empty shell, a prefab Trojan Horse stuffed to the vacant rafters with deception.

The building opposite faired no better. No scope for washing away the potential ills of *The Wilderness*. But it wasn't vacant. It wasn't a shell. It was refrigerated and bristling with our community. They were all there, Maddie, Julie, Annie's husband and two kids Jessica and Andy, Tom's wife Louisa and Gem, his son; the cold not only keeping them slow, but keeping them fresh.

Right now Eddie, Alex and Carl were becoming part of the community in a very real sense. The kind of sense that would have our cherished families gorging on their flesh, bellies opened to the frigid air and the gouts of steam rising, creating fleeting fog.

The Blakewell Spirit is alive and well, even in these, the darkest of times. Family and community transcends, that is clear to us. We embrace it, revel in it.

I took Annie's hand and we stepped into the compound.

"Shall we?" I said and she smiled serenely.

"Of course."

We went over to the refrigerated building where a viewing slot allowed us to observe our families lost, yet still loved. Others were joining us, others who needed to see their loved ones engage. Engorge.

And there we all stayed for an hour, watching them feed, their pale faces turned red, their clothes splashed with the life blood they craved more than anything.

I watched my darling daughter slurp a tendon as though it was a strand of spaghetti. I watched as Julia stuffed something red and grey into her yawning mouth.

I thought, as I often did at these moments, if others may consider our efforts to preserve our kin acts of inhumanity. Then The

Blakewell Spirit would rise and suffocate all doubt. I could look upon my Maddie, cradle her and her mother in my arms, even, if the freezer was cranked up high enough, and know she would always be with me. All she needed was fresh meat from time to time. How could I deny them that?

It was the same for Annie. And Tom. And the others who had rethought a life in order to stave off the undeath *The Sickness* had brought to our beloved village. We had to adapt, change the rules, so that we kept things the way they were before *The Sickness*. It kept us decent. It kept us human. And that made things right, didn't it?

Didn't it?

LULLABELLE

Rachelle Bronson

THE NIGHT SLOWLY SLIPPED OFF HER like an old dirty shirt, revealing more and more of the frigid morning, when a tapping on the window pane grew insistent.

A brief moment of dread and confusion froze her beneath her covers. Had they returned? Was it finally her turn to die?

She poked her nose out into the cold air and suddenly remembered that it couldn't really be them. After all the government was taking care of that issue.

She remained silent and unmoving for minutes until she was sure that it really wasn't one of them that had managed to elude the army. Only then did she throw out an arm to test the air. She shivered and curled back up into a ball.

Tap…tap…tap…

She groaned and threw off the blankets. "Fine! I'm coming already."

She rubbed her arms and blew hot breath into her hands. A fire would be the first order of the day. She moved quickly about the small attic apartment, throwing on her robe and slippers, building a decent size fire in the small stove, and putting the kettle on.

She remained crouched in front of the open door, letting the fire get air and her hands get warm, mesmerized by the dancing flames.

Tap…tap…tap.

"Alright then," she breathed, and moved to the tiny cabinet in the corner of the kitchenette. She pulled out a balled up paper bag, dumping its contents on the counter. She took a wooden spoon from its nail on the wall and began slowly smashing up the dried bits of bread into fine crumbs.

Tap…tap…tap.

She rolled her eyes, brushed the crumbs into her hand, and moved swiftly to the window. She slid the curtain back, opened the window, and dumped the crumbs on the window sill in a tiny pile.

"There. That's all I have right now…stop being such a pest." She didn't even glance at the pigeon before pushing the window back into its frame. Over the screeching kettle she didn't hear it pop back out gently.

She hummed to herself, a lullaby her mother used to sing to her, as she moved about preparing her breakfast of tea and toast with jam, not noticing the window inching open.

When she was done eating, she stoked the fire, threw her nightgown onto the bed, and padded to the bath in the opposite corner of the room. She ran the water for a few minutes and thanked God that today it was somewhat hot. She got in the tub and drew the shower curtain all the way around. Even though it did not have much pressure, she stood under the water for a long time, until her skin was red.

The telephone rang. She sighed deeply, wrapped herself in a towel, and raced to answer it before the downstairs neighbour's heard. She didn't want them to know she was home. She didn't notice that the window was wide open.

"Yes," she whispered.

"Anna. It's me." Her sister's voice seemed urgent.

"What is it? What's wrong?" Anna frowned.

"I need you to come and watch the children. Something's happened at the crematorium and they need me to come in early for my shift. Frank is there working late and can't make it home."

"Oh…have they got more of them coming in?"

"I think so."

"Alright. I'll be there soon."

Anna replaced the receiver in its cradle as a shiver racked her body. That's when she finally noticed that the window was open and the curtain was flapping in the cold October breeze. Her brow furrowed as she moved to close it but stopped cold when she felt a flutter against her bare feet. A sharp scream escaped her lips and she jumped back quickly, scrambling to get on top of the bed. The pigeon just sat there, unconcerned, its back to her, pecking at the floor.

"Oh, it's you. Well, aren't you a clever bird?" Still clutching her chest, she moved to get off the bed, but quickly stopped when the bird turned its head and stared right into her eyes. She gasped. It cocked its head to the side slightly and began slowly moving towards her.

"Shit!" She breathed through her teeth, as she finally noticed the blood matted in its feathers and oozing boils of pus. The usually black, bright and inquisitive eyes had been replaced with glassy milky pupils that seemed to not really see her, yet know exactly where she was.

How could this disease that had only infected humans before, making them into mindless flesh and organ eaters suddenly take over a bird?

But she couldn't deny the sign. She couldn't take the risk. She had to kill her little adopted pet before it attacked and infected her, or got away and tore into someone else.

She watched the pigeon she'd lovingly named Lullabelle, as she slowly tried to move off the bed. Left. Right. Left. It managed to sightlessly match her every move, all the while gaining ground. If she was to survive its attack she had to move now.

Anna jumped from the bed and ran to the kitchenette, losing her towel in the process, and quickly put her back against the cupboard.

And, just like she knew it would, the bird launched itself towards her, half flying and half running along the floor. It jumped and lunged for her so quickly, stabbing its beak, she barely had time to react. But she managed to slip a steel serving plate in front of her face before it could peck at the spongy softness of her eyes.

The loud clanging rang through the apartment, vibrating against the walls, through her fingers and up her arms, as its beak repeatedly hit the steel plate, making it hard for her to hang onto her only defense. Her hands throbbed, pecked and bloody.

She had to end this now. Quickly she brought the plate over her head and sliced through the air, bringing it down hard over the little bird's skull. She only stopped when she heard it crunch and shatter.

Anna took a deep breath, slid down to the floor next to it, examining its lifeless little body. But just as she thought she'd killed it, the pigeon jumped to its feet and resumed it single minded advance. Dead or not, it still wanted to eat her insides.

Anna didn't waste a second however. She scrambled up on her hands and knees, reached up and opened the drawer where she kept her utensils, and wrapped her fingers around the cold metal handle of her gun.

She shot the bird straight on. The shot took the pigeon's head clean off and sent it flying across the room.

Now it had to be dead. She squirmed when the headless body returned to its feet, undeterred by the blood pouring from its neck, leaving a sticky red trail as it pressed on towards her.

Exasperated, Anna grabbed a dirty pot from the sink, scooped up the writhing body, placed the lid over it, and popped it into the fridge.

No more time to waste, she had to get to her sister's house.

Anna stood motionless at the corner of the cobblestone street, watching her apartment building, making sure that nothing had heard her gun shot.

That they weren't following her. Noises alerted them. Caused them to converge and remind them that they were hungry.

The human population had nearly all gone from this town. The only people left now were the army and those that ran the crematorium. But she knew now that if a bird could be infected, than the other animals could too.

She listened. Under the street lamp she felt oddly safe, its soft glow illuminating the ash that fell steadily from the sky. She could see the morning sun trying to shed light on the world through the thick grayness all around her, but it never really shone bright like before. Now there was just dull daylight to let them know when it was day and when it wasn't. The street lamps were always on. Now that the crematorium had opened another facility, it ran 24/7 and there was no escaping the constant ash that covered the world.

She looked up, flakes falling on her face and catching in her long dark lashes. She tried to imagine that they were fat snowflakes coming down in swirls from the heavens. But that was only for a moment.

Suddenly she realised that it was eerily quiet. Too quiet. Though the town was mostly deserted, there was always the noise of army vehicles, the train, and the odd dog barking. Now, there was nothing at all but the wind whistling between the buildings.

Anna shivered and shoved her hands in her coat pockets, sighing deeply as her fingers felt the cold steel of her gun barrel, reassuring her that as long as she had it she was safer. She had taken it from her father's lifeless body, right before he'd been turned during the first wave of attacks. Though it had only been a few months so much had happened it seemed like a lifetime ago.

She turned quickly now and moved down the street, her rubber boots leaving prints in the ash. Halfway to her sister's she shook her hair and flipped up her hood, carrying on with her head down.

A dog barked. She stopped dead in her tracks, fearful of all god's creatures now; her ears staining to pick up running paws, but only picking up the sound of a train leaving the nearby station.

The train whistle blew as it made its way down the track towards to the mountain top where they had built the crematorium. She knew its multiple cargo containers were packed full of infected humans. Everyone from here knew its purpose.

The barking jerked her back to her purpose. The dog sounded closer this time, so she moved with haste in case it, too, was infected like her Lullabelle.

As she marched up the steps of her sister's large house she heard it bark again. Had it followed her?

Facing the street, unsure if she was shaking because of the cold or her encounter with the phantom canine, Anna brought an unsteady hand to her sister's door and gave a sharp knock. The door swung open quickly and something small shot out and attached itself to her leg.

"Hi, Aunt Anna," it said, words muffled somewhat by a face buried in her long wool coat.

"Hello, Elsa," she whispered back, still looking over her shoulder. "How are you?"

"Hungry."

"Your mother didn't get you breakfast? Let's see what we can do about that then." Anna pushed in through the door. "I'm here!" she called into the house.

"Mother left." The little girl said, finally unwrapping herself from her aunt.

"What?"

"She said she was late and couldn't wait for you any longer, and to mind my brother and not to use the stove while you weren't here and …"

"When did she leave?"

"A while ago…what took you so long?"

"Where's your brother then?" She ignored the question. She

hated lying to the children and how could she explain that she was nearly killed by a pigeon?

"In the backyard trying to get Smoky to eat something," Elsa replied crinkling her nose. "I think he's sick."

"Why do you say that?" she asked, removing her coat and boots, and making her way through the house.

"He looks sick."

Suddenly Anna flashed to her earlier encounter and she swallowed hard as her heart leaped into her throat. She ran towards the back of the house, yanked the kitchen door open with a hard swing, Elsa gasping behind her as it bounced off the wall, and rushed out into the backyard just in time to see the family dog writhing around under a rose bush.

"Ira, get away from him," she yelled grabbing the boy by the collar and dragging him towards the house. The boy yelped in surprise but wriggled away from her and raced back towards the dog.

"No. He's sick Auntie. I need to make him feel better."

"Ira…no!" she called after him. Only when hearing the fright in her voice did he stop and return to her.

"But—"

"Get in the house now. Take your sister with you."

He simply stood before her tears filling his eyes.

"Now please. Do as I say. I will go see about Smoky. And do not open that door until I say it's okay…got it?"

As much as she wanted to go into the house with them, lock all the doors and windows, and hide, she knew that with the war and everything the family had suffered, that dog meant more to all of them than anyone realised.

Only when she heard the door click shut did she make her way to where she'd seen Smoky. Anna moved slowly. Ira and Her scuffle with Ira had having risen ash from the cold ground and it now swished and swirled about into the air, obscuring her surroundings and creating a barrier between her and the dog.

She could barely see a foot in front of her. But she could hear the dog whining just at the edge of the yard. Anna waved a hand to clear the air, but she decided that following the dog's noises was easier. Just then her foot hit something hard and she cried out as she fell to her knees.

"Are you okay, Auntie?" She heard a soft whisper come from the house.

"Elsa, get in the house and stay inside with your brother," Anna said, whipping her head around. "I'm not going to say it again."

She heard the door click shut again and this time the lock turned in place. She took a deep breath and bent down, feeling through the soft ash for what she'd tripped over.

A long wooden handle surfaced and she quickly realized that it was the shovel her sister used to scrape the ash off the back stoop.

She used it to help prop herself up from the fall. Pain in her right leg registered as she tried to stand on it. Sucking air through her teeth, she looked down and noticed that her wool stockings were ripped and bloody. She must have cut her knee on the shovel.

Just then the dog started barking and she raised her head in its direction. She stood still, as silence seemed to swallow up all the noise around her. The same silence she'd encountered on the street. Even Smokey's barking seemed muffled, like it was underwater.

That's when she heard it, a swooshing noise that grew in intensity the more she strained to figure out what it was.

Anna waved a hand again to clear her line of sight, but the ash only danced and swirled around her head, making the shadows dart faster and the light seem like the enemy.

Just then she felt a flutter graze the top of her head. Instinct made her duck but surprise made her drop her makeshift crutch. She cursed under her breath and she bent down, blindly feeling the ground. She felt tiny razor-like claws sink into her injured leg.

She screamed out in pain as the bird didn't waste a second pecking with its sharp beak, tearing away her stockings and ripping chunks of flesh from her bloody wound. She only had enough time to pull it from her and throw it across the yard, before more claws descended from above, digging into her shoulders, neck and back.

Through all this she heard the dog whining and howling in pain behind her. She knew they'd gotten to him too. And by the time she managed to limp to the back door, he was silent.

"Open this door. open it right now!" She waved her arms wildly as she tried to bang on the door and keep the winged things off of her. Their wings flapping, their revelling cackles and the sticky sound of them ingesting her flesh consumed her senses, causing her to become disoriented.

"Please help me."

Just then light flooded from the house blinding her. With little hands grabbing at her, Anna gritted through the pain and scrambled into the safety of the house.

As her eyes adjusted to the kitchen lights, all she could focus on was the high pitched screaming coming from her niece and nephew. She strained to figure out the swishing and slicing sounds cutting through the air, but she soon realized it was a blade. Ira must have grabbed a knife. Then relief tickled her mind as she heard the thud of tiny feathered bodies hitting the ceramic tile after losing their attack.

"Stop screaming !" she yelled over them. She grabbed them both to her breast as she quickly took in her surroundings. The sight of her twelve year old nephew covered in blood, out of breath, and holding a butcher knife made her head spin and nausea rise in her throat.

"Auntie, you're hurt." She heard Elsa say as a rushing sounded in her ears. Before she could reply , Anna moved to the sink and vomited. She wiped her mouth quickly with the back of her hand. Finally noticing her gruesome wounds, she slid to the floor.

"Go get the first aid kit from the bathroom and then go to your parent's bedroom."

She saw the young girl hesitate.

"Go now, I'll be up there in a minute."

Elsa turned and ran through the kitchen, slipping and sliding on the blood soaked floor.

"Ira, go get my coat."

The boy didn't move eyes wide and teary.

"Ira, you did well. Your poppa taught you well. I'm proud of you. But it's not over. I need you to be brave now and go quickly. Get my coat from the foyer."

He was only gone a moment, but by the time he returned the bodies covering the floor had already begun to come back to life.

Ira opened his mouth in disbelief, too young to remember how the humans had behaved once infected. He screamed.

"Ok Ira. Now I need you to focus ... ok sweetie? One more

thing I need you to do." She searched his eyes for acknowledgement. There was none. "I need you to help me upstairs. We need to go up to your parent's room. Can you do that?"

Trembling he nodded and propped her up with his shoulders. They hobbled towards the staircase in the foyer, dead birds following their every move. Anna turned back and saw that the birds were gaining on them as they reached the bottom of the stairs.

"Ira, we need to go faster."

They tried to take the stairs two at a time, but her injuries prevented her legs from reaching that high. She had to think fast.

"Wait." She was reluctant to stop with the little army of writhing bodies nearly on them, but she had to do whatever it took to keep the children safe. She reached down into her coat and pulled out her gun. It seemed heavier than before but she quickly pushed it into Ira's little hand.

"Go upstairs now. Go in the bedroom with your sister,. You need to lock the door and push the dresser in front of it. You stay there till I come get you." She couldn't tell if his head was shaking from fear, denial or understanding. But before he could move, a guttural growl came from the bottom of the stairs. She'd forgotten about the doggy door.

"Smoky!"

Elsa's little voice echoed against the walls. Anna looked up to see her enthusiastically coming down the stairs, brown curls bouncing on her shoulders.

"Elsa, no. Stop!" she cried out, raising her hands. Before she could manage another thought the dog pounced, bounding up the stairs and sinking its sharp teeth into her flesh.

Anna cried out as burning pain shot through her right arm. The children screamed, as she shook her arm hard, trying to shake the dog free. Her shoe caught in the banister and she fell forward, head first down the stairs, taking the dog with her. Smoky only let go of her arm with a yelp when she landed on top of him, ripping a chunk of skin and muscle with him. The dog swallowed it, licking its lips before wriggling out from under her.

The dog got back on all fours quickly and sniffed the air. Its ears perked up and Smoky bared its teeth, dancing from one paw to the other. Panting…preparing…the amount of blood she was losing was obviously whipping it into a frenzy. But instead of wrapping her coat around her arm to curb the bleeding, she quickly threw it over the dog's head and scrambled for the solarium at the front of the house.

In her plight to save herself, she'd forgotten about the children. She turned quickly to brace herself against the doorframe and, as she did, everything suddenly seemed to turn into slow motion, like they'd suddenly become encased in honey. The dog broke free from her coat and started towards her. Ira raised the gun and a shot rang out. And just as Smoky lunged through the air, it howled in pain and crashed into her, sending her reeling backwards. Her socks slipped on the solarium's ceramic tiles. Her body was suspended in midair for a moment before it hit the wall of water below her.

Just when Anna thought she could simply let herself sink to the bottom of the pool until the dog's lungs filled with water, the children came to mind again.

She grabbed the dog by a leg as it tried to swim to the surface, astonished that the instinct to stay alive was still in there somewhere, but quickly realised that it was a grave mistake when

Smoky opened its vacant eyes and bit down hard on her hand, taking one of her fingers as a prize.

Anna opened her mouth in a silent scream and chlorinated water rushed in. She choked and gagged. She swam up and away from the dog, furiously kicking towards the surface. But before she could break for air she saw them. Dark little shadows circling and diving at her from above.

Futility overwhelmed Anna as the last of her air was pushed out by stinging water. And all she could think about was that she'd expected the water to be colder than it was.

ACCEPTABLE GENOCIDE

Shaun Hamilton

They gathered on the upper floor of their bleak concrete quarters, praying in silence. The fear of being heard by the Germans rippled through them as though it were electricity passing through water; they shivered on mass, their skeletons struggling to keep the dread under control. Starvation and hypothermia might one day take the blame for their deaths but it would be a heart no longer able to cope with the Germans' cruelty that would actually claim them. Either that or a bullet. They knew this as surely as they knew the loved ones they were no longer in touch with were already among the buried.

The men's squalid dormitory held fifty wooden bunk beds placed at 90° to each other, creating a maze within a labyrinth. They were told by their heavy-handed guards that it slept no more than a hundred but the true numbers were nearer a hundred and fifty. Those below eleven and over fifty weren't deemed worthy of a number—despite the one tattooed across their wrists. Some slept two to a bed, others gave their straw mattresses up to more vulnerable family members, choosing to sleep on the wooden floor using putrid cloth for their bedding. Such kindness stained their striped pyjamas with faeces and mud but gave them a clearer conscience. They shared their space with rats; rats and German boots which repeatedly kicked out, breaking bones or cutting flesh.

Not all of the men who made this place their home huddled together. Some lay on their beds and offered their own silent prayers; others ate at snippets of food they'd stolen or swapped for services rendered. One sat with a pile of leather boots on his bed, polishing and mending the officers' footwear with due diligence. His bony fingers shook as he thought of the consequences he'd suffer should one boot shine brighter than the others or a single lace be frayed when the rest straight and perfect. There was no electricity to give power to the room; no bulbs to give much needed light in his endeavours. To see close detail he had to take the boots to the wall where he would hold them up to the light from the security beacons outside, slicing into the room via the narrow windows tucked in tight below the ceiling. It was hard work but it was worth it: the last three pairs of boots had earned him a civil word and a single sausage. He had no kids. He held no loyalty towards anyone. He swallowed the sausage down so fast he almost vomited it back up. And if he had thrown it up, he would surely have eaten it again.

Whispers came from the far end of the room. The bed they surrounded was close to the stairwell; chosen so those on the floor below could hear the former Rabbi's words. Tobias had once been proud of his title. It filled his heart to know he could hear

God's voice and pass that word onto others. But to do so before the soldiers would surely result in his early death. He could not let that happen. Not yet. His God needed him here. Needed him to show these people that he still existed; that the horror they were forced to suffer was for a greater purpose. It was hard to get such a message through to those who had witnessed the rape and murder of their loved ones, or seen their land and possessions stolen by unworthy sinners, but now, more than ever, his commitment to the one true God was wanted. He had to show the people their God still loved them. That the day when they stand at his shoulder will be the day their suffering ends.

The Germans might succeed in claiming their lives but only God can claim their spirits

Kneeling against his bed the old man kept his head bowed, murmuring the Kabbalah; a holy text only a few knew. Not all knew why he chose these words but the most plausible rumour was they came from his home town. Tobias had lived in Sighet, Transylvania; a place where atrocities had taken place in 1943. Only a few knew of what Tobias had seen and the impact it held on the man.

His salt and pepper beard instilled wisdom; his furrowed brow and heavy eyes reminded of things wished unseen. The sugar-white skin hanging from his bones like curtain drapes was as rough as sandpaper. All who touched it seemed to know his age like reading brail. They grew strength from his very existence. As long as Tobias could pray on their behalf, their God knew of their unwavering devotion.

The noise came from downstairs.

The door had been kicked open. Heavy jackboots stomped across the floor, killing insects and lice. An angry voice called out. The rush of bare feet across splintered wood as Jews rushed to their beds failed to drown out the soldier's approachAll those on the upper floor knew of their brethren below was their own numbers were fewer. 300 refugees shared a ground floor space meant for 50 horses. Some of them screamed as German boots swung out and crushed bone and bruised flesh. None upstairs bore witness to the beatings but all knew the truth. They had seen it before; known it before—and knew they would know it again.

Like those only a few feet below them the prisoners moved. Beds were reached, mattresses laid up and sheets pulled up. Tobias moved slower than others, struggling to stand; a combination of age and ruthless beatings stealing his competence. A promising athlete before The Great War, too many years spent fighting and hoping had seen his summer seed pass beyond the harvest and draw towards the cold winter. Though it was true of all of those in there, he knew his time was coming. That his Lord would call for him and give him rest.

Dark metal helmets emblazoned with polished death's-head emblems emerged through the hole in the floor like the dead rising as four soldiers dashed up the stairs. The one up front—the eldest, whose scarred face was twisted in a vision of hatred—held a handgun close to his waist, the others wrapped their hands around the machine guns hanging from their shoulders. They passed Tobias without a glance; their shadows swallowing his lower bunk as search lights continued to strike the room through the glassless slits; they passed most of the room's occupants, determinedly winding through the maze as though being drawn by a magnetic field to their target. They stopped at the shoe polisher who had remained sitting as he worked, scared to move because to move would be to stop and to stop would surely mean another beating.

"What is this?" the first said, lifting his boot, stamping it on the man's frail thighs. Biting down on the scream the cobbler studied the immaculate black boot through his teary eyes.

"I...I see...see nothing."

"Nothing? You see nothing!" The guard punched the youngster in the face with his gun handle, breaking his jaw. The injured man dropped the boot he'd been working on and reached for his ruined mouth. "You sit there and say you see nothing, you pointless little bastard! Who the fuck do you think you are? Do you think you're better than me? Is that what you think? That your scrawny Jewish arse is far superior to my own?" He dug the boot's heel further into the man's thigh, driving through the finial of flesh until he reached the stick bone beneath. "Answer me, peasant! Is that what you think?"

Wildly shaking his head, blood and tears spilled over his pyjamas, smearing the yellow star on his chest all Jews were forced to wear.

"I can't hear you. Do you disobey me further by refusing to answer? Scuffing my boots and then trying to hide your incompetency is one thing, pig, but refusing to answer your betters is a punishable offence. Now answer me. Are you better than me?"

Trying to answer with mouse-like squeaks, the man's eyes scoured the room for help; for someone to give him the voice stolen by the jackboot. But no one spoke. They cowered. The hid. They closed their eyes and stuck their fingers in their ears. They pulled sheets over their heads and turned their backs. They did everything they could to save themselves.

"You screeching little shit! You disgust me!"

The bullet entered the cobbler's forehead, leaving a neat hole over his left eye that looked like a spare socket. It emerged with the force of a tornado, spraying the concrete with blood and brain that lost its embedment in the wall. A complete chasm erupted out of the man's cranium, smothering the bunk beds with small pulp lumps and sharp shards of skull.

Leaving the room in exactly the same manner they entered, the murderer called out, "Get that shit cleaned up before Selection or more of you will end up like him."

They laughed as they exited.

Her Kapo had beaten her for spilling the canister of soup.

Her Kapo was another prisoner who took perverted pleasure in administering the beating after the woman had struggled with the orders she'd given.

Her Kapo was another prisoner forcing her to work when they were both the same.

Even in this inhumane place such cruelty defied belief. How could someone who had already been beaten and raped by legions of soldiers turn round and hurt one of her own kind?

Because she had to.

She had to show who was boss in their dorm. Who was a favourite of the Germans. Who was the donkey and who was holding the whip. Muriel knew the woman was whoring herself to stay alive, but why the beatings?

If the Kapo had been doing her own job properly Muriel wouldn't have dropped the canister. Muriel was never going to be strong enough to hold such a heavy container. She was too frail. Too wasted by starvation. The oil drum had been filled to the lid with watery vegetable soup; its weight would have been immense even if she—or any other woman, man or child—were fit and healthy so what chance did she stand? She was a woman with tissue paper skin and brittle bones. What chance of carrying it from the Stores to the Kitchen?

None at all.

Men had initially helped to move it out of the stores but once outside they left her to their cigarettes. Then she and the Kapo manhandled it across the mud, each gripping a handle; each struggling to stay upright. The Kapo—who was fed on meat and drank hot coffee and wine—helped Muriel—who was fed stale bread and drank freezing water.

She lost count of the steps. It wasn't many. Even with both hands holding the handle it was only a matter of time before she fell. Four feet? Five?

Litres of bleached carrot and transparent potato chunks fell into the soil.

The Kapo managed to save most of the camp's weekly rations— Muriel stood with her back pressed against the closest hut in anticipation for the repercussions. Once the drum was set right. The Kapo strode over and kicked Muriel in the crotch; making her bleed like it was her monthlies. She would never have normally been pleased at the sight, but seeing the red seepage staining her dress confirmed there would be no German bastard. She couldn't be certain the multiple rapes had impregnated her, but none had used protection. She wept more at the thought of having their child than the actual rapes. Every day she checked her belly for growth. Every day she prayed to her God, 'Don't let it be so.' He spilt the drum for her; gave the Kapo the idea of kicking her there.

But now she had the pains. It felt like something inside her was ripped and could never be repaired. Her abdomen was swollen; bloated as though she were full. When she looked beneath her filthy striped dress she found skin as white as a piano's keys mottled with red and purple bruises. This reminded her of ink droplets on the blotting paper she used to use when writing her letters to loved ones. Her bones were so pronounced they held no secrets. Nothing suggested a good meal.

Her tears fell onto the soil at her feet. Some caught the breeze and slipped into the trench.

The grave.

Her punishment for spilling the soup had been severe. After the beating she and her dormitory had to go without rations for twenty-four hours. When she had finished her first meal in two days, she was forced to dig the trenches. Pits substituting for graves. Germans happily dumped the dead in great piles; slag heaps of limbs and broken torsos.

They said it was what the Jews deserved. Even the Kapo agreed when the officers taunted her. She would deny her race to save her own skin.

Only a few feet in front of Muriel rested a twisted mound of rotting bodies: men, women and children dragged off the land. Thousands of bodies wrapped around each other in a twisted, disgusting embrace. So many bullet holes perforating their malnourished flesh. Some had been pulled from their beds after their hearts had given up. Those carried out of the gas chambers were easily recognisable by the colour of their skin: green and cancerous; their yellow eyes bulging.

The stench was atrocious but Muriel was used to it. She had known the horror for too long. She could taste the putridness in her mouth; breathed the burned flesh constantly through her nose. Her skin was dusted in their ash, her hair greasy with their disease. She knew them all so well. So, so well.

The pit was more than six feet deep. Muriel was five feet tall when standing straight. The amount of bodies filling the pit was so high Muriel had to stand on her tiptoes and crane her neck upwards to see the peak. And still she and the others dug, making the hole wider. And still they dumped.

She had seen her mother's eyes in there, staring back at her.

"You're at peace now, mama," she whispered, turning away.

That earned her a slap across the cheek. The guard expertly cutting her paper-thin skin with her clunky ring..

Body and mind struggled with the effort needed to keep her alive. To stop working would mean death. To continue digging could kill her.

The blow was sudden and sharp, pushing her into the grave. She and the other women digging with her all suffered the same smash to the back of their heads; guards wielding coshes and gun butts, sending them spinning into the pits. Some died, their brittle craniums unable to withstand the blow; others were knocked unconscious, looking so much like their dead companions. The rest, like Muriel, struggled to stand on the rancid carpet, their bare feet becoming entangled in the spaghetti bowl of arms and legs, screaming mercy as the petrol was poured over the living and the dead.

The flames were hungry, tearing at the rotten flesh, devouring the living tissue. Their screams struggled to reach out of the fire; squealing bodily gases drowning out their pleas. A couple who hadn't fallen too far managed to drag their burning bodies towards the edge, blackened fingers scrambling at flaking mud. Soldiers shot through the outstretched hands, stealing the vestige of salvation.

Muriel forgot it all. Flames burst her skin and scorched her insides; vast waves of coal black smoke strangled her lungs but she left the nightmare behind. Forgot it all. All the hatred. All the pain. She turned away from the edge, showing her back to the laughing soldiers. Her mother's eyes found her from inside the heap's putrescent world. She saw her dead mother stand and smiled. Fighting to untwist herself free of the dead she struggled towards her daughter, arms outstretched in a reassuring embrace. Muriel's calls to her mother were choked off as her thorax split like bamboo. She didn't care. She had what she wanted. Beyond her mother's silhouette she witnessed the joyful Germans reaching into the pile with large spoons, gathering and spilling over the burning mound the litres of human body fat seeping from limbs and torsos. Wherever oil was thrown the flesh burnt ever more brighter. The soldiers clapped. Men and women applauded their atrocity.

But Muriel didn't care. She had mother.

The brick chimneys cast long shadows over the Birkenau death camp, their black smoke rising into the dull tin sky. Wooden huts stood in rigid rows; uniformed guards and tattered prisoners marched between them. The spacing between rows had been set out to ensure no despot could hide without being seen from one of the armoured towers dotted about the camp. The whole site was encompassed by an eight-foot high metal fence topped with razor wire; the base protected by wooden barriers and patrols walking with hungry Alsatians. Those not being marched stood in one great mass within the camp's central confines. Most assembled in lines—queues for doctors sitting at desks and their standing guards. The military men held clipboards they referred to as each captive passed. Weary men and women whose protruding bones had become their only features, stared at the healthy men in white coats with their dark hollow eyes. All were so emaciated they struggled to breathe. They wheezed together, their chests moving in sharp, shallow rises; others seemed to keep the air trapped inside for as long as possible, refusing to take in the chimney's poison as it sullied the land. They glanced up at the huge brick phalluses and knew the smoke's origin. They could not breathe properly; they would not breathe properly. They owed it to their friends and family.

The queues moved slowly.

"Name?"

"Ishmael Spiegel."

"Country of birth?"

"Hungary."

"Show me your wrist." The guard demanded. Reading the number scarring the wrist like a suicide wound he marked his papers with his pen before nodding to the doctor Taking this as his cue, opening Ishmael's arms out to the side, raising them above his shoulders and back down again. "What do you do about camp?"

"This morning I was fixing our hut's roof. This afternoon I am to move stones from one place to another."

"Do you think you can handle this work? It's not too much for you?" The doctor rudely opened the gaunt man's mouth and stared into the opening. Without a torch and in dull sunlight it was impossible for him to truly see what lay inside but he nodded in satisfaction.

"I can work," Ishmael answered in a voice so weak he must surely have been lying. The doctor sat back down.

"Good. You go to the left."

Doing as he was told, Ishmael shuffled into a yard to join a mass of other men, some of whom drew on rolled cigarettes as thin as a few strands of their shaggy, greasy hair.

The next one moved forward. The protocol repeated itself. Then the next, and the next and they all shuffled to the left.

But the next one?

"Name?"

"Mala. Mala Goldberg from Poland," she answered, her oft-practiced words spoken by instinct.

Mala shivered as the breeze passed through the crowds, her stinking dress wafting towards her midriff, showing more of her emaciated figure. She felt like she had become a metal hanger left behind in a wardrobe. There had once been a time when she carried curves men were desperate to hold; a time when her breasts, bum and hips had been her calling card. Now she was little more than a sack. A sack filled with sticks. Brittle, crooked sticks not even fit for burning. Who would want her now?

She broke off the self-revulsion by showing the doctor her wrist before he asked. Taking his eyes away from hers (did he spot something considered lost?) he glanced at the numbers, reading them off to the guard who nodded once in response.

"What is your job about camp?" the doctor asked?

"I…I'm a…a seamstress. I keep the German soldiers looking smart without the need to concern themselves about the expense of new clothes. I am good at my job. They come back. Always. Time and time again."

The doctor looked at her own wasted dress.

"Are you sure you are good at this?"

Mala stared at him in silence for a few seconds as it dawned on her what he was saying. She rubbed her hands down the dress's mottled front, feeling the horrid contours of her ribcage beneath

"I...er...I am too busy to care for my own clothes."

The doctor remained silent, studying her. Unlike the others, he hadn't stood up to check the suppleness of her limbs or to study her mouth's insides. "The soldiers," Mala continued, "they ask a lot of me. My hands are good...for the needles." She raised her left hand. It refused to stay still; as though the bones had been ripped out and the soft muscle snatched by a breeze. She dropped it back to her side.

The doctor maintained silence, He turned to the guard. They both shook their heads.

"Please no. Please, you cannot do this. I am good. I am strong." She thumped the desk, more in desperation than anger. "I can sew, I can farm. If I need to I will lift and carry." Still the doctor refused to speak. "I can...I can...if you'd like...I can...make your...your time in the camp...make it easier for you..." Her mind desperately scrambled for the singular reason the doctor might agree to keeping her alive.

"To the right."

Falling to her knees Mala screamed like an animal caught in a trap. Two male guards moved in. The first kicked her in the head. She fell, sprawling in the mud, unconscious.

Silently, others sent to the right retrieved their new companion.

Tobias began his incantation.

As the others scrubbed at the cobbler's body, preparing him for what they knew would be an indecent dumping instead of a respectful burial, Tobias sang. His voice held volume; he dragged it up from deep below his abdomen, setting it free into the murder room. His emphatic, gravelled singing spiralled around the room, bouncing off wood and concrete, reaching upwards towards the ceiling. Very quickly his echoes fell through the floor; both upstairs and down knew his words but realised little of their meaning. The man was known for his knowledge. His teachings. He uttered words others might say but never together, in sentences that made no sense.

His calling accompanied the cleaning. Using cold water carried from their own drinking troughs, men of differing heights but mirrored builds scoured at blood and scooped up the dead man's brain material. Each man retched as they gathered it in their freezing wet hands, scraping the amassed foulness into the exposed cranium. So hungry were they some wondered what the grey pulp tasted like. It looked like cold lumps of old porridge. It made them think of all the foods associated with cold porridge. Made them want the foods associated with cold porridge. But none performed the unthinkable…

A few hummed the former Rabbi's tune as though they knew what he was singing but they continuously lost the rhythm, exposing their naiveté. The remainder continued in silence, their tears washing filthy skin; tracks marking cheeks like slug trails across muddied leaves. Some stayed sitting and watched from their beds. A few turned to face the solid wall while one repeatedly butted his forehead into the concrete, splitting skin and smearing the uneven surface with his blood. He repeated his bashing in silence, no one thinking of stopping him.

No one could.

His voice booming, Tobias stood. Some looked at him with terrified eyes; the whites, yellowed with jaundice. They stared as though lying at the executioner's feet, watching the axe arch down towards their exposed necks. A few cowered, hiding further under their itchy blankets. More turned to face the concrete. Some edged towards the far gable wall, scared of the singing man's approach. The terrified urged him to shut up before the German's returned and punished them all for his insubordination.

A few cried.

But none felt the Rabbi's burning.

He reached the dead man. Those shivering with the cobbler's blood moved away, though none turned. All chose to keep their eyes on the powerful man with the white beard as they edged backwards, losing themselves to the shadows. None mimicked the other men's fears. A few even smiled as though Tobias's approach had broken through the crust of something that had held their souls for too long. They welcomed this.

The dead man lay sprawled on the bed.

A few of the terrified dared to look over. They did not understand. Why was this man so different? This cobbler? Why should this man take priority over the thousands already slaughtered by arrogant Germans psychopaths? And yet, instead of speaking, they watched. Watched Tobias lean forward. Watched him bend. Watched him sing his special words directly into the dead man's face before kissing the bullet's neat entry hole.

Tobias stood and turned away. As he approached his own quarters, the cobbler's cleaners returned to their work. Tobias sat, finishing his incantation with a single word:

"Return."

Not all killers are men.

The women continued to reach in and spoon the burning

with their own bubbling fat. Dozens of them watched the fires climb upwards, pulsing great tsunamis of smoke hundreds of miles across the country. A message being sent. The Germans are winning the war and they're winning in style. Their women do not sit at home and get fat like the Americans or kill themselves in the factories like the British, German women murder Jews. German women are vitriolic and as strong as their male counterparts. The bullets fired from a German woman's gun destroys many Jewish heads. The knifes pulled from their leather sheaths have gouged the eyes of men, women and children, all of whom wore the yellow star and carried that filthy blood in their veins. These women were proud of who they were and what they'd become.

The fires continued to rise as all before them lay dead and black. Jubilant with their endeavours, the soldiers celebrated by seeking out more to dig another ring to the pit.

An arm flashed out of the flames, grabbing the officer's ankle.

Surprised , she snapped her head round to see who was holding onto her. The sight of the blistered, charred skin reaching out from the flames ripped a scream out of her. She kicked at the thing, desperately striving to break free but the hand holding onto the trouser cuff was too strong. She frantically waved her leg about to set it free but nothing worked.

The arm, its strength beyond reason, pulled the her backwards towards the pit's edge. She cried more, beating at the flaking skin with the gun's heavy handle, breaking the skin until only dusty bone remained.

The soldiers turned en-masse towards her.

More women pulled themselves out of the pit.

As their bodies burned they stood, rising up like rag dolls

being pulled by strings. When they were upright their movements were as slick and graceful as the flickering flames. There were new bodies and old; those who had been set alight a few moments before joining those set alight half a day—even half a week—before. They rose as one like a wave rising on the ocean. Spilling from the pyramid of corpses they shifted towards the stunned soldiers; not walking but not running either. They weren't floating, nor were they jumping, leaping or flying. They just moved. They were the Lilly on the pond, pushed forward by the ripples caused by the thrown stone. Their stone was the petrol; their ripples the flames and their pond the bed of dead over which they travelled and encouraged their joining.

The soldiers scrambled for their precious guns, firing at what was already dead. Bullets ripped into charcoal torsos and still they walked. Machine guns stripped heads apart and still they walked. Handguns blew scorched limbs into the air and still they walked. Their flaming bodies edged closer and closer, reaching out at their persecutors, their hunger for the living as ravenous as the fire for their flesh. Some of the soldiers managed to get away but others stayed their ground, feeling the duty unbound to slaughter Jews again and again and again. They stuck their blades into dust; forced gun barrels into mouths and guts but they simply entered and left—the knife passing through as though stabbing a sandbag; the bullets passing through as though flying through paper. The flames caught their clothes, great tongues of yellow and orange bursting from the mouths of dead women to burn the starched thread. It reached for the flesh. It strived for the shorn hair, the soft eyes and leather skin. And it devoured. It turned their muscle to blisters, their blisters to ash. Billions of particles rushed high into the air to mix with the Jews' remains.

As the dead tore at flesh with brittle fingers and bit down on it with coal mouths, another wave followed. Then another and another.

The Birkenau pits emptied, seeking to feast on the taste of refreshing genocide.

They stood naked in the hut.

A tiny concrete changing room connected to a tiny concrete shower pen.

Wooden benches lined the perimeter and columns. Most of their warped seats were covered with the shitty rags worn by those women and children standing before them. Everyone shivered. Above the benches, hooks had been drilled into the walls, looking like a line of upturned thumbs. Instruction posters glued on every vertical surface screamedout orders in black German tongue: 'Don't Forget Your Hook Number' and 'Please Tie Your Shoes Together'. Only two doors offered any chance of freedom—one at each end of the compact room—but the smiling male guards watching them, each carrying cumbersome machine guns stopped anyone from daring. Besides, neither room offered true freedom. One led to the showers, the other back into the camp.

Four guards, all young, each barely capable of holding a razor to their cheeks, shuffled the women forward, pushing them towards the shower room. Some went willingly, most wanted to fight but their emaciated bodies and tired minds couldn't do it anymore. They couldn't reach into themselves anymore; couldn't find the strength behind the tears. So they submitted. Nude. Freezing. Ill with pneumonia, malnutrition and whatever plague the rats planted in them with their bites. Some had already seen their loved ones enter these huts and never leave. Others had watched them leave in wheelbarrows and taken to the pits. There had been a time the sight had sickened them; turned their stomachs and made them want to die. But this feeling subsided. Easing into upset. Appeasing into envy. Being shuffled into another room without windows, they felt acceptance. Relief. Salvation. Their hell would soon be over. No more beatings. No more starvation. No more hatred or fear or pain. Their bruises would fade, their broken bones would heal. They would be with their husbands, children, parents and friends once more.

But the others couldn't accept such defeatist logic . Others still knew of their loved ones. They saw them when the camps' occupiers merged; when the Auschwitz train transferred prisoners from one camp to the other. They had dreamed of being with that person once more in the flesh. To know their touch; their scent; their breath.

Their tears threatened to rip the concrete walls down—but the soldiers didn't care. They pushed the throng forward with steel gun barrels or kicked them with their steel toecap boots. A final bruise before the taking.

The squat room struggled to hold the 242 women and 67 girls. Above their heads pipes traced the ceiling like stretched sinew, connected to a series of perforated shower heads that stared down like a collection of incorporeal eyes. Below their bleeding feet a run of drains cut through the tiles, giving a mouth from where the stench of rotting could emerge, seeming to fill the room with a green haze that made some retch. Orders from Berlin insisted—dozens of Jews be forced into every nook and cranny of the poorly built concrete walls until no more room could be found. Time was short. The Allies were drawing close. Evidence had to be destroyed.

Some fell; their arms and legs trampled on as others struggled to help them to their feet. Children collapsed, pushed away from their mothers. Friends and siblings lost each other as the door was slammed shut and the padlock locked; its heavy click echoing through the door and into their prison. Separating the room created a vacuum that stole their screams. All stared upwards in silence, each holding their neighbours' hands.

A cascade of screams reverberated around the shallow room as the shower heads erupted into action.

Freezing water sprayed their icy bodies. Only the taller women seemed to get wet; their limp, dank hair looking ever more greasy as the downpour fell off their shivering forms. Smaller women and children felt the drips hit them like needles, sending arctic palpitations racing through their useless bodies. Tears merged with shower sprinkles, making it appear all were in mourning.

The water stopped.

The gas started.

Their deaths were quick. Their deaths were painful.

Like rats they scratched at their eyes and mouths, their nailless fingers reaching into their orifices to drag the poison out but to no avail. They crumpled in on each other like discarded scrap paper. They slumped to the floor, cutting and bruising on chipped tiles, no longer caring about being trampled on. Vomit and faeces slipped out of some who had managed to retain enough food to maintain natural bodily functions. Dry coughs spurted out of others whose faces found colour for the first time in months. Sputum and rabid foam flew from purple mouths like rotten ejaculations. As the last breaths entered the room, the pathetic shower fall cleansed their embarrassment. Small redemptions as they took their deliverance.

The last scream faded less than five minutes after the first dead face hit the floor.

As per regulation, the soldiers continued to pump the gas in for another ten minutes. You have to be sure.

They opened the door wearing their gas masks, talking to each other as though they were on their way to the pub. The door's weight was too much for one person. Two pulled, the other two pushed. When the slab was in place they reached for their wheelbarrows propped up against the benches now cleared of the rotting clothes. As the gas passed beyond them into the changing rooms and out into the chimney above or the open doorway beyond, they walked backwards into the shower room, pulling the wheelbarrows with them. They expected to trample over the dead.

They didn't.

They hit a wall.

Alive they had been cramped and packed; disorganized and unable to move. Dead they were regimented, standing in neat rows, unmoving, their bodies no longer shivering with a cold they could not feel.

Now it was the soldiers' turn to tremble. They turned around in silence, gasping when they saw the row of white faces looking back at them; black eyes darker than potholes boring into their poisoned hearts.

The girl—no more than seven and with three of her four fingers on her left hand bent backwards—rushed at the first soldier, biting into his knee. As he screamed the other men reached for their guns, swinging them round on their shoulder straps; pointing them into the crowd. The closest private didn't stand a chance—the swarm of women had him tumbling into his wheelbarrow and tearing open his chest with their blunt fingers before he could squeeze the trigger. A woman whose neck had been broken when she fell buried her head into the cavity and gnawed at the exposed intestines. Another ripped the youngster's gas mask off and bit down onto his nose, the blood filling her mouth like rich red wine. The two soldiers behind him managed to fire off half a dozen bullets before they were taken down – one even firing into a teenage girl's face without caring of the moral dilemma. Before she managed to dig her nails into his groin he remembered her as one of the many he had raped. This one claimed to be pregnant but he knew that to be just another Jewish lie because it was impossible for any Jew to be made pregnant by a German. She had been just a slut he happily carted off to the gas chamber. As she feasted on his testicles, tasting meat for the first time since passing beyond the sign above Auschwitz's gates bellowing "WORK MAKES YOU FREE," she looked up at him in a moment of quiet intimacy.

The mask was pulled from his face and he shared a kiss with another who bit through his tongue. Another pulled off his ear. With the mask's hose taken from around his neck, more smothered his throat with their own special kisses.

The last sprayed his bullets in front of him. Two hit his comrades in the back, killing the one up front and sparing him any more pain. The rest shredded the torso of a geriatric woman far too athletic for her age. He had been looking forward to killing this woman—almost as much as he enjoyed beating her. The sight of her had disgusted him. The notion of a Jew living so long filled him with a rage unsurpassed. Beatings to her back were his favourite—a wooden whip slashed across the spine bringing out squeals like shot rats—but the rapes had been particular fun. As she punched the gas mask and blinded him with the broken plastic he recalled the time he told her he could blind her whenever he wanted; stop her from seeing her precious family ever again.

The swarm passed over him and into the yard beyond with some eating everything they could until only skeletons wrapped in torn, bloodied rags remained.

Auschwitz escaped the outbreak.

Auschwitz had seen the start and witnessed the end but it escaped the blood and hunger.

As the dead in Birkenau ran, stuffing themselves with the fresh food they'd been deprived of when alive, the Germans ran into the huts and sleeping quarters of those deemed healthy enough to work and abuse. Some thought they were seeking solace with the living. They actually felt relieved at the Germans wanting something of them that wasn't cruel or painful. But when the soldiers started kicking them out into the yard to fend for themselves against the rabid waves running the two miles between the camps, they understood there would never be a place for a Jewish soul amongst the Nazis. There would be no place for them anywhere in a German society.

Some ran at the creatures wanting the end to come. Others waited, letting the time savour.

They were left wanting.

The dead ate. The dead feasted. The dead ripped, shredded, tore and destroyed.

The Germans.

Only the Germans.

The Jews ran free.

It ended with Tobias.

A German officer ran into his quarters and witnessed him

chanting. The dead cobbler was now alive, kneeling before the former Rabbi, his ruined body rigid as Tobias called out a stream of foreign words. Both men revealed only the whites of their eyes; each seeming to be staring back into themselves, looking towards the red that made them. The cobbler's silent mouth mimicked Tobias's; his fingers danced on his thighs, tapping out the rhythm. Those who had cleaned the dead man were sitting on those beds closest to the ceremony. Those terrified by what they saw moved back, pinning themselves tight against the far wall in fear of the walking thing turning its attention towards them. Of all the horrors they had seen in this Hell on Earth, this was the one that scared them more than anything.

The officer bursting through the door reacted on instinct.

Seeing the dead man he pulled out his handgun and shot him in the head. The cobbler remained where he was, his blind eyes focused on his Rabbi.

Sensing the bond between the two, the officer turned his gun on Tobias, ending his chants with a bullet between his eyes.

The creatures fell as one.

The cobbler slumped at Tobias's dead feet. Those scrambling around the pits lay down in their flames taking their German meals with them. Those running from Birkenau fell at the rail line, their bodies only metres away from the sheltering Nazis.

It began quickly.

It ended quickly.

Nothing official was ever said of the incident. Those Jews who escaped were quickly rounded up and murdered. Those who had witnessed the cobbler's rebirth were taken to the shower huts. Soldiers refused to speak of the incident other than to one man who visited them to discover all he could in aid of his battle against the British and Americans.

He was too late.

With a bullet in a bunker he took his story to his hidden grave.

SCARLET YAWNS

Stephen Bacon

Madness crouched at the edge of the woods, silently prowling the trees. Kessel watched through the window, across the endless expanse of white, imagining movement. He rubbed his eyes. It was probably just the falling snow, causing optical illusions in the afternoon's gathering darkness. Solitude can do that to the mind, he realised; he'd seen it often enough in the animals. As he waited with growing anxiety on that winter afternoon, he tried desperately to restart the electricity generator.

Fun Land was poorly named as a visitor attraction. Firstly, a collection of dilapidated funfair rides, several llamas, a herd of deer, some bemused wallabies, a rickety wooden rollercoaster, several caravans selling fast food, and an assortment of animals recently inherited from a local farm hardly constituted a fun land. Secondly, sitting midway between Aberdeen and Inverness, deep in the folds of the Glenlivet Valley, the park did little to attract visitors; more likely they stumbled across the place in their exploration of north-east Scotland.

It was mid January and the countryside was blanketed by a thick covering of snow which had been steadily increasing over the past few hours. The weather had resulted in the park being closed to the public for days, plummeting the skeleton staff that had remained further and further into their own personal abyss.

Kessel thumped the lantern down in frustration, wincing as the light flickered ominously. The battery-powered lamps were all they had left in terms of illumination. He'd seen a couple of hurricane lanterns in one of the old outbuildings, but he assumed the fuel had dried up long ago.

The clock on the wall chimed abruptly, signalling 4 pm. Tulson had been gone nearly an hour now. A kernel of unease began to unfurl in Kessel's stomach.

He tried the generator a few more times before giving up and closing the metal cover. He picked up the walkie-talkie and pressed the transmit button.

"Tulson? Tulson? Can you hear me? Over."

His reply was absolute static.

He stood and strode to the door, movement fuelled by dissatisfaction. Outside, the snow fell silently. Kessel felt his resolve weakening. He locked the door behind him and carefully stepped between the generator buildings, heading back to the staffroom. The trail of footprints he'd left on his way over here were already being obliterated by the snow, as if the weather was conspiring to remove all trace of him.

By the time he reached the staff section, the shoulders and hood of his coat were heavy with snow. The air was eerily silent.

McCourt glanced up from his magazine.

"Nothing. It's dead." Kessel's tone was clipped. "Looks like it might have burnt out."

McCourt returned to the magazine. "Told you."

"For Christ's sake, at least I tried!" The silence that followed Kessel's outburst was limitless. "At least one of us seems bothered."

McCourt shrugged. "Tulson had the right idea—get the fuck away as fast as possible."

"In case you haven't noticed, it's snowing like hell outside." Kessel pointed to the window. "We're in the middle of nowhere. The roads are blocked. The phones are down. The nearest house is about twenty miles southwest of here. Where the hell do you suppose he's gone?"

"How do I know?" McCourt turned the page with an air of nonchalance that made Kessel want to punch him.

Instead, he exhaled loudly. "What are we going to do? He's not answering the walkie-talkie."

"I'm hungry." McCourt yawned theatrically. "Do you fancy a walk to the food court?"

Kessel was aware that his companion was trying to antagonise him. There always seemed to be a permanent air of sarcasm surrounding McCourt. Kessel had noticed that, several days after starting employment at Fun Land back in March. Some of the others said that he was misunderstood; several thought of him as quirky; most just avoided him.

"I'll feed the animals first. It's getting dark," Kessel said. He thought about the things he might have seen at the edge of the woods. "Want to give me a hand? It'll be quicker."

"Why are you bothering with them?"

Kessel sighed and stepped outside again, closing the door behind him. The frozen air stung his face, but that sensation was preferable to any warmth that he might share with McCourt.

Inconceivably, it seemed to be getting worse: flakes thickening, the sky seeping darkness like blood into water.

He threaded his way between the service-area buildings. There was a shortcut that bypassed the main park compound, and he passed through the gate. Snow clung to the chain-link fence, turning it opaque, adding to his claustrophobia. The ground was perfectly unbroken by tracks.

He'd worked at the theme park for about eight months, so he was accustomed to being there after dark; nevertheless, the current emptiness of the place lent it an eerie tone. In the distance he could just make out the skeletal frame of the rollercoaster towering above the surrounding structures.

The grassy compound that housed the kids' petting farm had an adjacent brick building in which the animals took shelter. For the next twenty-five minutes he allowed his brain to switch to autopilot, enjoying the task of dispensing feed and water into the animals' pens, forgetting for a time the worry of how he would get home. The close proximity of the animals generated a calming warmth.

Once they were sorted—with only a minor unpleasantness from one of the llamas—his thoughts returned to the current predicament.

To say he was anxious about Tulson would be a slight overstatement. Concerned might be the best choice of word. Just before three o'clock, he and Simon Tulson—the head of the concessions department—had been crossing the perimeter of the service yard, close to the edge of the park, when they'd seen the strange sight in the sky. Their spirits had been high, albeit with an undercurrent of suppressed anxiety.

The adverse weather had at first seemed a novelty; it appeared that the snow front had arrived from Scandinavia quite unexpectedly, and had increased in severity over the past few days. January was a bleak time anyway for the park. It was usually semi-closed for restoration and overhaul at this time. Due to the weather, the managers had decided they would maintain status with just the barest amount of staff. Britain was in the midst of severe weather warnings from the Met Office, and it was decided that only a handful of workers should try to attend work. Due to the proximity of their homes, Kessel, Tulson, McCourt, and another worker, Lizzy Glendinning, had made it in. Unfortunately the heavy snowfall had left them stranded at Fun Land. The roads had become impassable, Britain was declaring a shortage of gritting salt-sand, and the government was urging people to remain in their homes for the coming few days until the expected thaw arrived. At first this had seemed exciting; all four of them were single so it was relatively undisruptive to be trapped at work; there was only the small problem of Lizzy's cat, but she had managed to get a call through to her mum before the phones went dead.

And then just before three o'clock, in the bleak darkness of northeast Scotland, they had spotted the lights.

Kessel and Tulson had been checking the generator. The electricity had stopped working earlier, but Tulson - who as a teenager had enrolled as an electrician's apprentice (withdrawn from the course after four months) - fancied he might possess a modicum of professional insight. Of course, he'd drawn a blank.

They were just crossing the service yard when Tulson had exclaimed and pointed into the sky above the fringes of the forest to the west. Kessel had glanced up, too late, just catching the streak of light as it disappeared beyond his line of sight. Tulson had said it looked like an aircraft in trouble, descending at an unnatural angle. The contrail that Kessel caught supported this.

Tulson had taken one of the electric lanterns and ventured into the woods, looking for any sign of the downed plane. Kessel had tried to argue that they should remain in the compound but his colleague had been firm in his resolve. For a few moments he'd considered accompanying Tulson, but the park responsibilities meant that he reluctantly agreed to await his return. When an agonising hour had elapsed, spent in constant contact with McCourt via the walkie-talkie—who appeared indifferent to Tulson's quest—and a desperate effort to restart the generator, Kessel had finally given up when the static had overwhelmed any remaining chance of communication with his missing colleague.

Kessel checked his watch as he left the animal compound. It was going to be a long night. The snow was still falling steadily. Across the forecourt of the arcade, a light burned in the window of the animal hospital. He knew that a Siberian Roe Deer had been sedated and quarantined for observation earlier in the week. Lizzy had been monitoring it for foot-worm; perhaps she was checking on its progress.

He pushed open the door and stepped inside, stamping on the mat to shake off the snow that had attached to his boots. "Lizzy?"

There was no reply. Kessel stared at her abandoned lantern that rested on one of the tables. The silence was eerie. He stood for a few moments, his ears straining for any sound. "Lizzy?"

Nothing.

From somewhere nearby came the barely audible click of a door closing. "Lizzy?" Kessel moved into the darkness. Rather than feeling scared, the shadows seemed to offer protection.

He reached the door of the office and pushed it open, peering into the room. The skylight was covered by snow, allowing a pale moon to filter through. It made the room deathly and unreal.

He paused and listened. A weird noise seemed to be coming from the animal care compound which lay beyond the next door. It was a wet sound, almost like fabric being torn. Kessel could smell something he couldn't quite place.

"Lizzy?" He pushed open the next door and stared in disbelief at what he saw.

The cage door was partially open. The roe deer was on its side, lying across the threshold of the holding pen, legs trembling as the final moments of its life shivered away. A figure squatted in front of it, leaning across its flank, bending forward and tearing strips of flesh from the carcass. The figure turned abruptly, allowing Kessel to see Tulson's bloated face, the mouth bathed in scarlet gore, bloodstained saliva looping from his chin. His eyes were black and glittering.

Kessel heard a hissing sound and realised absently that it was his own shocked exhalation. He took a step backward. Beyond Tulson's rising form a figure emerged from the shadows, rushing towards them both.

Fear propelled Kessel flat against the counter. He recognised the advancing figure as Lizzy, her hair writhing around her head. She resembled a demented gorgon. She swung something wildly and it connected with Tulson's grimacing face, knocking him sprawling onto the ground.

"Fuck's sake, Lizzy, what's going on?" Kessel stepped back and stared at his prone, blood-stained colleague. Thankfully he wasn't moving. He looked up at her. "Where has he—"

The butt of the tranquilizer shotgun connected with his jaw this time, and light exploded in his eyes.

Consciousness arrived in slow motion. Eventually he became aware of light seeping into his monochrome vision. He rolled onto his side and stretched, hearing the popping of his bones. His spine hurt from the hard surface upon which he was lying. He tried to raise his head but his neck felt stiff and disjointed. He opened his eyes instead. Every time he took a breath he felt a rawness in his nose. He fingered the dried blood that had caked around his nostrils from the impact of the strike.

It took him a while to recognise his surroundings. He was in one of the animal pens. A wall of bars separated him from the rest of the room. He stood and blew his nose, tenderly pressing the swollen flesh that burned above his mouth. He tried the door but it was locked. The smell of antiseptic was heavy in the air, despite his wrecked nose.

It was several moments before he noticed his companion in the adjoining cage. Separated by a distance of three feet, a motionless figure sprawled on the floor. Kessel bent and peered through the bars.

"McCourt?"

His colleague's face was pale, unnaturally so. Only the very faint movement of his chest betrayed the fact he was breathing.

Kessel squatted against the wall and ran his hands through his hair. Shit, what was happening? Where the fuck was Lizzy?

He moved to the bars and pressed his face against the cold metal. "Lizzy?" He could hear the desperation in his voice. They were locked in the observation suite. Had Lizzy transported them here?

He listened for a few moments but there was no reply. And that's when he heard the sound coming from McCourt's throat.

At first he thought the kid was choking. There was a deep, wet clicking noise coming from the other cage, which continued for nearly ten seconds. Kessel watched—fascinated and a little unnerved—at what he saw next.

McCourt's mouth was opening slowly, almost as if he was yawning. It looked grotesque and bizarre. His eyes remained closed. Kessel watched, rapt, as something began to emerge from between the kid's teeth.

It looked like a maggot, or a thin caterpillar. It probed the air hesitantly, almost searching. The clicking sound was still coming from McCourt's throat. Kessel watched the bulge of his colleague's neck as something moved beneath the skin.

Slowly, agonisingly, the pale worm revealed itself enough for Kessel to recognise it for what it was, even though his mind refused to accept the fact.

It was a human finger. As it flexed in the meagre light, Kessel could even make out the shine that caught on the surface of the nail. He began backing away from the bars.

A low moan spilled from McCourt's mouth, even though his lips were pulled back in an obscene grimace. His body shuddered. The head was tilted back at a sickening angle. By now almost an entire hand had emerged from the opening. Blood poured from the lips, running down the side of his cheeks and pooling on the floor. Kessel screamed.

The skin had torn from the extremities of the kid's mouth. More and more of the arm was revealed. The body was now wracked with spasms, almost vibrating with the shudders that had seized it. McCourt writhed against the back wall, struggling with what fought to burst from within. It looked obscene. He kicked against the wall and rolled to his left, out of sight.

For several minutes Kessel could hear horrible tearing sounds, blood gargling in the man's throat, the slap of his body against the tiled floor. The angle meant it was impossible to see what was happening but his imagination coloured the pictures.

"Lizzy!" By now he had lost all hope of a reply, but the physical effort of screaming lessened his panic.

Eventually the sounds stopped. The deathly silence that invaded the room did little to mask Kessel's fear. He pressed himself against the furthest reaches of the cage and stared wide-eyed at the door, waiting—praying—for Lizzy's return.

Nothing happened for about ten minutes. Then a series of curious noises came from McCourt's cage, still beyond the angle of sight; a wet, lapping sound accompanied by a rasped flurry of breathing. When Kessel had been a child, his family had owned a small Cairn terrier. The noise he heard now was similar to the one the dog had made as it devoured its food, pushing the bowl around the kitchen with its nose. Kessel felt fear itching at his scalp.

"McCourt? You okay?"

There was that tearing sound again, almost like someone biting into an apple. Kessel realised he was holding his breath, and he released it with a gasp. The sounds continued for about fifteen minutes; all the while Kessel's anxiety escalated. Several times he could hear McCourt retching. He listened, almost hypnotised by the feral randomness of the noises. Eventually it fell silent. Kessel stared into space, exploring the possibility that he had lost his sanity. The silence was acutely oppressive. He considered curling into a foetal position and trying to sleep. Several agonising minutes later, Lizzy's face loomed up at the window.

Kessel stood quickly as Lizzy entered, brandishing the shotgun like a talisman. "Lizzy, what the hell's happening?"

She stared at him for a moment, almost appraisingly. "Kess, stay back where I can see you."

"What do you mean? What's going on?"

She ignored him, instead turning her attention to the other cage. "Mac, you all right?"

A bare-chested McCourt suddenly stepped into view. Kessel stared at him, amazed at the man's appearance. McCourt gazed at Lizzy in a blank manner, his face slack and detached. Dark stains blended into the fabric of his jeans. He smiled mechanically at her. "Hi, Lizzy."

"Where's your shirt?"

He glanced down at himself as if noticing for the first time. "I…oh, I was sick on myself."

Lizzy nodded slowly. Considered.

"Where's Tulson?" asked Kessel.

She shrugged. "I don't know what happened. Something's fucked up. Big time."

"Let me out." Kessel gripped the bars.

She hesitated, manoeuvring the shotgun so it was aimed at him. "How are you feeling, Kess? You look a bit pale."

"I'm fine, other than a little freaked out." He laughed hollowly. "Seeing your co-worker trying to eat one of the fuckin' animals can do that."

"What was that shit?"

"Christ knows."

She approached the cages and began to unclip a bunch of keys from the fob attached to her belt-loop. Something in the far reaches of McCourt's cage suddenly caught her attention.

"What the fuck is that?" She stared at something beyond Kessel's view

At that precise moment McCourt lunged, his hands shooting through the bars with animal-like speed, grasping her head and wrenching it against the door. She shrieked, flailing her arms hysterically. He pressed his face against the bars and began biting her face and throat. Blood sprayed across the floor.

Kessel recoiled, terrified.

Lizzy screamed and twisted the shotgun at an angle, wildly pulling the trigger. The shot was deafening in the confines of the room.

McCourt stumbled back in a swathe of smoke and cordite. He managed to stay on his feet, his bloodstained grimace frozen in place. The entry wound glistened sickeningly where the blast had obliterated his chest. Fragments of ribcage were exposed like broken teeth. Lizzy collapsed, twitching on the ground as a dark pool gathered around her body. The jagged veins of the throat were lightening due to the blood oxygenating. Her eyes were open, rolled upward, as the death spasms seized her.

Kessel knelt and tried to grasp the shotgun, but the weapon lay agonisingly out of reach. His ears were ringing. He swore under his breath. Then a bolt of inspiration struck; he reached over and unclipped the bundle of keys that remained attached to Lizzy's belt. A low gurgle rattled between her clenched teeth, freezing his movement. When the noise died away, he straightened up and flicked through the assortment of keys. He forced himself to slow down, reminding himself that he was screwed if he dropped the bunch and it fell out of reach.

A couple of the keys looked like they might fit the lock but he didn't know what number pen he was imprisoned inside, so the labels were meaningless. He reached a careful hand through the bars and tried them, one by one, in the lock. Sweat conspired to slip the bunch from his fingers, threatening to send it skittering onto the tiles. The pool of blood was spreading across the floor. He threw a nervous glance at McCourt, who was quietly watching him with detached curiosity, absently licking the blood from around his mouth.

Kessel's heart surged as he felt one of the keys give in the lock. He twisted the barrel and the door clicked open.

The knowledge of his freedom left him anxious and trembling. Lizzy's tongue peeped through her gaping mouth. She was clearly dead. The smell of blood was overwhelming. He stepped over the puddle, made black by the poor light, and bent to pick up the shotgun.

Something yanked him back against the bars, and he turned in shock, feeling McCourt's gore-streaked fingers grasping his jacket. He tugged in the opposite direction, but the resistance was solid and unyielding. The effort squeezed a gasp from his lips. McCourt jerked again, drawing him against the steel bars, baring his teeth. He heard the gnash of the lunatic's bite, the rip of his coat's fabric.

Kessel thrust his elbow against the cage, feeling simultaneously the satisfaction of hearing McCourt's nose break, and the jolt of pain as he struck the metal. The inertia carried him forward and he fell in a heap.

He stood and picked up the shotgun. He pointed it at the shambling ruin that was once his colleague, and quickly pulled the trigger. The ferocity of the blast took him by surprise. McCourt's chin and mouth exploded in every direction, throwing him back against the wall. The recoil of the weapon stung

Kessel's arm but he barely felt it through the adrenaline that was coursing his body.

McCourt slumped at a sickening angle, displaying the inside of his broken head. He lay motionless.

Something weird caught Kessel's attention. He stepped closer to the cage and peered through the bars. On the floor in the corner of the pen, lying in a bizarre heap, was a bundle of bones and skin. A great deal of it had been eaten, by the look of it. Remnants of the discarded skull—flattened and broken by something of immense power—sported hair that matched the colour of McCourt's. Kessel dropped the shotgun, turned and vomited onto the floor, steadying himself with his outstretched hand.

Once the sickness had subsided, Kessel stood and picked up the shotgun, gingerly making his way to the door. In the improved light he examined the weapon. Both shells had been discharged. He knew there was a supply of cartridges locked away in the security office; it was a regulation of their zoological insurance that they kept live ammunition as well as tranquilizer rounds for sedating the animals. Kessel reasoned it would be wise to arm himself. He shouldered the door open and barged outside.

The cold air lessened his nausea. It had stopped snowing but the evidence of Lizzy's approach, and her efforts in transporting McCourt and himself across here, were just visible beneath the covering. Once again he was struck by the eerie sense of solitude that the weather had created. He clutched the shotgun in his arms as he would a comforter, and began to hurry towards the security compound.

The sky puzzled Kessel. He glanced at his watch. It was half past five. Half past five? He must have been unconscious for the entire night. The sky was losing its blackness, faint pale strands filtering into the edge of his vision.

He crossed the landscaped gardens, rendered vague and indistinct by the snow, and arrived onto the footpath that skirted the edge of the lake. The reeds and lilies that fringed the water looked delicate and precise against the black liquid. By now the light was sweeping across the horizon, painting the sky with a pale flourish. He was almost adjacent to the quarantine quarters when he heard the low bark of an animal nearby.

The snow had been broken and was turning to slush around the gateway. He passed through into the courtyard, and stopped dead in his tracks.

A deer stood on the snow-covered grass, shivering uncontrollably. A mournful bellow escaped its lips. On the ground before it, steam rose from the ravaged carcass of a sheep. Coils of intestines spilled from the gaping rent in its woolly flank. The deer turned at the sound of Kessel's arrival, and he saw the blood that coated its snout. The animal's lips drew back as it issued another sorrowful yelp—almost a bark—which echoed across the park like a klaxon.

Kessel noticed five or six other sheep beyond, cowering against the snow-coated fence that bordered the compound. A series of low bleats trembled from their lips. In the area between the huddled livestock and the quivering deer, a solitary sheep glanced around uncertainly. The wool on its back was stained with blood. Even in the dim light, Kessel could see the wound that stretched almost the length of its flank. The beast suddenly convulsed, dropping onto its haunches. Its eyes bulged hideously. A violent retching seized the animal and it jerked its head, tongue lolling unceremoniously to one side. The sheep's snout distended, lips pulled back in a sickening movement. And then something about six inches long spewed out from between its teeth, almost choking the animal. It rocked to one side and Kessel could see the protrusion for what it actually was—a hoof-tipped ovine leg. It coughed thickly as more of the leg emerged; almost to the joint this time. The cowering livestock in the background sounded like they were on the brink of a heart-attack.

Jolted from his reverie, Kessel noticed the first deer approaching with stealth; crouched low to the ground, ears flat against its head, blood-stained teeth bared. It was stalking him. He turned and sprinted out of the courtyard, slamming the gate behind and sliding across the bolt seconds before the animal reached him. He considered swiping at its head with the shotgun but decided the action would be futile. From here he could see through the outer glass wall into the animal quarantine, trying hard not to notice the prone figure on the floor.

Tullis. Kessel breathed a sigh at the body's limp state, and hurried back to the path surrounding the lake.

The madness that he'd witnessed in the last twenty-four hours was taking its toll on him, physically and mentally. His vision lurched; there was a leaden weight to his limbs. He moved with a sluggishness that was disabling. A feeling of sickness surged in his stomach and he bent over and retched, spooling strings of mucus from his mouth. His oesophagus spasmed and he coughed involuntary, trying to clear his airways. Something expanded inside his throat and he bit down, terrified of what was occurring. Swallowing what he could, he spat the contents of his mouth out onto the ground. His chest felt tight and constricted—but under control at least—although his breathing was ragged. He bent to examine what he'd vomited up.

It was the tip of a human finger. He pushed away the implications of what that meant and began to jog along the path. The cold burned his chest, searing his lungs. Plumes of breath whirled in a mocking dance before his eyes.

He was within sight of the security compound building when he felt the wetness on his left hand. He glanced down—at first, it looked like he was wearing a glove. Then he realised it was dripping in blood. He held up his hand and flexed his fingers, feeling a numb sensation extending the length of his forearm. The ground was stained with a sporadic trail of blood. He dropped the shotgun and unzipped his coat, examining himself frantically. And it was there, on the nub of his shoulder, that he felt the tear in his skin. That bastard, McCourt. He'd thought the material of his jacket had protected him. He'd been wrong.

Kessel looked out across the glass-like water of the lake. He could vaguely feel something in his gullet, something that wormed and probed. Madness was hiding inside him now, threatening to explode outwards. Instead of reaching the security compound and tooling himself up with as many shells as he could carry, he realised he would now only need one. He imagined the steel of the barrel against his teeth, wondering whether his big toe would be too numb to press the trigger.

He picked up the shotgun and began to run.

BONUS STORY

Print version only.

Does not appear in the digital version of this book.

OLD BONES

Peter Mark May

THE SCIENTIST CALLED IT *TH71Q*, until some bright spark in Utah blogging about the plague labelled it *H.I.Zee* and the name stuck; until there was no one left untransformed out of seven billion homo-sapiens to have any other thought but raging hunger. In Africa they called it the *Ethiopian Plague*; in Ethiopia they called it *Eritrean Aids*. In the Vatican they called it *Judgement Day*; in the halls of Westminster they called it the *New Black Death*. In Yeman they called it the *new gay plague* and in Israel the *Arab Alliance's final solution*.

Now there is no one left to call it anything, wars are defunct now, reduced to group squabbles over prey and one-on-one never ending fights to a death, that could never come. The real cause had been the apes and their immunity to the *TH71Q* virus they carried, and they had passed it on to humans without thought, or plan or evil intent.

Homo-sapiens gave way to Home-Victus-Mortuus and they roamed the planet feeding on any living creature that their slow lumbering decaying flesh could capture and devour.

Yet they were a species doomed for extinction, much like their former human selves. It happened in the blink of an eye, in relation to Earth's long history. A hundred years and there was nothing left but dust and bones. The apes moved out of the trees and the tigers hunted on cracked tarmac roads, seeking wild dogs and cats that had long forgotten their domestic past.

In a by the edge of a desert watering hole, under an overhanging slab of rock, the last remnant of the human race remained. In a life long forgotten, his name had been Dr. Henry Walsh, in his rebirth he had been hunter of flesh, regaining some of his former intelligence the longer his ungodly life continued, eating the flesh of anything living. He'd been under the rock like some old crab for a quarter of a decade, waiting for animals to bend their weary necks and sate their thirst at the water's edge. If they got too close he would pounce and with some success, hopefully keeping hold of the beast until his rotting teeth bit through its neck.

Yet there was little of him or his undead cadaver left now. Only a bit of old brain matter clinging to the inside of his bleached white skull, he had no eyes left to see they had gone fifty years ago, no ears left to hear they had gone ten years later, just some inner urgent hunger that sensed the vibrations on the wet sand.

His left leg a jackal had run off with into the night ten years ago and his right had long since turned to dust. The gristle in his left elbow had long since decayed to powder and only his skull, torso with its paper thin skin, and his right arm, with little flesh left, even moved at all.

In fact he hadn't moved for six months now, until today, vibrations echoing though the sack of cells that were left. Hunger reached into his blackness and with vile purpose his withered, near fleshless fingers dug into the shadow covered sand as he managed to pull what was left of his carcass from under the rock and towards the movement by the water's edge. The vibration was heavy and thumping in the dried scum of his brain matter and he reached up a flailing skeletal arm to gain more purchase on the wet sand to drag his earthly remains closer to his prey.

Then it happened. There was a click that he could not hear and all movement stopped. His jaw hung open like it had for three years ready for the cry of frustration he had no tongue left to utter and he fell into the mud of the shoreline, causing some of his lower ribs to splinter off like matchsticks. The left side of his chest caved in under the pressure of the fall and his teeth only met silt, not warm bloodied flesh.

The heavy vibration moved closer to his remains, a vast dark shadow that picked up his detached arm and, holding it at the elbow, looked at the last vestiges of human kind, as if it was something new, something he'd not seen before. The bony skull moved half an inch to the left making it sink lower into the mud causing the primate to shuffle back in surprise and then bring the arm down like a weapon of old upon the white skull breaking a hole in the top. Down and down, again and again, the half hairy arm smashed, breaking the skull into four large pieces. Then the arm was tossed long, with a splash into the water, and the primate jumped up and down on the skull fragments, breaking the brittle bones into even more tiny fragments, which ripped the last remnants of brain matter into slices of nothing. Finally bringing about man's extinction.

Night fell and the primates moved on into the jungles to hunt and escape the cold night air.

From the water something crawled with small powerful arms on its long eel-like body, with eyes much like a toad, reaching the remains of the skull it found what was left of the brain and feasted. Then it moved up under the now vacated rock and laid its eggs.

A year later its spawn laid its eggs in the same place in relative safety as the hunting primates had moved north to cooler climes.

A thousand years moved on and the things that crawled from the water's edge, lay basking in the sunlight for most of the day, under the rock they still spawned, but now not from eggs: straight from their wombs their young came onto the cool sand under the rock. The birth blood to be licked clean from their babies using round darting tongues.

Five thousand years later and the desert hand gone and the watering hole had grown into a huge lake. The creatures no longer lived in the water, but some racial memory still brought them back to birth under the rock, which now was a deep dugout cave.

One after the other they took turns to give birth in that place they kind thought of with reverence, hold their newborn young to their milk swollen teats.

Then, when they were old enough, these new young rose up on two legs and, with hunched backs, headed north in family groups, hundreds strong, to find broken cities that nature had taken back, and their faces mirrored on a thousand different images…

BIOGRAPHIES

Name: Gary McMahon
Website: www.garymcmahon.com
Last Publication: *Dead Bad Things* (novel; Angry Robot)
Next Publication: *Silent Voices* (novel; Solaris)
About the Author: Gary McMahon's fiction has appeared in various acclaimed publications and been reprinted in several "Best Of" anthologies. He is the author of six novels and several novellas. He has been nominated for the British Fantasy Award eight times. *The Concrete Grove* was awarded the This is Horror Award for Novel of the Year 2011. *What They Hear in the Dark* was awarded the This is Horror Award for Chapbook of the Year 2011.

Name: Mark West
Website: www.markwest.org.uk
Last publication: *The Mill*, from Greyhart Press
Next publication: *What Gets Left Behind*, a Spectral Press chapbook
About the Author: West has been involved in the small press since 1999 and has had sixty short stories, two novels (*In The Rain With the Dead* and *Conjure*) and a collection (*Strange Tales*) published. He has a raft of material due for publication and is currently working on a novel. He lives in Rothwell, Northamptonshire, with his wife and son and can see the A14 (the real location for "In Cars") from his study window.

Name: David Williamson
Last Publication: *The 8th Black Book of Horror* ("Boys Will be Boys")
Next publication: *The 9th Black Book of Horror*
About the Author: *The 28th Pan Book of Horror* ("The Sandman"), *30th Pan Book of Horror* ("The Good Samaritan," "The Not So Good Samaritan," "No Room at the Flat," written as Willam Davidson) The *5th/6th/7th* and *8th Black Book of Horror*. Also a Kindle edition entitled "Internet Dating…are you MAD?"… now, that's a REAL horror story! Dave lives in Worthing with his daughter and a three legged Lurcher called Othello.

Name: Selina Lock
Website: www.factorfictionpress.co.uk
Last Publication: *Lady of the Skies* (comic strip, illustrated by David O'Connell) in Ink+PAPER #1, November 2011.
Next Publication: "Lords of the Dance" in the *Stumar Press Book of Horror*.
About the Author: Selina edited twenty one issues of the award-nominated *The Girly Comic*, *The Girly Comic Book Volume 1*, and *The Girly Webcomic*. She wrote a column for *Borderline - The Comics Magazine*, and her comic strips have appeared in *Baddis*, *Sugar Glider Stories #2* and *WAR: The Human Cost*. She is a mild-mannered librarian from Leicester, and her daily life is spent in service to the god Loki, who currently inhabits the body of a small, black, scruffy terrier.

Name: Stuart Young
Website: http://stuyoung.blogspot.co.uk/
Last Publication: "Houses in Motion"—short story in the *Darker Minds* anthology
Next Publication: *Reflections in the Mind's Eye*—short story collection from Pendragon Press
About the Author: Stuart Young is a British Fantasy Award–winning author. His stories have appeared in various anthologies such as *Catastrophia, Alt-Dead, We Fade to Grey, Where the Heart Is, The Monster Book for Girls* and *The Mammoth Book of Future Cops*. He has published three short story collections: *Spare Parts, Shards of Dreams* and *The Mask Behind the Face*. Despite this he still finds writing his author bio far more difficult than it has any right to be.

Name: Joe McKinney
Website: http://joemckinney.wordpress.com
Last Publication: *The Red Empire and Other Stories*
Next Publication: *Mutated: Book 4 in the Dead World Series*
About the Author: The author of 14 novels and collections, Joe McKinney is best known for his zombie fiction, which includes the four part *Dead World* series and a string of short stories. His short stories have been collected in *The Red Empire and Other Stories* and *Dating In Dead World*. He's been nominated for the Black Quill Award and is a Bram Stoker Award™ winner 2012. He is currently a patrol commander for the San Antonio Police Department.

Name: Zach Black
Website:
Last Publication:
Next Publication:
About the Author: His work has been described as a mix of classic and contemporary horror fiction reminiscent of '70s and '80s pulp horror. Born and bred in Scotland, he is a native of the seaside town of Saltcoats, where he lives with his wife Kim, in the county of North Ayrshire—a land steeped in history and legend, by which he is constantly inspired.

Name: Shaun Jeffrey
Website: http://www.shaunjeffrey.com
Last Publication:
Next Publication:
About the Author: Shaun Jeffrey was brought up in a house in a cemetery, so it was only natural for his prose to stray towards the dark side when he started writing. He has had five novels published, *Killers*, *The Kult*, *Deadfall*, *Fangtooth*, and *Evilution*, and two collections of short stories, *The Mutilation Machination* and *Voyeurs of Death*. Among his other writing credits are short stories published in *Cemetery Dance*, *Surreal Magazine*, *Dark Discoveries* and *Shadowed Realms*. *The Kult* was optioned for film by Gharial Productions and has now been filmed.

Name: Richard Farren Barber
Website: www.richardfarrenbarber.co.uk:
Last Publication: Richard has had over 20 short stories published in publications such as *Morpheus Tales*, *Murky Depths*, *Trembles* and *Midnight Echo*, as well as anthologies including *Alt-Dead* and *Night Terrors II*.
Next Publication: Richard is included in Hersham Horror's next PentAnth title: *Siblings* to be published in September.
About the Author: During 2010/11 Richard was sponsored by Writing East Midlands to undertake a mentoring scheme in which he was supported in the development of his novel *Bloodie Bones*. This is now being shamelessly hawked amongst agents and publishers.

Name: Alison Littlewood
Website: www.alisonlittlewood.co.uk
Last Publication: Alison's first novel, *A Cold Season*, is published by Jo Fletcher Books, an imprint of Quercus.
Next Publication: Her short story, "About the Dark," has been selected for the *Mammoth Book of Horror #23*.
About the Author: Alison lives in deepest West Yorkshire, where she hoards books with the word "dark" in the title, avoids the sunlight, and tends the pet zombie she keeps in her cellar. Her short stories have appeared in magazines including *Black Static*, *Crimewave* and *Shadows and Tall Trees*, as well as the British Fantasy Society's *Dark Horizons*. She contributed to the charity anthology *Never Again*, as well as *Where Are We Going?*, *Full Fathom Forty* and *Terror Tales of the Cotswolds*.

Name: Jay Eales
Website: www.factorfictionpress.co.uk
Last Publication: *Mightier Than the Sword - in Faction Paradox: A Romance in Twelve Parts* (Obverse Books, May 2011)
Next Publication: As writer: *Zeitgeist - in Terror Tales* Volume 2, Issue 1. As editor: *Burning With Optimism's Flames* (Obverse Books, Summer 2012)
About the Author: Writer, Editor, Publisher, Designer, Journalist and all-round Renaissance Man. Editor of *Violent!* and publisher of *The Girly Comic* for Factor Fiction. News Features Editor for the award-winning *Borderline – The Comics Magazine*. His comics have also appeared in *Negative Burn*, *The Mammoth Book of Best New Manga*, *Lost Property, Robots, Predators* and *The BFS Journal*, and his fiction published in *Drabble Who?*, *Shadowsphere*, *The Speculator*, *Murky Depths* and *Faction Paradox: A Romance in Twelve Parts*.

Name: Adrian Chamberlin
Website: http://www.archivesofpain.com
Last Publication: *The Dark Side of the Sun* (collection of short stories), "Kriegsmaterial" (in Hersham Horror Books' *Fogbound From 5*)
Next Publication: *Beseiged* (novella in the Lovecraft-themed collection *Dreaming in Darkness*)
About the Author: Author of the critically acclaimed supernatural thriller *The Caretakers*; co-editor of *Read The End First*, an apocalyptic anthology from Wicked East Press; co-founder of Dark Continents Publishing; likes alcohol and hot cross buns; has heard of the concept of "spare time" but swears it's just a myth.

Name: Jan Edwards
Website: http://janedwards-writer.blogspot.com/
Last Publication: *Orbyting, The Hammer Out Book of Ghosts*, edited by Dexter O'Neill. January 2012
Next Publication: "Damnation Seize My Soul," *Dark Currents*, Edited by Ian Whates, Newcon Press March 2012
About the Author: Jan has had more than 40 short stories published and was short-listed in 2011 for the British Fantasy Award for Best Short Story and the Winchester Writers Festival "Slim Volume" prize. Other work includes reviews, interviews, poetry and magazine articles. She has recently also been part of a scriptwriting team for a TV spin-off. Jan has a BA in English Literature with Creative Writing. She is an editor with the award-winning Alchemy Press and lives on the edges of the Peak District National Park with husband Peter Coleborn, three cats and a selection of chickens.

Name: Katherine Tomlinson
Website: http://kattomic-energy.blogspot.com/
Last Publication: *L.A. Nocturne II: More Tales of the Misbegotten*
Next Publication: "Fire in the Blood" in *Drunk on the Moon* from Dark Valentine Press
About the Author: Katherine Tomlinson is a former journalist who prefers making things up. She is the co-creator (with illustrator Mark Satchwill) of the serial novel *NoHo Noir*. Her short stories have appeared in print and online. She lives in Los Angeles, where she is working on her first novel, *The Misbegotten*.

Name: Stuart Hughes
Website: www.stuarthughes.webs.com
Last Publication: "Busy Blood" (theEXAGGERATEDpress), a collection of eleven short shories Stuart collaboratively wrote with D.F. Lewis. "Adroitly written tales of the fantastic...A wonderful synthesis of mysterious delights and freakish surprises—expect the unexpected!"— Simon Clark.
Next Publication: Stuart will feature later this year with short stories in Hersham Horror Books's *Pentanth* series and *Morpheus Tales*. His second short story collection will be published by theEXAGGERATEDpress in 2013.
About the Author: Stuart was born in Burton upon Trent in March 1965. He started writing seriously in 1988 and his first short story was published a year later. Since then he has had over 80 short story credits in various anthologies, magazines and newspapers. In 1997, eleven of his short stories were published in the collection *Ocean Eyes*. For nine years Stuart edited the award winning magazine *Peeping Tom*, which won the British Fantasy Award in 1991 and 1992. Stuart is a member of the British Fantasy Society and the writers' group Derby Scribes. He is currently working on his first novel.

Name: R.J. Gaulding
Last Publication: "In Bits," in Hersham Horror Books' *Alt-Dead*
Next Publication: *The Chelsea Pensioners versus the Grave Zombies*, Hop'ung Press in 2013
About the Author: He lives in a remote part of Arbroath, Scotland, with his two cats "Glen & Fidditch". He is an ex-sergeant in the Royal Marines and loves walking, mountain climbing and scaring people off his land with shotguns. He has two tattoos, and loves to smoke his pipe and grow his facial hair.

Name: William Meikle
Website: http://www.williammeikle.com
Last Publication: *Carnacki: Heaven and Hell*, a collection from Dark Regions Press
Next Publication: *Night of the Wendigo*, a novel in hardcover from Darkfuse/Delirium
About the Author: William Meikle is a Scottish writer with fifteen novels published in the genre press and over 250 short story credits in thirteen countries. His work appears in many professional anthologies. He lives in a remote corner of Newfoundland with icebergs, whales and bald eagles for company. In the winters he gets warm vicariously through the lives of others in cyberspace.

Name: Rachelle Bronson
About the Author: Rachelle is the creator, producer and writer of the television series, *Legends*, optioned by Invictus Films Inc, and *Jaded* a sitcom optioned by Fastlane Entertainment. She's recently completed the short stories "Ishiah & Narantsetsik" and "Frozen," as well as two full-length feature films, *The Frozen Painter* and *Young Girl*, all optioned by Invictus Films Inc. In her free time Rachelle now works on her novel *Tarzwell*, which is based on her real-life experiences living in a haunted house. "Lullabelle" is her first publication.

Name: Dave Jeffery

Website: www.davejeffery.webs.com

Last Publication: *Campfire Chillers* collection was released in September 2011 at Fcon, Brighton. His story "Frigophobia" was included in the popular *Phobophobia* anthology (Dark Continents Publishing) released in December 2011.

Next Publication: The contemporary novel *Finding Jericho* will be released through Hidden Thoughts Press. This book is on the BBC: Headroom recommended reading list as well as being featured by the BBC Health website. It is also supported by the mental health charity MIND. *Finding Jericho* is released in April 2012. His story "Ice Rage" will be featured in the forthcoming *Read the End First* anthology (Wicked East Press).

About the Author: He is best known for his pulp zombie novel *Necropolis Rising*, which has gone on to become a UK #1 bestseller. His story "Daddy Dearest" appears in the award-winning *Holiday of the Dead* anthology (Wild Wolf Publishing). His *Campfire Chillers* collection (Dark Continents Publishing) is currently on the longlist for the prestigious 2012 Edge Hill Prize. When he is not writing and spending time with his family, Dave has a real job that takes up whatever time he has left.

Biographies

Name: Shaun AJ Hamilton
Website: http://shaunhamilton.wordpress.com/
Last Publication: "Bastard Thing" in *Crack the Spine* ezine
Next Publication: Story to be included in Mark West's *Ill at Ease 2* collection
About the Author: Recently completed latest stage of transformation. Following insertion of latest wires and battery, cyborg status is now on line. Always been pissed off with existence, no matter how much metal I have inside me—or the number of volts.

Name: Stephen Bacon
Website: www.stephenbacon.co.uk
Last Publication: A short story called "Cuckoo Spit," which was published in *Black Static*.
Next Publication: His debut collection, *Peel Back the Sky*, to be published by Gray Friar Press in 2012.
About the Author: Born in 1971, Steve lives with his wife and two sons in South Yorkshire. His short stories have been published in various areas of the small press, including *Murmurations - An Anthology of Uncanny Stories About Birds*, edited by Nicholas Royle; *Where the Heart Is*, edited by Gary Fry; *Alt-Dead*, edited by Peter Mark May; and *Shadows & Tall Trees*, edited by Michael Kelly. He will have a story in the forthcoming issue of *Crimewave* from TTA Press. In her summation for *Best Horror of the Year 3*, Ellen Datlow described him as "an extremely promising writer of dark fiction whose work is well worth searching out."

Name: Peter Mark May
Website: http://darkside6869.webs.com/
Last Publication: *Hedge End*, a novel published by Samhain Horror 2012
Next Publication: *AZ: Anno Zombie*, also from Samhain Horror in December 2012
About the Author: He is the author of *Demon* (2008), *Kumiho* (2010) and *Inheritance* (2010), published under the name P. M. May, as well as short stories published in genre Canadian & US magazines and the UK & US anthologies of horror *Creature Feature*, *Watch* and the British Fantasy Society's 40th Anniversary anthology *Full Fathom Forty*, plus a novella called *Dark Waters*, released in 2011. He has edited three Hersham Horror Books anthologies so far, but is letting others have a play now, but somehow found the time to co-found Karōshi Books with Johnny Mains and Cathy Hurren in 2012.

Name: Joy Sillesen
Website: http://indieauthorservices.com
Last Publication: *Drunk on the Moon*, a horror anthology from Dark Valentine Press
Next Publication: *Blood Will Tell*, a science fiction adventure romance from Dark Valentine Press
About the Designer: She is a publishing industry veteran who has designed everything from websites to event posters, but her real love is book design. She is also a multi-published author under the pseudonym Christine Pope.

COPYRIGHT PAGE

Thus Spoke Lazarus © Gary McMahon 2012
In Cars © Mark West 2012
Blind Date © David Williamson 2012
Love and Level Sands © Selina Lock 2012
White Light, Black Fire © Stuart Young 2012
Bugging Out © Joe McKinney 2012
The Rhyme of Albert Greentree © Zach Black 2012
'Til Death Do Us Part © Shaun Jeffrey 2012
Checking Out © Richard Farren Barber 2012
Soul Food © Alison Littlewood 2012
Imaginary Kingdom © Jay Eales 2012
The Third Day © Adrian Chamberlin 2012
Midnight Twilight © Jan Edwards 2012
Dead End Jobz © Stuart Hughes 2012
Pyramid Power © Katherine Tomlinson 2012
Ultimate Ana © R.J. Gaulding 2012
The Silent Dead © William Meikle 2012
Ascension? © Dave Jeffery 2012
Lullabelle © Rachelle Bronson 2012
Acceptable Genocide © Shaun Hamilton 2012
Scarlet Yawns © Stephen Bacon 2012

Old Bones, Fogbound From 5, Alt-Dead, Alt-Zombie, Siblings, Hersham Horror Books © Peter Mark May 2011/2012

```
This book may also be used as a weapon in the
        event of a zombie apocalypse.
```

Stumar Press

STUMAR PRESS BRINGS YOU QUALITY HORROR FICTION

DERBY SCRIBES ANTHOLOGY 2011

Eleven short stories featuring Simon Clark, Conrad Williams and Neal James, plus Derby Scribes members including Richard Farren Barber, Stuart Hughes and Christopher Barker.

COMING JUNE 2012

Soul Screams—a collection of thirteen horror stories from Sara Jayne Townsend. "Townsend writes accomplished, powerful stories of mystery and fear, with places and themes we all recognise, and delicious twists in the tail."—Tim Lebbon, author of *Echo City*

COMING JULY 2012

Spare Parts—a collection of six horror stories by British Fantasy Award winning author Stuart Young. "Young serves up six stories on the theme of love and loss, and the quiet desperation of ordinary lives suddenly transformed by accidental magic."—Simon Morden

COMING 2012

Ten Terrors Volume One—featuring ten horror stories from Graham Joyce, Mark Morris and eight other writers to be announced soon. Volume two will feature Tim Lebbon and nine other authors.

Coming Soon From Hersham Horror Books

SIBLINGS

Is the next in our *Pentanth* line of 5-story horror anthologies featuring the talents of:

Stuart Hughes

Sara Jayne Townsend

Richard Farren Barber

Simon Kurt Unsworth

Sam Stone